Praise for the novels of Mary Carter!

THE THINGS I DO FOR YOU

"A touching novel."
—*Publishers Weekly*

"A marvelous combination of wit and heart."
—*RT Book Reviews*

THE PUB ACROSS THE POND

"The ending is as enchanting as the Ireland she describes,
and this is guaranteed to become one of the books
on your shelf that you'll want to read again."
—*Fredericksburg.com*

"A fun, quirky read."
—*Publishers Weekly*

MY SISTER'S VOICE

"At once a story about love and loss, family and friends,
the world of the hearing and that of the deaf,
My Sister's Voice satisfies on many levels."
—Holly Chamberlin, author of *Summer With My Sisters*

"Gripping, entertaining and honest. This is a unique,
sincere story about the invisible, unbreakable bonds
of sisterhood that sustain us no matter how far they're buried."
—Cathy Lamb, author of *My Very Best Friend*

"Carter's talent continues to evolve, as evidenced in this solid
offering. The unique spin Carter takes on the familiar theme
of self-discovery gives this a welcome, fresh feeling."
—*Publishers Weekly*

"Carter's latest contains compelling characters that you
will want to root for. Numerous surprises keep
the plot fresh and the reader engaged."
—*RT Book Reviews*

Books by Mary Carter

SHE'LL TAKE IT

ACCIDENTALLY ENGAGED

SUNNYSIDE BLUES

MY SISTER'S VOICE

THE PUB ACROSS THE POND

THE THINGS I DO FOR YOU

THREE MONTHS IN FLORENCE

MEET ME IN BARCELONA

LONDON FROM MY WINDOWS

HOME WITH MY SISTERS

Published by Kensington Publishing Corporation

HOME WITH MY SISTERS

MARY CARTER

KENSINGTON BOOKS
www.kensingtonbooks.com

KENSINGTON BOOKS are published by

Kensington Publishing Corp.
119 West 40th Street
New York, NY 10018

All Kensington titles, imprints, and distributed lines are available at special quantity discounts for bulk purchases for sales promotion, premiums, fund-raising, educational, or institutional use.

Special book excerpts or customized printings can also be created to fit specific needs. For details, write or phone the office of the Kensington Sales Manager: Kensington Publishing Corp., 119 West 40th Street, New York, NY 10018. Attn. Sales Department. Phone: 1-800-221-2647.

Kensington and the K logo Reg. U.S. Pat. & TM Off.

eISBN-13: 978-1-61773-709-1
eISBN-10: 1-61773-709-7
First Kensington Electronic Edition: October 2016

ISBN-13: 978-1-61773-708-4
ISBN-10: 1-61773-708-9
First Kensington Trade Paperback Printing: October 2016

10 9 8 7 6 5 4 3 2 1

Printed in the United States of America

Dedicated to my sister, Melissa Carter-Newman.
I couldn't have asked for better.

ACKNOWLEDGMENTS

I'd like to thank the usual suspects: my agent, Evan Marshall, and my editor, John Scognamiglio. And as always I would like to thank my readers and my family for sharing in my stories and encouraging me to continue.

CHAPTER 1

Bells jangled as Austin Rhodes held open the door to the bustling Winter Biergarten. The scent of bratwursts sizzling on the grill leapt out to greet him, and he could already taste the first tangy sip of his India Pale Ale. Add a heaping scoop of German potato salad and these simple pleasures would go a long way to soothe him when he lost yet another Scrabble game to Yvette Garland. "Silent Night" rose above the chatter of customers, and Christmas lights strung about the room cast everyone in a cheery glow. A giant wreath topped with a big red bow hung above the stone fireplace already crackling and popping with a roaring fire even though it was just a little after noon. Snow was predicted later on and folks were hunkering down as if it had already arrived and making a festive day out of it. Winter was the busiest season of all for this Bavarian town nestled in the Cascade Mountains, thanks in part to the many festivities designed to charm the snow pants off the tourists. Yes, indeed, there was no better place to celebrate the holiday season than Leavenworth, Washington. Even a Scrooge like him could feel a little bit of magic in a day like today. Austin tucked the Scrabble board under his left armpit and extended a hand to his elderly neighbor who was taking her time coming up the walk. "No ice or snow yet," she said, ignoring his hand and instead grabbing the doorframe and hoisting herself up into the space.

"Maybe I just wanted to hold your hand," he said with a wink.

"Stop grinning and winking. People are going to think we're Harold and Maude."

Austin raised an eyebrow. "Who are they?"

She waved him off and headed for their usual booth along the window. Besides walking slower than usual, when she lowered herself into the booth, she failed to disguise a wince. Austin immediately looked away. Yvette Garland was not only a fiercely proud woman, she could also strike like a rattlesnake if you were foolish enough to irritate her. Austin was reminded of something his grandfather always said about getting old: *It's a hell of a time of life and I'd avoid it if I were you.* At least they had a good meal coming and undeniably the best view in the house.

From here they could see the Cascade Mountains framing the background, and all along the base towering pines colored the landscape with emerald green, striking a vibrant contrast with the gunmetal gray sky. Austin had lived here for ten years and hadn't once tired of the view.

However—if one *was* to tire of the mountains, and sky, and the towering emerald pines, a simple shift of the gaze was all it took and one could absorb the sights and sounds out the window. Boutiques, and pubs, and restaurants spilled out on either side of them, drawing tourists and locals alike. It was a shifting panorama of people, shopping bags, children, ice skates, and careening sleds. Teams of horse and carriages were making pilgrimages around the town, their drivers suited up in traditional Bavarian garb: suspenders, flowing shirts, and hats adorned with decorative plumes. A young mother walked by with a child tugging on each gloved hand, a bounce in their step as they eagerly awaited the first few flakes to fall. You could smell snow in the air. Austin loved that smell. Heck, he loved everything about Leavenworth, and nothing had surprised him more. He always thought he'd be a wanderer, yet here he was, a homebody.

Austin set up the board as the waitress brought their tea and pint. She set the tea in front of Austin, and the Pale Ale in front of Yvette. Yvette waited for her to leave before rolling her eyes and switching their drinks. "She's horrendous," Yvette said in a loud voice. "She didn't even take our order."

"She's new," Austin whispered.

"She doesn't care, and that's horrendous."

"You never know what a person is dealing with," Austin said.

"You're bringing your work home with you again," Yvette chided.

Austin laughed. He was a manager at a suicide prevention hotline center. Sadly, this was one of their busiest times of year. "I'm too caring?" he said.

"Exactly. She doesn't care, so why should I?"

Austin shook his head. Yvette said whatever was on her mind. And there was a chance she was right. Maybe the waitress wasn't carrying around a world of ennui, maybe she just didn't care. Austin would rather live his life erring on the side of caution, but he wasn't going to antagonize Yvette with his philosophies.

Yvette glanced in the direction of the waitress again. She was standing by the register painting her nails. Yvette turned back and treated Austin to a long look. He laughed. "In my day, jobs were scarce. When you got one, you appreciated it." Yvette removed a flask from her purse and added whiskey to her tea. "Fights off colds," she said when Austin gave her a look.

"Uh-huh." Austin knew the doctor had told her to stop drinking—it wasn't a good mix with chemo—but she wouldn't hear a word of it. He knew she had just gotten her latest scan results, but so far she hadn't said a word about them. He wouldn't push. He set up the Scrabble board as the waitress finally caught on to Yvette's glares and sauntered over to take their order. Austin ordered his usual, a cheeseburger and fries.

Yvette, who usually devoured a bratwurst and sweet potato fries, and apple pie à la mode, shook her head. "I'm not hungry."

Austin knew it would happen, but he loathed watching this powerhouse of a woman lose her appetite. "Maybe some soup?"

Austin suggested. He looked at the waitress. "What's the Soup of the Day?"

The waitress looked at Austin as if she wanted to stab him in the eye with a fork. "I don't think there is one."

Yvette shook her head and threw up her arms. "There's always a Soup of the Day."

"Is that what you want, then?" The waitress smacked her lips.

"How should I know until I know what it is?" Yvette barked. The waitress simply stood and stared.

"Maybe you should go ask another waitress, or one of the cooks," Austin said gently. The waitress flounced away. Yvette shook her head until she returned.

"There's no Soup of the Day," the waitress announced in a smug tone. "There are *soups*. More than one." Austin and Yvette waited, the waitressed simply stared.

"Why don't you tell us what they are?" Austin prodded.

"Broccoli and cheese, or lentil." The waitress twisted her pencil in a strand of her hair, snapping her gum as if to keep her from dying of boredom.

Yvette gingerly lifted her tea and stuck out her pinky. "This will do."

"That will do what?" the waitress asked, staring at Yvette's pinky as if expecting it to perform tricks.

"Bring us a bowl of the broccoli and cheese, and extra crackers," Austin said before the waitress could flee. "I'll eat it if you don't," he added as he doled out their tiles. "Ladies first."

Yvette began to hum along with the Christmas carol playing in the background as she placed her first word on the board. There it was, her tongue poking out of the side of her mouth that always showed up when she was thrilled with her word. He stared at it for a long while before challenging her. "Glitty?" She smiled and nodded. "What the hell is 'Glitty'?"

"Language!" She smiled nonetheless, then gestured around the restaurant. "All the Christmas lights and sparkling snow makes Leavenworth all glitty," she said. "Triple score."

"Uh-huh," he said. He stared at his letters, then at the board.

Outside the sun struck an icicle hanging from an eave outside. It was kind of glitty.

"Hurry up. I don't have much time left."

Austin played *Gulp*. Yvette played *Stay*. Austin played *Hope*. Yvette gasped and threw open her arms just as the waitress arrived with the soup. Austin reached across the table the second he registered the impending collision, but it was too late. Yvette smacked the bowl, and cheese soup splattered all over the waitress. She screamed.

"Oh no." Austin was on his feet, thrusting his napkin into the waitress's hand.

"Look what you did," she wailed at Yvette. "This is the worst thing that could have happened."

"That's the worst thing that could have happened?" Yvette asked.

"You could have scalded me!"

"But I didn't. You know how I know? Because that soup has been sitting in the window for ten minutes. It's probably not even warm, let alone scalding."

"Lucky for you or I could have sued you!"

One of the older waitresses scurried over. "Is everything all right?"

"She poured soup all over me," the waitress cried.

"It was an accident," Austin said to the waitress. "I'd give you some water, but—"

"She didn't bring any," Yvette finished for him.

"Go get cleaned up, these things happen," the older waitress said. The younger one stomped off. The older waitress sighed. "Sorry. She's new."

"The worst thing that could have happened," Yvette muttered. "Charmed life, that one."

"No worries," Austin said with a nod to the older waitress, who finally took off. He looked at Yvette. "What's going on?"

"I told you I wasn't hungry." Yvette pushed the board away and tears came into her eyes.

"It was an accident," Austin said as he reached to touch her hand across the table. "She'll be fine."

"Of course she will," Yvette said. "She's young and healthy, isn't she? The worst thing that's ever happened to her is some old lady spilled cheese soup on her." She jerked her hand away and took out her flask. Her hand was shaking. Austin had never seen her this upset.

"What is it?" he asked again.

"Put it away." She eyed the board as if it were her mortal enemy, then turned her head and refused to look at it. Austin quickly ditched his joke about winning by default and put away the board.

"What about apple pie à la mode?" he said. She shook her head. "Yvette, what is it?"

She stared out the window. "I know I'm an old lady and this is what happens when you're old, so I can't believe how utterly shocked I feel." She turned to look at Austin. "My cancer has spread." She ran a shaky hand along the tabletop. "They're stopping chemo. He said I probably won't see more than a few days into the new year." Austin stared at her, mouth open, searching for something, anything to say. When he couldn't think of a single darn thing, he reached for her flask and helped himself to a generous swig. They sat in silence as "Frosty the Snowman" began to play and lights twinkled, and outside the first few flakes of the winter storm began to fall. Yvette tilted her head in the direction of the music. "At least it isn't 'Silent Night' again." She glared in the direction of the speakers. "That's just the song a dying woman wants to hear."

Austin leaned forward. "Doctors are wrong all the time."

"Can it. I'm dying. And that's the least of my worries."

Austin took the bait. "That's the least of your worries?" Yvette nodded. "What then?"

She reached across the table, grabbed Austin's hand, and squeezed it hard. "What are we going to do about Roger?"

CHAPTER 2

Yvette said she didn't want anything from the store, but Austin stopped anyway, insisting she needed to have a few things on hand in case the snowstorm hit hard. She stayed in the truck while he picked up soup, milk and cereal, apples, cheese and crackers—her favorites—plus some salt for her walk. She was dying, and he couldn't believe whom she was most worried about.

Roger. The creepy caretaker who squatted on her property. Lived in the cabin out back and shuffled around, mumbling to himself. Austin didn't know if he was a drunk, or on drugs, or was mentally disabled. And if that was the case, he felt bad, he really did, but Yvette shouldn't carry someone else's burden to that degree. Why was she so worried about him? Yvette wasn't exactly the warm and fuzzy type. Maybe it was just the fact that Roger had been around for so many years, or maybe there was a lot more to the story than he'd ever been told. Austin didn't like people prying into his business; he heard enough of people's pain all day long at work, and he wasn't the type to pry. But he couldn't stand seeing her so worked up. He'd ask around at the churches; maybe there was a shelter or home Roger could move into, maybe that would help ease Yvette's worries. She certainly couldn't expect whoever bought the property to let the old man keep living there.

Austin was almost out the door when a silver ornament dangling on a display tree caught his eye. Silver letters spelled out the word JOY. Neither he nor Yvette had celebrated Christmas in a long time. And she'd probably hate it. But maybe she wouldn't. Maybe it would make her smile. He returned to the register to pay for the ornament, then tucked it into the bag and headed for his truck.

"Why did you buy those?" she asked, pointing to the apples the minute he returned to the truck.

"They're good for you."

"Don't be a fool." She shook her head. "It's too late to keep the doctor away."

"It's never too late."

"If I didn't know better I'd say you're hoping for a Christmas miracle."

"Would that be so bad?" As Austin started the drive back home, he purposefully avoided her gaze. He needn't have bothered. Yvette stared out the window.

"The real miracle is that I made it this far," she said.

Me too, Austin thought, but he didn't voice it. Would have sounded cruel coming from a thirty-two-year-old regardless of the fact that quite often that was exactly how he felt. Life could do a number on you if you let it. They fell into an uneasy silence as he took the curves and climbed higher up the mountain road to her sprawling property. He couldn't help but wonder who would inherit her estate. The place had belonged to her late husband, Rupert Harris, who had run a sled and skating outfit in town in the winter and horseback riding all other times of year. Rupert Harris had come from money and his first wife died in a car accident. She passed young so there were no kids, and by the time he fell in love with Yvette, both of them were well into their sixties. Yvette had a son from her first marriage, but Austin had never met him, and the one time he pressed Yvette on it she simply said: *He's gone.* The set of her mouth and the pain reflected in her eyes made him back off. Austin didn't know whether that meant he had passed away or he had taken off. He never brought up the subject again.

If Yvette had any other family or friends, they didn't come around. She had twenty acres and a gorgeous log home that resembled a mini ski lodge. He hoped whoever inherited or purchased it would love it and take care of it the way she had.

Leavenworth was such a charming place; he'd hate to see the house abandoned or torn down for God knows what a developer might come up with. A hotel, or actual lodge, he supposed. With its twenty pine-tree-filled acres, and skating pond, and hills to sled, surely someone would be thinking along those lines. He'd buy it himself if he could afford it, but he could barely afford his own three-room cabin and two acres next door. Not that he needed more room, it suited him perfectly fine. But he sure didn't like the thought of having new neighbors. Not that this was any time to be thinking about himself. He had to find a way to cheer her up. They pulled up to the black iron gate that secured the entrance. Austin rolled down the window and punched the key code into the security system. A few seconds later the electronic gates slid open. He thought it was cool that Rupert had combined modern technology with the old-fashioned gates. Austin pulled in and took the half-moon drive up to the house where he put his truck in park. Then he grabbed the groceries with one hand and with the other he helped Yvette up the steps to the wraparound porch and into her house.

They entered into a mudroom. Austin put the groceries down and pulled off his boots, then hung his winter coat on the rack on the wall. Yvette had already slipped out of her coat and boots and had headed into the house. Austin followed.

The main floor reminded Austin of an expansive loft apartment. There was a fireplace with a stone chimney that took center stage on the main wall, towering at least fifteen feet up to the start of the second level. An arrangement of soft leather sofas faced the fireplace, and a bank of windows overlooked the expansive grounds. A few feet behind the sofas was a marble island with stools all around, delineating the chef's kitchen behind it. With so many windows, the place definitely had an indoor-outdoor feel, and the natural light helped offset all the wood—from the thick planks in the floor to the logs in the walls. Had it been closed in, the effect might have been suffocating, but with all the space and cathedral ceilings, it transformed into something artistic and welcoming.

Yvette's room was on the main floor down a hall to the right, and the second story housed at least five guest rooms, but Austin had never been beyond the main room and kitchen. Not that he felt any need to nose around, he certainly would never let anyone poke around in his little cabin.

He knelt down in front of the fireplace, added a few logs and kindling from the bin sitting next to it, and tossed some crumpled-up newspaper on top. Just as he had struck a match and lit the newspaper, a horrifying scream rang out. It had come from Yvette, who was in the kitchen area putting away the groceries. Austin dropped the match into the fire, then shot to his feet and hurried toward Yvette.

She was standing stock-still, mouth open like a rendition of *The Scream*. Dangling from her fingers was the ornament. *JOY.* He watched her stare at it like it was a snake ready to strike.

"What on earth is the matter?" Austin heard his own voice echoing back, sounding slightly hysterical. His heart was thumping in his chest. Yvette's eyes flicked to the windows, and Austin turned around and looked. Roger was standing in the yard, staring into the windows. He was a tall man, with broad shoulders. He wore a cracked leather jacket and always had on a red cap. The way he silently appeared and stared always made Austin think he was an alien, sent here to observe human life but not participate in it. That was the nicest comparison Austin could make about the older man. He was younger than Yvette, probably in his fifties. Before Yvette passed away Austin was going to have to find out what the guy's deal was. The last thing he'd stand for was somebody scamming her for an inheritance. "Did he scare you?" Austin said. "I told you that guy is creepy. I'll go talk to him." Austin headed for the door.

"It's not him," Yvette said. "It's you."

Austin turned back to Yvette. She wasn't making any sense. "Me? What did I do?"

"What is the meaning of this?" Yvette was literally shaking as she bobbed the ornament up and down.

Why is she so worked up about a freaking Christmas ornament?

"Who are you?" she said. "Some kind of Ghost of Christmas Past?"

That stopped him in his tracks. "What?"

"What is this?" She flicked the ornament with her index finger and they both watched it swing for a second.

Austin shrugged. "I thought it might cheer you up."

Yvette recoiled. "Why are you doing this to me?"

"I'm sorry it's upsetting you so much."

"What's the third one?"

"Do you need me to get you something? Water? Your pills?"

"Just get it over with. Say her name."

"Say whose name?"

Yvette shook her head, then removed a flask from one of the kitchen cabinets and took a long swig. How many of those did she have lying around? Maybe a bit of paranoia was a side effect of stopping chemo or being told you wouldn't live much past the new year. Who did these doctors think they were, giving Yvette news like this at this time of year? He turned back to see if Roger was still skulking on the lawn. Not only was he still there, but he had edged closer to the windows.

"Don't stare at him, it's not polite," Yvette said, coming up behind him.

"He's the one standing out there just staring into the windows," Austin said.

"He's not hurting you."

"Yes, ma'am."

"Go on home now. I need my rest."

Austin really wanted to know why she was so worked up about the ornament. Not only had he not cheered her up, she seemed even more upset than before. "Have a little faith," he said. This time in addition to letting out another bloodcurdling scream, Yvette Garland lifted a rolling pin and charged him.

CHAPTER 3

Hope Garland paced her tiny apartment, clutching her iPad and practicing her pitch. "It's been five years since the three of us spent Christmas together." She stopped. Could it be longer? Definitely longer since the three of them spent Christmas with their mother.

"Can you do that somewhere else?" Michael called from the sofa. She glanced at the top of his head, dark hair sticking up in the middle. He'd been glued to the television for the past hour, captivated by some kind of extreme fishing show. Bigger boats, more waves, hairier fish. *Gawd*. He hadn't even taken her suggestion of watching *It's a Wonderful Life* seriously. Another piece of evidence that he wasn't the right guy for her, bagged and sealed and placed in the evidence locker. Truthfully, she'd known it after their first month together, when it became obvious that he wasn't a dog lover, but she'd spent the next five months trying to talk herself into him. Every time she wanted to break up with him, she could hear her older sister, Faith, in her ear. "Not everyone is a dog fanatic, Hope. *Must Love Dogs* is one thing. *Must Think Life Revolves Around Dogs* is you being psychotic. Give people a break!"

Faith was never one to tiptoe in on little cat feet. So Hope tried. She'd given him multiple breaks. Maybe she was the one who was broken. Or maybe, she knew it all along. He just wasn't the guy for her. Why did she think she had to turn him into a villain to admit it wasn't working out? She hadn't fostered a dog since they'd started dating, and she couldn't wait to get to work every day just to be around those big eyes and wagging tails. She missed having a dog lying at the foot of the bed, snoring away. She missed the click of their nails on the wood floor, and the exuberant joy when it was time for a walk. Dogs taught people how to live in the moment. She felt bad that Faith couldn't see that. But that wasn't the only reason she wanted to end things with Michael. And maybe all her reasons were all little things, things other women would consider trifling—but the little things added up.

"Look at the size of that bass!" he said. "That's a whopper."

"Wow," Hope said. "Size does matter." She could see him nod. He didn't register sarcasm. She felt mean. But seriously. Did he expect her to get excited over a fish? She didn't understand the male brain. Slippery, and elusive. Like a fish? Just because one lived in the Pacific Northwest did not mean they loved freaking fish. Maybe, if he had ever tried to get excited about dogs, she would have tried to get excited about fish. At least dogs were incredible companions. And smart. So, so smart. Could you say the same about fish? Could you cuddle up on the sofa with a bass? Was it all about stringing it up and posing for the picture? Sometimes she thought men weren't just from different planets, they were off in their own solar system.

Be nice, Hope. As soon as the holidays were over, she was going to end this relationship as neatly as possible. She would let him down gently. She would put it in a language he understood. *As you know, Michael. There are plenty of fish in the sea.* Holidays should not be about heartbreak. Would Michael be heartbroken? She doubted it. Hope tucked a strand of hair behind her ear and went back to silently begging her sisters to spend Christmas with her this year.

"As long as you're pacing, would you get me a pilsner?" Michael called out. Hope rolled her eyes, knowing he'd never turn around to see it. She headed for the fridge. He was on his third beer within the hour. She shouldn't be counting, it was Sunday, they weren't going anywhere, but she knew by the end of the day the six-pack would be gone, and he might even rummage through her cupboards for some hard liquor, and he would fall asleep on the sofa and snore. She was twenty-eight. Not married, no kids. Was this really the life she wanted? He wasn't a drunk now, but if he kept this up, what would he be like in ten years? It was too reminiscent of her parents. But she didn't say a word. She didn't want to fight. She handed him another beer and headed for the hall between the living room and her bedroom where she could pace in relative peace. She wished he'd just go home, but in order to get her wish, she'd actually have to have a conversation with him. One she didn't want to face right now. Right now she had to focus on her sisters.

Christmas with their mother, or Carla as they'd been ordered to call her, hadn't happened for at least six years. Maybe seven? And Carla was definitely out this year—she'd already announced she was going to Cuba with her latest boyfriend, but her sisters hadn't made any such proclamations. Yet. Hope had a small window; if she wanted to nail down plans for Christmas, she was going to have to pounce.

Last year they told her she'd waited too late. "Sorry, Hope," Faith said. "We're going to visit Stephen's mother. If only you had said something earlier."

"Same here," Joy said. "It's too late to change my plans as well."

"What plans?" Hope asked.

"Friends on the east coast," Joy said, leaving it at that. Hope was convinced Joy had no such plans, but accusing your little sister of being a liar usually didn't go over so well.

The year before, they said she'd asked too early. "I can't even think about Christmas this early," Faith said. "Let us get through the start of the school year, would you?"

"I don't even know what I'm doing tomorrow let alone Christmas," Joy said. Hope didn't know when her sisters had morphed into Goldilocks—too hot, too cold, too porridge-y!—but if they didn't start celebrating with her, they were going to turn her into the Grinch. This time she was asking at exactly the right time. Just a few days after Thanksgiving. Not too early, but still plenty of time to arrange travel and plan exactly where they would spend Christmas.

She took a deep breath and imagined they were in the room. Faith, tall and leggy, would no doubt be looking sexy in designer jeans and some kind of trendy top with lace, or shimmery material, something practical but uber-feminine. Long brown hair flowing past her breasts. A slightly superior look on her face. At thirty-two Faith was the oldest, but she still sported a flawless complexion, no doubt the result of what Carla called "her hippy-dippy California ways."

Joy, on the other hand, twenty-four but still the baby of the family, would be splayed out on the La-Z-Boy, her athletic figure practically hidden underneath her tattoos, and colored sweatpants with JUICY on her derriere, and her pretty face slathered with dark makeup. Maybe a neon-pink streak running through her choppy platinum hair. Joy thought of herself as the forgotten child and maybe to some extent she had been. Her mission in life seemed to be to make Hope feel that everything she said was a complete waste of breath, or at least worthy of an eye roll.

She felt bad for judging her sisters, but she couldn't help it. How did they see her? Did they look at her as the dutiful middle child? Did they think her boring with her girl-next-door look, her honey-colored hair that she'd never touched with highlights despite the two of them begging her to "mix it up," and her natural brows they'd salivated over tweezing? Did they long to take a lint roller to her T-shirts covered in dog hair? Most likely. No matter.

She began her plea again, making eye contact with the apparitions of her sisters. "You two can come to Portland, or Joy and I could go to San Francisco, or we could all meet in Seattle."

Joy probably wouldn't go for meeting in Seattle; she'd told Hope she was in between apartments, whatever that meant. Regardless, Joy would have a fit if Hope didn't at least include the *possibility* of spending the holidays in her home turf. It was so ridiculous, all three of them lived on the west coast, but given the protestations of Faith and Joy every year, you'd think they lived on opposite ends of the earth. Every year Hope tried everything she could think of to convince them to spend it together, and every year they deflected her request with a sorry excuse. Faith's usually revolved around family:

We're going to spend it with Stephen's mother this year, sorry.

The kids just want to spend it at home.

I'd rather wait until we could all afford to go somewhere nice, somewhere away from here.

Joy's excuses ran the gamut and were often filled with a Shakespearean-esque passion:

I'm not celebrating that Hallmark holiday this year!
Bob (Mark, Jeff, Greg) and I are:

    a)   Hiking the Appalachian Trail
    b)   Buying a yurt
    c)   Going to Vegas

Hope was always defeated. *Not this year, sisters.*

But short of kidnapping them, Hope wasn't quite sure how to get her way this year. She thought about involving Stephen, but she never really felt comfortable around Faith's husband. There was nothing wrong with him per se, but he was a bit stiff. And he always seemed to want Faith to go to his mother's house for Christmas. No matter what, it was probably going to take several attempts, so she might just as well make the first call. But to whom? If she called Faith first, Joy might complain that she'd been an afterthought. But Faith always had to call the shots, so she wouldn't be receptive if Hope and Joy had it all worked out in advance.

"I can't believe you're this worked up about Christmas," Michael called from the sofa.

"That's because your family is normal," she said. "They just get together. My family talks about getting together like scientists talk about taking trips to outer space. *Maybe. Someday. You never know.*"

"Hurry up and call because if you three aren't getting together, I had a few thoughts of my own."

"What thoughts?"

"Let's just say—we're going to have a merry Christmas whether you get together with your sisters or not."

"I have to get together with my sisters. If we don't start doing it, we'll forget how."

"Then call already."

She hoped he wasn't planning anything big. Couldn't he see that they weren't right for each other? What was wrong with this picture? The guy she didn't want to be with was sticking to her like glue, and the two women she did want to be with were dodging and evading. Regardless, he was right. She needed to get over herself and call. She clicked on the video icon and clicked on the picture of Faith's smiling face.

Hope smiled when they connected and took a deep breath to start her pitch.

"I can't this year," Faith said before Hope had uttered a single word. "I just can't." Hope realized a second too late that her lips had begun to flap, ironically like a fish caught in a bait. "And don't bother with Joy. She and her latest boyfriend are opening a coffee shop. In Seattle," Faith added when Hope didn't respond. "Across from a Starbucks." Hope continued to stare. "Maybe next year," Faith said. A noise erupted in the background, a thud. It could have been something falling, it could have been thunder, it could have been the sound of Hope's heart free-falling. "I gotta go," Faith said. "Maybe next Christmas." She clicked off. Hope hadn't said a single word.

CHAPTER 4

It took more sips from the flask, a whole lot of talking—mostly apologizing—for Austin to calm Yvette down this time.

"What is going on?" he said when she'd finally stopped wielding the rolling pin and had sunk into the sofa. "Did you stop a medication you weren't supposed to?"

She pointed to a bookshelf that lined the far wall. "*Little Women,*" she said. "Bring it here." He retrieved the book and handed it to her. "Sit."

He sat next to her as she opened the book. He hoped she wasn't going to read to him. He was exhausted and really just wanted to go home. Instead, she removed a slightly faded photo from the book and handed it to him. It was a color photograph, lined in a thick white frame that dated it at least twenty years. It was dog-eared and wrinkled, but its subjects were still clear. Two little girls in green and red dresses sat in front of a Christmas tree with their legs splayed out. The girl on the right held an infant in her lap. The girls looked to be about four and eight, and the younger one held the baby in her lap. Big smiles were planted on their faces. The baby, whose mouth was open in a scream, must have just come home from the hospital. Austin looked at Yvette. "Are you one of these girls?"

Tears filled her eyes as she shook her head. He'd never seen Yvette cry, not even at Rupert's funeral. "Those are my grand-daughters."

That was a shock. She'd never mentioned grandchildren. She pointed at the girl in the middle. "Hope." She pointed at the infant that Hope was holding. "Joy." She pointed at the girl on the right. "Faith."

Austin took a minute to process it. *Hope. Joy. Faith.* He'd played *hope* in the Scrabble game, then bought the *JOY* ornament, then said, *Have a little faith.* Good God. What were the odds of that? He had absolutely no explanation other than the Santa-in-the-sky. "You're kidding me." His left arm erupted in goose bumps.

"You swear you didn't know?"

"I swear I didn't know." No wonder she freaked out. That was weird.

"Someone is working through you," she said. "Sending me a message."

"Like Santa Claus?" Austin joked.

"Like my son," Yvette said, deadly serious. "Their father."

"His ghost?" Austin said. "Are you talking about ghosts here?" He'd better be careful. Just because Austin didn't believe in stuff like that didn't mean he wanted to argue with a dying old woman about whether or not there was an afterlife. So her son must have passed away. Austin wondered what happened to him. Why was she estranged from her granddaughters? Maybe he could do something for Yvette after all. "I know what he could be trying to say," Austin said. Yvette narrowed her eyes. If he wasn't careful she'd be slinging that rolling pin around again.

"What?" There was an edge to her voice, she was on guard.

"You need to have them come home for Christmas," he said. As soon as it was out of his mouth he prayed that nothing horrible had happened to them.

"I couldn't do that," she said.

Oh God. *Had* something horrible happened to those adorable little girls? Austin tensed. "Why not?"

"This is the last time I ever saw them," she said, picking up the picture. "It was the middle of summer."

"Then why is there a Christmas tree?"

A little smile played out on Yvette's face. "Because their daddy loved Christmas. He wanted it to be their Christmas card the following Christmas. So he set up the tree to take the picture."

"That's sweet."

"The only time he ever put up an artificial one, mind you. For real Christmas it had to be a real tree."

Austin wondered where she was going with all this, but he didn't want to rush her. "I agree. Nothing beats a real tree. That wonderful pine smell when you walk in the house."

"I thought you hated Christmas as much as I do?"

"Doesn't mean I hate everything about it. I think Christmas trees are beautiful. I like a white Christmas. I've been known to hum a carol or two." Austin handed the picture back. "These seem like really good memories. You should try and get in touch with them."

"I'm sure they don't even remember me."

"What happened?"

"Their mother took them away. From their father. From me. She destroyed his life."

Austin wondered what that was all about. "I'm sorry. I really am. But whatever their mother did—it wasn't their fault. How old are they now?"

Yvette caressed the picture with her fingertip. "The baby, Joy, is twenty-four, Hope is twenty-eight, and Faith is thirty-two."

"You see?"

"See what?" Yvette snapped before he could finish. "That I've missed their entire lives?"

"They're adults now. Why not at least reach out?"

"I wouldn't know where to begin to find them."

"I'll do it," Austin said. "I'll find them for you."

"You're just saying that because I'm dying."

"So? Can you think of a better reason?"

Yvette took her time walking to the window, then stood staring out at her property. "Rupert loved Christmas. Remember how he'd turn the yard into some kind of extravaganza? The kids who used to come skate on the pond? Cutting down the Christmas tree? The carols?"

"I remember," Austin said. Apart from the downtown celebrations, Rupert's was always the place to be.

"If you find my granddaughters, and they're willing to come see me before I die, there's one nonnegotiable condition."

"Shoot."

Yvette turned from the window and stared at Austin. "There will be no Christmas."

"Pardon?"

"No tree. No decorations. No singing. I'm not going to spend the last few weeks of my life mired in this commercialized, expensive, stressful bull. No Christmas."

"You're talking to the choir. But don't they have a right to celebrate Christmas if they want?"

"Oh, rights shmites. They can celebrate Christmas next year. Besides, I've got a little gift that might just make up for it."

"What's that?"

"If they follow my rules, I'm leaving the three of them this place."

Wow. That would be an easy choice. At least for him. Still. If you were a Christmas lover it was a bit Scrooge-like. He shifted. "There are more rules?"

"Austin. This is life. There are always more rules."

CHAPTER 5

Hope strode through the corridor of Portland Paws, treating herself to one last glance at all the empty cages, thrilled that all of their dogs had been adopted well before Christmas. It was a record, thanks in part to the Whine and Cheese event she had orchestrated. As a no-kill shelter they could host only fifteen dogs at a time, and if it took a while for certain dogs to get adopted, the staff would often foster them. But since all the dogs were adopted by the end of the event, the team of six was now on break until just after the new year. Hope was just about to turn the sign to Closed Until January 2nd, when the door pushed open and an enormous bloodhound burst in, dragging a petite woman behind him. Hope took one look at the woman's face and she knew what the woman was planning. Shoot. Michael was waiting in the car. She told him she'd be out in five. The bloodhound lunged for Hope, and the woman dropped the leash along with a fifty-pound bag of dog chow. "Merry Christmas," she said. "He's all yours." Yep. That's exactly what Hope thought she was going to do. The dog jumped up and stood eye-to-eye with Hope.

"Manners." Hope gently pushed the dog down, making a mental note to suggest a breath freshener. "I'm sorry, we're closed for the holidays," she said to the woman in a friendly but firm voice. Friendly but Firm was Hope's new motto.

"I'm not staying," the woman said. She whirled around and made a beeline for the door.

"Stop," Hope said. She rushed after her.

The woman reached the door first and yanked it open. The dog planted its giant front paws on the counter and began sniffing.

"We can't take him until January second," Hope yelled, hoping to reach her in time. The woman was already out the door.

"He's not mine," she said, racing down the walk.

"I need a history, a name, background, an age," Hope said. "Come back here."

"His owner died. Don't know his name. Don't care. He smells. And I don't know how old he is, but I'm too old to deal with this shit." With that the woman disappeared into a black BMW waiting at the curb and roared off.

"Merry Christmas to you too," Hope said.

A beep sounded. Hope turned her head toward the curb where Michael was parked. He beeped again. Did he not notice that a bloodhound came in but didn't go out? Was it really too much to step out of the car and speak to her?

Hope gestured for Michael to come in. Finally his head popped out of the passenger side window. "Why aren't you getting in the car?"

"Did you not see what just happened?" Hope said.

"Our reservations are for seven o'clock."

"That woman just abandoned a dog here."

It was getting dark, but Hope could see Michael looking around. He'd missed it all. He'd probably been buried in his smartphone. "What woman?"

"Come in," Hope said, then turned and ran for the inside. Michael didn't want to come in, he was anxious to get to the restaurant in time. This was definitely going to cause another fight. She couldn't waste time arguing with him, there was an enormous dog sniffing around inside. She pushed open the door and almost smacked into him. He was chowing down on a sea of dog food. The large bag lay on the ground, ripped to shreds, pellets spilled across the floor.

"Oh God." Was he starving? Poor thing. "Okay, okay," Hope said, stepping around him and the mess. How much should she let him eat? This was a nightmare. She grabbed the broom and dustpan and neared the lake of food. Half of it seemed to disappear in the seconds she'd turned her back. "Take it easy," she said. "You don't want to get sick, do you?" When the broom neared the food he lifted his head an inch and emitted a long, low growl. Bloodhounds weren't known to be vicious, despite their size, but any animal could lash out if they hadn't had a good meal in a while. She was going to have to coax him into a back kennel, get him some water, and call for help. But there was no way she could let him eat an entire bag of food.

"Hey, you," she said, loudly. The dog didn't even lift his head. Hope turned and grabbed a stuffed toy from the counter, a stuffed elf someone had left behind. "Lookie here," she said, waving the elf in his peripheral vision. "Lookie here." The dog did look, then lunged for the elf. When he got it between his teeth, he nudged forward. He wanted her to play tug-of-war. He was just a big baby. She began walking backward, holding on to what little of the elf wasn't in his giant, slobbering mouth. Little by little he was coming with her. "My elf," she teased. "You better hang on."

The dog shook his head violently, and Hope's hands jerked along with it. "He doesn't want to be a dog's toy," she said, glancing at the stuffed elf while trying to pick up the pace. "He wants to be a dentist." Just then the door opened and Michael came barreling in.

"Watch out," she yelled. Michael slipped on the lake of dog food and cried out. The bloodhound whipped around, dropped the elf, and flew across the room before Hope could stop him. By the time she reached Michael, the dog had him pinned on the floor, each of his four huge paws trapping Michael underneath him. His big face was right in Michael's face. Oh no. Michael didn't even like dogs from a distance. The low growl was back. Michael had stopped screaming, in fact was too terrified to utter a word, but Hope could see him shaking.

"He's just a big baby," Hope said, grabbing the dog by the scruff of the neck and pulling him off her boyfriend. The dog let her tug at him and soon she had at least two paws pointing back toward the kennel. Michael was breathing heavily, on the point of hyperventilating.

"Come on, big boy," Hope said. "Let's go lie down."

"Help," Michael said quietly.

"He's not on you anymore." Hope tugged a little harder, and after a few forced steps the dog hurried back to the elf, snatching it up and looking expectantly at Hope.

"Good boy," she said.

"Bad dog," she heard Michael say. "Bad, bad dog."

"I can't believe you don't like dogs," Hope said.

"I'm allergic," Michael yelled.

"That's code for 'I hate dogs,' " Hope said. "You should get off the floor. It's pretty rank." She entered the kennel with the dog happily following. But when he saw the empty kennels, little jail cells from which all the other prisoners had escaped, he turned back to the door with a mournful howl. "Only for a very short time," she said. "You'll get water, and a pillow, and I pray Olivia will take no more than thirty minutes to come pick you up." His big eyes blinked at her. *Oh God. Those big, silky, floppy ears and hanging jowls. What a face. God, dogs were so freaking cute. How could Michael hate them?* She wanted to blame the fact that he hadn't grown up with dogs, but neither had she. "Unless you count my sisters," she said to the dog out loud. He tucked his head down. "Come on." She pointed to the first kennel on the right, which still had a big pillow in it. He went in, curled up on the pillow with the elf tucked under a big flap of skin, and sighed. "I'll bring you water," she said softly, closing the door to the kennel. She filled the largest bowl she could find with water and headed back to the reception area, where she found Michael hunched over, one hand resting on his back.

"Dinner is out," he said with what looked like an exaggerated grimace. "Let's just go home. I need a muscle relaxer."

"Sorry," Hope said. "I can't leave until Olivia gets here to take the dog."

He sighed. "How long?"

"Olivia didn't pick up the phone so I have no idea."

"I had such a nice evening planned," Michael said. "A big surprise."

"I'm sorry. We'll do it another night." She tried to keep the irritation out of her voice, but really, what did he expect her to do?

"This is supposed to be the start of our holiday."

Holiday. It no longer felt like Christmas to Hope. Another holiday without her sisters. And now this. The man she wanted to break up with laying a guilt trip on her. "Unless you want me to take the dog with us, there's nothing I can do."

"Funny."

"I wish you liked dogs."

"Don't start. I'm *allergic*. Can't you hear how stuffed up I sound?"

"You should throw in a few fake sneezes." The phone rang. Hope snatched it up.

"Hey," Olivia said in a guarded, almost accusatory tone. Was everyone going to blame Hope for the poor dog being abandoned? "I got your message. What's up?"

"A woman literally dumped a dog on me and took off," Hope said. "I need you to come get him."

Olivia groaned. "Did you tell her we were closing for the holidays?"

"Of course. She didn't listen."

"You should have had the door locked."

Hope took a deep breath. She had to keep calm. Just because she was miserable at Christmas didn't mean she had to take it out on others. "Can you come get him?"

"No, I'm leaving tomorrow for New York."

Hope could hear the excitement in her voice. New York at

Christmas. She'd often imagined herself there with her sisters. Taking in the tree at Rockefeller Center, ice skating in Wollman Rink, perusing the decorative windows of Saks and Macy's. But no, they'd never agreed to that either. Olivia was never going to cancel her trip, but Hope gave it her best try. "You're up for fostering next."

"And there were no dogs to foster."

Thanks to my event. "Well, what am I supposed to do?"

"Can you take him?"

"No, I'm having Christmas with my sisters." Taking the dog would mean admitting defeat. And Hope wasn't done with her sisters yet.

"That's great," Olivia said. "Finally, right?"

Hope had complained to everyone about her sisters not spending Christmas with her. Olivia sounded truly happy for her. Hope felt like a heel. "Should I start making calls?"

"I'm ahead of you there," Olivia said. "I'm waiting for a few people to call me back."

"Anything promising?"

"A friend of mine might be in to take him."

"And if she doesn't?"

"He."

"Can I have his number?"

"Look, I'm doing the best I can."

"I'm sure. But I have to take off too."

"You shouldn't have left the door unlocked."

"I didn't think anyone would just storm in and abandon her dog."

"Don't get snippy. I'm doing the best I can."

Hope sighed. "Okay. Did your friend say he'd call or come in, or what?"

"He's looking into it. I'll call you back." With a click she was gone.

Michael threw open his arms. "Let's just take him to another shelter."

"I can't take him from a no-kill shelter to a kill shelter."

"They might find a home for him."

"They might not."

"It's the holiday season. All they have to do is throw some antlers on him and someone will take him."

Let's throw some antlers on you, see if anyone takes you. "I can't take him to a shelter."

"Of course you can't." His sarcasm was as thick as his skull. He took out his cell phone, dialed, and then hung up with a heavy sigh. "Why is the reception so bad in here?"

"Too much concrete," Hope said, looking at the thick walls.

"Looks like I'll have to go outside in the damp and cold to cancel our reservation." He pushed open the door. A burst of cold air rushed in. A few seconds later the door swung open again and a man stepped in. He was tall, around Hope's age, and good-looking in that rugged, west coast sort of way. Olivia had come through fast.

"I'm so glad you're here," Hope said.

"You are?" He had a nice baritone voice.

"Are you Olivia's friend?"

"Yvette's," the man answered. Hope frowned. She didn't know any volunteers named Yvette. It didn't matter, as long as he was taking the dog.

"Great," she said. "You're a lifesaver." He tilted his head and stepped closer. He had that cowboy look, with brown hair that appeared tossed rather than combed, a leather jacket with a flannel shirt underneath, stone-washed jeans and cowboy boots. He had green eyes and a few days of stubble on his jaw. He was gorgeous but didn't act like he knew it. That made him even more attractive, which was just ridiculously redundant.

"How's that?" His voice was warm and genuinely curious.

"I just didn't think anyone would come for him. My boyfriend was worried I'd be stuck here all night." For a split second Hope wished she hadn't said the word *boyfriend.*

"I think there's been a misunderstanding," he said. "Are you Hope Garland?"

"Yes, yes. Sorry. You're in the right place. Olivia told me you might be coming."

"She did?"

"Yes."

"And who is Olivia?"

"She's the owner." Hope frowned. Why was she telling him that? He was Olivia's friend, wasn't he?

The man held his hands up. "Let's start over. My name is Austin Rhodes." He stuck his hand out. Hope shook it. He had a nice grip.

"Sorry. I don't mean to be rude or rush you. It's just this woman abandoned the poor guy at the last minute and I'm supposed to be starting my holiday break."

"Holiday break!" he said, as if he were terribly excited for her. "That's perfect."

Hope cocked her head until she realized that she'd probably picked that up from dogs, then casually tried to straighten it before he made the same connection. "Yes, well. Thank you. I'll just grab the dog."

"Wait." He held out his hand and for a second she thought about taking it. "What dog?"

Gorgeous but not very bright. That is too bad. "The dog that was just abandoned," Hope said slowly.

Austin put his hands up again. "Sorry. I'm not here for a dog."

"Then why are you here? Who's Yvette?"

"What dog?" They spoke at the same time.

"Do you like dogs?" Hope asked. Even if he wasn't sent by Yvette, maybe he was sent by Santa to take the dog.

"I love dogs."

Was that big smile genuine? Maybe he was a con artist or a criminal. She couldn't hand the poor dog over to a criminal. God, she hoped he wasn't a criminal. He was way too good-looking to be an outlaw. Although that would make him a gorgeous bad boy, and what woman didn't like that? Between his looks and that adorable bloodhound, who knew how many innocent victims he could lure into a van? Hope put her hands on her hips. "Do you have a van?"

He wrinkled his brows in confusion. "No, a truck."

"What kind of a truck?"

"A pickup."

Well, that was a relief. Kind of hard to hide a victim in the
back of a pickup. Unless . . . "Open back or an enclosed cab?"

"Pardon?"

"Is the back of your truck open or enclosed?"

Austin folded his arms across his chest. "Open."

Hope breathed a sigh of relief. "Do you want to meet him?"

"I really should stay focused. Are you almost finished? Can
we go somewhere and talk?"

Was he some kind of creep? He might have an open pickup
truck, but that didn't mean she would just take off with him,
right? She couldn't. Could she? She glanced outside. As much
as she hated to admit it, she wished Michael wasn't here. She
liked the idea of being kidnapped by this cowboy. She'd better
get a grip. Plenty of psychopaths had been attractive. "Talk
about what?"

"I'd rather tell you in private." He looked solemn.

"Tell me what?"

The door burst open and Michael barreled in. "Is he taking
the dog? Can we finally get out of here?"

"He's not taking the dog," Hope said. "Yet."

"I'm not taking the dog," Austin said.

"You've got to be kidding me," Michael said. He began to
pace the tiny reception area. "He has to take the dog."

"He's not Olivia's friend. It's a misunderstanding," Hope
said. Although she still had no idea who he was or what he was
doing here.

"Then why are you here?" Michael took in Austin, and squared
his shoulders. Was he jealous?

"Michael," Hope said. In case Austin wasn't a criminal or a
creep, she didn't want Michael to make him feel bad.

Michael turned to her. "We have plane tickets to Hawaii."

"What?"

"We leave for Maui tomorrow morning and we'll be there
through the new year."

"Through Christmas?" Hope said.

Austin held his hand up. "You might want to hear me out
first."

"Surprise," Michael said.

"But what about my sisters?"

"Exactly," Austin said. "Think of them."

Hope glared at him, then turned to Michael. "You booked tickets to Maui without asking me?" Hope said. She couldn't believe he did that. She'd told him she wanted to see her sisters for Christmas, that she was going to make a real effort this year. Hadn't he been listening to her?

"I think the words you're looking for are—*Thank you,*" Michael said.

"I wanted to spend Christmas with my sisters," Hope said. "Remember?" Sure they'd flat out rejected her again, but that didn't mean she had given up. She still believed in Christmas miracles. Sort of.

"Good," Austin said. "That's very, very good."

Hope swung her gaze to him. Who was he to tell her what was good let alone very, very good? "Who are you?"

"I live next door to your grandmother," he said.

"You live next door to a cemetery in Florida?" Hope put her hands on her hips and arched her eyebrow.

This time Austin cocked his head. "No," he said. "I live in Leavenworth, Washington."

Leavenworth, Washington. Hope had heard of the little Bavarian town, but she'd never made it there. Every year she tried to get her sisters to go somewhere with her. There were so many great little trips in this area of the country. Victoria, B.C., Vancouver, Alaska even. But her sisters never wanted to go anywhere. "My grandmother is buried in a cemetery in Miami," Hope said.

"Yvette Garland," Austin said.

"No," Hope said. "Wait. Who?" Garland? He couldn't possibly be talking about her father's mother, could he? Goose bumps suddenly raised on her arms, and her stomach clenched as one word flew through her head: *Daddy.*

"So you're not taking the dog?" Michael said.

"You know what?" Austin turned to Michael. "I would take the dog for her. But I sure as heck wouldn't do it for you." He turned back to Hope. "And I sure wouldn't want you to miss out on Hawaii with Mr. Wonderful here—"

"Hey—" Michael said.

"—but I'm here because your grandmother is dying and her last wish is to spend Christmas with you, and Joy, and Faith."

"What?" Hope said. Oh God, he knew her sisters' names. He was talking about her paternal grandmother. Why wasn't he mentioning her father? Could this really be the year they found him? Now that would be a Christmas miracle. No. He wasn't alive. He couldn't be. He never would have abandoned them. Never. Hope's heart gave a painful little squeeze.

"Who are you and what are you trying to pull?" Michael said.

"My paternal grandmother," Hope said, testing out the words. *Daddy.* She'd almost cried it out. No matter how old she got, part of her was stuck at the age where he'd left her. Left *them.* Did Austin Rhodes know her father? She held her breath, biding her time before she asked, terrified of the answer.

"That's right," Austin said. "Yvette Garland. She's my neighbor."

"You said that," Hope said, not unkindly.

"How do you know he's telling the truth?" Michael said.

"Here," Austin said. He handed Hope a picture.

She took it and stared at it in disbelief. It was of her and Faith and Joy. Joy was just an infant, Hope was holding her. She must have been at least four in the picture, but she had no memory of it. Where were they? Who took the picture? She peered closer. There was a Christmas tree in the background. Rage swelled in her. "This isn't real," she said, thrusting it back. But Austin refused to take it. His eyes remained steady on hers. "Joy never spent a Christmas with Dad. She was born in the summer. He didn't come for us. Not ever. She never spent Christmas with him."

Austin held up his hands. "Your grandmother said your father loved Christmas. He put up an artificial tree when she came home from the hospital because he wanted it to be your Christmas card the next year. It was the only time he put up an artificial tree because he preferred the real ones. Me too. I like 'em natural."

"Are we still talking about trees?" Michael asked.

Austin shook his head as if trying to shake Michael off. He held the picture up. "You're right. It was summer. She said so."

"She?"

"Yvette. Your grandmother."

Hope didn't know what to believe or what to say. "How did you find me?"

"I Googled you," Austin said. "You've done a lot of good work with the shelter. I was really impressed. Your Whine and Cheese event sounded brilliant."

Hope was stunned for a moment. "Thank you."

"Your what?" Michael said.

"Never mind," Hope said.

"Anybody can Google," Michael said.

"What does that have to do with anything?" Hope said to Michael. He crossed his arms across his chest and shrugged. She looked at Austin. "What about my father?" She could barely get the question out and her voice cracked.

"You can call your grandmother if you'd like," Austin said. "Or just about anybody in Leavenworth. They'll tell you I am who I say I am."

"What about my father?" Hope asked again. "Is he with her?"

Michael stepped in front of her as if trying to block out the sight of Austin. "Don't get worked up. This guy could be lying."

"I don't know anything about your father," Austin said. "But Yvette does. She won't share the details with me, so you'll have to ask her yourself."

"Have you talked to Joy or Faith yet?"

"No, you're the first."

"Why?"

"Yvette thought as the middle child you'd be most likely to persuade the other two."

"She was wrong," Hope said. "They never listen to me." They'd flat out rejected her again. But would they reject an invitation from their estranged grandmother? Could Hope be getting her Christmas wish after all? From the back room came a very long and very loud howl.

Hope looked at Austin. He held eye contact. The dog continued to howl. "Is my grandmother allergic to dogs?" she asked.

"No," Austin said. "I don't think so."

The dog howled again. Hope smiled. "Good. Put me down for a plus one."

A smile crept over Austin's face, the kind of smile that made a girl almost swoon. "You got it," he said.

"But we have tickets to Hawaii," Michael said.

"You have tickets to Hawaii," Hope said.

Michael stared at her. Then pointed at her. Then shifted his weight. Then shook his head as if shaking her off. "We're done," he said. "Completely over."

Oh, thank God. "Peace on earth," Hope said, and flashed him a smile. He narrowed his eyes, then turned and walked out the door, out of her life. She wished him well and mentally tossed him a fishing pole.

CHAPTER 6

"You can't seriously tell me you're getting into a truck with a total stranger and that slobbery beast and taking off for Leavenworth instead of coming to Hawaii with me?" So much for getting rid of him that easy. Michael cut her off just as she was about to climb into the passenger side of Austin's red pickup. The beast was already in the truck along with Austin.

"I've taken precautions," Hope said. She'd taken a picture of his driver's license and had posted it on all her social media sites in case he was a serial killer. Austin didn't put up an argument. Most serial killers probably would. She'd also called Yvette Garland and confirmed Austin was her neighbor and she had sent him. It was probably the shortest conversation of her life, and Hope now had more questions than ever. She had to meet this woman, she had to find out what happened to her father.

"If you do this, we're over," Michael said.

"You already ended it ten minutes ago," Hope pointed out.

"I was hurt. I'm giving you a second chance."

"No thank you," Hope said.

"I mean it. We're done."

"I understand." She wasn't smiling, was she? She would have to be careful not to show her relief.

Michael shifted, thoroughly flummoxed. "I'm just trying to get through to you."

"She's my grandmother."

"Who abandoned you."

"My father abandoned me. I can't blame that on her."

"You're being manipulated."

"I'm going to Leavenworth to meet my grandmother."

"If you make it there alive," Michael said.

"If he says or does anything weird, I'll ditch him."

"I can't believe you're doing this to us."

"We've only been seeing each other six months."

"So?"

It looked like Hope wasn't going to completely get out of the breakup portion of the relationship. "The six-month gift is perfume or a nice necklace—not a trip to Hawaii."

"You can pay me back."

"I don't want to pay you back. I don't want to go."

"You don't want to go to Hawaii, or you don't want to go to Hawaii with me?" There was hurt stamped in his eyes. She bet he had an extreme fishing adventure planned in Hawaii and that kept her from feeling too sorry for him.

"I don't think we're a match."

"Obviously," he said.

"Pardon?" She didn't know why she was letting him goad her. She should just let him say whatever he wanted as long as she ended up free.

"How could you turn down a trip to Hawaii? That's insane. I even have a deep-sea fishing excursion booked!"

She knew it. "I hate fish."

"What?"

"I. Hate. Fish."

"You're just trying to upset me."

"No, it's true. I loathe them. Scaly, slimy, foul-smelling, hideous things. I have nightmares about them."

"I can't believe you."

Hope threw her arms open à la *What are you going to do?* "Well, I'm glad you found out now. Better than slogging through another six months, right?" *Or six days.* She was never going to fall in love again. It was torture being trapped with the wrong person, pure torture.

"You're unbelievable."

"I don't know what else to say. Bon voyage. *Mele kilikimaka.*"

"What?" Michael said, mouth open.

"That's the island greeting that they send to you from the land where palm trees stray."

Michael just stood and stared. Austin laughed quietly in the background. Hope hopped into Austin's truck. His laughter grew louder.

"What?" Hope demanded.

"It's *sway.*"

She had no idea what he was talking about. "What is?"

"From the land where palm trees *sway.*"

"What did I say?"

"Stray."

"I did not."

"You most certainly did."

Hope opened her mouth to protest again and then laughed. "Guess I still have work on my mind." This time they shared the laugh. Hope exhaled.

"You okay?" Austin said.

"Let's go," Hope said.

"Is he writing down my license plate?" Austin was staring through the rearview mirror.

"And posting it to Facebook, Twitter, Pinterest, and Instagram," Hope said.

Austin laughed. "I didn't understand half of what you just said, but I'm okay with it."

So he was a mountain man who was also out of touch with the popular world. It made her like him even more. Joy was completely obnoxious on social media and so was her mother.

Austin stared at her. She didn't know what he was waiting for. She felt a flash of heat on her face as they looked at each other. "Where to?" he said at last.

Oh, duh. "My place so I can pack. Then, as long as you're fit to drive this late, Joy is in Seattle," Hope said.

"Fit as a fiddle," he said with a grin.

Hope purposefully avoided raking her eyes over his strong jawline and muscular arms. "But we're probably going to have to take her by force."

"As soon as I get coffee I'll be fit to keep driving, but I'll leave the force to you," Austin said.

"May the force be with me," Hope said. "Got it."

Austin laughed. "You're funny," he said. A warm flush worked its way through Hope. Michael had never laughed at her jokes. Austin massaged the top of the dog's gigantic head. "And there's not much room. We'll have to throw this guy in the back."

"Save that decision until after you meet Joy," Hope said.

An hour later, after stopping for Hope to throw some clothes in a bag and get coffee and gas, Austin's truck rattled along the highway with Christmas carols playing on the radio. When he got to the station playing them, Hope started to hum along with it. His hand was halfway to the knob as if he'd been about to change it, when he stopped. It wasn't lost on Hope that he'd left it on for her. Michael wouldn't have even noticed that she'd been humming along. Not that it meant anything.

She tried calling Joy and Faith. Neither of them picked up their phone. Were they screening? The thought that they would see her name flash across their screen and not pick up was beyond painful. She'd never done anything to them. She wasn't bossy like Faith and she didn't badger anyone for money like Joy. Yet still they ignored her. Well, not this time. This was a family emergency of sorts, wasn't it? She'd keep trying on the drive. She was going on to Leavenworth whether they came or not. Maybe her grandmother would tell her where she could find her father. Joy and Faith claimed to have no interest in confronting him, but there were some days it was all Hope thought about. She at least wanted to look him in the eyes and say, *How could you? Do you know how much we missed and loved you? Are you even sorry? Even a little bit?* But most of all she wanted to know that he was still alive, and doing okay. As okay as a man who abandoned his three daughters could be. Would he have left them if they were boys?

The dog was lying half on the seat and half on Hope. God, he was just a big sweetie. She loved running her fingers along his soft, floppy ears. With the heater going in the truck, and the music gently playing, and her close proximity to Austin, it struck her as ironic that here they were, perfect strangers, in a uniquely intimate setting. She thought she could even smell a touch of wood smoke on him. He glanced at her and she quickly averted her gaze, feeling her face heat up yet again. Thank goodness it was dark. She always liked riding in a car at night. The gentle hum of the road, the glow of streetlights, a dog's body heavy and comforting across her lap, the feel of him breathing in and out, and a gorgeous man at the wheel. Total strangers, yet they felt so familiar, and truth be told she was loving every second of it. That was the really weird part. She tried calling Joy again and once more it went to voice mail.

"Are you and your sisters close?" Austin asked. From the soft tone of his voice she knew he had picked up on the fact that they were anything but.

"We used to be," she said. *When we were children. When we had nothing but one another.* She didn't say any more at first, and Austin didn't pry. He just nodded. It wasn't a distracted nod either. She could tell he was really listening to her. It prompted her to say more. "But I keep trying."

"That's good," Austin said.

"Is it?" Hope mused.

"It is. You should never give up on family. Never."

He sounded passionate about it. She liked that about him. If only her sisters felt the same way. "Do you have brothers or sisters?"

He shook his head. She thought she caught a look of grief

pass across his face, but she was only looking at him in profile and in the dim cab it was hard to tell. She decided not to ask any follow-up questions; she was here for her grandmother and answers, not because the neighbor was wildly attractive.

"Are you hungry?" Austin asked. "We could stop for a bite."

"Starving," Hope said. "I was supposed to be going out to dinner tonight."

"And Maui tomorrow," Austin said.

Hope glanced at him. "I broke up with him," she said.

"I'm sorry," he said.

"Are you?" She got the feeling he hadn't liked Michael, so why let him get away with lying.

"Am I what?"

"Sorry that we broke up?"

Austin's eyes didn't leave the road. "Why wouldn't I be?" His voice took on a deeper tone. Husky was the word that came to mind. He didn't answer the question, and he wouldn't look at her. Did that mean anything?

"I didn't think you liked Michael. That's all."

Austin smiled. "Still have to work on my poker face."

"So I was right."

"Does it matter?"

"Yes, it kind of does."

"Why?" Austin asked.

"Why?" The nerve of him. To ask why. Because she wanted to find out if he liked her, that's why. "Forget it."

"If you're upset, then I'm sorry." This time Austin did glance at her.

God, he is gorgeous. He knew that, right? There was a definite jolt whenever they locked eyes. She looked away. "I'm not upset. At all. In fact I was just waiting until after the holidays to break up with him. Does that make me a bad person?"

"No, it makes you human."

"He was a nice guy. Just not the guy for me."

"Glad I could help."

"I never said you helped." Austin flashed his green eyes and smile on her. It wasn't fair, giving a man eyes like that. She turned her attention to the dog.

"What are you going to name him?" Austin asked.

"Our grandmother can name him," Hope said. She closed her eyes, just for a second, it had been such a long day. When she opened them again, her head was against some kind of soft material wadded up near the window. There was a little drool on it. She jerked up and a sweatshirt fell into her lap. It was his. Somehow Austin had made a makeshift pillow for her using one of his sweatshirts and placed it under her head. While driving or did he pull over to the side of the road? She didn't want to know. And she wasn't going to swoon over the fact that he wanted her head to have a soft place to land. Darn him.

"Good nap?"

Hope looked out the window and gasped. They were nearing Seattle; the Space Needle glowed ahead, with the skyline spreading out on either side of it. She glanced at her phone; it was nearly ten at night.

"I can't believe I slept the whole way."

"You must have needed it."

"It's so late."

"Do you want to stay at a hotel and then roll up on her in the morning?" Austin asked. "We can pick up some takeaway as well." Hope glanced at her purse she'd thrown down by her feet. She made enough money to barely pay her bills. That was the new American dream. "Your grandmother factored it into the budget," Austin added when she didn't answer.

"She did?"

Austin nodded. "She insisted that this trip couldn't set any of you back financially."

"Don't tell Joy that," Hope said. Then regretted it. Even if it was true that Joy was always scheming for money, Hope didn't like complaining about her sisters with a total stranger. But Austin just laughed, a deep sound that filled the small cab with extra warmth. Even the dog looked up and seemed to be smiling.

"Yes, let's do that," Hope said. "Food and a good night's sleep is just what I need."

"Tell me where you want to pick up food, and where you want to stay, and your wish is my command." Hope was silent for a while, hoping he'd never know that she was replaying the sound of him saying that to her over and over again. *Your wish is my command.* She'd never had a man say that to her before and might never again, and so she wanted to savor it.

CHAPTER 7

We Three Kings motel was a low-budget, two-story affair located within walking distance to Pike's Market but tucked behind a viaduct and set back from the main part of the city, giving the place a bit of an abandoned feel. Even though Austin insisted they had enough money to stay at a decent hotel and eat at a nice restaurant, Hope chose a fried chicken joint and the sketchy motel. The fried chicken because she had a craving, and the motel because they allowed dogs. An added bonus was the hope that the musty odor of the room might just cancel out the dog's stink bombs. She was glad somebody had been feeding him something, but this poor guy needed some consistency. One whiff and even the most loyal of dog lovers would be tempted to turn away. She'd tried to foist him on Austin for the night, and to her surprise he'd agreed, but instead of following Austin into his room, the dog trotted into hers and commandeered the bed.

"Well," Austin said with a grin, "looks like he made his choice. Can't say I blame him." He treated her to a long look and a wink before softly shutting his motel room door. Hope had to admit that a part of her wished the old sitcom scenario of there being only one room left at the inn and being forced to share it with Austin Rhodes had crossed her mind. One tiny little bed for the two of them. But, of course, that didn't happen. This was where motels went to die and there was plenty of room at the inn.

Hope stood out on the communal balcony, taking in the crisp air and scrolling through Facebook on her iPad. Christmas lights strung around a potted tree in the parking lot blinked on and off. Joy was awake and online. She was posting about her new coffee shop. *GIVE TO THE CAUSE,* one posting said with a link to Joy's Kickstarter page. Since when was coffee a cause? Hope clicked onto Joy's Kickstarter page. She had only $57 in donations. Looked like Hope wasn't the only one who didn't think coffee was a cause. She navigated back to Joy's Facebook page. Who was her sister? Would they be friends if they weren't related? There was a time she knew Faith and Joy like they were a part of herself.

Faith had been a protective older sister, and scrappy to boot. A girly-girl and a tomboy rolled into one. It was like having a little soldier on your side, always armed and ready to do battle. Faith could equally braid Hope's hair and then defend her when the redheaded boy across the street tried to pull it. She'd scold Norman, the old German shepherd next door who growled whenever Hope tried to sneak a pet, and Faith even rescued Hope from their mother's moods. All it would take was for Carla to say "I'm getting a headache," and Faith would whisk Hope off on an outdoor adventure. They'd trip down to the corner store and buy lollipop rings, potato chips, and cans of soda. Arms loaded down with their treasures, they'd head to the beach. If it was raining they'd make forts in their bedroom, using up every bedsheet and blanket in the house. They'd curl up and color, or read Nancy Drew, or make up stories about princesses in castles.

Hope had always felt so safe, so protected around Faith. And when Joy came, she had two little soldiers protecting her. Hope remembered feeling like Joy belonged to her and Faith. They changed diapers, and fed her, and bathed her, and dressed her. They were the first ones up in the middle of the night when Joy would cry. Often their mom would go out on dates and leave them all by themselves. Looking back, it was child abuse, but at the time it felt like freedom. Freedom from Carla's tears, and headaches, and stale beer and cigarette smoke. Freedom from the barrage of awful things Carla would say about their father and why he wasn't coming for them. Faith would pretend to be the mother and boss Hope and Joy around, but in a fun way.

She'd decide what was for dinner (always macaroni and cheese), what they would watch on television (*Animaniacs,* and soap operas, and talk shows—they were glued to Jerry Springer; it was like watching long-lost family members), whether or not they would take a bath (usually not), and what book they would read before bed (*Harry Potter*). Sometimes they'd have to spend hours calming down a crying Joy, but most of the time they created elaborate, imaginary lives. They were orphans living in Russia, they were triplets going camping, they were runaways hitching a ride on the nearest train.

Many of Hope's childhood memories were a blur. But she remembered how she felt about her sisters. Loved. Inseparable. *The Three Musketeers,* their mother used to say with a trace of jealousy. They grew up together; they battled sunburns, and knee scrapes, and Carla, and their missing father. They made up all sorts of reasons he hadn't come for them—the favorite being that he was a spy. He wanted nothing more than to see his girls, but it would put all of America in danger. But he watched them, and loved them, and protected them from afar. And they continued to protect one another. For a while anyway. For as long as it lasted. Her sisters; herself. There was a sliver of time when Hope never could have imagined it any other way.

And then one day Faith was gone. Fled to California at seventeen. The usual reasons. Pregnant by a summer boy. To Hope the west coast might as well have been Siberia, and losing Faith felt like losing a limb. She kept reaching for her, thinking she was by her side, only to discover over and over, more and more shocked each time, that Faith was really gone. All Hope was left with was long-distance phone calls that always ended too soon. It was as if a giant undertow had stolen her sister and whisked her out to sea.

Hope stuck around for Joy, though. Tried to fill Faith's shoes. But Joy was always the wild one. The older she grew, the more she resisted Hope's efforts to mother her. She was probably more like Carla than any of them. The second she turned eighteen, Joy ran off to Seattle without so much as a thank you. And even though they were basically estranged, Hope couldn't stomach the thought of being on the opposite coast from her sisters, so she soon followed to Portland. They were circling one another's orbits without getting too close. They saw one another every couple of years. Not nearly enough for Hope. Maybe this Christmas was the excuse they needed to really commit to one another again.

Hope brought her attention back to Joy's Facebook page. This is how she knew her sisters now. From social media.

Every other picture was coffee, or foam, or Joy and a handsome young black man gazing at coffee or foam. This must be her new boyfriend. Hope hadn't heard about him first-hand, of course, but Faith had mentioned him. His name was Harrison, they'd met on some dock looking at sailboats. Hope didn't even know Joy liked sailboats, let alone went looking at them on random docks. Faith said the only reason Joy talked to her more was that she was always angling for money. Faith was extremely well-off; turned out getting pregnant by Stephen hadn't been the worst thing that could have happened. He was wealthy, and his parents even made sure Faith finished high school and went to college. They now had a beautiful home in San Francisco, two kids, and a two-car garage. Hope had only been there a handful of times—mostly because of Faith's busy schedule.

It was too late to call Faith, but Hope left a message on Joy's Facebook Feed. *I'm in the Emerald City, sis. Call my cell!* A few seconds later Joy logged off of Facebook. Hope stared at her cell and waited. And waited. Why that little scoundrel. When had

Joy stopped loving her? Hope had sensed a year or so back that she'd done something to tick Joy off, but she seriously didn't know what it was. She asked Faith over and over, but Faith insisted she didn't know either. "Joy is Joy," Faith said. "Whatever it is she'll get over it. You're lucky she's not calling, all she does is ask for money."

For the heck of it Hope checked her mother's page. Carla Garland. There she was, smiling, her naturally dark hair colored the lightest shade of blond Hope had ever seen on her, and the latest post read: *Heading for Cuba for Christmas with my sweetie!! Thanks, Obama!!* The picture was of her mother and a smiling Cuban-American man standing on a sailboat, champagne glasses raised. Hope's eyes welled with tears. When would she stop crying over the mother she wished she had? People needed to be themselves, didn't they? Her mother had raised three girls practically on her own, and despite their father being the love of her life, Carla was not a woman who could be alone. She'd had a string of men since Thomas, but not one of them had ever stuck. Hope suspected Carla had never stopped waiting for Thomas to come back to her. In a sense, each of them was a little bit stuck in the past, still waiting. Not that any of them would ever admit it.

Hope closed the cover on her iPad, hugged it to her chest, and leaned into the rail. Her eyes fell on another set of blinking Christmas lights surrounding the WE THREE KINGS motel sign. The *g* was missing, making it WE THREE KIN S motel. Another message had been added below: WE THREE KINGS WELCOME YOU. At least someone welcomed her.

Hope turned and headed back for her room. Austin's curtains were drawn, but she could see he had a light on. Did he have a wife or girlfriend? She didn't get that feeling, but then again he'd said very little about himself.

The flatulent bloodhound was taking up more than half of the bed. Hope crawled in but instead of pushing his snoring body out of the way, she simply formed herself around him. She loved the sound of dogs sleeping. She made one more attempt to call Joy, and once again got her voice mail. She hung up. Tomorrow morning she would park herself outside of Joy's apartment and ambush her.

Hope woke to the sound of her cell phone blasting out "Jingle Bells." She pawed the nightstand until she made contact with it, then glanced at the screen. Faith. Who else would call before seven a.m.?

"I was asleep," Hope said.

"Do you want to FaceTime?"

"God, no."

"Why not?"

"Because I don't even have a face yet." Hope covered her eyes with her hand. Even the dog was still sleeping.

"I'm returning your call."

"From yesterday."

"I just got back from a run." Faith always had to workout-drop. It was worse than name-dropping. *Oh, I just got back from the gym. Oh, I just got back from Pilates. Oh, I just got back from lifting weights. Oh, I just ran a marathon and bought a kale farm.*

Hope stretched out on the bed, opened one eye, and glanced at the empty box of fried chicken by the bed. The dog was still snoring on the floor beside her. His giant paws were covering his head as if he, too, had been rudely awoken by Faith. "Me too."

"You too, what?"

"I went for a run this morning." Hope had woken up in the middle of the night to run to the bathroom. She was going to use it.

"You went for a run?"

Hope gripped the phone and tried not to let Faith's obvious sarcasm get to her. She *could* have gone for a run. "Just got back."

"Liar."

"Why would I lie about going for a run?"

"You're cutting into my kale smoothie time."

"I'm drinking mine now," Hope said. Should she make a slurping noise or was that taking it too far?

Faith sighed. "What's so urgent?"

"Are you sitting down?"

"I'm stretching in the kitchen. Seriously, in twenty seconds I'm putting kale in the blender."

Why didn't she just tattoo her accomplishments on her forehead? I'M HEALTHIER, FITTER, SMARTER, RICHER, MORE IN LOVE, HAVE CHILDREN. SO MUCH BETTER THAN MY SISTERS. "Guess who invited us over for Christmas?"

"Who?" Faith was immediately on guard.

"Over the river and through the woods."

"I'm hanging up."

"To Grandmother's house we go."

"You want to spend Christmas in the cemetery?" There was a grunt. Faith was still stretching. Maybe she wasn't as limber as she claimed.

"Yvette Garland."

"Who?"

"Dad's mother. Our paternal grandmother."

There was a clatter, then swearing. Faith had dropped the phone. When she spoke again, she was out of breath. "Dad's mother?" Panic was evident in her voice. They rarely talked about their father and when they did their voices always resorted to higher pitches.

"Her neighbor showed up at the shelter yesterday looking for me."

"Looking for you? Why did she look for you first?"

"He."

"What?"

"The neighbor is a he."

"So? Why did he come to you first?"

"Maybe our grandmother is a wicked witch and he was ordered to bring back one of our hearts on a silver platter."

"Oh, and you're Cinderella, and we're the Wicked Stepsisters?"

"And how!" Hope laughed. Faith did not.

"My kale is wilting," Faith clipped.

Holy night. Faith was jealous. It didn't matter how old they were, they could succumb to their childhood roles within seconds of speaking. Faith, as the oldest, always felt she was entitled to be first. "He probably came to me first because I'm closer to Leavenworth."

"Seattle is closer to Leavenworth. So if it was a geographical decision, then Joy should have been first."

"Oh my God. Who cares who he approached first?"

"It just doesn't make sense." Everything had to make sense in Faith's world. Which meant everything had to agree with the way Faith saw the world.

"Our paternal grandmother is not only alive, but she's requesting to see us. Can we focus on that for a second?"

"Why does she want to see us now?"

"She's dying. This might be her last Christmas, Faithy. She wants to spend it with us."

There was a snort. "Too bad."

"Don't be like that."

"What about Dad?" Hope could actually hear the lump forming in Faith's throat. Maybe this was why they never got together. It reminded them that there was a piece missing to their family puzzle. The one who had torn a hole in all of them. The one who never came for them. He happened to be the one who loved Christmas the most, even gave each of his three daughters holiday-themed names. Maybe they never got together because then they'd have to face the pain of losing him all over again. Being rejected year after year when he didn't call, or show up, or send a freaking Christmas card. They didn't even know if he was alive or dead.

"Austin doesn't know anything about him."

"Who's Austin?"

"The neighbor."

"His name is Austin?"

"Why would I make that up?"

"Is he an old man?"

"No."

"Is he attractive?"

Hope looked at the wall between her room and Austin's and lowered her voice. "What does that have to do with anything?"

"Just wondering how a total stranger convinced you to go and visit that woman."

"She's our grandmother."

Faith snorted. "I have to go."

"She had a picture of the three of us. You and I are in dresses. Joy is just a baby and I'm holding her. I must be about four in the picture, which would make you eight or nine—"

"Eight," Faith said.

"I don't remember it at all," Hope said.

"The day Joy came home from the hospital," Faith said. "Grandma Garland came to visit. The first time we ever met her."

"How can I not remember it?"

"I don't think she stayed long. She was tall. I remember that."

"Like you," Hope said.

"I'm nothing like her," Faith said. "I remember her as scary. With a hard look on her face."

"You were just a kid."

"After she left I asked Dad—'Was that woman a witch?' "

"You did not."

"I swear."

"What did he say?" Hope loved hearing a new story about her father, a borrowed memory she could steal as if it were her own.

"He laughed and said, *Sometimes.*"

Hope laughed. They fell into a comfortable silence. Faith was the first to snap out of it. "Count me out." And without so much as a satisfying click, Faith was gone.

Hope flopped back down on the bed and caressed the dog. He treated her to a yawn. As long as Hope could get Joy on board, then Faith would come around. If there was one thing the oldest Garland girl could not endure, it was being left out. Hope sighed. Her sisters had no idea how much work she did behind the scenes, orchestrating everything without taking any of the credit. Yes, the middle child was the unsung hero of siblings. Oh ye of little Faith, and Joy to the world. "Watch me pull off a Christmas miracle," she said to the dog. He yawned in return. Looked like she'd have to show them all. Kale didn't wilt, did it?

CHAPTER 8

Austin's truck pulled up to the last known address for Joy, a busy shopping street located in the heart of the Capitol Hill District. It was usually filled with skateboarders, tattoo artists, and homeless teens. Hipster shops snuggled up against eateries, bars, and coffee shops. A community college nearby supplied an endless stream of youth. At ten in the morning, however, it was a ghost town. Forget *Sleepless in Seattle,* they slept just fine here. In fact, hardly any of the shops opened before noon. Ironic given that Hope thought of them as the coffee capital of the world. Hope suddenly wished they'd brought the dog. Then at least they could walk him up and down the street while checking things out. Instead, they'd taken him for a morning walk and then fed him and left him in the room where he happily commandeered the bed and didn't even look up as Hope left. They would come back for him at checkout, giving them exactly two hours to find Joy. "This can't be right," Hope said. The exact address Joy had given was a giant shopping market that was currently closed. The sidewalk in front was littered with homeless teenagers, most sound asleep, their signs resting at their sides.

Hope counted six teenagers and two pit bulls. Austin dug around in his pockets and pulled out some change.

"They're so young," Hope said. "Do you really think giving them money is the solution?"

"You can't always see change," Austin said. "Doesn't mean it's not happening."

"I think that's exactly what it means."

"It's not about them, it's about me."

"How so?"

"Makes me feel a little better. So I do it."

"You know pot is legal here now, right?"

"And?"

"The number of runaways to Seattle and Colorado has increased dramatically. Would it make you feel good if you knew you were supporting their decision to wake and bake?"

"If I give, I give. It's not my place to be judgmental."

Ouch. She did sound sort of judgmental. She was cranky that Joy had lied about her address. She was tired of being punished for an unknown offense. Austin stepped out of the car and approached the kids. They were paired off, a boy and a girl sitting close but not touching, their heads resting against a brick wall, and another pair asleep with their hands entwined and heads on each other's shoulders. One girl lifted her head as Austin approached. From the car, Hope took in the platinum blond hair and blue eyes. It was Joy. She gasped. Was her baby sister actually sleeping on the streets?

Hope's first instinct was to barge over there. Her second instinct, honed by years of being stuck in the middle, was to duck. She slid as far down as she could go, praying no part of her was visible. She heard the truck door open and there was a long silence as Austin stood taking her in.

"I have to ask," he said at last.

Hope made eye contact. "Are they still there?" she whispered.

"Who?"

"The kids you gave money to. The blond girl with the black boy. Are they still there?"

Austin's head popped up and he looked off into the distance. "Actually—they're getting on bicycles." He sounded surprised.

"How much did you give them?"

"None of your business."

"How much?"

"It's the holiday season," Austin said. "A time for giving." Hope shot up and looked down the street. Sure enough Joy and Harrison were pedaling away.

"Follow them," Hope said. She put on her seat belt.

"What? No way."

"That's my sister."

"You're kidding me."

"Nope, you just helped fund her coffee shop."

"That's not so bad."

"She's not homeless."

"How do you know?"

"Because Faith would know. Follow them." Oh yes, there was no way Faith would have kept this nugget to herself. She would have been the first to organize an intervention. Timed to coincide with the Seattle marathon perhaps. Austin was still standing outside. "Let's go," Hope said. "Follow them."

"Do you know how slow bicycles go?"

"We can keep circling, or pull over once in a while as if we're checking directions."

"Guys don't ask for directions."

"Please."

Austin sighed and got in the truck. It didn't take long for them to pull up behind Joy and Harrison. Pretty soon they were passing them and taking the hill down to Pike's Market. Here the bikes could really fly. Austin hung back just enough to keep them in sight. The bikes swerved onto the sidewalk a few seconds later in front of a fancy condominium high-rise.

Hope took in the doorman as Joy and Harrison locked their bikes up to a stand in front of the building. "They can't live here, can they?" But sure enough Joy and Harrison were greeted by the doorman and enthusiastically ushered in. Hope noted how Joy had ditched her homeless sign.

"I can't believe your sister just swindled me." Austin sounded slightly impressed.

"I wonder if there's even a coffee shop," Hope said.

"At least she's not on the streets," Austin said.

"Are you always so cheery?"

"No," Austin said. Hope immediately regretted the question. A dark look settled over his face. She wished she could take it back.

"What now?" Austin asked.

"We go in," Hope said. "We've got her cornered." But instead of making a move, Hope sat in the truck and pulled out the picture of them as little girls.

"We look so happy. Like we loved each other. Like sisters."

"Joy is kind of screaming her face off," Austin pointed out.

"Okay. But she eventually grew to love us."

"I'm sure she did," Austin said softly. "Does."

"I don't know what happened to us," she said. "I barely remember us being these girls."

"Barely is a start."

"You're right. Let's go." Hope took a deep breath and got out of the truck.

Unlike the smile he'd flashed Harrison and Joy, the doorman greeted them with an impassive face. "May I help you?"

"That girl who just came in," Hope said. "The blond one?"

"Who are you here to see?" The doorman stood taller as if bracing himself for a tackle.

"Joy Garland. My sister. You just opened the door for her."

"Who may I say is calling?" The doorman opened the door and allowed Austin and Hope to step into the lobby. An artificial Christmas tree took center stage in the marble and glass lobby. The tree's decorator had been a purist; purple tulip-shaped glass bulbs were the only ornaments that adorned it. A starfish sat at the top, and little white lights twinkled from nearly every branch. With the plethora of pines on the west coast, couldn't this fancy condo building afford a real tree? And was it trying to be edgy and artistic? All purple? *Don't try so hard to be cool, tree!* she wanted to shout. *Nobody likes a hipster.*

"Tell her it's her sister, Hope, and that I'm right here in the lobby."

"I'm afraid the residence does not belong to your sister and therefore you are not on the approved guest roster."

"Who does this residence belong to?"

"I'm afraid I can't give out that information."

"Well. You could call her, tell her I'm here, or we'll just wait in the lobby until she comes down."

"I cannot have unapproved guests waiting in the lobby."

"You'll call her then," Hope said. It wasn't worded as a question. There were a couple of leather chairs in the waiting area so Hope sauntered over and sat down. "Comfy," she said. "I could wait here all day." Austin took the other seat.

"Mrs. Mann wouldn't like this," the doorman said.

"Harrison's mother?" Hope said, making a wild guess.

"Are you here to see Harrison then?" the doorman asked.

"I believe we are," Austin said.

"You're not on the guest roster," the doorman repeated again.

"This is a family emergency," Hope said.

"Please," the doorman said, gesturing for them to leave. "You are free to call her. Why don't you leave the premises and call her. I'm sure she'll meet you somewhere."

"She's not answering her phone," Hope said. "Either her battery died, or she's lost it, or she's ignoring me."

"You cannot stay here. Please. I need you to exit the building."

"Do you have siblings?" Hope asked.

The doorman looked around as if she might be directing the question to an unseen person behind him. "Yes," he said finally. "I have two brothers."

"Are you the middle child?"

"How did you know?" His voice perked up. Hope didn't know, but she was happy she guessed right.

"I can tell by the confident way you hold yourself. We middle children have to always be the peacemakers, don't we?"

"Yes, yes," he said excitedly. "I have often kept my brothers in line." Hope nodded her encouragement. "And when I say 'in line,' I mean out of jail."

"I doubt they appreciate it, though, do they?"

He shook his head, then lifted it toward the ceiling as if praying. "They always ask for more."

"Right?" Hope said. "Where's the love?"

"Where's the love?" the doorman repeated. "Where is it?" The second time he sounded as if he was genuinely asking her.

Hope shook her head. "You're an unsung hero."

The doorman put his hand on his heart. "That's me."

Hope nodded. "And what if you had a family emergency and had to get ahold of one of them, but through no fault of your own they weren't talking to you?"

"I cannot believe they would put me in this position," the doorman said, sounding more and more worked up.

"Right? It's all on you. You have to do everything."

"They make me so tired."

"They certainly do."

"And angry. I am so, so angry."

"Well, I say enough."

"Enough!" He slammed his hand on the reception stand.

"Call her, will you? Call my sister and tell her we have had enough!"

"Enough!" the doorman said. He swept up the phone.

Austin flashed Hope a smile. "Well played," he said under his breath. Hope held her palm out and after a moment Austin gave her a discreet high five.

The doorman put down the phone and approached with a smile. "She'll be right down."

Yeah, right. Joy was probably scrambling down a fire escape as they spoke. "I appreciate you so much," Hope said. He blushed and grinned some more. Hope grinned back. The doorman scooted even closer. Hope stared at a purple glass tulip dangling from the hipster Christmas tree. Suddenly Austin cleared his throat and threw his arm around Hope.

"We both thank you," he said. "Right, babe?"

"Right, cowboy," Hope said. The doorman nodded, then trudged back outside with a few forlorn glances back. Austin retracted his arm. Hope wished the doorman would walk back in. The minutes ticked by. When she could stand it no longer, Hope got up and wandered to the elevators.

"What are you doing?" Austin said.

"She's not coming down," Hope said.

A pizza delivery boy entered. Joy loved pizza for breakfast. It was now 10:30. She'd probably found the one place that started delivering for lunch this early. "I can take that up," Hope said, grabbing the box out of his hand.

"Twenty-two bucks," the kid said.

Hope looked at Austin. "Can we get this out of the granny fund?"

"Got it." He peeled off twenty-five dollars and handed it to the kid. "Keep the change."

The kid hurried away. Hope looked down at the order. Apartment 2801. Hope glanced outside. The doorman had his back to them. Hope pushed a button and the elevator dinged. She slipped into the elevator and pulled Austin in after.

"The twenty-eighth floor?" Austin said as the elevator started up.

"Something tells me Mrs. Mann doesn't know her son is spending his days pretending to be homeless." The elevator dinged, announcing their arrival. There were only two penthouses on the twenty-eighth floor, and 2801 was to the left. The door was already swinging open when Hope approached. At the sight of Joy's sleepy face and patch of platinum blond hair, Hope's heart gave a little squeeze.

"Pizza!" Joy shouted. Then her eyes landed and locked on Hope.

Hope meant to start with "Hello" or a hug. Instead, the words rushed out of her mouth before she could stop them. "Why are you pretending to be homeless?"

"Shit." The door slammed shut.

"Still got the pizza," Hope said to the closed door.

"Where's the za?" a male voice asked from within.

"With my psychotic sister," Joy said.

Hope felt her face flush and she didn't dare look at Austin. Soon she could feel his mouth near her ear. "Crazy women are the best," he whispered. Hope laughed and finally looked at him. "She's pretending to be homeless and I'm psychotic."

Finally the door swung open. A handsome black man stood in front of Joy. He had a boyish face, the type of face you liked instantly. "Manny actually let you up?"

"I'm Hope," she said, ignoring the question and handing him the pizza. "Nice to meet you."

"I've seen you on Joy's Facebook page," Harrison said. "You're the one who works with dogs." He stepped back and Austin and Hope stepped in.

"Don't let her in," Joy said, hurrying away from them with the pizza.

"Already in," said Hope. She stepped through a hallway and into the living room. There were floor-to-ceiling windows and a panoramic view of Seattle. The floors were pristine cherry and all the furniture was white. "My God."

"His mother is a news anchor," Joy said, opening the pizza on the gorgeous sofa. Hope wanted to yell at her not to eat on what appeared to be a twenty-thousand-dollar sofa.

"Why are you pretending to be homeless?" Hope asked.

Joy didn't even look up as she dug into the pizza without a plate or napkin. She shook her head. "Let the lecture begin."

"We were in Capitol Hill. I saw you begging for money. This is Austin. He gave you money. You took off on your bicycles—and here we are."

"Man, I told you some dude was following us," Harrison said. He grinned at them. "I made you, man. I made you." Austin smiled and shrugged.

Joy lifted her head and considered Austin. "Thanks for the contribution, man. It's going to a good cause."

"Give it back," Hope said.

Joy stared at Hope. "You're always trying to shame me."

"You were pretending to be homeless."

"We're saving for a coffee shop."

"You should be ashamed of yourself," Hope said.

"You've got it all wrong," Harrison said.

"Don't bother," Joy said.

"Tell me," Hope said.

Joy stood up, articulating with her hands as she talked. "Do you know what the rest of those kids are doing with the money dropped into their cups? Taking drugs and drinking. I'm saving for a coffee shop. And I should be ashamed?"

"Why not take out a business loan?"

"I tried. They wouldn't approve me."

"Go back to college. Get a credit card and start building your credit."

"Stop," Joy said. "You're not my mother. There's no shame in being an entrepreneur."

"You should earn the money, not pretend you're homeless."

Joy looked around the condo. "Technically this isn't my home so I'm homeless."

"I guess I'm not," Harrison said. "But I'm dating a homeless girl, so I was just there for support." He grinned.

"If you're sleeping here, you're not homeless," Hope said. "What happened to your job?" Last she'd heard, Joy was working at a tattoo parlor.

"I had an epiphany," Joy said. She lifted her shirt. There was a tattoo of a coffee cup surrounding her belly button.

"What is that?" Hope said.

"Inspiration," Harrison said. He thumped his heart with his fist and flashed the peace sign. Then he lifted his shirt to reveal an identical coffee cup tattoo around his belly button.

They must have been drunk out of their minds. "Is there more?" Hope asked.

Joy cocked her head. "More what?"

"Gee, I don't know. Do you at least have a business plan tattooed on your bum?" Austin laughed.

A look of hurt flashed across Joy's face. "Why can't you just once act like a friend instead of a hall monitor?"

Hope stepped up. "We're just worried about you."

"We?"

"Faith and I."

Tears came to Joy's eyes. "What part of 'we're starting a coffeehouse' do you not understand?"

Hope wanted to hug Joy and congratulate her. But she also didn't want her rushing into this crazy scheme without giving her honest feedback. If sisters couldn't tell you the truth, who could? "Faith says it's across from a Starbucks."

"So?" Joy was defiant, forcing Hope to be honest.

"So. That doesn't sound too smart."

"Are you saying I'm dumb?" Joy dropped her pizza.

"It's the perfect way to stick it to the man," Harrison interjected.

"It's business-suicide." Hope thought she saw Austin flinch, but she didn't have time to find out what that was all about.

"It's strategic," Joy said. "Our guests will be anti-Starbucks. We're making a statement."

"Funny, because the statement you seemed to be making just a short while ago was—'Help! I'm homeless!' "

"Creative fund-raising," Joy said. "Or something else entirely."

"What does that mean?" Hope couldn't believe how quickly things had escalated. She wished she had a do-over.

"I don't owe you an explanation." Joy shook her head and literally turned away from Hope.

"Give Austin back his money so we can take it to a real shelter for the homeless."

"They're not any better than us."

"They're actually homeless."

"So am I."

"You're not homeless!"

"You try living with his mother."

Harrison laughed, then looked at Hope. "She's cool. Just. You know. Not to us."

"I'm sorry we have to meet under these circumstances," Hope said. He seemed nice. She wanted to apologize for her sister but that would start World War Three for sure.

Harrison grinned. "It's cool."

"What are you doing here anyway besides spying on me?" Joy leaned back on the sofa and crossed her arms.

"I have some news that might come as a shock," Hope said.

Joy leaned forward. "Grandma Garland is dying and she wants us to spend Christmas with her."

Hope was dumbstruck. For a half a second.

Faith!

Of course. The sister grapevine was in excellent working order. Faith had already spilled the beans. Which meant she'd called Joy and, unlike when Hope called Joy, Joy had actually picked up the phone for Faith. Hope couldn't believe it. Or rather, she could believe it, which was even more aggravating. Hope literally wanted to jump on top of Joy and pummel her. Instead, she grabbed the nearest pillow and screamed into it.

"That's cashmere," Joy said, grabbing the pillow back.

"So you're answering Faith's calls but not mine?" Hope could hear the anger in her voice. She didn't want to get into a childish fight in front of Austin. But she equally wanted to take the pillow again and bash Joy over the head with it. Multiple times.

Joy pinned her pretty sky-blue eyes on Hope. "Faith doesn't lecture me like you do." Hope shook her head. Faith also didn't stick around for Joy, Hope did. Why didn't Joy appreciate that? Joy's eyes slid to Austin and stayed pinned on him. "Who are you?" she asked again. "Besides being totally hot for an old dude, and quite generous."

"Thanks for the Benjamin, man," Harrison said, thumping Austin on the back.

"Sure," Austin said.

"You gave them a hundred dollars?" Hope was flabbergasted.

"We're going to buy a sign with it," Joy said. Her hands fanned the air. "Coffee and Cream. Just like us." She leaned over and started kissing Harrison.

Austin waited a few seconds and then cleared his throat. "I'm Austin. Your grandmother's neighbor."

"Wow. Isn't she lucky?" Joy winked at Austin until he blushed. Hope couldn't believe the things Joy got away with. Like opening a coffee shop across from a Starbucks. "So. Is she really dying?" Joy leaned in for the juicy details.

"Joy!" Hope said.

"What?"

Hope shook her head. "You can't just say whatever comes into your mind!"

"You should try it sometime," Joy said.

Hope clenched her fists. *Get stuffed. Is that what you want me to say?*

"I'm afraid she is," Austin interjected. Joy and Hope stared at him. "Really dying. Your grandmother."

"Grandmother," Joy said. "In name only."

"It's terminal cancer. Her doctor said she might not live much into the new year."

"Is our father there?" Joy asked. And there it was. Her pitch went up. They all resorted to squeals when it came to their father.

Austin glanced at Hope. She purposefully averted her eyes. She didn't want to cry. Or scream. Or jump from the balcony. "No," Austin said softly. "I don't know anything about him."

This was Hope's chance. She stepped forward. "He doesn't know anything about Dad. But she will. We need to see her. We need answers."

"Does she live in a shack?" Joy asked Austin.

Hope put her hand on his arm. He got the hint and stepped back. Hope fixed her gaze on Joy. "When did you become this person?"

"What person?"

"Greedy," Hope said.

"That's your interpretation," Joy said.

"How else am I supposed to interpret that question?"

"I just wondered if she lived in a shack because of the way Mom used to talk about her."

Joy was right. Their mother never had a nice word to say about their paternal grandmother. But that didn't mean Joy had to sound so heartless. Who cared if she lived in a shack? "This is about a family member who doesn't want to die alone."

Joy waggled her finger at Hope. "Why are you going to see her? The woman never so much as sent a birthday or Christmas card."

"I don't think she knew where you were," Austin said quietly.

"She could have found out," Joy said. She squinted at Hope. "She's nothing more than a stranger to me. I'm not going."

"Suit yourself." Hope turned and headed for the door.

Joy started to follow. "What are you expecting from her?" Hope opened the door and headed for the elevator. Austin followed. "Where exactly does she live?" Joy yelled down the hall. Hope clamped down on Austin's arm before he could shout back an answer. "I can get the address from Faith," Joy yelled down the hall.

"I don't care," Hope said.

"Why do you want to see her?" Joy was out of the apartment now, running down the hall. A few seconds later she stood breathless in front of Hope. For a second Hope flashed back to all those years when it was just her and Joy. Sometimes they would be walking to or from the beach and Joy would get stubborn about something, stop wherever she was, and refuse to budge. Hope would simply wait her out. The middle child was nothing if not patient. Eventually Joy would come running after her, almost panicked that Hope would leave her. Now here she was, all grown up, but still the same stubborn little girl. If Hope was going to meet their grandmother, there was no way that Joy was going to be left out. Hope held eye contact with Joy. She wanted nothing more than to get through to her. Get along with her. She wanted to take her in her arms and squeeze her until Joy loved her again. She wanted her to grow up. The elevator doors slid open. Hope and Austin walked in. Joy stood there, staring. Just as the doors were about to close, Hope thrust her arm in between them and took a step out. "I don't just want to see her. I want to see you and Faith. Every Christmas you two blow me off."

Joy sighed. "It's so complicated when we get together."

"It doesn't have to be."

"Then stay. Spend Christmas with me. Forget about that woman."

Hope shook her head. "I want to meet her. And I'm tired of not knowing where our father is."

Joy considered her for a moment, then reached her hand out for Hope. Tears came to Hope's eyes as she clutched her baby sister's hand. Maybe she did lecture her too much. But it was because she loved her. Feared for her. Wanted to protect her. "Okay, okay," Joy said. "Don't cry." She looked at Austin. "We're going to need gas money."

Hope wedged her foot against the elevator door and threw her arm up as if barricading Austin. "He gave you a hundred dollars."

"We used it to pay for the pizza," Joy said.

"I paid for the pizza," Hope said. Joy shrugged, then stuck her tongue out. Hope shook her head, then stepped back and laughed. Joy joined in and was still cackling as the elevator doors shut.

"So that was Joy," Hope said as they started to descend.

"Technically your grandmother paid for the pizza," Austin said.

"Joy," Hope said. "They named her Joy." Austin arched his eyebrow. Did he have any idea how sexy he was?

"Yes?" he said. "They named her Joy. And?"

"And?!" Hope said. "That's like naming an alligator Fluffy."

Joy headed back into the apartment, closed the door with a sigh, and leaned against it. "Why didn't you tell her?" Harrison asked from the sofa.

"Because," Joy said, walking toward Harrison, then cuddling up with him on the sofa. "She didn't ask. She just jumped to conclusions." Joy and Harrison had gone to Capitol Hill to talk to Elsie, a homeless girl they'd befriended. She was an artist and a darn good one. They'd spent all night discussing the sign that Elsie would make for their coffee shop. They'd fallen asleep on the sidewalk with her in solidarity. Austin woke them by approaching and giving them the hundred-dollar bill. Before they took off, they gave the money to Elsie to help pay for the sign.

Joy reached under the coffee table and brought out the scrapbook she'd been working on. COFFEE AND CREAM was written on the cover. Inside were all her ideas, and plans. Hundreds and hundreds of hours of planning.

Harrison glanced over. "That's way too much to tattoo on your bum," he said.

Joy laughed. "It had better be," she said.

Harrison reached over and took her hand. "You should show that to your sisters."

"It wouldn't matter. No matter what I do or say, I'm always just the baby. Someone they need to lecture, and scold, and worry about."

"Don't give up," Harrison said. "Maybe they'll come around."

"And maybe Santa will bring us our coffee shop," Joy said, laying her head on Harrison's shoulder. "And every angel will get her wings, and elves will picket Starbucks, my sisters will finally see me as the woman I am instead of the little girl I used to be."

"Dang," Harrison said. "All I want is a toaster."

Joy laughed and kissed him. "Easy to please," she said.

"A four-slicer. None of that two-slice nonsense."

"A man needs his bread," Joy said.

Harrison nodded and squeezed her tighter. "A man needs his bread."

CHAPTER 9

Faith Garland turned to look out over Fisherman's Wharf just as her cell phone rang. It was a crisp day, and although the air had a distinct winter bite, the sun was shining full force. The ring of the phone melded with the sound of barking seals and the hum of voices along the wharf. Faith stared at her screen. Joy's nose ring and thick black eyeliner stared back at her as her finger hovered over DECLINE. She should find a less angry picture of Joy, but for that she'd have to go back to childhood. Faith answered the call.

"Guess who just ambushed me?" Joy plunged in before Faith could even say hello. Even though Faith already knew the answer she let Joy ramble on about Hope. "Either she really wants us to come, or she wants the inheritance all to herself. Which do you think it is?"

Faith was glad that Stephen was in the restroom and the kids were heading closer to the seals carrying on at the end of the dock. Faith didn't need to get any closer, she could smell them from here. She hated getting into arguments with her sisters in front of them. Her family unit—the one she'd created for herself—saw her as calm, put together, and in charge. Sometimes just a few-minute conversation with one of her sisters could make her feel irrational and totally out of control. If only Hope would stop pushing her sisterly agenda. "What inheritance?"

"She's got some kind of a house, doesn't she?"

"She probably owes on it. Believe me. We're poor going back many generations on both sides of the family tree."

"You never know. Hope was just here, playing me."

"I don't think Hope is playing you." Hope, however awkward about her approach, was never diabolical. She was just needy. Needing for the three of them to have some kind of special relationship—the product of too many Afterschool Specials and novels where sisters giggled and painted each other's toenails and shared their deepest, darkest secrets.

"Now we have to go! I'm bringing Harrison."

"You're going to our grandmother's house?"

"It's so weird to hear you call her that. We don't have to call her that, do we?"

"We don't have to do anything."

"Good. Well, I'm going. Just in case."

"Just in case there's a big inheritance." Faith couldn't keep the disdain out of her voice and she didn't even try.

"I have a coffee shop to open. This could be fate."

It wasn't fate. It was life being life. Faith didn't bother to say that; Joy was a spark plug, always ready to blow. "I'll think about it," Faith said. She clicked off and dropped the phone back into her purse.

Brittany and Josh were close to the edge of the water now, a couple of upright humans amidst all those stinky, barking seals. She didn't know how Hope worked amongst stinky barking dogs all day. Couldn't be much better than the seals. She could not believe that both of her sisters were now planning on visiting this woman. What would their mother say?

Stephen finally emerged from the restroom and for a few seconds Faith wondered what he'd been doing in there so long. Not that it was any of her business anymore. She still found him attractive, that was the irony of all this. He'd maintained his athletic body with his daily runs, he didn't have any horrendous habits, he made great money but was still able to pull off a work-life balance, he moderated his extracurricular activities that didn't include her like golf and business dinners. As a rule he didn't come home late. On paper, he was perfect. She was the one who was finally accepting who she was and who she wanted to be with. She was the one driving their family off a cliff. Yet here he was, playing his part. He took one look at Faith and furled his eyebrows in concern. "What's wrong?"

He knows you. One look at your face and he knows something is wrong. Would anyone ever know her like that again? A grenade of guilt exploded in Faith. He'd tried so hard to be a good husband, and she'd ruined it all. She hated seeing the pain in his eyes every time he looked at her. And something else. A bit of desperation. He wanted to save this marriage despite the fact that she was in love with someone else. She saw it every time she looked at him. If he hadn't walked in on her and Charlie in a compromised position, she probably would have never ended the marriage. That made her both sad and guilt-ridden. "Joy is going too. With her new boyfriend. They're both going to visit that woman."

"Okay." Stephen put his hands in his pockets. "I'm pretty sure I know what's coming."

"I can't let them go without me."

"The Garland Girls Reunion Tour," Stephen joked. Faith tried to smile, but she didn't have it in her. Stephen ran his hands through his hair. The fact that he still had a full head of hair was reason enough to try to make the marriage work. What was wrong with her? "We're supposed to go to my mother's for Christmas," she heard Stephen say. "It was going to be our last Christmas together as a family." The bitterness crept into his voice. There it was. Faith had been waiting for it. She knew anger had to be simmering underneath his polite façade. She certainly couldn't blame him. Often she'd imagined this from his point of view.

How would she have reacted if she'd come home to find him on the sofa with another woman? She definitely wouldn't be taking it as maturely as Stephen appeared to be taking it. They'd agreed not to make any decisions or say anything to the children until after the holidays. They had no idea Charlie even existed. How strange. Was Faith really going to do this? Was she really going to follow her heart? Was that even wise?

That huge dilemma aside, Faith still didn't want to spend yet another Christmas with Stephen's mother, pretending everything was okay. The woman had never really accepted her as a daughter-in-law, and it was going to be even worse when she found out Faith was leaving her precious son, her golden boy. Stephen's mother had taken Faith in when she was seventeen and pregnant. Saw to it that they married. Helped raise Josh. Made sure Faith finished high school and even went to college. Yet the woman had never loved her. Faith didn't blame her, but she was tired of pretending. At least this year she wouldn't have to open yet another pair of socks from her mother-in-law and pretend that it was a fabulous gift. Especially when everyone else did get fabulous gifts. Maybe she was psychic, sensed that one day Faith would cheat on her darling son, and the years of socks had been punishment in advance.

"We went to your mother's last year. And the year before that."

"Your sisters are welcome to come."

"What part of dying grandmother do you not understand?"

"You never even met the woman."

"Actually, I did. We did. We met her twice." Faith didn't know she was going to say that until the words came out of her mouth. It was as if a veil lifted and the memory of meeting her a second time came pouring in.

She was inside a trailer. The smell of whiskey and cigarettes actually hit the back of her throat. She could picture her grandmother standing in the kitchenette with her hard, wrinkled face. A smoker's voice, low and gravelly. Oh, she remembered her all right. She'd called Hope chubby and pinched Hope's cheek until she cried out, asked their father when he was going to "shut that thing up" (Joy), and tried to get Faith—who was only eight years old—to run to the store to buy her booze and cigarettes. Her father laughed as if it were a joke, but Faith remembered the look in her grandmother's eyes. The woman had been deadly serious. And she'd had cash clutched in her hand. Instead, her father went to the store, leaving them alone with that woman. Faith couldn't even remember her looking at them or talking to them the entire time he was gone. If she had cookies she didn't place them on a plate in front of them; in fact, it was truly as if they weren't even in the room. Their grandmother stood staring out one of the windows in the trailer and began talking about their mother. Words Faith didn't even understand at the time, but she knew they were all bad. When her father came back from the store they left immediately. Once she had her cigarettes and her beer, the rest of them didn't exist. Nothing about that woman had felt like a grandmother.

So if she was summoning them to her home now, Faith knew there was a motive, and wanting to make up for lost time, or bequeathing them some generous gift, was not going to be it. Not even close. The truth was—no matter how much she complained about them—she couldn't let her sisters face that woman alone.

She had enough guilt over abandoning her sisters. At least that was Hope's version of what Faith had done to them. To this day there was this hurt, Why-did-you-leave-us? look in Hope's eyes. What was she supposed to say? She was their sister, not their mother. Yes, she'd taken on that role, but could she really be expected to carry it on forever? Didn't she have a right to live her life? Besides. It had all happened so fast. One summer. One summer had completely changed the trajectory of her entire life. That magic number seventeen. Seventeen-year-olds shouldn't hold the power to make life-changing decisions, but that's what happened when you didn't have parents. She loved her mother, but Carla Garland could not be called a parent.

There was so much about Faith's life that she'd kept hidden from her sisters. Not out of spite, but to protect them. She'd always wished she would have had an older sister to look out after *her*. Tell her everything would be all right. Back then Hope was so sensitive to change, so clingy, but Joy was independent. Faith knew Joy was going to be all right without her. And Hope was just going to have to learn. Faith didn't have a choice, she needed to look out for herself for once. It was just one night, one kiss. And it changed everything.

The barking of seals brought her back to the present. Stephen was watching her. She flushed as if he knew everything she'd been thinking.

"What?"

"You three should go," Stephen said. "My mom will understand."

I was already going. You just have to act like it's your idea. "Thank you."

"But you can't bring Charlie." He spit out the name with the usual emphasis and sarcasm. "That's my only rule."

My God. Who did he think she was? Why in the world would she want to drag Charlie into this? "You know I wouldn't do that."

"I really don't," he said. "Do I?" Just then, as Faith was watching and Stephen was shooting her with another little stinger, Josh turned and looked directly at her. *He looks sad.* Fifteen didn't seem to be an age he was enjoying. Was there any way that he knew about Charlie? No, it wasn't possible. She and Stephen had gone to great lengths not to let on. What was happening to her sweet little boy? He used to be a mama's boy. Always clinging to her. He was shy, and sweet, and thin and scrawny. He wasn't going to be a jock or the leading man. That filled her with pain for him. But he seemed content to be smart and kind. That is, until this year. The change that had come over him was so startling. Usually sullen, and sometimes angry. And then last month she'd actually walked in on him after he'd taken a few test swipes to his wrist with a razor. And although he had sworn up and down he was just goofing around, that maneuver had landed him in weekly psychotherapy. Faith was even more unsure now about splitting up. She loved Charlie, but Josh took priority. Faith couldn't help but feel like she was being punished somehow. As if she shouldn't dare to be happy.

Not that she had gone about it in the right way. But was there a right way to fall in love with someone outside of your marriage? If she had been honest, truly honest with herself, she never should have married Stephen. Was she supposed to just swallow those choices now for the sake of her children? Wouldn't it be better for them to have a happy mother?

"It's hormones," Stephen said, watching her watch their son. "I was like that too."

"Did you try to slit your wrists?" Faith snapped. Oh, she shouldn't have said that. This wasn't Stephen's fault. He was actually handling all of this much better than she was. *Be nice, Faith.*

"He said he wasn't really going to do any serious damage to himself."

"And you believe that?"

"I want to," Stephen said.

"It was a cry for help."

"And he's getting help."

"Mental illness runs in both of our families."

"My family?" Stephen asked.

"Your mother." All of Josh's traits both physical and emotional mirrored Stephen and his side of the family. Except for his eyes. He had her father's piercing eyes. *He's an old soul,* people used to say after looking into her father's eyes. Josh was an old soul too. And he was hers to protect.

"Are you sure Josh is better off with the crazies in your family rather than mine?" Stephen asked.

"Not sure whatsoever," Faith said.

"So why do this? You never want to spend Christmas with your sisters—"

"Don't put words in my mouth."

"Hope is always making an effort and you're always rejecting her."

"Wait. Are you trying to get me to stay, or are you trying to get me to go?"

Stephen sighed. "I don't know," he said. Seals barked in the distance. Josh and Brittany began running back to them.

"No matter what," Stephen said, "this year just isn't going to feel like Christmas."

Faith was sorry to realize that for once, she wholeheartedly agreed.

Hope and Austin were only half an hour from Leavenworth when Faith's name lit up the screen of her smartphone. "She's coming," Hope said with a grin. Austin turned down the radio as Hope answered.

"Hi, Faith."

"You do know that Christmas is still three weeks away."

"Your point is?"

"Why are you headed there so early?" Faith sounded annoyed. Probably because none of this was her idea and Faith thought she should be the one spearheading everything.

"I'm on break and Austin generously offered me a ride." Austin gave a smile and a nod at this. Hope wondered if Faith could hear her smiling through the phone. Her sisters were coming! She was off this early in the season thanks to her Whine and Cheese event, but if she mentioned anything about her work with dogs Faith would roll her eyes. And even though they weren't video chatting, Hope would still be able to feel that eye roll through the phone. Faith was even less of a dog person than Michael. Hope glanced at the hound. A long piece of drool dangled from his jowl. Hope wiped it off with her sleeve. The dog thanked her by licking her chin. She gently pushed his big face away. Faith was not going to be happy to see the lovable beast. The thought made Hope smile even wider.

"Austin said there's room for all of us at the house—kids, husbands, boyfriends." *And dogs.* "I guess our grandmother's late husband was loaded." She wondered the minute it was out of her mouth if Austin would think she was being callous, but if he did, he didn't let it show.

"Joy will be overwhelmed."

"That's not what I meant." Hope really didn't want to discuss Joy's motives for visiting with Austin listening.

"I remembered meeting her a second time," Faith said.

"I don't even remember the first time," Hope sulked. Austin glanced over. Hope looked away.

"She lived in a trailer. Dad went out to buy her cigarettes and we waited for him. She insisted on getting a picture of us before we left."

"How come I don't remember that?"

"You were only four. We didn't stay long."

"Was Mom there?"

"No, just us."

"I don't remember."

"Just as well."

"What do you mean?"

"Prepare yourself. From what I remember she was a nasty old woman. She didn't care about us at all. Definitely didn't act like a grandmother."

"Are you sure it was her?"

"Unless Dad introduced some other random, nasty woman living in a trailer as our grandmother. Yes, I'm sure."

"I was just asking." Hope needed to change the subject, get the focus off of her. "I met Joy's boyfriend."

"And?"

"He was a lot nicer to me than she was."

"She likes to hold a grudge."

"Oh my God. You do know why she's mad at me."

"I do. But I'm not going to tell you."

No one else on earth could make Hope feel so childish than her sisters. Within seconds. It was insane. "You have to tell me!" She hated carrying on like this with Austin in the car. He was whistling softly, looking out at the scenery, pretending he couldn't hear a word. The dog on the other hand had cocked his head and was staring at the phone like he wanted to eat it. Which he probably did. Hope was pretty sure the beast was part goat. He had eaten a huge chunk of the comforter out of the We Three Kings motel.

"Who's going to break the news to Carla?" Faith laid it on thick when she pronounced the name and Hope could imagine her rolling her eyes.

"Maybe she'll come too," Hope said.

"Dream on."

"Does she know why Joy is mad at me?"

"You have to stop caring."

"Why? How?"

"Because it's going to turn you into a doormat. Call Carla." There was a *click* and Faith was gone. She glanced at Austin. Finally, he met her eyes.

"Everything all right?"

"I need to make another call."

"No problem."

"Can we find a bar first?"

"A bar?"

"I have to call my mother. That's going to require a stiff drink first."

"Say no more. We're almost to Leavenworth. I'll drop you off in town. There's a ton of restaurants and bars. I'll point to some of my faves. I can give you some time to explore on your own, pick you up before we go to Yvette's?"

Hope didn't realize she'd been holding her breath until she let it out. "That sounds perfect."

CHAPTER 10

Austin dropped Hope off at a small tavern that specialized in beer and regret. It was dim and smelled like ale and shoe polish. Flanking the entrance were a couple of plaster figures dressed in Bavarian costumes and holding out a plate with a giant sausage.

"There are nicer places," Austin said. "But it's quiet here."

"It's perfect."

"I'll give you some privacy. Text me when you're ready."

"Are you sure?" she asked.

"It will give me a chance to do some Christmas shopping," Austin said with a wink. He was such a nice man. If he liked her grandmother, she couldn't be as bad as Faith said. Or maybe the years had mellowed her into a nicer person. Hope was looking forward to meeting her. But first she had to break the news to her mother. No matter how happy Carla seemed, she was still haunted by their father's disappearance. And Yvette Garland was at the top of the list when it came to whom she blamed. "That woman is keeping him somehow," she said once, her hair plastered to her forehead by sweat. This was before their mother went on meds. The longer her husband stayed away without contacting her, the more paranoid she became. At some point they just stopped discussing their father. It was too painful.

There were only a few old men at the bar, so she was able to curl up at a back booth and call her mother. The tavern had free Wi-Fi, so first Hope thoroughly depressed herself by scrolling through Facebook. All her Facebook Friends seemed amped up on Christmas cheer. Posting recipes, and holiday plans, and family pictures, and reindeer already. Twinkling lights, and ugly sweaters, and cat memes. Kissing. Bragging. Cheering. Happy times twelve—as if all her friends were mainlining peppermint-laced steroids. These are my Facebook Friends. These are my Facebook Friends on Christmas. Bah humbug!

Hope knew Facebook wasn't real life, but she couldn't help feeling a twinge of panic whenever someone posted memes about sisters. Everyone, it seemed, cherished their sisters. And it was mutual. Heart emojis, smiling faces, cradle to grave proclamations. Hope was determined to get her sisters to feel the same. To rekindle the bond they once had as children. That couldn't just disappear, could it? Back then Faith would have wrestled an alligator if it was threatening either Joy or Hope. Probably Joy. Who else would provoke an alligator? They used to fight too. Hope even missed the fighting. You knew you were loved when you made someone so angry they physically wrestled you to the ground. Faith once pummeled Hope for stealing her first McDonald's French fry. Not the last fry, which may have been forgivable. The first hot, salty one out of the box. Hope was twelve, which meant Faith was sixteen. Hope, of course, had no idea she only had one more year left of living with her sister. They had gone to the beach and then McDonald's for dinner. Against Faith's warnings, Hope had decided to order an apple pie instead of a meal, but when she smelled those fries, she had to have one. She reached for Faith's fries one second, swiped a long one out of the box, and the next thing she knew she was down on the dirty linoleum with Faith on top of her pummeling away, her normally beautiful face swollen with homicidal rage. Joy stood over them with a grin sucking on a strawberry milkshake. You had to really love someone to fly into such a rage you'd kill them over a French fry. God, she missed her sisters.

But now she had to deal with her mother. She could video chat with Carla, but Hope didn't actually feel like looking at her. She dialed her number instead.

"Yes?" her mother answered on the third ring. Why couldn't she just say hello like a normal person?

"Hi, Carla." Even though they had been doing it for years, it still felt weird to call her mother by her first name.

"Hope, sweetheart. I'm off to Cuba for Christmas."

"I heard." *On Facebook.* "I was hoping I could talk you into coming here for Christmas."

"Next year you girls are coming here and I won't take no for an answer. Maybe we'll all go to Cuba." Suddenly her mother was in love with Cuba. She'd always wanted things she couldn't have.

Hope took a deep breath. There was no easy way to say this, she was just going to have to come out with it. "Grandma Garland contacted us. She's dying. We're going to Leavenworth to spend Christmas with her and we want you to come. In fact, I'm here now." There was silence on the other end.

"Your father?" The words sounded as if they'd been torn from her mother's throat.

"I don't know. Austin—that's her neighbor—he's the one who brought me here. He says we'll have to ask her. And I intend to do just that."

"You haven't already?"

"I haven't met her yet. We just rolled into town. I'm at a pub. I wanted to call you first."

"Don't do it. Don't ruin our Christmas."

Hope didn't know what she expected from her mother, but it wasn't this. How was she the one ruining Christmas? "What?"

"We've been doing fine, haven't we?"

"What if he's alive?"

"If he's alive, then he abandoned us. And I want no part of that."

"And if something happened?"

"Then it's going to ruin Christmas. For all of us."

"It's too late to turn back now. I'm here."

"I forbid you to see her."

"You can't."

"Do it for me."

"Mom." Her mom sniffled. And she didn't reprimand her with a "Carla." Hope hated upsetting her. Especially around Christmas. "Join us. Let's face this together. Maybe it's actually a gift." Hope stopped short of saying a Christmas miracle. She couldn't shake the feeling that her father was guiding them here. At Christmas of all times. That he wanted them to have answers. To have peace. The trauma of losing him was the wound that kept all of them from being close. If they could just heal, then they would have a chance at being a real family.

"A gift?" Her mother sounded furious. "A gift is something you can exchange for cash."

Hope made a mental note to always give her mother cash from now on. "I'd rather know the truth than spend the rest of my life in the dark. We've been without him for the past two decades. I have to know what happened to him and the one person on earth who probably knows is dying."

"I can't believe you girls would do this to me."

"She's our grandmother."

"You think she's going to leave you something?"

"Of course not." *Joy does.* Hope kept that to herself.

"That woman is a master manipulator."

"People change when they're about to face death. I think she just wants to see us before she passes on."

"That old witch will live until a hundred, mark my words."

"I'm sorry. I didn't mean to upset you."

"You did."

"I just want to be with my mom and my sisters for Christmas." Hope could feel the tears coming. She didn't want to cry, but she was suddenly so exhausted.

"Don't you cry. This is supposed to be my pity party," Carla said.

Hope sighed. She knew her mother never got over their father breaking her heart. But they'd lost a father. Why didn't she see it that way? "Merry Christmas. Call us from Cuba. Don't let Castro change his mind and kidnap you. Bring back cigars." Hope didn't want to end things on a bad note. Maybe it was for the best that her mother wasn't part of this. Maybe her grandmother would open up more if it was just the girls.

"I'll have a better time if you tell me you're not going."

"We're going. But we'll have a miserable time. Is that better?"

"Don't tell me anything. Unless I ask. Promise?"

"I promise."

"Your sisters are going too?"

"Yes."

"Well, you finally got what you wanted. Congratulations."

"That sounds insincere."

"Are Stephen and the kids coming?"

"The kids are, but I don't think Stephen is."

"Did I tell you I suspect Faith and Stephen are having problems?"

Hope sighed. She had told her. Multiple times. "Everyone has problems."

"Do you think it's good for your sister to go through this when her marriage is falling apart?"

Hope wasn't going to take the bait. This wasn't her fault. She wasn't responsible for everyone's problems. "Don't smoke too many cigars."

"Fernando says hello. He can't wait to meet you."

An image of Carla's boyfriend, Fernando, commandeering his sailboat flashed through Hope's mind. He stood at the wheel, looking into the camera with a gap-toothed grin. He was dark skinned and wore a white visor on top of thick black hair, sported mirrored sunglasses, a pot belly, and red swim trunks littered with parrots. He seemed like he was all about fun, fun, fun. Hope prayed he was nice too. Her mother often fell victim to bad boys, her father being the worst of them. Thomas Garland had been young, tatted-up, and had ridden into Carla's life on a Harley. He'd been wearing a Santa cap too. That might have been adorable, had it not been for the reason for the Santa cap: a holiday pub crawl. Thomas was drunk the first time they met—and driving.

Even so, Hope could only imagine what Thomas would have thought of Fernando and his parrots. "Hi back. Later, Carla." Her mother had just started to say something else when Hope clicked off. She'd never know for sure she'd been hung up on. It was petty, Hope knew, but sometimes she had to get her jollies, no matter how microscopic.

Hope texted Austin that she was done with her phone calls but added that she wanted to look around the main street a bit before leaving. She stood outside the tavern on Front Street gazing at all the colorful Bavarian shops. The backdrop of the Cascade Mountains was stunning. It was easy to imagine oneself in an old-fashioned German village. The hamlet had been given its new theme in the sixties, a ploy designed to save the town from extinction and bring back tourists. It worked. Leavenworth was a winter wonderland. There was even a nutcracker shop. Nussknacker Haus. As Hope entered the shop, she immediately felt lighter and joyful. The shelves were stacked with nutcrackers from all over the world. Christmas carols played in the background. A shop clerk greeted her enthusiastically.

Hope wanted to buy a pair of nutcrackers—there were so many—such a variety of Christmas themes and craftsmen. What a perfect gift to offer her grandmother upon meeting. They were quite expensive. Perhaps Hope would have to buy something simpler, an ornament perhaps. The shopkeeper must have sensed her dilemma for he soon showed her a tiny discount section where there were two adorable nutcrackers in Santa outfits. They had slight defects, the products of too many tourists handling them, but the markdown was enough that Hope decided to spring for the pair. Maybe she could set them up on either side of the entrance to her grandmother's house. Hope liked the thought of the nutcrackers being there to greet Joy and Faith when they arrived. Hope was going to get them all into the Christmas spirit, so, whether they liked it or not, here comes slightly damaged nonreturnable nutcrackers. *Take that, Faith. Take that, Joy.*

She wanted to buy more, and she also wanted to go to the store and get ingredients and supplies to make her famous Christmas sugar cookies with buttercream icing—isn't that something you do with a grandmother and your lovely sisters at Christmas? But it was probably best to wait until a little later. Tucking a nutcracker under each arm, and gazing once more up and down the quaint street, positively glowing with lights and cheer, she called Austin and told him she was ready. She couldn't wait to explore this adorable town further. But now she was ready to meet her grandmother. A ripple of excitement hit her. This was the quintessential place to spend Christmas. Magic was in the air. She had a very strong feeling that this year was going to be life changing. And she, for one, couldn't wait for it to change.

Austin's pickup rambled up, and Hope peered into the cab. The slobbery face of the dog greeted her, and he eyed the nutcrackers like they were juicy bones. "Not for you," Hope said. Austin got out of the truck, which was rather gentlemanly of him, and although he reached to take the nutcrackers out of her arms, he looked alarmed.

"What's this?"

"Aren't they adorable?"

Austin pointed. "This one has a chip on its nose—"

"At least it's not its shoulder," Hope interrupted.

"And this one—"

Hope swatted his finger away. "They were marked down."

"The island of misfit nutcrackers?" Austin joked.

"Something like that. I thought we'd surprise my grandmother. We can prop these babies up on either side of her front door."

Austin held a nutcracker under each arm and glanced back at the store. "I think we should return them."

"Why? Because they aren't perfect?"

"Of course not."

"I love them."

"There's something I forgot to tell you."

He looked so handsome. And serious. "What?"

"Your grandmother doesn't want to celebrate Christmas."

"That's because she was dying alone. She has us now."

"No, she really doesn't want to celebrate. I was supposed to tell you. I didn't know you were going to buy these."

Hope grabbed the nutcrackers back and placed them in the cab of his truck. "I'm keeping them," she said. "You told me. Mission accomplished. Now let me deal with Christmas and my grandmother."

Austin still looked worried, but he nodded. Hope gently shoved the dog out of the way as she got in the cab. "Move over, Mr. Jingles."

"Mr. Jingles?" Austin said.

"It just came to me." If Yvette didn't like Christmas, she was going to have to say so herself.

Austin patted the top of the dog's gigantic head. "Mr. Jingles," he repeated. "Suits him."

"Do you like Christmas?" Hope asked Austin as the truck pulled out, cruised down Front Street, then took a left at the end and began heading uphill.

He glanced at her for a second and then kept his eyes on the road. "No," he said softly.

"Why not?"

"I think it puts an extraordinary amount of stress on people."

"Oh." He sounded pained. "I take it you're not close to your family?"

"Not anymore."

There was definitely a story there, but Hope wasn't going to push for it. This was the opposite of the happy Facebook front. This was real life. Imperfect, frustrating, beautiful, real life. "I'm sorry."

"You're pretty much in the same boat, aren't you?" Now there was a defensive edge to his voice. Austin Rhodes did not like talking about himself.

"I agree that for a lot of people Christmas can be lonely, or way too stressful. But it doesn't have to be that way," Hope said.

"Society makes it that way by putting so much pressure on the holiday," Austin said. "Capitalism at its finest."

"It's not supposed to be like that."

"But it is. You can't deny it."

Hope didn't want to argue about politics, or religion, or economic greed. She just wanted to enjoy the season. "Look at this place. It's a winter wonderland. Can't people just truly enjoy connecting with nature, and loved ones? Did you ever consider it's just as simple as that?"

"Says the woman who just dropped a ton of money on a pair of overpriced nutcrackers for a woman who doesn't even want them."

"They were on clearance. This one has a bite taken out of his jolly nose, and the other one is missing a finger. One guess which finger it is."

Austin threw his head back and laughed. The sound of it warmed Hope. Soon the truck was nearing the end of the road. Ahead of them was a private drive. The road turned from pavement to dirt. Trees hugged the entrance.

"Life is what happens when you're busy expecting something else," Hope said softly, taking in the enormous estate barely visible behind an iron gate.

"Good one," Austin said. "Who said that?"

"Santa's elves," Hope said.

Austin smiled. "Who knew?"

"I'm sure they had to learn that the hard way."

"Not easy pleasing kids all over the world," Austin added.

"It's a thankless job."

Austin stopped the truck before the gate and turned to study her. "You're certainly not what I expected."

Hope didn't ask him to clarify. She was too busy gaping at the estate. "Are you taking me to a ski lodge for lunch before you take me to my grandmother's?"

"No," Austin said.

"This is her place?"

"Yes, ma'am."

It was enormous. And postcard-perfect. And dripping with wealth. "Oh, holy night," Hope said. Her sisters were going to freak. And then Joy was going to smell money. And then they were going to freak out. For a split second Hope wanted to whisk her grandmother out of the enormous log house she could glimpse just beyond the gate and take her somewhere less enticing. Let Joy and Faith get to know her without distractions.

"Are you ready?" Austin said.

"Not at all," Hope answered. "Not at all."

CHAPTER 11

The truck idled in front of a massive iron security gate. Austin leaned out and pushed the code into a numeric keyboard hidden on a pole.

"A fortress? Out here?"

"Neighbor kids would come in and try to skate on the pond."

"Is that so bad?"

"It is if they fall through and no one is around."

"Ah." And that was the downside of life. Everything that could bring a bit of happiness was also a risk. She couldn't believe her grandmother lived here. Why wouldn't her father be here too? *He's not alive.* Otherwise wouldn't he be here? Or had they had a falling out? Maybe money wasn't important to him. What was important to him? If he was alive, then certainly not his own daughters. Was their grandmother as furious as they were? How could a woman who lived in a winter wonderland not want to celebrate Christmas?

"I can't wait to meet her," Hope said as the gate swung open and Austin pulled in. He gave her a look that was easy to interpret: *Be careful what you wish for.* Just ahead of them was a massive log house, almost a mini ski lodge with green shutters and a wraparound porch. The land surrounding it seemed to go on forever in all directions.

"It's huge," Hope said.

"Twenty acres," Austin said.

"My God." The mountains rose and fell in the distance, snow covering their peaks. Hope could imagine what an astonishing sight it was to see the entire place covered in a blanket of snow. "Do you think it will snow for Christmas?"

"Sooner than that. It's supposed to be one of the snowiest winters on record. We've already had several big snowfalls."

"It must be breathtaking covered in snow."

"It's always breathtaking."

"Where's the pond?"

"Out back a ways."

"And you can skate on it?"

His eyes flashed on her, and she watched him register the fact that she liked to ice skate. It had been so long since a man had paid such close attention to her. "Skate in the winter, swim in the summer. As ponds go, it's gigantic."

Hope scanned the windows for her grandmother but couldn't make anyone out. "I imagined her standing on the porch, eager to greet me."

"She's taking a rest. In fact, I'm going to show you around the grounds first."

"Oh." That was slightly disappointing. She really couldn't wait to meet her. Would she see any family resemblance? Would she feel familiar? Oh, why had she waited this long to get in touch? Until there wasn't much time left. It wasn't fair.

Hope opened the door to the truck and Mr. Jingles jumped out. Before she could even consider putting a leash on him, he leapt forward, then tore off across the lawn. "Oh no. Mr. Jingles. Mr. Jingles!"

"He'll be all right. This has to be a dog's idea of heaven."

Hope spread her arms and breathed in the crisp mountain air. "This has to be everybody's idea of heaven."

"You'd be surprised," Austin said as Hope reached for her

bag. He gently put his hand out to stop her. "Yvette said Roger would bring your things in."

Hope scanned the area as if expecting a bellboy to materialize out of thin air. She wouldn't have been surprised given that the house did resemble a boutique hotel. When nobody appeared she turned back to Austin. "Who's Roger?"

"He's the caretaker, I guess you would say. Lives in a cabin out back and helps Yvette with odds and ends."

"That's nice." A funny look came over Austin's face. "Isn't it?"

"To be honest, I'm not quite sure what to make of him. But Yvette sure is attached to him." Hope nodded, unsure of what he meant or what to say. "Are you up for a little tour of the property?"

"Absolutely." He glanced at her feet. She was wearing sneakers. "Something wrong?"

"We won't trudge the entire twenty acres, but there may be muddy spots. Did you bring boots?"

"I'm from Oregon," Hope said with a grin. She went to her bag in the cab of the truck and dug through it until she found her hiking boots. She sat on the porch and put them on. When she looked up, Austin was staring at her. Their eyes held slightly longer than ever before and she felt a jolt of electricity move through her body. *He's attracted to me, and boy am I attracted to him.* He looked away first. Shoot. Maybe *she* should have looked away first. But he was so easy to look at.

"Where is your place from here?" She kept her voice light, friendly. He didn't look back at her.

"Thataways," he said, gesturing to the right. Either he was shy, or he had a girlfriend, because a definite wall had just come down. *Get a grip, Hope. You just broke up with Michael. Aren't you supposed to feel sad or something?* All she felt was relief every time she looked at Austin. She had to remind herself that she was here to meet her grandmother and spend Christmas with her sisters. She was not here to pick up the boy next door, no matter how attracted they were to each other.

She gazed at her tennis shoes on the porch, already feeling at home. She stood. "Ready."

Austin pointed to the tennis shoes. "I'll put those in the cab."

"No thanks." Hope glanced at the rest of the porch. There wasn't much to make it homey. A severe-looking bench. It could do with some plants, and comfortable chairs, and why on earth wouldn't you hang a gorgeous wreath above this door? She could already see it strung with Christmas lights, twinkling in the night. She couldn't wait to decorate. She might even make a wreath for the door. There were certainly tons of pinecones around. She could get Joy and Faith to make it with her. One giant wreath made by the three wise women. They could pose in front of it, smile like the world was nothing but snowflakes and angels, and post it on Facebook. *CHRISTMAS WITH MY SISTERS!! Heart emoji, smiley face, thumbs-up, wink. NOWHERE I'D RATHER SPEND THE HOLIDAYS!*

Hope couldn't believe she was in the middle of a winter wonderland and instead of enjoying it she was mentally composing fake posts on Facebook. She took a deep breath and tried to shove the image of the wreath made with sisterly love out of her mind. They probably would have made her stand in the middle anyway, getting squeezed from both sides.

Austin was still staring at her shoes.

"What?" Hope said.

Austin shifted uncomfortably. "Yvette might not like that."

"We're in the country. They're a pair of shoes on a log porch. What's not to like?"

"She has her ways."

"Well, so do I. If she wants me to remove them, I'd like to hear it from her."

"You got it."

Hope knew she was being silly, but she really wanted her shoes on that porch, wanted a place that felt like home, wanted to be welcomed and loved.

"Shall we start with the pond?" Austin said.

"Love to." Hope hopped off the porch and followed Austin. "I'll have to buy some skates in town." She could already imagine herself skating at night with glittering stars overhead and

Christmas music playing. Now that would be romantic. Did Austin skate?

Austin laughed. "No, you won't. The barn is filled with skates. Rupert rented them out."

"To whom?"

"The whole town."

"Really?" Hope liked the sound of that. This place should be shared. Wasn't that what Christmas was all about?

"He sounds like a character."

"On one hand he was Mr. Christmas."

"And the other?" Hope asked.

"Well, he was a shrewd businessman, I'll tell you that."

Hope nodded as she gazed at the property. His estate was certainly proof that he was a shrewd businessman. Hope didn't think wealth was obnoxious if one actually worked for it and gave back at the same time. "My grandmother didn't want to carry on the tradition?"

"There's too much to running a business. And a lot of liability. She probably would have done it if she was younger."

"Or if my father had been around." Hope hadn't meant to say it out loud, but it was already out of her mouth. To her relief Austin didn't comment on it. He seemed good at knowing when to leave things be. As they walked around the back of the house, a large red barn came into view. Next to it was the pond. It was even bigger than Hope had imagined. Perfect for skating! And tearing around the edges was Mr. Jingles.

"Is it frozen?" Hope asked.

"Solid as a rock," Austin answered. A fantasy of Austin's abs flashed through her mind.

Hope forced herself to stare at the pond. "Thank God. If Mr. Jingles fell through I was going to send you in after him."

Austin laughed. "I think he's even too heavy for me." To the right of the pond was a free-standing deck with a sunken hot tub. In the other direction thick pine trees lined the perimeter, and the mountains framed the background. It would truly be an effort to feel anything but peaceful out here.

"That's the basic layout," Austin said. "Do you want to hike through the woods?"

The cold air whipped Hope's cheeks. She imagined herself plopped on a cozy sofa with a mug of hot chocolate and a good book. She could gaze at the winter wonderland by the warmth of a fire. "Could I go inside and rest up a bit?"

"Of course," Austin said.

Hope breathed a sigh of relief. "It's been a long twenty-four hours."

"No problem. It's a big house. Even if she's still napping you'll have most of the place to yourself." They headed back to the house, with Mr. Jingles at their heels. She would have to set him up with food and water right away. That's when he would know that he was home.

"Can I have him in the house?"

"For now there's a mudroom. I'm sure that will be fine until you get a chance to ask Yvette about it."

They headed to the truck. Her bag was gone.

"Roger," Austin said. They glanced up. Sure enough her bags were sitting next to the front door.

"That's so sweet." Hope gazed at the bags. "He doesn't go inside?"

Austin shook his head. "Never. Although Yvette has certainly tried."

"He says no?"

"He doesn't talk at all. She calls to him and he just stands at a distance, staring."

"Staring?"

"I think he might have some developmental delays."

"Oh." Hope glanced around again. She couldn't see anyone, but there were plenty of places to hide. She wondered if he was behind a tree somewhere, watching and listening. "I'm glad he has a place here then."

"Please don't quote me on that. I'm just totally guessing."

"Of course. I won't say anything to anyone." She glanced at her running shoes. Next to them sat a giant pinecone. It hadn't been there before. It almost looked like a mini Christmas tree.

Hope picked it up. "It's gorgeous." She inhaled and caught the wonderful scent of the outdoors. She didn't know how anyone could live anywhere but the Pacific Northwest.

"Roger must like you," Austin said, eyeing the pinecone.

"That's sweet." Hope tucked the pinecone back into her shoe for now. Then she noticed the nutcrackers. They were positioned at either side of the door. They looked fantastic. She beamed. "Roger must like Christmas."

"Yvette doesn't." Austin headed for the nutcrackers.

"Leave them," Hope said. "If she doesn't like it, I'll deal with the fallout."

"Suit yourself." He headed back to his truck. "Good luck."

"You're leaving?" She didn't mean to sound so panicked, but the thought of going into the house alone felt like breaking and entering. She'd gotten so used to Austin in such a short period of time.

Austin gave her a reassuring smile. "I live right next door." He pointed to his left. All Hope could see was a parade of trees.

She smiled. "Thank you. For everything."

"You're welcome."

"Are you sure you don't want to come in?"

"You'll be all right. The key is under the mat." She glanced down. A faded mat said: WELCOME. She lifted it up and sure enough there was a key. Iron security gate with a numeric PIN, yet there was still a key under the mat. She laughed at the irony. Austin had his back to her as he headed for his truck.

"I'll see you later?" Hope called after him.

Austin turned, then stared at her with a grin that was slow to develop, but he nailed the landing. "Going to miss me?"

Heat flushed through Hope and she felt like a child who had just been caught doing something she shouldn't be doing. As crazy as it sounded to her, she felt like she missed him already. She hadn't once felt like this with Michael. "No, I just assumed—"

"I'm just teasing. I will definitely see you later." Their eyes locked and a feeling of joy spread through her. Up until now she'd had limited experience with lust at first sight. At the end of the day, there was this mysterious thing called chemistry, and she'd finally met someone who made her spark just looking at her. He broke eye contact first, gave her a nod, got in his truck, and backed out. The gate slid open as his truck neared. But before the gates closed, Austin began to back up. At first Hope had this crazy thought he was coming back for her, but soon she saw a flash of silver metal. An SUV was pulling in.

Hope was thrown for a second. Faith didn't have an SUV, did she? Didn't she say she wasn't going to be here until closer to Christmas? The SUV had Washington plates. Faith and the kids must have flown into Seattle, picked up Joy, rented the SUV, and then pedal-to-the-metal all the way here. And both of them had been so adamant about not coming. Typical. Reverse psychology was a powerful thing. Hope bounded down the steps as the SUV pulled into the gates. Not only was Faith at the wheel, but Joy was in the passenger seat, her platinum hair shining in the winter sun. Her sisters were here. For the first time in years, the Garland Girls were going to be together for Christmas.

CHAPTER 12

Hope had looked forward to this day for so long, yet there was too much to take in at once. Her grandmother standing on the porch, tall and regal with a look that could only be interpreted as harsh, Joy and Harrison tumbling out of the van, a porcelain hand entwined with one the color of caramel, their laughter ringing out into the mountain air, and Faith frozen in the driver's seat, gripping the wheel as if she was terrified to let go. Joy and Harrison planted their feet on the ground, smiling and looking around as if they were expecting imaginary paparazzi to jump out from behind the evergreens to snap their photo.

Faith was now on her cell phone. Hope felt the first stab of disappointment. Who was she calling? Couldn't it wait? She could at least get out and say hello to her sister. Was common courtesy too much to expect? Brittany and Josh jumped out next, loaded down with backpacks and each carrying an iPad. Nobody moved, and Hope didn't know where to turn first, so she shouted hello and headed for Joy, arms thrown open. Joy let go of Harrison's hand and looked at Hope, but she didn't return any signal that she wanted to hug, forcing Hope to throw her arms around her little sister's stiff body. She smelled slightly musty. Most likely pot, or maybe she hadn't showered in a few days, or maybe she was still using that natural stone deodorant, or all three, and what had happened to her sweet baby sister? If Hope had taken a different approach with her after Faith fled, would things be different now? The first few months after Faith was gone Joy slept in Hope's bed. Every night Hope would tell her as many stories as she wanted to hear until she fell asleep. Mostly stories about how soon they would be back with Faith. Or maybe they would go to California to live with her and take care of Faith's baby too.

"Why doesn't she come back?" Joy would ask. "The baby can sleep in my room."

"She'll come back," Hope would say. "You'll see." But she never did. Maybe Joy blamed Hope. Or maybe it was just life. Life had a way of taking away the people you loved. But they were here now and Hope was determined to make the best of it.

"Why aren't you hugging me back?" Hope knew she sounded hurt, almost as if she was pouting, and it wasn't the way she wanted to start things off.

"I only hug trees," Joy said.

"And me," Harrison said with a bright grin. His teeth were so white and so straight that Hope found herself staring at them, almost mesmerized.

"My uncle is a dentist," Harrison said with a wink.

Hope stepped out of the embrace, turned to Harrison, and held out her hand. "Nice to see you again."

"You too," Harrison said with enthusiasm. "I forgot to thank you for the pizza." Joy rolled her eyes. Hope ignored the eye roll and turned to her niece and nephew. Oh, they were growing up so fast. Brittany was a lovely girl with long, shiny chestnut hair, freckles on her nose, and bright hazel eyes, just like Faith. Josh was taller than Hope now, and lanky. He had Stephen's sandy hair and intense blue eyes. Brittany was ten now and Josh was fifteen—almost all grown up. Where did all the years go? Hope enveloped Brittany in a hug. Thankfully her niece didn't limit her affection to trees and hugged her back. She smelled wonderful, her hair like strawberries. Then she hugged Josh, who was a little shy, but at least put his unwilling arms around her and halfheartedly patted her back.

"Faith?" Hope called. Faith held up one finger, still talking on the phone. Brittany and Josh exchanged a knowing look. Hardly five minutes had passed and everyone was silently sharing secrets with each other, leaving Hope to feel like the odd man out. That was okay. It had been awhile. They just had to get the cobwebs out. A few weeks in the mountain air would do them all wonders.

Speaking of wonders. She glanced around for Austin, but he was gone. She hadn't even noticed him leaving. The dog was gone again too. She was pretty sure Austin wouldn't take Mr. Jingles, especially since he didn't have his food, so he must have wandered off again. Her sisters were probably giving off a bad mood scent. She wondered if he missed his owner. Probably more than her sisters missed her.

"What's Granny like?" Joy asked, sidling up to Hope and lowering her voice.

Hope snuck a glance to the porch, where their grandmother was standing like a statue. She hadn't made one move to greet them. "Haven't met her yet. She was napping." They both turned to Yvette, who as they watched bent over to pick up the pinecone next to Hope's shoes. She held it up, dangling it from her fingers as if she had a rat by the tail. Then she tossed it out into the yard. Hope winced. She loved that pinecone. She'd get it later. Why were all her relatives so surly? She made her way up to the porch and stood at the base of the steps looking up to her grandmother.

"Hello," she said. "I'm Hope."

"Are those your shoes?" Yvette pointed to Hope's sneakers.

"They sure are," Hope said. Yvette glared at them. Hope was relieved Austin wasn't here to say *I told you so.* "I can bring them inside."

"Shoes go in the mudroom." Bossy and exacting. Faith definitely got the grandmother gene.

"Got it," Hope said. "Shoes and dog in the mudroom."

"Dog?" Yvette looked around, startled.

"Mr. Jingles," Hope said. "Austin said you were a dog lover."

"I'm no such thing." Yvette x-rayed Hope and Joy with her eyes. "The dog can live in the barn." Hope bit her tongue. The dog wasn't going to live in the barn, but it was too soon for a fight. Yvette turned to the nutcrackers. "What on God's green earth are they?"

"They're nutcrackers," Hope said.

"I know what they are," Yvette said.

"Then why did you ask?" Joy piped in.

Yvette narrowed her eyes and crossed her arms. "Why are they here?"

Hope couldn't believe they were arguing about little wooden men. "They're a gift. From the shop in town."

"Why would the shop in town buy me a gift?" Yvette barked.

"No, I bought them. For you."

"Put them in the mudroom," Yvette said. Yvette stared at Hope until she picked up the nutcrackers. She held one under each arm, feeling like an idiot. Joy grinned.

Harrison trudged up the steps loaded down with what appeared to be everyone's luggage.

"You brought your own bellboy?" Yvette said, giving Harrison the eye.

Not only was their grandmother surly, she was a racist. This visit wasn't going to last. Hope glanced at Harrison, who still sported a grin. "This is Harrison. Joy's boyfriend."

"My friend, my business partner, and my lover," Joy said.

"And sometimes the bellboy," he said, dropping the bags in his right arm and holding his hand out. Yvette just looked at it.

"Are you a racist, Granny?" Joy asked.

She's braver than me, Hope thought. *She says the things I only dare to think.*

"She's fine," Harrison said. "Mrs. G and I will work it out."

"She won't shake your hand," Joy said. "Because you're black."

"That's not true." Yvette stuck her hand out. It trembled violently. "Don't squeeze too hard," she said. "I'm dying." Hope left the porch to see what was taking Brittany and Josh so long. She set the nutcrackers down on the steps.

"No," Yvette said.

Hope sighed, picked up the nutcrackers, and headed for Faith's SUV. She yanked open the back door and threw the nutcrackers inside. Faith was still yakking on the phone. Unbelievably rude.

"Get out and say hello," Hope yelled. Faith gave her the middle finger. Hope slammed the door. *And to all a good night.*

Hope turned to see her niece and nephew standing stock-still, looking left and right as if expecting an imminent attack. Brittany finally made eye contact. Hope smiled, then gave a head nod toward Faith. "Who is she talking to?" Hope asked, making a concerted effort to sound chipper.

"She talks a lot," Brittany said. "A lot a lot." Josh just stared at her as if trying to tell her something telepathically. Hope loved her older sister, but it wasn't easy always being bossed around by her, and Brittany and Josh had to feel the same at times. She wanted to scoop them up and tell them everything would be fine. But they were too big for that. She wished someone would scoop her up and tell her everything would be fine. Joy and Harrison disappeared in the house with Yvette and the bags. Hope's shoes had disappeared as well.

"She seems cranky," Brittany said. "I miss Carla."

Hope rolled her eyes. Brittany ought to be calling her Grandma, not Carla. How did she end up with such a wacky family?

"We'll feel right at home," Josh said. He dug at the dirt with his shoe.

"Look at all this land," Hope said. "You guys must be so excited." More stares.

"What are we?" Josh said. "Farmers?"

"Can we skate on the pond?" Brittany said.

"We sure can," Hope said.

"Can we do it now?" Brittany asked.

"We should probably visit awhile," Hope said. "But soon."

"Do you think it's going to snow?" Brittany said.

"We'll wish for it," Hope said with a wink.

"Wishes," Josh said. He glanced at Faith, who was still on the phone. Hope wanted to open that car door again and pull her sister out by her hair. Instead she threw an arm around her niece and nephew. "*I'm* not cranky," Hope said. "And I'm so happy the two of you are here." With one arm around Brittany's shoulders and the other around Josh's waist, she maneuvered them toward the porch, and they clomped up the stairs and opened the door. They entered into a tiny mudroom where Brittany and Hope started to take off their boots and shoes.

"Do we have to?" Josh asked.

"He has stinky feet," Brittany said, looking at Hope with wide eyes.

Hope laughed. "He'll fit right in," Hope said. "Looks like everyone else has taken theirs off."

Josh groaned. Hope stifled another laugh. And here she thought it was only teenage girls who could be dramatic. Poor kid. Hope remembered the pain of being a teenager. It was obviously just as intense for boys. "It's a log cabin," Josh said. "Wood floors. How could my shoes possibly do any damage?"

"He's been difficult lately," Brittany said, suddenly sounding like she was twenty years older.

"Shut up." Josh poked Brittany. She poked him back. Hope quickly stepped into the main house, wanting to avoid the progression to shoving. She was going to have to find out where the nearest liquor store was.

Hope couldn't believe how expansive the house was inside. It felt a little bit like a ski lodge or a mountain retreat. She couldn't help but think that it had to be worth a fortune. Who was Yvette leaving the property to? Hope honestly didn't think it was going to be left to them, nor did she feel any claim to it. What she really wanted to know was—where was their father? If he wasn't here, could Yvette tell them where to find him? She was going to have to ask Yvette at the first opportunity.

The main room stretched out like a giant loft with a wrap-around balcony on the second level where you could stand and look below. The kitchen was in the middle of the floor with a vast marble island giving the kitchen a sense of separation from the living room. A stone fireplace would have been the focus of the living room had it not been for a never-ending series of windows bringing the outdoors in. You could take in all of the side yard, as well as a portion of the barn and pond in the back. It was a wonderful blend of indoors/outdoors. Paradise was the only word that came to mind.

Joy and Harrison were already propped up on stools along the kitchen island as if they were a pair of skiers on their honeymoon ducking into the bar. Yvette stood behind the island just staring at them. Hope urged Brittany and Josh to follow her as she made her way up to Yvette.

"I'd like you to meet Brittany and Josh," she said. "Faith's children. Your great-grandchildren."

"Nice to meet you," Brittany said. She gave a little bow as if she wasn't quite sure what the protocol was. Seeing what a sweet girl Brittany was made Hope long to have a child of her own.

Yvette stepped forward and brought her great-grandchildren into a group hug. "Aren't you two precious," she said, releasing them and stepping back. "Would you like some milk?"

"I'm lactose intolerant," Josh said.

"Nonsense," Yvette said. "It's fresh milk."

"Do you have any juice?" Josh said.

"You have some in the van," Brittany said.

"I'd love some of that fresh white milk," Harrison said, nudging Joy.

Joy laughed. "Not me. Do you have any chocolate milk?"

Yvette eyed the pair. "In my day," she said, "we only drank one kind of milk."

"What exactly do you mean by that?" Joy asked.

"Now you've got soy milk, almond milk, goat milk." Yvette shook her head like it was a travesty.

Joy whirled around in her stool. "I don't like what you're implying, Granny."

Harrison nudged her. "I think she's just talking about milk."

"Don't be so naïve," Joy said.

Yvette began taking things out of the refrigerator one by one. "I'll show you everything I've got," she said. "It's not much, but it's yours."

"We can make a list and go to the store later," Hope said.

"Why do you need to go to the store?" Yvette barked. "Look at all I have. I'm not even done yet."

Hope was just trying to be helpful. Being loving and kind wasn't going to be easy with this group. She already felt like picking up items and throwing them at the windows to see if she could shatter one or two. But was she going to do it? Of course not. Why couldn't everyone else be like her and keep their rage bottled inside?

"I'm here, I'm here," Faith called out, stumbling into the room and dropping her Coach purse as if it weighed a hundred pounds. Then she stood surveying the room, hands on hips. She was so tall and thin. Her brown hair was longer than Hope had ever seen it, wavy and free, hanging down past her breasts. Faith was definitely getting better with age. Hope watched as her older sister made a beeline for Yvette and threw her arms around her. Why hadn't Hope felt free to do that? Where did that kind of confidence come from?

"I remember you," Faith said, stepping forward and staring at Yvette. She thrust her chin up. "Do you remember us?"

Yvette nodded. "Joy was the screamer, Hope was the chubby one, and you were a bossy little thing."

Chubby? Did Yvette just call me chubby?

"Faith is still the bossy one," Joy said.

"And you're still a screamer," Harrison said, nudging Joy.

"I'm not chubby," Hope said.

Yvette's eyes flicked over Hope. "So I see." She said it like it was a bad thing.

"Why are you taking everything out of your refrigerator?" Faith said, stepping up and eyeing the items lined up on the counter.

"This is what I have. I'm giving you everything I have."

"Where's our father?" Joy asked. "Do you have him?" Hope gasped. A heavy silence fell. Hope felt a slippery sort of panic enter her body. She had wanted to control this herself, ease into it. It was like being in an airplane when unexpected turbulence bounced you around. What's done was done. They stared at Yvette, awaiting an answer.

Yvette picked up a gallon of juice and slammed it down. "My house, my rules."

Faith squared her shoulders. "We all want to know."

Hope's heart hammered in her chest. She was ready for the question. She wasn't so sure she was ready for the answers. But the saying was true. You couldn't un-ring a bell. Hope imagined sleigh bells ringing. She missed her father like no time had passed at all since he'd thrown her up in the air and caught her on the way down. *You're my girls,* he always said to them with a look of fierce pride in his eyes. *You're my girls.*

"Your father is no longer with us," Yvette said. The words felt like stones being aimed directly at Hope's heart.

"What does that mean?" Hope heard herself ask. Yvette turned her back and began putting the items back in the fridge. Hope took a step forward. "You mean, he's not here?" Hope said. "Like he's in another state?" She heard the pathetic quiver in her voice. Yvette slowly turned around and locked eyes with her. Hope saw a world of pain reflected in Yvette's eyes. The pain of losing a child. Oh no. Yvette headed for one of the stools at the kitchen island, her steps slow and deliberate, as if she were walking with an invisible cane. Harrison jumped up and pulled out her stool. She sat, then took a deep breath, and looked each one of the girls in the eye.

"There was a car accident. Your father died in a car accident." There it was, the question that had been on all of their minds the past two decades, answered so matter-of-factly. Hope felt the sensation of something clawing at her insides. She wanted to throw something. She didn't like this woman. Maybe Carla was right. Maybe Yvette was a liar. But even Hope couldn't cling on to that thought. She may have been stoic, but the pain in Yvette's eyes wasn't something even an award-winning actress could pull off.

"When?" Hope asked.

"Twenty-four years ago. Shortly after you girls were taken from him."

Taken from him?

"No," Faith said. "Daddy. No." Faith buried her head in her hands and began to sob. Brittany hurried up and threw her arms around her mother's waist. Josh stared out at the yard.

"At least we know now," Joy said. Hope wanted to smack her. She'd ruined everything. Why did she always have to blurt out whatever was on her mind? Hope wasn't ready for this. She hadn't wanted to know this soon.

"Tell us everything," Hope said.

"Now who's the bossy one?" Yvette said.

"Tell us everything," Faith said.

"Or we walk," Joy said. The three of them stood, chins up, staring at Yvette. Hope felt sad that this was what it took to unite them, but happy to know they had her back.

"Six months after you were taken," Yvette said. "A few days before Christmas. He was on his way to get you girls back."

We weren't taken, Hope thought.

"We weren't taken," Joy said.

"Six months after they separated?" Faith asked.

"Separated?" Yvette said. "Is that what she told you?"

"What who told us?" Joy asked.

"That woman. The woman who ruined my life. My son's life. All of our lives!"

"You blame our mother," Faith said.

"She is to blame," Yvette said.

"They were young. They were in an argument," Faith said. "Carla was running to her mommy. That's all. She said he'd follow. We've been waiting for him."

"Well, looks like the wait is over," Joy said.

He drank a lot, Hope thought. She kept it to herself, she wasn't here to throw her father under a bus.

"Your parents didn't separate. My son woke up one morning and you were all gone. You call her your mother. I call her your kidnapper."

CHAPTER 13

A thick silence blanketed the room. Hope could hear the ticking of a clock somewhere, birds chirping, and a dog barking excitedly in the distance. That was probably Mr. Jingles. Hope wanted to tear out and look for him. He was definitely having a better time out there than they were in here. They appeared to be stuck in some sort of avant-garde tableau, or permanently frozen in a game of tag. This could be next year's Christmas card. *Hey, remember this moment? This is where our estranged, dying grandmother told us our father was long dead and our mother was a kidnapper. Good times. Happy new year from the Garland Girls!*

Harrison broke the silence. "For real?" He looked around the room as if waiting for someone to declare it a joke.

"We weren't kidnapped," Joy said. "Your son abandoned us."

"Old enough to remember, were you?" Yvette said.

Oh, snap. Joy glared but said nothing.

"You want to see the police report?" Yvette asked.

"Sure," Joy said.

"If he was coming to get us, then he had to know where we were," Faith pointed out.

"She'd threatened to do it before it happened. Said she'd take you all to Florida. But he didn't know where. And he didn't know she was actually going to do it. He woke up one morning and you were gone. Broke his heart into a million pieces."

Hope felt herself sway and sank into the nearest chair. Was she telling the truth? Her own heart felt like it was breaking as she imagined her handsome young father waking up to find them all gone.

"There was a snowstorm predicted for the day he left. I told him to wait. But he wouldn't. He said he had to make it to you girls by Christmas."

No, no, no, no, no, Hope thought. *That sounds like something he would say. No, no, no, no, no.*

"What happened?" Josh asked.

"His car hit a patch of ice, spun out, and crashed into the woods on the other side."

"Oh my God," Faith said.

Anger surged through Hope. She sprung off the chair and faced Yvette. "Why? Why didn't you find us then and tell us? Why did you make us wait all these years?"

"How was I supposed to find you when the police couldn't?"

"Did you even try?" Hope said.

"I lost my son. I was grieving."

"Is that a no?" Hope asked. The anger was driving her.

"I did the best I could," Yvette said.

"So did our mother," Faith said. "She wasn't hiding us. She didn't kidnap us. In fact, she spent almost every day of her life waiting for my father to walk through our front door. She loved him. She wanted him to find her."

"I forgot about that," Hope said. An image of Carla rose to mind. Their young mother sitting on the dirty floor in a yellow sundress, dark hair falling about her pretty face, back against the kitchen cabinets with her long, tanned legs pulled up, smoking a cigarette, staring at the door and waiting. "She literally sat on the kitchen floor for days. Was that what she was doing? Waiting for him?"

"Of course that's what she was doing," Faith said. "What did you think she was doing?"

"I don't know," Hope said. "That's why I asked."

"Where was I?" Joy asked. "Was anyone taking care of me?"

Hope wanted to zap Joy with a nasty retort. In Joy's world, it was all about her. But the truth was, she was the one who had lost the most. Faith, who was eight when they took off, had years of memories of their father; Hope at four didn't have nearly enough, but what she did remember she clung to; but poor Joy had none. She had a right to be a little bit selfish. She'd missed out on the best dad in the world. Well. In certain moments he was the best. He loved them fiercely. He was young, and so not a perfect man, but he did love them fiercely.

"You've been filled with her lies. I expected as much." Yvette stood her ground.

Hope stepped even closer. "We had a right to know. We had a right to go to his funeral. We *loved* him." Hope could feel years of tears filling up in her eyes. She suddenly wished Austin were here. She was missing a total stranger, wanted him to take her in his arms while she sobbed.

"I'm dying," Yvette said. "What more do you want?"

"Where is he buried?" Harrison asked. Joy shot him a look. "It might help you get closure," he added, taking her hand. Hope felt a pang of jealousy. He was such a nice guy. Joy had better not let this one go.

"He was cremated. I spread his ashes on this land. He's part of it now. Just like you can be part of it now." Yvette gestured around her as if their father were part of the dust mites in the air.

"Happy we're all together for Christmas now?" Joy said to Hope.

"Yes," Hope said. *Am I?* It just didn't feel right to answer, *Sort of.* "And our father would be happy too."

"Speaking of Christmas," Yvette said. "I have a few rules."

An image of the nutcrackers stuck in the backseat of Faith's SUV flashed through Hope's mind.

"Rules?" Joy said. Her nostrils flared and Hope found herself staring at Joy's silver nose ring.

"My only son died around Christmas. I lost you three girls too. I haven't celebrated a Christmas since Rupert passed and I don't intend to start now."

"But you invited us here for Christmas," Hope said. *And it might be your last one.*

"I invited you here," Yvette said. "It just happens to be around Christmas. If I could have postponed my death until Easter, I would have."

"We could celebrate Kwanzaa instead," Joy said.

"What's that?" Yvette said.

"See?" Joy said, turning to Harrison. "Racist."

"Oh, do give us an informed rundown of Kwanzaa, Joy," Faith said. She pulled up a spot on the floor and began doing yoga stretches.

Harrison shook his head. "I don't celebrate Kwanzaa. But I do love me a Merry Christmas."

"Not the point," Joy said.

"Mom?" Brittany said. "Are we really not going to have a Christmas?"

"Of course not," Faith said. She was now lying on her back and tilting her legs over her head. "We'll celebrate Christmas."

"And Kwanzaa," Joy said.

"You really want to rob your only great-granddaughter of celebrating Christmas this year?" Faith yelled from the floor. Watching Faith do yoga was really stressing Hope out. She had an urge to make Christmas cookies. Or just eat fudge icing with a spoon. Heck, her finger would do. Just give her the container. Maybe she could wash it down with a candy cane martini. She made a mean one if she did say so herself.

"You can celebrate Christmas after I'm gone," Yvette said. She leaned in toward Brittany. "I'll give you five hundred dollars to skip Christmas this year." Brittany's eyes widened.

"We'll take it," Josh said. He stuck out his hand like a businessman shaking after a deal.

"No tree, no cookies, no lights, no decorating, no singing?" Brittany said.

"Correct," Yvette said. "None of that nonsense, period."

"You can keep your money," Brittany said. "I'd rather have Christmas."

Thatta girl, Hope thought.

Faith un-pretzeled herself from the floor and turned to Josh and Brittany. "Why don't you two go outside?"

"I'll take the money to not celebrate," Josh said. He held out his hand.

"Me too," Joy said.

Hope bit her lip to literally keep herself from turning to Joy and saying, *Of course you will.*

"Nobody is taking money," Faith said. "I will draw up a plan for Christmas that everyone can agree to." Faith turned to Yvette. "You won't have to lift a finger."

"No," Yvette said. "No Christmas. End of story."

"I don't want the money," Brittany said. "I'll take Christmas, please."

"Good luck getting Hope not to celebrate Christmas," Faith said.

There she was, singling Hope out, mocking her. As if there was something wrong with wanting to celebrate Christmas. Hope took the higher road and did not say a word.

"What about Kwanzaa?" Joy said.

"This isn't happening," Hope said.

"*A Christmas Story!*" Harrison exclaimed. "With the leg lamp and the little dude that gets his tongue stuck on an icy pole. Have you seen that one, Mrs. G?"

"Do this for me, and every single one of you will be set," Yvette said. "You will never have to work another day in your life."

"Five hundred dollars would last our whole lives?" Brittany asked.

"Not just five hundred," Yvette said, pinching Brittany's cheek. "This whole house and land. All yours. Well, your mom would own one-third of it. Sounding like a better deal now?"

"Give up Christmas and we get this house?" Brittany said.

"Deal," Josh said. He stuck out his hand once more.

"Leave my children out of this," Faith said.

"The whole house?" Brittany said. "The skating pond?"

Joy's head seemed to float above the crowd. "You're leaving us this entire place?" Hope could almost see her eyes glowing.

"Kwanzaa it is, baby," Harrison said. They high-fived.

"I intended to leave the estate to you three girls," Yvette said. "Whosoever follows my rules. I'm hoping it will be all three of you."

"Whosoever," Harrison repeated, drawing it out.

"Christmas is out this year!" Joy said. "It's too materialistic anyway."

"Says the girl who pretends to be homeless for spare change," Hope said.

"What?" Faith said.

"What are the rest of the rules?" Josh asked.

"You might want to get paper and pen," Yvette said.

Joy held up her smartphone. "Siri. What is paper and pen?"

Yvette looked around wildly as Siri robotically explained what she found on the Web for paper and pen. "What's happening?"

"What do you mean, pretends to be homeless?" Faith said, yanking the phone out of Joy's hands. Joy turned on Hope. She was practically snarling. "I should have known you wouldn't keep your mouth shut. You love thinking the worst of me, don't you?" Joy jabbed her finger at Hope. There it was again. The not-so-veiled hint that Hope had once done something terrible to Joy. What in the world was it?

"Why don't you just tell me what grudge you're harboring against me so we can be done with this?" Hope said. She loved her baby sister, natural deodorant and all. But why did Joy have to be so mean?

"And Mom says we fight a lot," Brittany said to Josh. What an awful example they were setting. They should have waited until they were alone. Fighting in front of the kids and their dying grandmother. It was a good thing they weren't going to celebrate Christmas, Santa was definitely going to skip them this year.

"Somebody tell me what 'pretends to be homeless' means in very concrete terms or I'm going to scream." Faith didn't literally stomp her foot, but she might as well have. Hope and Faith stared at Joy.

"It's nobody's business!" Joy grabbed her phone back from Faith.

"I thought you weren't ashamed of it," Hope said.

"I'm not." Joy thrust her chin up, then furiously typed something into her phone. Great. Hope could only imagine all the tweets Joy was sending out about her. #mysisterssuck. It made her sad. And furious. Although maybe she should have kept her mouth shut about Joy pretending to be homeless. Nah, it would not have been humanly possible to keep that to herself.

"We were funding creatively," Harrison said.

"Exactly," Joy said. "Crowd sourcing."

"Crowd sourcing?" Hope said.

"Like the Kickstarter," Joy said. She narrowed her eyes. "Did you guys get the link?"

"If you were legitimately crowd sourcing, then what's the big deal if I tell Faith?"

"Go ahead," Joy said. Her left eye began to twitch.

Hope turned to Faith. "She and Harrison were on the streets of Seattle with a group of homeless kids, holding up a sign that said, HUNGRY AND THIRSTY. Austin gave them a hundred dollars."

Joy shrugged. The twitch grew more pronounced.

"How could you do something like that?" Faith said.

"A hundred dollars?" Josh said. "Just for carrying a sign?"

"Don't get any ideas," Faith said. She turned back to Joy. "You should be ashamed of yourself." Hope felt a twinge of guilt for starting this in front of everyone. She hadn't meant to. Sometimes things just flew out of her mouth.

"I had no choice. I'm starting a business. It's not like my rich older sister was willing to give me a loan."

"You shouldn't be starting a business if you don't have money," Faith said.

"That's what I was doing. Raising capital," Joy said.

"I need to lie down," Yvette said. "We'll go over my rules later."

"I'm sorry if we upset you," Hope said. "We really do love each other." Faith stretched her arms behind her back, Joy buried herself in her phone.

"My room is down here at the end of the hall. There are six bedrooms upstairs. I'll let you take your pick. Joy, you will not be sharing a room with Harrison. There will be no comingling in my house while I'm here."

"What about when you're not here?" Harrison said.

The Garland Girls gasped in unison.

Harrison held his hands up. "I don't mean not here as in— *not here*—I meant—out. Like Christmas shopping. Or Kwanzaa shopping." He winked at Joy.

Joy turned to their grandmother. "Is it really a rule, Granny? Or more like a guideline?" Faith pinched the bridge of her nose as if pained.

"Hard and fast rule," Yvette said.

"Do you need anything?" Hope asked Yvette gently. She couldn't believe they'd just been ordered not to celebrate Christmas. Worse, her sisters seemed to have no problem with it. There was no way Hope was going to go along with it. But she certainly wasn't going to push it before Yvette's nap.

"I can manage," Yvette said. She took a few steps along the hall to the right of the front door. She stopped for a moment and turned back around. "I'm glad you're all here," she said. "Even you." She pointed at Harrison. He beamed and gave her a thumbs-up. Joy pulled him in for a selfie.

"We're happy we're here too," Hope called after Yvette.

"Can we go outside?" Josh said.

"Yes, pretty please?" Brittany said.

"Knock yourselves out," Faith said. She began taking an inventory of the fridge as the kids made a beeline to the mudroom to don their coats and boots. Hope sat at the kitchen island. "No kale," Faith said. "I knew it."

Hope caught Joy's eye. Joy mouthed "Oh no!" then smacked her hands over her mouth and gave a muted laugh. Hope felt thrilled to be teamed up with Joy for once, instead of being on the receiving end of it.

Harrison looked at the three of them, one by one. "I think I'll have a walk around too." He got up.

"I'll come with," Joy said.

Harrison put his hand on her shoulder. "No," he said. "Why don't you hang with your sisters?" Joy considered this, then shrugged and flopped down on the sofa.

Hope gave him an appreciative look. He was the only thing about Joy at the moment that gave her any hope. Brittany and Josh reappeared, all suited-up like Eskimos. Hope loved winter. The padding, the chill in the air, coming in after a winter's day to the warmth of a fire. They could all have such a good time here if only they would let themselves. Thank goodness for children. They were built to be happy.

"I have a dog with me," Hope told Harrison and the kids. "You might run into him out there."

"Of course you do," Faith said.

"He's a gigantic bloodhound," Hope added.

"Of course he is," Faith said.

"He's friendly. Name is Mr. Jingles." Hope ignored Faith and grinned at Brittany.

"Mr. Jingles," Brittany said, grinning back.

"Try and bring him back with you if you find him," Hope said.

"Got it," Josh said.

"Are you sure he doesn't bite?" Harrison said. Hope went to her bag and retrieved treats and a leash.

"He's enthusiastic but harmless." She handed the leash and treats to Brittany. She started to jump up and down.

"Can we bring him in the house?"

"No," Faith said.

"Eventually," Hope whispered in Brittany's ear. Brittany grinned. The three of them headed outside. Hope watched from the window.

"They're so grown up," she said to Faith. "And so sweet."

"Not always," Faith said. "But they're mine and I love them."

"Brittany said that Josh has been a bit moody lately," Hope said.

"He's a teenager," Faith snapped.

"I think he's very bright and sweet," Hope said. She looked out the window and watched Brittany twirling in the yard. Then she fell backward and began to make a snow angel. *Yes,* Hope thought. *You go, girl.* Josh and Harrison headed for the woods. Hope focused her attention back inside and soon her eyes landed on a couple of large objects wedged between the refrigerator and the wall.

"The nutcrackers," Hope said. She hopped off her stool and pulled them out one by one.

"I didn't want them in my car," Faith said.

"Why stick them here?" Hope asked.

"I did it," Joy said. "Wanted to see how long it would take you to find them."

Hope patted their little heads. "I should put them back on the front porch," she said.

"Looks like we'll be splitting this estate in two," Joy announced.

"Excuse me?" Hope said.

Joy blinked, then thrust up her index finger. "Nutcrackers are a celebration of Christmas. I think that disqualifies you."

Hope stared at her younger sister, tears welling in her eyes. "What in the world did I do to you?"

For a second Joy's lip quivered as she met Hope's eyes. She opened her mouth as if to finally tell her. Then her veil of steel slammed down again. "Nothing."

Hope whirled on Faith. "Tell me!"

Faith threw up her arms. "I'm not getting involved."

"Since when?"

Faith opened her purse and took out a pill bottle. She popped it open and downed one.

"What is that?" Hope said.

"Prescription Xanax," Faith said.

"Can I have one?" Joy said.

"No," Faith said.

"Can I have one?" Hope asked.

"No," Faith said.

"Why would she say yes to you if she said no to me?" Joy demanded, turning on Hope.

"Because she knows I'm not going to try to sell them on craigslist," Hope said. "How's that for a start?"

"Is this why you wanted us all together? So you could be nasty?" Joy sounded genuinely hurt.

"I was joking," Hope said. "I knew Faith wasn't going to share. Since when does Faith share?"

"Hey," Faith said. "If I had kale I'd be force-feeding both of you right now. It's obvious your bodies are toxic."

"Do we have any alcohol?" Joy asked.

"Toxic, toxic, toxic," Faith said as Joy began rummaging through the cabinets.

"Granny sure likes her whiskey," Joy said, holding up a bottle of Johnnie Walker Blue.

"Like Dad," Faith said. The three of them stared at the bottle.

"I'll pick up some vodka in town," Hope said. "I'll make us my famous candy cane martinis."

"Kale smoothies is what we need," Faith said.

Joy leaned on the kitchen island. "I'd kill for a joint."

Hope ambushed Joy with a hug from behind. "I missed you two. I missed the Garland Girls."

Joy groaned. "I hated when Mom called us that."

"Dad called us that first," Hope said. "And we loved it."

"It's not fair. I never got to know him." For once Joy didn't sound sarcastic. Faith came up from behind and put her arms around both of them.

"He was so thrilled when you were born," Hope said. "I think you were his favorite."

"Really?" Joy's voice was tinged with the sound of a deep ache.

"He barely even let Mom hold you when you were back from the hospital. It was like you were a part of his arms."

"I can't breathe," Joy said. Faith backed off, then Hope. They plopped into stools at the island. "Was I really his favorite?" Joy asked.

Faith nodded. "He said you completed the set." She laughed and soon Joy and Hope joined in.

"God, he was funny," Hope said.

"And fun," Faith said.

"And devastatingly handsome," Hope said.

"They did make such a beautiful couple," Faith said.

"It seems like beautiful couples are always doomed," Joy said. "Did they fight a lot?"

Faith snorted. "Do active volcanoes get a little hot?"

"We used to hide under the bed," Hope said.

"Only when he'd been drinking," Faith said. Joy stared at them wide-eyed.

"But it was mostly good," Hope said quickly. Now that he was gone, she certainly didn't want to taint his memory.

"I can't believe he died all those years ago and we never knew," Joy said.

"I can't believe he was coming for us," Hope said. "Should we tell Mom?"

"It can wait," Faith said. "Far be it for us to ruin Christmas in Cuba."

Joy picked up a nutcracker and held it. "Mom told me not to believe a word that woman says."

"She told me the same thing," Hope said.

"Maybe he wasn't really coming to see us," Joy said. She put the nutcracker down and picked up the other one. Then she smashed them together as if they were kissing.

"I wonder if he was drinking and driving?" Faith said.

"I was wondering the same thing," Hope said. She didn't realize she'd started crying until she felt the tears dripping down her cheeks. Suddenly Faith was in front of her, enveloping Hope in a hug. Joy, nutcracker in each hand, wrapped her arms around Faith, who was still hanging on to Hope.

"Group hug," Faith said. Then she abruptly pulled away. "Joy—are you showering?"

"Americans are so hung up on daily showers, and deodorant, and perfume. We're supposed to be natural."

"Mission accomplished," Faith said. "You smell like a caveman."

Joy sniffed her armpits. She looked as if she were about to protest, then laughed. "I'm rank," she said.

"There's deodorant in my pink bag by the door. Find a bathroom and stop communing with nature."

"We need to talk," Hope said. "We need to stand up to Yvette's rules. Starting with Christmas."

"We'll talk when I can breathe," Faith said, waving her hand as if to ward off a smell.

Joy rolled her eyes, then set the nutcrackers on the kitchen island, one lying on top of the other.

"No comingling in this house," Hope said, separating the nutcrackers. Joy and Faith each let out a cackle. It warmed Hope from the inside. She laughed too. Soon the three of them were in hysterics. When they settled down, Joy bounded off to retrieve the deodorant. She found it and thrust it up like it was the Olympic torch. "I've missed you guys," she said, looking at them for a second, then grabbed her bag and crossed over to the stairwell leading to the second floor. She pointed at them. "I get dibs on the room. Nobody interrupts my shower. No talking about me behind my back."

"Don't worry," Faith said. "If we do we'll be sure to repeat everything to your face."

CHAPTER 14

Hope and Faith bundled up and headed outside. Joy seemed like she was going to spend hours in the shower, which Hope and Faith agreed was a very wise move. The air was crisp and cold, and smelled like snow. Although they couldn't see the others, laughter and voices rang out from the woods. A dog barked. Hope smiled, confident they had already met Mr. Jingles. Faith caught her smile and shook her head and rolled her eyes. "Not coming in the house," she said under her breath. *So coming in the house,* Hope thought to herself. Sometimes it was a lot easier to win arguments when she kept them in her head.

They headed across the expansive lawn to the pond. As they walked, Hope tried to think of nonthreatening ways to bring up the topic of Stephen, but they were getting along nicely and she didn't want to ruin that. Instead, she opened her arms and twirled around just like she'd seen Brittany do a bit earlier.

"Look at this place," she said. She took in all the tall pines. "Christmas tree, anyone?"

"Do you really think she's going to leave it to us?" Faith said.

"This is a Norman Rockwell Christmas here. Dad would have loved it. Are we seriously not going to celebrate Christmas?"

"Of course we're going to celebrate Christmas," Faith said. "Otherwise my children will report me for abuse. Granny will warm up to it."

Hope wasn't so sure about that. The one trait that they all had in common was stubbornness. "And if she doesn't?"

"We'll work on her." They were just about to reach the pond when Faith pointed to the deck near the barn. "Is that a hot tub?"

"Sure is," Hope said. Faith made a beeline toward it. Hope ran after her. By the time Hope reached the hot tub, Faith already had the cover off. She found the controls and fired it up. "It works!"

"Looks pretty clean too," Hope said.

"We're definitely coming out here with cocktails," Faith said.

"Candy cane martinis or kale smoothies?" Hope teased.

Faith swatted her. "Let's check out the pond." They headed over. It looked so pristine, so inviting. Hope couldn't wait to go skating. There was a fence around it as well as benches on either side for sitting and putting on skates. Hope wished she could go back in time to when this property was open to the public during the Christmas season. If the Garland Girls adopted the house, they could bring back the tradition. That is, if they could keep Joy from selling it to the highest bidder. "Is Stephen coming for Christmas Day?" Hope kept her voice light and casual.

Faith looked away. "I don't know."

"Everything okay with you two?"

"What does Mom say?" Faith leaned against the fence and poked at the edge of the pond with her toe.

"She thinks you're having trouble."

"Is she posting it on Facebook?"

Hope laughed. "She only posts parrots and booze."

Faith started laughing along with Hope. "Who knew she'd turn into Jimmy Buffett in her golden years." Hope wondered what their mother was doing now. Sunbathing on a sailboat?

Dancing with a rum and Coke in her hand? Smoking a Cuban cigar?

Hope gazed at the mountains. They were so solid, so comforting. This truly was God's country. "This business about Dad is going to break her heart."

"She said not to tell her anything unless she asked."

"Let's hope she doesn't ask."

"God, they were so young," Faith said. "Just kids."

"Who shouldn't have had kids," Hope said. It felt like a betrayal to say that, but it was so true. Maybe they would have held it together better if they'd been older.

Faith gave a little shrug. "We survived."

Hope focused on a pine tree in the distance. She loved the stark green, the spikey needles, the crisp scent the trees infused into the air. "But he didn't."

Faith crossed her arms. "He might not have been coming for us."

Hope had never considered that. Why did she always believe everything everyone said? Had he been coming for them? "You think she lied?"

"I don't think she lied about the accident. But how are we supposed to know whether or not he was coming to see us? He died not far from here. He could have been going anywhere."

"I guess we'll never know." Hope sighed. She didn't want to think about it.

Faith kept going. "He was a fast driver. And often drinking. Remember?"

Hope nodded. "Mom always yelling at him to slow down."

"Slow down, you're going to get us killed," Faith mimicked.

They fell silent and looked out at the land. Faith pointed. "Is that a man hiding behind that tree?"

"Where?" Hope followed the trajectory of Faith's finger. Sure enough there was a man with a red cap and beard, early fifties, hiding behind a tree, watching them. "That must be Roger," Hope said. "He's the caretaker. Austin thinks he might have some kind of brain damage. I guess he does that a lot."

"Creepy."

"I don't think so," Hope said. "He gave me a pinecone and put my bags on the porch."

"Maybe he's a good egg then." Faith lifted her hand to Roger and waved. He stared for a minute, then slowly raised a gloved hand and waved back. Then he turned and trudged away. Faith tracked him for a moment. "Seems harmless," she concluded.

"He lives in that cabin out back."

"Should we go say hi?"

"I think we just did," Hope said. "He seems a bit shy."

"Granny is like you. Always taking in strays."

"Why have you and Joy taken to calling her Granny?"

Faith laughed. "Because she looks like she'd hate it."

Hope laughed too. God, it was good to be around her sisters when they were happy. She just had to make sure they all stayed happy. "We should go into town. There are a ton of cute shops."

"How did she get the money for this place?" Faith wandered in the direction of the barn. Hope followed.

"Her late husband, Rupert. He owned a sledding and skating outfit in town. Visitors used to come here, too, to skate on the pond, sing Christmas carols, the works." Faith stood at the doors to the barn. They were shut tight and padlocked. "I think all the skating equipment is still in there."

Faith laughed. "You are a plethora of information." She tugged on the padlock. "Wonder why all the security?"

"I think she's trying to keep the past under lock and key," Hope said. Faith shrugged and walked toward the pond. Hope hurried after her. "We could start that up again, you know."

"We?" Faith didn't turn around.

"Yes, the three of us. We could keep the house and start up the business again." They stopped at the edge of the pond. Hope could just imagine the neighbors gathered to skate. Christmas was supposed to be the season of giving. Imagine, year after year, giving back by inviting their neighbors to enjoy such a magical place. Hope could definitely see herself stepping into a life like that. And no, it didn't hurt that a man like Austin lived next door, but that wasn't her only motivation.

"I live in San Francisco." Faith looked at Hope, as if waiting for her to continue her pitch.

"I could manage the property," Hope said. She'd been thinking about it a lot. She could do it. She could live here.

A little smile broke out on Faith's face. "Ah. So you want to keep the house to yourself."

"Not at all. It's all of ours."

"What about the dogs?"

Look at all this land. I could adopt a ton of dogs. "I wasn't going to do that forever."

"Could have fooled me."

There she was again, subtly putting her down. Hope had had enough. "You really thought I was going to work at an animal shelter the rest of my life?"

"Yes," Faith said.

"Well, you're wrong. I will always be involved in the welfare of animals, but that doesn't mean I don't have goals."

"What are they?"

Shoot. She had no idea. Getting closer to her sisters. Didn't that count as a goal? "I can see myself managing this place. Starting an outreach to the community." She thought of Austin and his work with suicide prevention. Maybe at-risk kids could come to this place, like a retreat. Faith was fact-based, Hope wasn't going to start pitching at the daydreaming stage.

"Joy will never go for it." Faith started walking toward the woods, and once again Hope followed. Faith was always leading the way, but Hope didn't mind. She wanted to be with her sister, and it didn't matter where they went as long as they were together.

"Joy could be persuaded," Hope said. *As long as we present a united front.*

Faith laughed. "Good luck with that."

"She could sell coffee to the skaters."

"We could build her a little coffee hut on the premises," Faith said.

"Exactly."

Faith stopped. Hope almost ran into her. "Where's your boyfriend?"

For a second, Austin flashed through Hope's mind. His smile. His stubble. Muscles buried in flannel. "Hawaii."

"Are you kidding me? Without you?"

"He had a ticket for me too."

"Why aren't you there?"

"Because I wanted to be here. With my sisters. His idea of Christmas lights is probably a string of colored bikinis on the beach. This is more my idea of where to spend Christmas."

"How'd he take it?"

"Surprisingly well given that I broke up with him."

Faith snuck her arm around Hope and started walking again. "I didn't like Michael."

"You never met him."

"I could hear it in your voice."

"Hear what?"

"He wasn't treating you right."

"He didn't like dogs."

"Maybe I was too quick to judge."

Hope slapped Faith lightly on the back. "Wait until you meet Mr. Jingles."

"I do not want to meet Mr. Jingles."

Just then, the little group emerged from the woods. Mr. Jingles was in the lead, pulling on the leash that was attached to poor Brittany.

"Speak of the devil," Hope said. "Let go if he pulls too hard," she yelled to Brittany. Josh and Harrison emerged next. Harrison waved.

"What do you think of the Black Stallion?" Faith whispered.

Hope shook her head at the reference. "He's cute. And very nice."

"I agree. Joy seems happy. With him at least."

Hope looked back at the log house, then lowered her voice. "Am I allowed to say that I like him better than I like her right now?"

"Absolutely."

"She's going to want us to sell this place."

"Probably for the best. It has to be worth a fortune."

"We should keep it. I meant that."

"Having money might be a better option."

"You don't need money."

Faith's eyes narrowed. "You don't know that."

So she and Stephen were having trouble. Hope wished they were close enough to confide in each other. It was a really bad sign if you couldn't share secrets with your sisters. Then again, it wasn't something you could force. Hope didn't press Faith for any more details. "Granny said there were more rules. Wonder what they are."

Faith was still watching Harrison. "Do you think it's an easier life these days for mixed-race couples?"

"Easier, yes. Easy? No," Hope said. She wished it were easy. She wished people would confront their own racism.

Faith must have been thinking the same thing. "Do you think Granny Dearest was just talking about milk?" she asked.

"No," Hope said. "I don't."

"Me neither." She sighed. "So our grandmother is a racist."

"I think a lot of people harbor racist feelings and thoughts. But it's so taboo to admit that—even to ourselves. What if we could all just examine what we think, feel, and say—admit it—then dig deeper to the root of those beliefs. Honesty, self-scrutiny, and being open-minded. I think people who say they 'don't see color' are lying and also quite insulting. Why not see color and like what you see? Honor other races and cultures."

"Yeah," Faith said. "Don't think Granny is going to tackle that in the time she has left."

Hope shook her head. "Probably not."

Just then Brittany let go of Mr. Jingles and he made a beeline to Hope and Faith. Faith started to scream.

"Calm down," Hope said. "You'll excite him even more." But Faith didn't, or couldn't, calm down and Mr. Jingles directed his kinetic energy straight for her. Before Hope could stop him, he lunged. Faith went down onto the grass with Mr. Jingles on top of her, excitedly barking. Soon he had a large paw planted on either side of her head and his big tongue was less than half an inch from her mouth. Hope practically had to lie on top of the dog to wrestle him off.

"We're selling," she heard Faith say the minute the dog was away from her. "We're definitely selling." Hope would have been depressed at her utterance but was soon distracted by the skies. It began to snow.

CHAPTER 15

Hope stood on the sidewalk of the adorable downtown with her petulant sisters and company. They'd had their first big snowfall, and the town was covered in a beautiful white blanket. Yet her sisters were still moody. Faith had risen with the sun to go for a run, but when Hope peered outside she saw Faith pacing by the side of the barn, talking on her cell. Was she arguing with Stephen or was something else going on?

Joy, on the other hand, had spent the morning sucking up to their grandmother. Waxing poetic about the commercialism of Christmas and trying to sneak in the merits of espresso. Finally, Hope had corralled everyone into this trip downtown. Yet Faith and Joy were sporting sour faces. What in the world was it going to take to break through to those two? How could anyone gaze at these snow-covered mountains and pout? Brittany and Josh were lagging behind, and Harrison still seemed conscious of letting the girls have some alone time. Joy wasn't having it. Any time he pulled away, she grabbed his arm and clung to him. Oh well. They were still together, even if Joy didn't have eyes for anyone but Harrison. Surely they would be just as charmed by the downtown as she was. Because even if Yvette didn't want to celebrate Christmas up at the log home, the town was certainly celebrating it down here. Christmas lights were strung in the windows of every shop, electronic reindeer grazed in a patch of snow in the median, wreaths dotted doorways, shop windows boasted decorative themes, and in the center of the town was a gigantic Christmas tree. There was a tree-lighting event coming up with costumes, and singers, and lantern parades led by old-fashioned Santas, and swarms of people swept up by the spirit of Christmas. Hope was going to have to find a way to get everyone to attend. Forcing them to have a good time was another matter altogether. At least they were here now. Having fun. Weren't they?

"Isn't it adorable?" Hope said, gesturing to the quaint street.

"Picture-perfect," Faith agreed, staring at the chalet façades.

"Too perfect," Joy said. "Wonder what weirdness lurks underneath."

"Like a Stephen King novel," Harrison said.

"Let's stick with Norman Rockwell," Hope said.

"Who?" Josh said.

Hope ruffled his hair. "A famous artist. He painted a lot of quaint, small-town scenes just like this one."

"Okay," Josh said in a tone that conveyed *whatever*.

"Look," Brittany pointed. Across the street you could see kids careening down a snow-covered hill on sleds. The overnight snowfall had brought all the outdoor activities to life. Farther still, Hope could make out a horse and carriage making the rounds. "Can we do that?"

"Yes," Hope said.

"No," Faith said.

Hope nudged her. "You used to love sledding."

"That was before I was a mom. One of these two will break an appendage and spend the rest of their holiday in a cast."

"It's sledding," Hope said. "Not skiing down Black Diamond."

"Today we're just going to wander the shops and get a bite to eat." Faith forged ahead without awaiting a response.

"We'll go soon," Hope said, looping her arm around Brittany. She tried to bring Josh into the mix, but he deftly avoided her touch.

"I love sledding," Brittany said.

"We can ice skate on Yvette's pond too," Hope said.

"I love this place." Brittany grinned.

"I do too!" Hope said. Why couldn't her sisters be as enthusiastic and happy? Or her nephew. He was definitely scowling. She turned to him. "How about you, Josh? Willing to try out the hills or the ice?"

"Nah," he said.

"Why not?" Brittany asked. She looked at Hope, then glanced at Josh. "*Moody.*"

"Shut up," Josh said.

"We can build snowmen and have snowball fights too," Hope said. "Then make hot chocolate and string popcorn."

"This is going to be our best Christmas ever," Brittany said.

"Ironic," Josh said. "Given that our great-grandmother said we're not to celebrate it."

"We're celebrating already," Hope said. She took a deep breath and tried to convince herself she was having a good time.

"Do I have to come?" Josh asked as he caught up with Hope and Brittany. Faith was still bulldozing ahead, and Joy and Harrison were lagging behind.

Hope tried to keep her tone light. "What's wrong? Aren't you looking forward to a good Bavarian meal?"

"No," Josh said.

"Told you. Moody," Brittany said.

Hope put her arm around Josh. "I'm sure they'll have cheeseburgers and fries on the menu too."

Faith had already disappeared into a shop but by the time Hope caught up, she couldn't be sure of which one. Hope wanted to go into the first shop anyway. It was a cooking shop, and in the spirit of Christmas you could smell sugar cookies baking in the oven. She tried to get Joy's and Harrison's attention. She waved frantically and called their names until a look of pure horror on Josh's face brought her to a stop. Yikes. She was now at the age where she was embarrassing teenagers in public. She would get a grip; there was no need to worry where everyone was.

"Come on," she said to Brittany and Josh. "Let's check this one out." A bell chimed as they stepped in. It was warm and welcoming. A kitchen was set up in the middle of the store with a counter filled with a tray of just-baked cookies, along with a rolling pin and icing waiting to be piled on. Cookie cutters were lined up along the counter. Hope took in all the different shapes. Santa, reindeer, trees, and ornaments. Customers were busy squeezing bags of icing onto their creations, laughing if too much squirted out. This was what family and friends were for—laughter, and doing things with one another. Hope wished Joy and Faith were here, ready and eager to decorate cookies together. If this were a Hallmark movie, they'd all be here, squealing, connecting, and maybe even getting icing in one another's hair.

"Can we decorate a cookie?" Brittany asked, jumping up and down.

Josh rolled his eyes. "Don't be such a baby." Brittany winced.

Hope grabbed Brittany's hand and began jumping up and down too. "Christmas gives us license to act any age we want," she said. She grinned and grabbed Josh's hand. He shook his head, and finally a little smile escaped from his lips. Hope stopped jumping, laughed, and ruffled his hair. She headed for the cookie line. "Let's also decorate one for Faith, and Joy, and Harrison."

"Do you think they have any non-Christmas cookies for Great Grandma?" Brittany asked. She was taking on Hope's old role: The Peacemaker.

It took all of Hope's restraint not to reply: *What's so great about her?* "Why don't you go ahead and make her a Christmas one. I don't think she'll mind if it comes from you two."

"Using us to force her to celebrate Christmas," Josh said. "You're diabolical, Aunt Hope."

Hope laughed and hugged him. It was like hugging an irritated ironing board.

"Where's Mom?" Brittany said, looking around.

"Probably making one of her phone calls," Josh said.

There was something in his tone. Bitterness. He and Brittany exchanged a look. What did it mean? One of her phone calls. To Stephen? Someone else? She wanted to ask more, but Josh turned away. "I'm going to wait outside." They were next in line.

"Please," Hope said, hooking his arm and pulling him in. "Decorate this." She grabbed a tree from the tray and shoved it at Josh. Next she nudged a bag of green icing toward him.

"You're crazy," he said. But he picked up a bag, hovered it over the cookie, and began to squeeze.

Brittany giggled and grabbed a reindeer from the tray.

"This is so much fun." Hope picked up an ornament. Then two more. She would make three—Faith, Hope, and Joy. Surprise her sisters.

"You have to pay for those," a nasal voice said from behind. Hope whirled around to see a surly girl with blond hair and an apron glaring at her.

"Before we decorate them?" Hope said.

"After," the girl said.

"I was planning on it," Hope said. "No such thing as a free cookie for Christmas, is there?"

"The first one is free. But you have three."

"I said I'll pay for them. They're for my sisters." Brittany's head popped up when Hope's voice grew a little sharp. She tried to smile. Why was she letting some clerk in a small-town shop get her all worked up? Why was everyone so grumpy about Christmas? It was one thing to reject commercialism and embrace the spirit instead, but where was the spirit? After she decorated her cookies and paid for the whole lot, she spied some reindeer antlers on a shelf and grabbed three. She put one on her head, then plopped one on Brittany and Josh. "I'll pay for those too!" she said.

"Aunt Hope?" Brittany said.

Josh went to take his off.

"We're celebrating," Hope said. "We're having fun."

"I'll wear two," Brittany said, swiping up Josh's antlers and putting them on her head.

"'It's beginning to look a lot like Christmas,'" Hope started to sing.

"You guys are weird," Josh said. "I'm going outside." He dropped his cookie on the counter.

Brittany's hand snuck over and snatched it up. "I'll finish it," she said. They were almost out the door when Brittany tugged on Hope's sleeve. Her face was somber.

"What's wrong, sweetie?" Hope asked.

"I'm worried about Josh," Brittany said. "He really is moody."

Hope smiled. "All teenage boys are moody," she said. "But it probably doesn't help to keep pointing that out."

"Okay," Brittany said. "But he's so different."

Hope put her arm around Brittany and gave her a half hug. "Moodiness is in our genes," she said. "It's definitely in our genes."

Josh wasn't outside when Hope and Brittany emerged from making cookies. There was no sign of him or any of the others. They stood gazing at the people, and the lights, and the snow.

"It's magical," Brittany said. "I wish my dad was here."

Me too, Hope thought about her own dad. She smiled at Brittany. "He'll be joining us soon, won't he?" Hope eyed her niece, ready to catch any shift of expression that might indicate trouble.

"Depends on work, I guess," Brittany said with a shrug.

"I'm sure he'll be here for Christmas," Hope said.

"Nobody really wants to celebrate this year."

"I do," Hope said. "Don't you?"

"I do," Brittany said. Her eyes had a twinkle. Now that's what Hope wanted. That was the spirit, right there. All these grown-ups so focused on themselves. Brittany would only get so many Christmases as a child.

"We're already celebrating," Hope said. "We just made cookies."

"Not all of us."

"Let's find them. Eat cookies in front of them. Make them

feel guilty." Hope nudged Brittany and kept nudging until her niece laughed.

"Do you think Grandpa Garland would have liked me?" Brittany asked.

Hope stopped in her tracks. She'd been so focused on the fact that she'd lost out on a father she hadn't even considered that they'd lost out on a grandfather. And her father would have adored them. She knew it beyond a doubt. "No," Hope said. "I think he would have loved you to death." Brittany beamed and then nodded. They turned into a shop with thick hand-knit sweaters displayed in the windows. An image of Austin flashed in her mind. He would look good in one of those. Not that she was going to buy a Christmas present for a man she barely knew. Although he had driven all the way to Portland to pick her up, hadn't he? Of course she was going to get him a present. She tucked the sweater idea away.

"There they are," Brittany said. Hope looked up to see Faith, Joy, Josh, and Harrison standing in front of the Winter Biergarten restaurant, looking around as if waiting for them. And the expressions on their faces were anything but festive. Brittany hurried up to them and Hope followed. Faith immediately threw her arms up in the air.

"Where have you been?"

"Looking for you guys," Hope said.

"Josh said you were baking cookies."

Brittany dug one out of her bag, stuck it in her mouth, and handed one to Hope with a wink. They bit into their cookie at the same time.

"You'll spoil your lunch," Faith said. She actually reached to take the cookie out of Brittany's mouth.

Hope slapped Faith's hand away, giving Brittany time to finish the cookie. "It was my idea. Since you weren't there to make them with us we were going to tease you."

"Real mature," Faith said.

"Sorry, Mom," Brittany said.

Hope couldn't believe poor Brittany felt guilty about eating a cookie. They were on vacation. It was Christmas. Hope was going to kill Faith if she didn't get into the spirit of things. "Why are you so angry? We were supposed to check out the shops and you disappeared. I'm the one who should be angry."

"We decided we were going to eat first," Faith said.

"When did we decide that?"

"In the car."

"Brittany, Josh, and I didn't know that."

"Well, Joy and Harrison did."

"No, they didn't. They were making out on the street corner."

"Do you have a problem with that?" Joy said.

"I don't know," Hope said. "Were you charging for it?" Harrison laughed, Joy glared.

"Can we just eat now?" Josh said.

"Selective hearing," Faith said, opening the door to the restaurant and storming inside. Why on earth was she making such a big deal about this? Had she mentioned it in the car? Hope didn't remember that. Would it be anti-Christmas of Hope to give her sister a beating with a pair of fake reindeer antlers?

CHAPTER 16

They were seated at a large booth by the window, right next to a roaring fireplace topped with a giant wreath. Christmas lights were strung along the ceiling and carols played softly in the background. Outside, it began to snow again. Hope could stare at the flakes coming down forever. Nature was certainly a thing of beauty. After they had some food in their stomachs, and had relaxed, maybe they could focus on actually having a good time in this adorable village. "I'm getting a greasy cheeseburger and fries," Hope announced. She glanced at Josh and Brittany. "How about you guys?" Their heads immediately snapped toward Faith. She shook her head. Brittany buried herself in the menu again, but Josh continued to stare at his mother.

"Why not?" Josh demanded.

Faith kept her voice calm. "It's not good for you."

"Aunt Hope is having one."

"If she wants to pollute her body with toxins, I can't stop her."

"Hey," Hope said. Since when was it a crime to have a cheese-burger and fries on holiday? Hope had a nice body and normally she ate very healthy. There was definitely something up with Faith.

"I'm vegetarian," Joy said. She had a smug look on her face. Hope suddenly wished she hadn't tried to get together with them at all. She wished Austin hadn't come into the animal shelter that night. Deep-sea fishing with Michael would be better than this.

Liar. You like him. She did like him. She wondered where he was. What was he doing right now? Had he been thinking about her? Her sisters might be giant pains in the rear, but Austin was still here.

"You're vegetarian?" Faith was saying. "Since when?"

"Since forever," Joy said.

"You ate chicken the last time you were at my house," Faith said.

"That was two years ago," Joy said.

"Pardon me. I didn't have the converter to tell me that two years equals forever. Oh, right. That's because there isn't one."

"Guys," Hope said. "Can we just all calm down?"

"I think everyone should stop participating in the butchering of innocent animals," Joy said.

Brittany squeaked. A look of guilt was stamped on her face. Hope snuck her hand across the table and took Brittany's. Unlike Faith, Brittany squeezed her hand back.

"We're supposed to be having a nice lunch," Hope said. "Not scarring children with our current political whims." Hope knew it was a mistake the minute it was out of her mouth.

"Current political whims?" Joy gripped her fork and leaned toward Hope.

"Never mind," Hope said. "Let's just order." She looked around. The service in this place was abysmal.

Joy let her fork clatter to the table. "You've never taken me seriously."

Please don't start, Joy, please don't start. Hope was so tired of fighting. "It came out wrong. I'm sorry."

But Joy was not satisfied. She turned to Faith. "I told you. I told you."

Hope's eyes darted to Faith. "Told me what?" Faith shot Hope a warning look and shook her head. Hope turned to Joy. "Out with it."

"You really don't remember?" Joy demanded. Hope shook her head. "That time you, me, and Mom had a meeting with my teacher? Well, you didn't have the meeting and I probably wasn't supposed to be there, but Mom couldn't find a babysitter so she took us along." Joy stopped and waited for Hope to validate.

Hope's mind raced. Did she remember that? Meeting, teacher. Meeting, teacher. Nope. She had nothing. "When was this?" Hope asked.

"Oh my God," Joy said. "I can't believe you."

"I just asked how old we were." My God, she was livid. And Hope didn't really remember.

"I was nine, so you were thirteen or fourteen," Joy said.

"Thirteen," Hope said. Joy was always acting like Hope was over four years older and she was almost exactly four years older.

"Do you remember now?" Joy picked up the fork again.

"No, so just tell me what I did."

"The teacher said I was a bright girl if I would just focus and you said—'She's not bright, she just copies me!'" Joy stabbed the table with the fork and shot daggers at Hope.

Hope waited for more, waited for the bad thing that she'd supposedly said to come. Instead, Joy stared at her, fuming, as if she'd already said it. "That's it?"

Joy threw up her arms. "You publicly belittled me!"

"Like sisters do," Hope said. She glanced around the table with a smile. Harrison and Faith were suddenly buried in their smartphones, Brittany and Josh were staring openmouthed and eyes wide.

"You meant it. To this day you don't think I'm smart."

Hope couldn't believe Joy was serious. She felt a pang of guilt. "I was joking. I was being sarcastic."

"So you do remember it?"

"No, I don't."

"Then how do you know you were joking?"

"Because it's not that big of a deal."

"To you. It's a huge deal to me."

"Obviously."

"You're not even taking this seriously now."

"Joy, listen to yourself. Faith? A little help here?"

Faith rearranged her silverware. "I'm not getting involved."

"Right," Hope said. "Because you weren't there anyway." A heavy silence descended like an axe.

"Why wasn't she there?" Josh asked.

"Never mind," Faith said.

"Don't blame her," Joy said. "This is between you and me."

"Oh my God," Hope said. "I was probably just trying to get attention." *Trying to survive without Faith.* "I'm sorry if you think it was some diabolical plan to make you feel as if you weren't bright."

"You were telling the truth. You've never thought I was smart. You still don't."

"Oh my God," Hope said. "Is this for real?"

Harrison and Faith nodded their heads. "You're really that upset over this still?" Harrison and Faith continued to nod. Hope took a deep breath. "I'm so sorry. I don't remember saying that. I must have been jealous. Of course I think you're smart. I think you're so smart. And brave, and adventurous, and wacky. I love you, Joy. You're my sister."

"Wacky? You think I'm wacky?"

Joy used to be wacky. Wonderfully wacky. When she was four she ate popcorn with her feet. She could pick up kernels with her toes and bring it up to her mouth, ensuring she'd have the entire bowl to herself. And when scolded she used to give this incredible little laugh, a trill that pleased the ears and instantly made Hope forget whatever it was that warranted the scolding in the first place. The woman before her was not laughing. Hope was truly sorry now; just speaking the words and seeing Joy's face crumple into tears filled her with spiky needles of guilt. Maybe she had bullied Joy a bit without realizing it. Maybe she had been jealous. But she definitely thought Joy was smart. Why had Joy buried this all these years? How could

Hope pay for a crime she didn't remember committing? "You're my beautiful, sweet, smart, smart, smart baby sister," Hope said, getting out of her seat and kneeling down by Joy. She hugged her knees. "Please forgive me."

"Okay," Joy said, sniffing loudly and wiping underneath her eyes. "So you believe I can make this coffee shop work, too, right?"

Oh God. Really? This? Hope gritted her teeth as she slid back into her seat. Joy was smart. She had just outfoxed Hope. Got her feeling guilty and literally groveling at Joy's feet, and now Hope was going to be forced to publicly declare Joy's coffee shop a great idea. And no doubt this was all going to come back to haunt her when they were arguing over whether or not to sell the property. Hope shot a look at Faith. Was she going to help her now?

"You should show her the plans," Harrison said.

"Like they care," Joy said.

"We're not going to talk about your coffee shop right now," Faith said. "I'm not sitting here talking shop, am I? Hope, thank God, isn't blathering on about dogs."

"How could you talk shop?" Joy asked Faith.

Faith blinked. Her nostrils flared. "What?"

"You don't have a job."

"Being a stay-at-home mom is the hardest job in the world," Faith said.

"Give it a rest. Oprah is over," Joy said. Hope took her seat and looked around for the waitress.

"What should I get, Mom?" Brittany stared at the menu like it was written in Swahili.

"A turkey sandwich and soup," Faith said.

Brittany's face scrunched up. "Turkeys are animals."

Faith glared at Joy. "You need to start watching what you say around my children."

"I'm not a child," Josh said. "And I still want a cheeseburger."

"I have a right to state my beliefs." Joy thrust her chin up.

"You don't eat any meat at all?" Brittany asked.

"I'm trying to cut down on eating anything with a face," Joy said.

"Except for me," Harrison said. Joy laughed and nuzzled his neck.

Faith slammed her fist on the table, jiggling silverware and sloshing water. "Enough! You two think you're so cute. You're not. You're totally transparent and immature."

Hope raised an eyebrow. Faith normally kept her cool. Something was definitely going on in her personal life to make her so edgy. Hope had to at least try to restore order. "Why don't we all order what we want, just this once, and also—maybe we should stop talking until after we've eaten. I think we might all be suffering from low blood sugar."

"Now you're telling us not to talk?" Joy said.

Faith piled on. "Who's the bossy one now?"

Forgive me, Father Christmas. All I want this year is to beat my sisters to a pulp. Just once. But thoroughly. So that all they'll wish for Christmas is their two front teeth. Hope scanned the restaurant. "Is it just me or is the waitress atrocious?"

"Can we talk, Mom?" Brittany asked.

"Of course," Faith said.

"Can we go sledding?" Brittany asked.

"Asked and answered," Faith said.

"But Aunt Hope thinks it's a great idea."

Hope was going to physically go and find the waitress. Maybe pummel her. She felt like telling Brittany that right now drugs seemed like a great idea too. It was too bad Faith was so stingy with her Xanax. Not that it was working. Despite her best efforts, Faith was the poster girl for anxiety. Definitely having marital problems. And taking it out on all of them.

"You like sledding, right, Aunt Hope?" Brittany's shining eyes were pinned on her. Faith glared at Hope even though she had yet to answer.

"I like sledding," Hope said carefully. It was true. She did like sledding. How could you not like sledding? "But," Hope said with a smile, "it's always a good idea to eat kale before you go sledding."

"Why?" Brittany asked.

"Cut it out," Faith said to Hope.

"Mom, if I eat kale can I go sledding?" Brittany asked. Hope slid down in her seat.

"No."

"But Aunt Hope—"

"If Aunt Hope had children she'd understand."

Hope threw down her napkin. "I am so sick of you saying that to me." Joy's head jerked up. She smelled blood. Hope had always gotten the feeling that Joy loved it when Faith and Hope fought.

"It's true," Faith said, stabbing her fork into the table. "Fur babies don't count."

"I don't call my pets my fur babies," Hope said. "But I think I'm perfectly capable of stating that I don't think it's too dangerous for your children to sled down a freaking hill in the middle of a winter wonderland!"

A waitress finally slid up to the table, alarm stamped on her face. "Sounds like you guys are hungry." She dumped a basket of bread on the table. Josh reached for it, but Faith grabbed the basket and handed it back to the waitress.

"We don't want to spoil our appetite," she said.

"Speak for yourself." Joy grabbed the basket back and handed it to Harrison. "Want to spoil your appetite, baby?" she said.

He beamed. "I want to spoil you," he answered.

Josh grabbed the basket out of Harrison's hand and snatched a roll and butter, before throwing the basket back down and glaring at his mother. He picked up the butter knife. "Can I use this, Mother, or is this dangerous too?"

"Josh," Faith said. Her voice came out in a choke. Hope saw tears come to her sister's eyes. What was going on? Faith's hand dropped to her purse, where she rummaged around, then discreetly (or so she thought) slipped something into her mouth. Another Xanax. How much of that stuff was Faith taking? She would have to get Faith to tell her exactly what was going on. The table fell into an uneasy silence that continued until the waitress came back to take their order.

Everyone managed to place their order, including Hope, who changed her order to a chef salad because she didn't want to eat a cheeseburger and fries in front of Brittany and Josh. Maybe she'd come back later by herself and satisfy the craving.

"You caved," Joy said, sounding gleeful.

"What?" Hope said.

"You still let Faithy boss you around."

"I didn't tell her what to do," Faith said.

"I'm taking the higher road," Hope said.

"By switching from cow to pork?" Joy said.

"What?" Hope said.

"Chef salad has ham, and eggs, and bacon."

"And here I meant to order green eggs and ham," Hope said.

Josh laughed. "Good one, Aunt Hope."

Joy shook her head. "Do you know how smart pigs are?"

"Pigs wallow in *muck*," Josh said, stressing the word *muck*, as if Faith had already forbidden him to say the other word.

"They have the intelligence of a three-year-old," Joy said.

"What about turkeys?" Brittany asked with alarm.

"Dumb as doornails," Hope said to her with a wink. She meant it as a joke. Brittany nodded solemnly.

"So smart animals deserve to live, but dumb animals deserve to die?" Joy said. "So, Hope. Maybe all your ways of signaling to me that I wasn't smart was really just your repressed desire that I was dead."

"Joy!" Hope said. This was going beyond an argument. Joy was pathological. "You know that's preposterous!"

"Do I?" Joy said.

"You'd better," Hope said. "I'm not going to sit here and take this."

"So how much do you think the property is worth?" Joy asked.

"What does that have to do with anything?" Hope said.

"You and Faith were already discussing it behind my back. You want to keep the property and turn it into some year-round Christmas celebration!"

"Oh my God," Hope said. "Did you even take a shower?"

"We weren't making any decisions," Faith said. "We were just discussing the possibility."

"I'm not changing my mind," Joy said.

"We're here to celebrate Christmas with our grandmother," Hope said. "Right now it doesn't belong to us. It's her home."

"We're not here to celebrate Christmas with her because she doesn't want to celebrate Christmas, remember?" Joy said. Brittany, once again, looked traumatized. The poor kid. Why was her family so dysfunctional?

They fell into a surly silence and finally the waitress came with the food. Her chef salad was slammed down in front of her. Thick slabs of ham stared at her. "Disgusting," Joy said.

"Funny," Hope said. "I was just thinking the same thing." She dropped her napkin on top of the plate. Hope didn't want any of it now. Her sisters had officially ruined her appetite. Hope got up from the table, walked out the door, and just kept going.

CHAPTER 17

The air had turned bitter (just like them) and the snow was coming down sideways. Hope was no longer in the mood to Christmas shop. Maybe not celebrating was the way to go. It would certainly save her a lot of money. It was going to be a long walk back to the estate, but she didn't have any other choice. She certainly wasn't going to return to the restaurant with her tail between her legs. Maybe she'd go back to the cabin and pack her bags. Why go to all this trouble for people who didn't want to be around you in the first place? She was just buying into the hype. *Family is everything. You have nothing if you don't have family.* But what if your family hated you? What if they were all crazy?

Well, she'd tried. She'd much rather be in the shelter with dogs. She couldn't wait to see Mr. Jingles. She wished she'd video-taped him slamming Faith to the ground. He'd earned his keep with that little good deed. Maybe he was all the family she needed. She would go back to Portland, buy Mr. Jingles a Christmas sweater, and watch *It's a Wonderful Life* while drinking candy cane martinis.

Just then a horn beeped. A truck rumbled beside her. Hope

knew it was Austin without looking; his pickup had a distinctive hum. "What are you doing?" he called out. The sound of his voice was a welcome relief.

"What does it look like?" Hope gave him a pained smile.

Austin glanced up the hill. "Glutton for punishment."

"It will be good for me."

"That's the glutton part." He idled a second. "Are you going to get in or what?"

"Fine," Hope said. *Thank God.* She didn't really want to walk, and she wanted to see Austin one more time before she left. He smiled as Hope came around to the passenger side and got in. He hummed as he started back up. "The sooner I get back and pack, the sooner I can get out of here."

He shifted and the truck lurched forward. "What happened?"

"This was a huge mistake." He was wearing cologne. Not too much like some men poured on, but just the right amount. The amount that made you want to get a lot closer to the person wearing it. Now that she saw him again she realized that the sweater from town would look great on him. The navy would really complement his brooding eyes. If only she was staying.

"Tomorrow is a new day," Austin said.

"And I'll be back in Portland."

"What about your grandmother?"

"She's trying to manipulate us."

"How do you figure that?"

"No Christmas. Whosoever follows my rules will inherit the estate."

"She said that?"

"She did, indeed. Joy has fallen for every inch of it. My younger sister now sees me as an opponent to eliminate. And don't even get me started on Faith."

Austin nodded, and Hope looked out the window. The snow was piling up now, blanketing the roads and the grounds and the trees. "It's so beautiful," Hope said.

"We're going to get a big one."

"How far is the closest airport?"

"It's easier to drive. You should wait a few days."

"How far is the nearest car rental?"

Austin sighed. "You won't make it far with what they're expecting."

"Then you can take me to a hotel." Austin pulled into the estate. He rolled down the window and leaned down to punch in the code.

"I finally see your grandmother in you," he said as they waited for the gate to open.

"How so?"

"You're stubborn mules, the pair of you."

"You would be stubborn, too, if you had to survive in this family."

"I had a brother."

Had. Past tense. Austin's voice was low and filled with pain. "What happened?"

"He's no longer with us."

"I'm so sorry." Hope wanted to ask a million questions, but it was obvious by his clipped answer and pained expression that he was only opening up a little to help her. Whatever had happened to his brother he did not want to talk about it.

"Don't give up on them," he said. "No matter what."

"Okay." She wanted to touch him, take his pain away.

"How's your niece and nephew?" Neither of them seemed in a hurry to get out of the truck. With the snow falling, the heater still running, and Christmas carols playing gently in the background, Hope could stay in here with Austin forever.

"Brittany is a doll. The only one who loves me."

"I very much doubt that. What about the boy?"

"He's a bit surly. You know teenagers."

"He reminds me of my brother."

Maybe he was moving toward talking about what happened. Hope kept her voice light. "In what way?"

"Surly." Austin gave a small smile.

Hope waited, but he didn't say anything else about it. Maybe it would help if she opened up first. "Yvette said our father died a long time ago. In a car accident."

Austin's head snapped toward her. "A car accident?"

"Yes. What?"

"Nothing."

"That wasn't nothing. Tell me."

"It made me think of Roger."

Hope was suddenly on high alert. "What made you think of Roger?"

"I confronted Yvette recently about him."

"I don't understand."

"I didn't like the thought that he might be scamming her in some way. Trying to get her money when she dies."

"You also thought something might be wrong with him."

"She said he has TBI—traumatic brain injury."

"Okay."

"From a car accident he was in a long time ago."

Hope tried to process that. Had he been friends with her father? Were they in the same accident? If so, Yvette had been lying about him coming to see them for Christmas. "A drunk driving accident?"

"What makes you ask that?" Austin's piercing eyes were suddenly on her. He had this way of making her feel as if she was the most important person in the world. Maybe that was a skill he'd picked up from his job.

"My father drank. Mom was always warning him he was going to get killed. And take us with him."

"I'm sorry," Austin said. He was a really good man. A man, it seemed, who had a lot of secrets of his own. Something kept him all to himself up here. She wondered what it was.

"Yvette said our father was on his way to see us the night he died. Maybe Roger and my father were in the same accident."

"So you think he was bringing Roger along to come see you?"

"No, I think maybe he wasn't coming to see us at all. I think maybe he was drinking and driving with his friend Roger instead."

"Maybe I shouldn't have brought it up."

"No, I'm glad you did."

"Why?"

"I used to want the fantasy. Comfort myself by imagining our father still loved us. That there was a reasonable explanation for him disappearing from our lives. Tearing us apart."

"And now?" Austin asked softly.

"Now I just want the truth."

"Does it make a difference?"

"Of course. How can you even ask?"

"I'm just saying. No matter what he did or didn't do, it doesn't mean he didn't love you girls."

Hope wanted to say that it meant exactly that. But she couldn't. Because she remembered how much he loved them. More, Hope thought, than anyone had ever loved her or maybe ever would. Even so. It hadn't been enough. She wanted to stay in the truck forever, but definitely wanted to change the subject. "Do you have to work today?"

"Just returning."

"Did it go okay?" Hope didn't want too many details, but she wanted him to know she was interested in his life.

Austin nodded. "We're pretty busy this time of year."

"It sounds like a pretty stressful job." *And sad.*

"It can be," Austin said. "It can also be uplifting."

"How did you get into it?"

"These sound like the kind of questions you ask on a date." Austin's eyes slid to her; then he looked away with a smile.

Hope felt emboldened. "Are you asking me out on a date?"

Austin got out of the truck. Hope did too. He glanced at the mountains. "Not if you're leaving."

Hope stood and stared at him for a moment. Of course she didn't want to leave. But she also didn't want to face her sisters again. Why couldn't they just get along? "If I pack now would you take me to a motel?"

"It can't be that bad."

"I can't stay. I won't let these people ruin my Christmas."

"If that's what you want."

"Thank you." Hope ran toward the house. She spotted Roger, standing closer than he'd ever been, about ten feet away. He had a startled look on his face. Did he hear her tell Austin she was leaving? What did he care? He waved at her. Hope felt a pang of sadness. She waved back. "I'll be packed in two seconds," she called. She looked at Roger. "Have you seen Mr. Jingles?" she yelled. He just stared. "My dog?" She glanced at Austin.

"I'll look for him," Austin said. The snow was still coming down. Hope knew she was being dramatic, should probably just make peace and stay. But the other part of her wanted to flee. She was tired of not being appreciated. The middle child. Joy got to be wild and throw fits, and Faith got to boss everyone around. And Hope? She was just stuck. The middle sucked and everybody knew it. How many people actually liked the middle seat in airplanes? Nobody. That's who. Because the middle sucked. She stormed into the house. Her grandmother was standing at the window watching Roger.

"Roger is standing really close to the house," Hope said. "He waved at me."

Yvette turned around. "He likes you." Yvette offered a small smile. *Was he in the car with my father? Is that what you're hiding?* "Where is the rest of your gang? We're getting a big storm."

Tell her. Tell her you're leaving. "They'll be here any minute." Right? Hope fumbled in her purse for her phone. Should she call Faith, tell her to come home now? She'd pack first and do it when she came down. Yvette turned back to the window and Hope hurried up the stairs. God, this house was beautiful. She ran into her room, the smallest room, even though she was here first—and began throwing clothes into the duffel bag she'd brought. It didn't take long. She scooped up her things from the bathroom and upended them into the bag. She ran downstairs. She would throw her bag in the truck first and then say her good-byes.

She snuck out to the porch. But just as she headed to the truck, she caught sight of Roger. He was standing in the side yard with three boxes around him. He headed back to the barn. Hope heard Yvette scream; then her grandmother flew out on the porch, nearly knocking her down. "Roger! Roger!" Yvette cried, hurtling herself down the stairs and across the field. Hope was stunned. She didn't know a dying old lady could move that fast. Austin came around the corner followed by Mr. Jingles. Mr. Jingles made a beeline for Hope and lunged. He planted his large paws on her chest and almost knocked her down. "Roger! Roger!" Yvette cried again. By the time Hope made it to her grandmother's side, her grandmother was standing by the boxes, staring down at them. Tears were streaming down her grandmother's face.

"What's wrong?" Hope's heart hammered in her chest.

Her grandmother reached in the box and lifted out a string of Christmas lights. "He wants to decorate," she whispered.

"Oh," Hope said. She screamed because of that? Hope almost had a heart attack.

"Quick," Yvette said. "Get the nutcrackers."

"What?"

"Put them on the porch."

"Why?"

Yvette whirled around and grasped Hope's hands. She had a vise-like grip. "It's because you girls are here." Yvette let go of Hope and clasped her hands under her chin as if praying. Her eyes were shiny with tears.

Hope rubbed her hands, hoping to get the circulation back. "How do you know?"

"He's never done this before." Roger came out dragging what appeared to be a sleigh.

"Good God," Yvette said.

"Are you going to stop him?" Hope said. She didn't want Yvette to stop him, but she was curious. Yvette seemed to like Roger better than she liked her granddaughters. Austin hurried over to help Roger with the sleigh. Yvette began digging through the box, removing strings of lights and setting them on the ground.

"You should get your coat on," Hope said.

"Or what?" Yvette said. "I'll freeze to death?" She glared at Hope. Then laughed. "You should see the look on your face. Are you going to help me unpack these boxes and decorate, or are you leaving?"

"How did you know?"

"You announced it right before you trounced in the house." Yvette looked at Roger. "And I'm glad you did."

"Let me get this straight," Hope said. "You're willing to celebrate for him?"

"Yes," Yvette said.

"Why are you willing to celebrate Christmas for your caretaker and not your three granddaughters?" Hope was more curious than angry. Yvette didn't seem like the type of woman who routinely did an about-face.

"He's like a new man." Yvette clasped her hands underneath her chin once more, smiling, eyes shining.

And you're like a new woman.

Hope wouldn't have believed this was happening if she wasn't watching it with her own eyes. "How did you meet Roger?" She tried to keep her voice casual. She prepared herself for a lie.

Yvette turned and stared into Hope's eyes. "He was your father's best friend."

Hope didn't know what she was expecting, but that was not it. She did not remember her father having a best friend. Then again, why wouldn't he? Hope would have to have a talk with Carla. "Why won't he talk?" Hope wasn't going to let on that Austin had already told her everything.

"He has TBI."

"What's TBI?"

"Traumatic brain injury."

"Oh. That's so sad. What happened?"

"Car accident," Yvette said quietly.

This was the moment Hope had been waiting for. She whirled around. Yvette refused to meet her eyes. "Was he in the car with my father that night?" Hope felt a lump in her throat as she asked it.

Tears pooled in Yvette's eyes. "Yes," she said.

Hope felt her stomach drop, but she couldn't stop now. "Was my father driving?" Yvette nodded. Hope didn't want to ask the next question, but she didn't have a choice. She had to know. "Had he been drinking?" Yvette swallowed. Her wrinkled Adam's apple brought a pang of grief straight to Hope's heart. For a second she didn't see a cranky grandmother dishing out ulti-matums. She saw a mother who had lost her only son. She saw a woman in a great deal of pain. Yvette simply nodded again.

Hope sidled up and took her grandmother's hand. At first it was cold and limp. And then her grandmother squeezed her hand back as Roger and Austin returned carrying reindeer be-tween them. Roger met her eyes and Hope smiled. He winked. Hope bit the side of her mouth. Did he ever talk? Could he talk? She would ask more questions later; from the way Yvette was almost collapsing beside her, the old lady had answered enough questions for now. But God, Hope prayed that he could talk. And remember. She prayed he could tell them whether or not her father was really coming for them.

CHAPTER 18

Twenty-four years ago . . .

Hope sat beside Faith with Joy squirming in her lap. The sun was beaming in from the window behind her, warming her back. Faith, as always patient and still. Their father was dressed as Santa Claus, but even with the long white beard he hadn't fooled them for a second. He had a large bag slung over his shoulder and Hope was wide-eyed anticipating the gifts within.

"Tom," their mother called from the kitchen, a cigarette propped between her fingers. "Christmas is six months away."

"Christmas is a frame of mind," their father said. "Besides, this is the perfect card." He looked at Hope and winked. She giggled. *Don't let Mom ruin this!*

"I can wait," Faith said. *Of course she can.*

"I can't," Hope said.

Joy let out a loud belch. Everyone laughed, including their mother.

"Do you know what's more fun than getting presents?" their father said.

"Decorating the tree?" Faith said, her brows furled in concentration.

Hope couldn't think of a single answer, although she did like decorating the tree, and singing Christmas carols, and watching *Rudolph,* and *Frosty,* and *The Year Without a Santa Claus.*

"Eating cookies?" Hope finally said.

"You're being ridiculous," Faith said, lifting her chin. "It's giving Santa cookies and milk." Hope felt the hot flush of humiliation wash over her. Oh. She thought of herself before Santa. That couldn't be good.

But her father wasn't mad, he just laughed and set the bag down. He began to remove brightly wrapped packages from the bag and put them under the tree. They had just decorated it for Baby Joy. Hope could tell her father loved Christmas just as much as she did. Maybe even more. And he was telling the truth, it didn't seem to be the present part that he liked most. He liked giving to others. He liked giving to his girls. He always went overboard, as their mother always told him.

Joy started to scream. Her mother took her out of Hope's lap. Hope cheered. Joy was too heavy. "What do you want for Christmas, Daddy?" Hope asked, lurching to her feet and clutching his hand. Her fingers were sticky from a candy cane she'd just inhaled, but he didn't seem to mind. He hoisted her up and swung her around.

"I've got everything I ever wished for with you three elves," he said.

"We're not elves," Faith said. "We're your daughters."

Their father threw his head back and laughed. "They're not elves," he called to their mother. "They're our daughters." Their mother stabbed out her cigarette and rolled her eyes.

"Too bad," she said. "Elves have jobs."

Faith pulled into the estate, and for a minute thought she was seeing things. There were Christmas decorations splayed out all over the yard. A ladder was propped up next to the largest pine tree on the estate. Lights were already strung around the bottom branches. So far there were reindeer and a sleigh, a mechanical angel, red bows, and wreaths. Hope, Austin, that strange caretaker, and her grandmother were all involved in one decorating activity or the other. There looked to be at least half a foot of snow covering the grounds and it was still coming down.

"What the freak?" Joy said. Faith had already lectured her about swearing in front of the kids and she was doing a pretty good job of containing herself.

"Told you," Harrison said. "Snow makes white folks all freaky."

"You squealed when you saw it was snowing and you know it," Joy said.

"Yes, yes, yes," Brittany said. "We're celebrating Christmas!" She was the first to unlock her door and tumble out. She made a beeline for Hope.

"She likes Hope better than me," Joy said.

"Can I go into the woods?" Josh said.

"Everyone's decorating," Harrison said. "Come on, Little Dude. Let's help."

"Don't ever call me a little dude again."

Harrison laughed. "Deal. Come on, Big Dude. Let's go see if they need help." Josh rolled his eyes and the two got out of the car and headed for the group. Faith waited for Joy to leave. She wanted to call Charlie and she wanted to pop another Xanax. Why wasn't Joy racing off after Harrison?

"Hope wins again," Joy said.

"What?"

Joy pointed out the window. "Look what she's making them do."

"So what?" Faith said. She was a little tired of all the arguing, and she didn't want to give Joy the impression that she was on-board for ganging up on Hope. Being this close to her again was bringing back those protective feelings. Hope was always so . . . well—*hopeful*. Faith felt the familiar guilt tugging at her heart. Maybe she should have taken Hope and Joy with her. Then again Stephen's mother didn't even like her; imagine if she had had all three of them. And even though she knew it was painful for her, Faith realized now that the separation had been good for Hope. She was a lot less clingy than she used to be. And she was making an effort. Faith applauded that. If only Joy was a little more like Hope.

"She should be eliminated from the inheritance," Joy said as she began to pace.

Faith turned to Joy and stared her in the eyes. "You're not seriously thinking that Hope would have been cut out of the estate?"

"Granny said—"

"I'm not talking about what that old lady says. You don't seriously think we would have cut Hope out of this, do you?"

Joy shrugged, that pouty, defiant look on her face that Faith remembered so well. "If she leaves it to us at all, then it will belong equally to the three of us," Faith said.

"What do you mean 'if'?"

"I don't trust her," Faith said. "She's toying with us."

"So you think it's fair to split it equally?" There was an edge to Joy's voice. She was referencing the fact that Faith made more money. Again. They'd failed her. They'd spoiled Joy to death and babied her, and let her get away with pretty much everything. And now the little brat had turned into a big one. Why had she picked a fight with Hope in the restaurant when it was Joy they should be straightening out? She needed to be back in San Fran so she could relax with a Pilates class. And she was definitely crankier without her kale smoothies. Hope could chide all she wanted, but kale was magical. And Charlie. She missed Charlie. Waiting until after the holidays were over to be together was the right decision, but it was so, so hard. She needed the Xanax. Even if she was taking a bit too much. Who didn't overdo it during the holidays?

"We're not entitled to any of this, anyway," Faith said. "It belonged to her late husband, who wasn't our grandfather and never even met us."

"We'll sell it, won't we?"

"Would you even be here if it wasn't for the inheritance?"

Joy looked at Faith. If captions appeared above her head they would read: CALCULATING ALL RESPONSES TO SEE WHICH SUITS ME BEST. Faith had an urge to shove her out of the truck. "Probably not," Joy said in a singsong voice and then opened the door, jumped out, and slammed it shut. Faith's hand shook as she reached for her friend, her only friend these days, the little orange bottle. The pills themselves were only temporary friends; it was the bottle that housed them all that gave her comfort. How many had she taken today? If she was being honest—and she would be honest with herself—it was only when you weren't honest with yourself that it was a problem, right? So she'd taken two more today than she should have. Just two more. That wasn't too bad. This would be her last one for today. She needed the bottle to last through Christmas and even a little beyond—unless she could get a call in to her doctor and have them refill her prescription.

She dialed Charlie, and there it was, the tell-tale pounding of her heart. "Pick up," she said as she listened to it ring. "Please, pick up." Charlie was mad at her. Mad for coming here alone. What was Faith supposed to do? Introduce her new lover to the kids before she announced the divorce? No way. She was going to end up the bad guy no matter what, but she wasn't going to be the bad guy and the Mom Who Ruined Christmas Forever. She wanted to wait until way after the holidays—let them get used to the divorce first. Maybe they could announce it in March—were there any holidays in March? Just Saint Patrick's Day. That was certainly better than Easter.

Charlie's voice mail picked up. Faith hung up. Charlie was screening. Or was Faith just being paranoid? She couldn't expect Charlie to just sit around waiting for Faith to call. Maybe she should force herself to stay with Stephen until the kids were out of the house. Another three years for Josh, but Brittany had a ways to go. Faith certainly didn't want to rush those years. But she didn't want to lose out on love either. Would Charlie wait that long? Not a chance. Charlie didn't have children, and was already making allowances for Faith. Three years was ridiculous to ask of anyone. Besides, she'd already told Stephen everything and she certainly wasn't going to do that to him. She looked outside. Everyone was just a blur through the snowflakes. She clutched her phone in one hand and bottle of Xanax in the other. "Merry freaking Christmas."

Hope was following Roger through the woods, enjoying tromping in the snow. They had done as much decorating as they could, and when Roger turned for the woods, Hope decided to follow him. Besides, she loved walking at night in a snowstorm. Then again, she was going to have to turn around and retrace her steps if she lost sight of Roger. Even though he hadn't turned around and acknowledged her, she got the feeling he knew she was following. She had just decided to pick up her pace when someone grabbed her arm. She let out a scream and whirled around to find Faith towering over her.

"You scared me," Hope said.

"What are you doing out here?"

Up ahead Roger stopped but didn't turn around.

"I'm exercising."

"Try again."

I could be exercising! "Just exploring."

"You're going to get lost."

"I don't think he would let that happen." Hope pointed at Roger, barely visible through the falling snow.

Faith tipped her head back. "They look like stars," she said as the snowflakes hit her face. "Snow stars."

Hope laughed. "Snow stars," she repeated. She linked arms with Faith. "Let's not keep our tour guide waiting." They started up again, and a few minutes later so did Roger.

Faith released her arm but kept walking. "I think my kids hate me."

"Brittany adores you," Hope said.

"Okay. I think my son hates me."

Hope thought of the look on Josh's face and the way in which he said, *One of her phone calls.*

"What?" Faith stepped closer.

"I didn't say anything."

"You were thinking something." There was barely any light to see by, so Faith had been reading Hope's energy. It was like that with family. "Out with it."

"Just who are you calling all the time?" The words tumbled out of Hope's mouth.

Faith stopped. "What do you mean?"

Hope sighed. She didn't want to get into another fight with Faith, but the only thing worse than opening your mouth around her was not talking once you started. She was going to have to see this through. And maybe it was time. "Josh made a comment about 'one of your phone calls.' "

"Oh," Faith said. "I don't think he's upset about that."

"He sure sounded upset. And then he and Brittany exchanged a look like they'd been discussing that very topic." Hope felt instantly guilty for betraying her niece and nephew's confidence, but she also wanted them all to resolve this.

"It couldn't be that," Faith said. "I'm sure they don't know anything."

"Don't know what?"

"Never mind."

"Listen. You want to keep secrets from me—go ahead. And you might think you're fooling Brittany and Josh with whatever it is you're doing, but you're not. They might not know everything, but they certainly know something."

"It's nobody's business," Faith called.

"Whatever you say," Hope said. "If you want to walk with us, walk with us. Otherwise, leave me to enjoy the woods."

"He doesn't talk at all?" Faith whispered when they had come to a stop at a clearing. Roger turned around.

"I can talk," he said. "I can talk." The words were slow and labored coming out of his mouth as if they had taken considerable effort. His voice was gruff and scratchy, like an old record that hadn't been played in years. Hope knew her jaw had just dropped open, and she tried to be subtle about closing it.

"Good," Faith said. "That's good."

"Good," Roger repeated.

"You knew our father?" Hope said. She stepped closer.

"What?" Faith's voice rang with alarm.

Hope turned to her. "I just found out."

"You knew Daddy?" Hope cringed a little when Faith said it—it was hardly fitting for a grown woman to still use the term *Daddy*. Hope could hardly judge her, she had done it herself. Roger turned away from them. "Hello?" Faith said. "Did you understand me?"

Hope tugged on her coat sleeve. "Take it easy," she said.

"Were you friends?" Faith persisted.

"Good friends," Hope whispered. She smacked Faith lightly across the stomach. With all the padding it couldn't have hurt, but it elicited another flash of anger from Faith.

"Don't hit me," she said.

"No hitting," Roger said.

"Roger was in the car with Dad," Hope whispered. "He has traumatic brain injury."

"Oh," Faith said. "My God."

"I don't know how much he remembers."

Faith looked at Hope. "That means he wasn't coming to see us."

"We don't know that."

"Why would he bring Roger with him?"

"Moral support?"

"She was lying. He was just out, driving drunk—probably going to a party."

"We'll never know."

"Do you remember our father?" Faith asked. "Do you remember where you were going?"

Roger stared off into the distance. Then he pointed to a little path in the woods. "Home," he said. Roger gave them a wave without turning around and headed off in the direction opposite of the path he told them to take.

"I think he just blew us off," Faith said.

"That would be a great guess."

"That means he understood me, right?"

"How do you figure?"

"He's purposefully avoiding the question. You can't dodge someone like that unless you fully understand what you're trying to wriggle out of. Right?"

"Maybe," Hope said.

"Definitely," Faith said. She tore off after Roger.

"Hey." Hope had to really lift her knees to run in the snow. It was still coming down. "Let it be." She grabbed Faith by the coat and tugged. Faith stumbled back and then fell. She landed on her back in the woods. "Oh God," Hope said, standing over her. "Sorry."

"You're a jerk," Faith said.

Whew, if she was yelling, that meant she was okay. "If Roger remembers that's a good thing," Hope said. "Pushing him too fast is a bad thing."

"It's pretty out here," Faith said, not bothering to get up. She wrapped her legs around Hope's leg and started to tug.

"Hey," Hope yelled. Faith tugged harder and Hope fell to the ground beside her. The snow muted her fall, but Hope still cried out. Faith laughed. Hope smacked her, then lay down next to her. All she could see was the darkening sky, and darker forms around it that she knew to be trees, and little flakes pelting her face.

"Are we having fun yet?" Faith deadpanned.

Hope started laughing and then couldn't stop. Finally, Faith joined in. Hope snuck her gloved hand out until she found Faith's and took her hand in hers.

"Let's do something Christmas-y tomorrow. Anything. What do you want to do?" Faith asked.

"I think we should look for the perfect Christmas tree."

"I love it. We'll do it tomorrow. If we can ever get up." They lay there for a few more seconds until Mr. Jingles came barreling down the path toward them. Faith tried to get to her feet, but Mr. Jingles was faster. His big droopy jowls and large pink tongue dangled life-threateningly close to her face.

"Help," Faith said. "Get him off."

Hope grinned. "Is this a good time to tell you what I want for Christmas?"

CHAPTER 19

The entire gang gathered around the crackling fire in the log house, including Austin. Faith whipped up hot chocolate and Hope saw to the popcorn. Outside, the decorations glittered in the darkness. Hope couldn't believe she could now look out onto the grounds and see a sleigh framed in white lights, led by mechanical deer, also aglow. Standing at the helm was a mechanical Santa who actually waved. Beside them, two pine trees were swathed in colored lights. The angel shone its lights onto the snow, and glittering stars hung from the trees. A big bowl of popcorn sat on the coffee table awaiting eager hands.

Yvette and Harrison were playing Scrabble. Yvette had her tongue poking out of the side of her mouth. It was cute. Brittany was drawing a Christmas scene on a blank canvas.

"Where's Josh?" Austin said.

"In his room," Faith said. "You know teenage boys." Hope started to laugh and then caught the look on Austin's face. He looked worried. He'd said earlier that Josh reminded him of his brother. Was that why he had that look on his face? What had happened to his brother? Maybe she should go up and find Josh, see if she could talk him into joining them. Would that turn her into the annoying aunt instead of a beloved one? It had been a really long day. Maybe it was better to just let him have some peace. *Peace on earth.* She'd settle for it in her own family. At least tonight everyone was relatively calm, and Hope might even dare say festive.

"Hurky?" Harrison said. "What kind of a word is *hurky?*"

"You just used it twice in a sentence," Yvette said. "Triple score." Harrison panned the crowd, trying to see if he had any support.

"Her house, her rules," Austin said. "Her house, her rules."

Harrison nodded; then a big smile broke out on his face. He laid down his tiles with a flourish. "Boom!"

"Holla?" Yvette yelled. "What is holla?"

"You're doing it, Granny," Joy said.

Yvette's eyes narrowed. Austin got her attention. "If you ask me," Austin said, "he's getting a bit too glitty."

Everyone looked confused but Yvette. "Indeed," Yvette said. She turned to Harrison. "I'm pulling out all the stops now."

Harrison opened his arms. "Bring it, Mrs. G. Bring it."

The next day after a hearty breakfast, they commenced the search for the perfect tree. Yvette was feeling weak, so she stayed back with Harrison and Joy. Harrison was still sleeping and Joy had morphed into Florence Nightingale, fluttering around their grandmother, trying to soothe her. Austin showed up as the group headed back to the woods. Roger took the lead with an axe.

Hope kept glancing back to the house. She hoped Joy truly liked Yvette and wasn't just trying to ingratiate herself because of the inheritance. "You're obsessing on Joy," Faith said after she came up alongside her.

"She's using our grandmother. Doesn't that bother you?"

"First of all, she's making her tea and keeping her company. Second of all, don't think for a second that that woman isn't smart enough to see through Joy."

"But she's weak, and sick."

"She's still a Garland, isn't she?"

"I just hate to see Joy being so manipulative."

"She has the least good memories of all of us."

"I know. I know. But at what point does a person have to stop being a victim and start taking responsibility for his or her life?"

"Do you remember how Mom's face would light up whenever Dad was in a good mood?" Faith asked.

Hope remembered. She also remembered how every Christmas their father lifted them up to place an ornament high on the tree, how their tiny apartment filled with the smell of popcorn, how the Christmas carols played so loud that eventually the neighbors pounded on the walls. How they went to bed, beyond exhausted, filled with popcorn, and icing from making sugar cookies, their father's laughter still ringing in their ears. So young. He was younger than Hope was now. Nobody ever told them these were all the years they would get. Death was a thief forever stealing the moments you should have had.

After they'd left the west coast and their father, Christmas in Florida was always depressing. Once their mother had given up on their father ever returning, she never fully embraced Christmas celebrations again. Oh, they went through the bare minimum motions of celebrating, but there was no sparkle in their mother's eye, no sounds of laughter, and no more stringing popcorn, spontaneous singing, or decorating sugar cookies with colorful icing.

"That's why we have to make this the best Christmas ever," Hope said. "Let's give Joy something really great to remember."

"You got it. Although . . ."

Hope heard the hesitation in Faith's voice and wished she could sweep it away. "What?"

"Don't you think it's kind of insulting that our grandmother would agree to celebrate because of Roger, but not because of us?"

"Think about it. Dad is the one who caused the accident. Roger is brain-damaged for life. She feels guilty. That's why she lets him live here, and that's why she's willing to celebrate Christmas."

"I wonder how much he understands. It's hard to tell."

"He looks happy. That's easy enough to tell."

"I have an urge to shave his beard and hair off and see what he really looks like."

"He's a mountain man all right."

"Like Austin?" Faith had a devilish glint in her eye. Hope could feel her face heating up. Faith noticed it, too, for she cackled. "I don't blame you. He's hot." Austin glanced over and made eye contact with Hope.

"Not another word," Hope said to Faith under her breath. Faith just batted her eyelashes.

Roger had just stopped underneath a giant pine tree. It was tall and lush, and its branches were reaching out, a peacock spreading its tail.

"This," he said, gesturing to the tree. "Ours."

"It's perfect," Hope said.

"I've never seen such a beautiful tree," Brittany said.

"I have to admit," Austin said. "This one could win contests."

"Can I chop it down?" Josh asked.

"No," Faith said, but Roger gestured for him to come forward. Josh stopped and looked to Faith for permission. Faith glanced at Hope. Roger continued to gesture for Josh to approach. Faith finally relented. "Just be careful."

Josh approached and from a distance they watched Roger gesture and imitate how Josh should swing the axe at the base of the tree.

"He'd be killer in Gestures," Hope said. It was true. He clearly conveyed which way the tree would fall, and everyone gave it a wide berth. Josh followed his instructions and after a few awkward swings Josh finally got in a few good ones. He drove the axe into the base of the tree with steady, violent strokes. Soon he was sweating and out of breath. "More," Roger said. Josh nodded, then with a startling look of determination attacked the tree again. Soon the sound of wood splitting rang out into the woods and the giant pine tree fell. They cheered. Roger actually beamed. Josh grinned. Hope realized with a start that this was the first time since they arrived that she had seen Josh smile. And out of all of them, it was Roger who coaxed it out of him. Talk about "Don't judge a book by its cover." She'd underestimated Roger. They all had.

Austin informed them that he would drive the truck back so they could load the tree into it. He asked Josh if he wanted to join him. Josh looked at Faith and this time she didn't hesitate.

"Go for it."

"Can I drive the truck?"

Faith laughed. "That depends on whether or not Austin wants to live dangerously." Everyone glanced at Austin.

"Always," Austin said.

"Yes!" Josh said. The two headed off. Brittany took Hope's hand. Roger smiled and began to walk away.

"Thank you," Hope called after him. He did not stop or turn around, but he lifted his hand in a wave as he disappeared.

Everyone agreed. The tree was indeed the most gorgeous thing any of them had ever seen. Tall with lush branches that spread out like wings taking flight. It stood in the middle of the cabin out far enough so that you could walk completely around it and take in its glory. They'd purposefully waited until early evening to decorate. Yvette sat on the sofa with her spiked tea, while the rest of them sifted through boxes of decorations. Austin had already strung the colorful lights on the enormous tree. It was magazine-perfect. For once, Hope felt as if they all were in sync, ready to enjoy the holidays. Everyone except Roger. They'd done everything they could to get him to come inside and help decorate, but instead he stood outside, gazing at it from the window and once in a while gesturing to Austin to readjust a light or hang an ornament in a different location. When he was satisfied with the tree, Roger disappeared, most likely off to hide in his cabin.

"Wait," Yvette said. "There's one more." She smiled at Austin and pointed to a paper bag on the floor. Hope dug into it and found an ornament that said *JOY*. She gave it to her sister. Joy's face was still for a moment as she considered the ornament; then she broke out into a genuine smile.

"That almost got me gored by a rolling pin," Austin said, pointing to the ornament. Hope looked at him. "Long story." He winked. Joy stalked the tree like she was a lion and it was prey, painstakingly looking for the perfect place to hang it. Faith and Hope shared a look and a smile. Finally Faith swooped in, grabbed Joy by the waist, and lifted her up.

"Hey," Joy said.

"Just hang it," Faith said. Joy laughed and plopped the ornament onto a branch.

Hope asked Yvette if she had a radio they could turn on. Instead, and even better, she had an old stereo and a Bing Crosby Christmas album. Soon his rich voice filled the room.

"We need cocktails," Hope said when they were several minutes into decorating.

"Yes!" Josh said.

"Shirley Temple for you," Hope said, ruffling his hair.

"Make that two Shirley Temples," Austin said.

"Three!" Brittany said.

"I'll take another shot of Johnnie Walker," Yvette said.

"I'll have a martini," Faith said.

Hope wanted to ask her if she was sure she should be drinking with Xanax. She'd seen her sister sneak at least two pills today. Was she abusing them? Things were finally starting to go relatively well; Hope didn't want to mess things up. She made a mental note to make Faith's drink light on the vodka.

"In Europe kids my age drink wine," Josh said.

"And go to boarding school," Brittany said.

"Don't tempt me," Faith said.

"You're tempted to give us wine?" Josh asked.

"No, I'm tempted to send you to boarding school."

"Yes, yes, yes!" Brittany said. "I want one in the French Alps." Hope laughed.

"I just want a cocktail. Or a glass of wine," Josh said.

"You're already full of whine," Faith said.

"I hate this place." Josh got up and headed for the stairs.

"Come on," Faith said. "We're having fun for once. You didn't really think I was going to let you have a drink, did you?"

"I'm not drinking," Austin said.

"I'm not having fun," Josh said.

"Why don't you go outside and play?" Faith said.

"In the dark and cold?" Josh said. "Some mother you are." He stomped up the steps and soon they heard the slamming of a door.

"Josh?" Hope yelled up the stairs. "We'll all have Shirley Temples!"

"Just leave it," Faith said. "He'll come back down when he's ready."

"I just wish he was having a better time of it," Hope said.

"I suppose that's my fault," Faith said. "Everybody blames the mother."

"Where's my Johnnie Walker?" Yvette said. Joy jumped up to get it for her.

Hope glanced upstairs. "Maybe if I go up and talk to him—"

"I said leave it," Faith said.

Hope regretted that she'd brought up the cocktails. She had made it sound kind of fun. Why didn't she tell them she could make great nonalcoholic ones? She didn't know Josh was going to want a cocktail. Faith was right—she didn't have children, and she didn't know what constituted a good role model. She should have waited until the kids were in bed. Then again Josh didn't ever seem to sleep. Some nights she heard him sneaking through the house. Did he have insomnia, or was he snooping on something in particular? Hope had come out one evening to literally see him tiptoeing down the stairs. Maybe he was already sneaking drinks. Either way, she'd already offered so she set about making Shirley Temples and candy cane martinis. She could hear Austin asking Faith about Josh, wondering if he had any good friends back home. It was hard to be a kid. Even at Christmas. Hope was standing in the kitchen, regretfully making the drinks, when Austin joined her.

"I think your instincts are right," he said.

"To throw myself over a bridge?" Hope said. Then she remembered what Austin did for a living. "Oh my God. I didn't mean to joke like that."

"It's okay," Austin said. "I knew you were joking." He placed his hand on the small of her back for a tiny second. She felt a warm tingle up her spine.

"I forgot what an awkward time it is," Hope said, glancing upstairs. "Being a teenager."

"I'm worried it could be more than that," Austin said.

"What do you mean?"

"Would you just—leave this where Josh—only Josh—can find it?" Austin slipped her a folded-up piece of paper.

"Sure," Hope said. She glanced at it.

"Would you mind not reading it?" Austin said. "It's just between us guys."

"Sure." He was passing Josh a private note? Was that sweet or weird? She was dying to read it. But Austin had been good to her. To all of them. She would honor his wishes.

"Thank you." Austin searched the counter. "Show me how to make those Shirley Temples," he said with fake enthusiasm. Hope laughed and the two of them began making drinks. The folded-up piece of paper in her jeans pocket actually felt warm. What did it say? Was Austin right to be so worried? Should Hope be doing something? Did Austin know that the cologne he was wearing was driving her slowly insane?

"Try this," Austin said, handing her a drink.

Hope looked at the sparkly red drink. "Is it with or without alcohol?" she whispered.

"For you?" he said, leaning in with a grin. "Definitely with."

His eyes were bright, almost gleaming. Every time she was around him she felt a little bit like a kite rising into the air. Another spark passed between them. She smiled. "Cheers to you," she said. They clinked glasses.

"Thank you," he said softly.

"For what?"

"It feels like Christmas," he said, his hand sneaking over and touching hers. "For the first time in a very long time, it feels like Christmas."

CHAPTER 20

The next day the Garland Girls agreed to spend the morning doting on Yvette. Hope rose early to feed Mr. Jingles and give him some attention. He seemed perfectly happy sleeping in the mudroom at night, and was eager to return to the outdoors, no matter how cold. They also left a portion of the barn open for him so he could curl up in the hay whenever he needed a break. Once Mr. Jingles was taken care of, the mission was breakfast in bed for Yvette. Hope was the first to wake and she ventured into each of her sisters' rooms and roused them. Faith practically bounced out of bed, which made Hope hate her just a little, but Joy reacted like a drunk who had just passed out. She flailed and moaned, and threw a pillow over her head. Faith yanked it off, grabbed her feet, and then began to pull Joy out of bed. There was a lump under the covers beside her. "If you don't get up I'm telling Granny that Harrison is sleeping in your bed."

Joy cursed underneath her breath. "Okay, okay. Stop. I'm coming." Hope figured it was a rare day that Joy was up before the sun—yet another reason she should reconsider her coffee shop—but she trudged downstairs with them nonetheless. Hope immediately set to finding a bowl to mix the pancake batter, and Faith grabbed a frying pan and bacon. "'I can bring home the bacon,'" she started to sing.

"'Fry it up in a pan,'" Hope joined in.

"How's the rest go?" Faith said. "'Never ever let you forget you're a man.'" She sang into Hope's wooden spoon and swayed her hips.

"'Cause I'm a woman,'" Hope crooned, joining in on the dance as well. Faith and Hope exploded into laughter, and then they shushed each other.

"You guys are weird." Joy sauntered over to the windows overlooking the backyard.

"Mom used to sing that," Hope said. "Remember?"

"Does it look like I remember?" Joy said. Faith looked at Hope and rolled her eyes.

It was a crisp day. Hope predicted more snow would fall. Maybe today they could try out skating on the pond. This crew needed something to cheer them up.

"It's so peaceful," Joy said.

Thank God. Maybe she was starting to feel it. Maybe she was starting to recognize its importance. "Doesn't it feel like home?" Hope said as she cracked an egg into the silver bowl.

"No, it feels like the answer to my coffee shop," Joy said.

"Don't start," Faith said. "I haven't even had coffee."

"See? If I had a coffee shop you could stop in and have some whenever you want."

"Who are you kidding?" Faith said. "You'd probably charge us double."

"A sister's surtax," Hope said.

Joy turned around and treated them to a smug look. The only thing she was missing was her tongue sticking out. Hope wanted to fling pancake batter in her face. Maybe Faith was right—no talking without coffee.

"How about you start practicing your skills?" Faith said to Joy.

Joy crinkled her face. "What do you mean?"

"Make a pot of coffee, dork," Faith said. Hope laughed, then clapped her hand over her mouth.

"This is why I hate spending time with you two," Joy said. She grudgingly moved toward the coffeepot.

"I'm not laughing at you," Hope said. "I'm laughing at Faith. She used to call everybody a dork. I'd forgotten that."

"Finally, something I remember," Joy said. "Didn't she make a sign for her room that said 'Stay Out Dorks!' . . . ?"

"She did!" Hope said. "It took me a week of puzzling over that sign to realize that Joy and I were the dorks."

Faith laughed. "Is that why you didn't pay it any attention?" Faith glanced at the tree. "We need mood lighting." She left the bacon sizzling, then hopped over to plug in the tree. The lights reflected in the window behind them, each color glowing back. The sun still wasn't up, but the darkness was a comforting hush. Hope wanted to capture this moment forever, freeze it in time. If only that were possible.

"Your boyfriend was asking me a lot of questions about Josh last night," Faith said out of the blue.

"Harrison?" Joy whirled around, as if ready for a fight.

"Austin," Faith said.

Joy started the coffeepot gurgling and hopped onto the counter. She never was one for stools. "You and Austin?" she said to Hope.

"Faith is just teasing," Hope said.

"Am not," Faith said. "You have a total crush on him."

Joy pointed at her sister. "You still turn bright red when you're lying."

"Shut up." Hope lobbed enough butter in the pan to satisfy a hedonist.

"Not saying I blame you," Joy said. "He's hot. For a white guy."

"I really like Harrison for you," Hope said.

"What do you mean 'for me'?" Joy said.

"I mean—he's a nice guy." Hope sighed. Why was it that Joy took every single thing out of her mouth as a hostile act? Sometimes it was just exhausting to be around Joy.

"You're supposed to be helping," Faith said, eyeing Joy on the counter.

"I made coffee," Joy said.

Faith thrust a bowl of apples at Joy. "Wash and cut these."

"I'll check on the coffee," Joy said. She hopped off the counter, stood in front of the coffeepot, and stared at it.

Faith tried to engage Hope in a look, but Hope kept her eyes on the first batch of pancakes threatening to bubble in the pan. She didn't want to gang up on Joy. But she did want apple pancakes in the next batch, so she headed for the apples. Just as Hope had reached the sink to wash them, Faith stepped in front of her.

"Joy is going to do that."

"I don't mind," Hope said. She stepped left. Faith cut her off again. "Faith!"

"I already asked Joy to do that."

"What is your problem?" Joy said. "I'm making coffee."

"No, you're watching a coffeepot. The job is done. Move on to the next task."

Faith grabbed the bowl of apples. Hope didn't loosen her grip. They played tug-of-war. "Let go," Faith said.

"What is your problem?" Hope said.

"Same as yours," Faith said. "It's just what you were talking about." Faith shot a look of disapproval Joy's way. Oh no. Faith was going to get her in trouble. What had Hope said to Faith about Joy?

"How's that?" Joy asked.

"We both think you've become a spoiled brat and we're sick of it," Faith said.

"Oh God," Hope said. "Why?" She let go of the bowl and Faith stumbled. An apple tumbled out and rolled across the floor.

"Couldn't wait to get together again to bash me down," Joy said.

"Those weren't my exact words," Hope said.

"You want to talk about spoiled?" Joy said.

"Let's not," Hope said. "Say, what do you two crazy girls want for Christmas?" Hope waved her wooden spoon in the air. Maybe she should grab a paper towel and make a little white flag. "Come on, guys, we're supposed to be making breakfast for our dying grandmother here. Remember?"

Joy stepped up to Faith and jabbed her index finger at her. "Josh is a walking time bomb. He hates everybody and everything. And Brittany is absolutely starved for attention."

Hope watched Faith's nostrils flare. It was just as fascinating to watch as when they were teenagers. Gorgeous Faith would suddenly morph into a horse. A raging stallion. Her nostrils were the most expressive Hope had ever seen. "You have no right to judge my children."

"I'm not. I'm judging *you.*"

"How dare you. I'm a good mother. You have no idea how hard it is."

"It must be. After all, you're sneaking off every two seconds to take Xanax and make phone calls. Who are you calling? And where's your husband? If your life is so freaking perfect—"

Faith slammed the bowl down on the counter. "I never said my life was perfect. It's not perfect. I'm not perfect. Are you happy?" Faith plucked an apple out of the bowl and lobbed it at Joy. She ducked and it hit Hope in the chest.

"Ow," Hope said. "Stop that." She stomped back to the pancakes just as smoke curled up from the pan. Saved just in time. Someone would like them a little crispy. She began slipping them onto the spatula and dropping them on a plate.

Joy stormed up to the bowl of apples and began gathering them in her arms. "You're rich, you're married, you don't have to work, you have offspring as you remind us every single time we talk to you. Oh, boo hoo, what a tough life!"

Hope whirled around. "I swear to God, if you throw those apples," she said to Joy.

"You'll what?" Joy said. "Gang up on me along with Miss Perfect here?" Joy lobbed an apple at Hope's head. She barely ducked in time. The apple whizzed by her and smacked against the window.

"Oh my God, you're going to break something," Hope said.

"I was aiming for your head," Joy said. She held another apple up threateningly.

"Cut it out!" Hope yelled.

"I'm getting a divorce." Faith's voice cut through the air.

Hope had been poised to pour the next round of batter into the pan. Instead of making separate little circles, she was so startled she just dumped the entire thing in the pan. "Faithy," Hope said. She put down the bowl and approached Faith, who was separating greasy strips of bacon and hurling them at the pan.

"The kids don't know. Don't you dare say a word."

"We won't," Hope said.

"What did he do?" Joy said.

"He married me," Faith said.

"Well, that was his first mistake," Joy said. "But still."

"I'm the bad guy, all right? I'm the one having an affair." Hope was about to respond, although she hadn't quite figured out what to say—*Ms. Perfect was having an affair?*—when the sound of footsteps running along the upper hall echoed down. Faith's head snapped up. So did Hope and Joy's. They didn't see anyone, but a few seconds later heard the sound of a door slamming.

"Oh God," Faith said. "It's one of the kids. Oh God. They heard me."

"You don't know that," Hope said.

"Of course she does," Joy said. "Didn't you hear the running and the slamming?" Hope gave Joy a dirty look. Joy stuck her tongue out.

"Oh my God," Faith said again. "What am I going to do?"

"Who are you sleeping with?" Joy asked. She sounded way too excited for the details. Changing Joy was going to be a life-long project.

"Charlie," Faith said. "I'm in love with Charlie." She gave a little laugh. Joy looked at Hope and mouthed "Charlie?" Hope shrugged.

"Does Stephen know?" Hope asked gently. She'd been so sure that Stephen had done something wrong she felt a little guilty.

"He caught us on the living room sofa," Faith said.

"Awesome," Joy said. Faith and Hope both looked at her sharply. "Oh, come off it. I happen to applaud a wild spirit. Stephen was too stuffy for you, and Hope—you said so yourself."

Oh God. None of them could keep their mouths shut. This was why they never got together. Hope suddenly had a hard time remembering why that ever bothered her.

"Stephen is a good man, and a good provider, and a good father," Faith said.

"And yet," Joy pointed out, "you're sleeping with Charlie."

"I never said anything against Stephen," Hope said.

"You said he's stuffy," Joy said. "And closed-minded."

"Don't you ever know when to shut your mouth?" Hope said. She turned her back on Joy. "Faithy. I didn't mean it."

"Oh yes, you did," Faith said. "Looks like you talk about both of us behind our backs."

"What about you two?" Hope said. "Just because you talk about me in front of my face you think that makes it okay?" Joy pulled her right arm back and hurled another apple across the room. It thunked against the wall, then burst open like a mini-grenade sending shards scattering before it smashed to the ground.

"Those aren't baseballs!" Faith said. "You're so freaking immature."

"So?" Joy threw another one.

"Stop it!" Faith screamed.

"Something's burning," Faith said. Sure enough the big blob of a pancake had little stacks of smoke rising from its center. Hope lunged forward, turned off the stove, and removed the pan.

"What in the world?" Yvette raced into the room. She could move really fast for someone in her condition. "Where's the fire?"

"We got it," Hope said. "Sorry."

"Sorry, Granny," Joy said. "We were trying to surprise you."

"Oh, I'm surprised all right. Didn't know you were in that much of a hurry to kill me off."

Hope picked up the empty bowl from the counter and shoved it at Joy. "Pick up the apples before someone falls and breaks a hip."

"Is that a veiled reference to me?" Yvette said.

"No," Hope said. "Anyone could fall and break a hip."

"I might be riddled with cancer, but my bones are perfectly strong, thank you very much," Yvette said.

"I'm sure they are," Hope said.

Joy snatched the bowl out of her hands. "There's coffee," she called to Yvette. "I made it myself."

Brittany and Josh stomped down the stairs. Faith looked stricken. From their expressions, both of them knew about Faith's affair by now.

"Who wants crispy pancakes?" Hope said.

CHAPTER 21

The breakfast was a disaster. Faith wouldn't stop chattering at Josh and Brittany. Hope watched, fascinated as her sister turned into a deranged parakeet, flapping her clipped wings and chirping nonsense. "Did you hear us down here?" she asked.

Brittany squeaked, Josh elbowed her. "Hear what?" Josh said. Hope had to hand it to him, he had a steady hand. But there was a bite to his voice. He knew about the affair and he wasn't going to let Faith off easy.

"We were acting," Faith said, her eyes flicking between her children.

"Acting?" Josh said.

"Yes," Faith said. "Making up scenes like we did when we were kids. You know. Soap opera stuff."

Brittany and Josh looked at Joy and Hope as if scouring their faces for the truth.

"Soap operas are trashy," Yvette said. "Your mother always loved them." Hope clenched her fork and shoved more pancakes into her mouth. How much syrup would she need to consume before putting herself in a peaceful coma? When were the holidays over again?

"That's us," Joy said. "We've always been trashy."

Hope was hurtled into a memory. Her parents were standing in the kitchen section of their trailer. It was their first home together. Joy was the lump in her mother's belly. Faith was coloring, and refusing to share all shades of red. Hope literally crawled along the hall toward the kitchen. She was pretending to be a dog. She stopped when she heard what sounded like arguing.

"She thinks I'm a piece of trash!" her mother wailed.

"Screw her." Her father pulled her mother into him. "She's a self-righteous cow."

"Why does she hate me so much?" Hope started to growl, low in her belly. She would be a guard dog. The next time she saw her grandmother, she would bite her.

"Because you've stolen my heart," her father said. Hope couldn't remember what happened next. A lot of her memories were like that. Fuzzy blips. The reception on an old television going in and out. Maybe their mother melted into his arms. Maybe they kissed. Maybe they noticed Hope and took her for a walk. Or maybe their father opened a bottle of whiskey and disappeared for the next three days. Her mother had loved her soaps. And Hope used to curl up on the sofa and watch them with her. Her mother was very vocal, drawing Hope into the story but filling her in. Pointing at the television, talking about the characters and their scandals as if they were all neighbors. Hope loved it. Whenever the soaps were on, the attention was off of their own lives. They made her mother happy.

Hope forced herself to concentrate on the present, took a deep breath, and stared across the table at their grandmother. "We're not trashy," she said. "Neither was our mother."

"Is our mother," Faith corrected.

Hope thought of their mother's latest Facebook post: bikini, red lipstick, deep tan, margarita as big as her head. "Is our mother," Hope echoed.

Yvette swiped her index finger between the three girls. "You're the ones acting out soap operas."

"Which soap opera?" Brittany asked. Hope could hear both desperation and doubt in her voice. Hope could tell that she wanted to believe her mom, but part of her knew the truth.

"I only bring it up in case somebody heard me saying something that sounded odd," Faith said. "That's all."

"Everything out of your mouth right now sounds odd," Yvette said. "What is going on here?"

"It's none of your business, Granny," Joy said.

"I'm not hungry." Josh shoved his plate. It knocked into his milk. They all watched as it sloshed over the side.

"Can I have your pancakes?" Brittany said.

"You'll get fat," Josh said. "But what do I care."

"Josh!" Faith said.

"What? You're the one who's always telling her that." He sounded so hostile. Hope thought of the note Austin had slipped her. She had placed it on Josh's nightstand the previous evening. Had he read it? If so, it certainly hadn't cheered him up much.

"You're going to kill her self-esteem," Joy said. She turned to Brittany. "Your body is beautiful and you don't need to worry about calories."

"Thank you," Brittany said.

"But you might want to avoid eating anything with a face."

"Now that's just nonsense," Faith said. Brittany squeaked. "Not you, darling. Your body is beautiful. But everyone has to think about what they're putting into their body. And cut it out with that 'I don't eat anything with a face!' diatribe. My children will eat protein!"

"Pancakes don't have faces, unless you make them into little Mickey Mouses," Harrison said.

"I love when you do that, baby," Joy said. They rubbed noses.

"Like you're the expert on self-esteem," Faith said, stabbing her food.

"That's what I love about my girl," Harrison said, putting his arm around her. "My girl is confident."

"And I certainly didn't learn that at home," Joy said to Brittany. "So don't worry. You can acquire the skill too."

"There is nothing wrong with Brittany's confidence," Faith said. "You don't know the first thing about being a parent."

Joy had that look in her eye. Hope tried to get her to look at her so she could talk her out of whatever was going to come out of her mouth next. "Apparently neither do you," Joy said.

Hope looked at Josh and Brittany. Confusion was stamped on their faces as they tried to figure out whether or not they had just been insulted. "Sorry, guys," Hope said. "This has nothing to do with you. We always end up squabbling when we're together."

"Good thing you don't get together much, huh?" Brittany said. Hope felt a sear of pain in her heart. She bit her bottom lip. She hadn't planned on weeping during breakfast. Maybe they should have a "No Talking" rule at the table.

Josh shoved back from the table. "I'm going outside."

"I think you should go to your room," Faith said.

"Why? What did I do?" Josh's voice rose.

"You're giving me attitude, and talking back," Faith said. "Your father and I have addressed that issue with you repeatedly."

"My father isn't here now. Or haven't you noticed?"

"That's it. Go to your room."

"I don't have a room."

"You know what I mean."

"I really don't know what you mean. I mean, you could be acting right now. Are you? Am I in the middle of another trashy soap opera?"

Faith stood. "You apologize to me at once."

"No."

"You're grounded."

"I don't give a shit."

"That's double for swearing."

"I don't care."

"I'll make you care."

"How?"

"Don't push me, Josh. Not in front of all these people."

"You're a hypocrite."

"How did I raise such an ungrateful child?"

"Ungrateful? You bet I am. You're a liar. You're a cheater. You're cheating on Dad!"

Brittany wailed. She slapped her hands over her ears. "It's not true, right, Mom? It's not!"

Hope froze in horror, although it was somewhat of a relief that they were done pretending. God, this was a mess. How were they supposed to have a happy Christmas now? Should they even try?

"Cheated?" Yvette said.

"She has a lover," Josh said. "Charlie."

"Stop, stop," Brittany said. She commandeered Josh's plate of pancakes and began shoveling them into her mouth.

"Let's talk about this in private," Faith said, her voice cracking and quivering.

"Save it." Josh got up from the table and walked toward the coats hanging by the front door.

"We'll talk about this," Faith called after him.

"Not if I can help it," Josh said. "I'm calling Dad to come get us."

Fat tears rolled down Faith's face. Hope reached over and took her hand. A second later Joy's hand snuck over and she laid hers on top of the pile. It was a nice moment. For a moment.

"I expected more of you girls," Yvette said. She got up from the table, entered the kitchen area, and removed a bottle of whiskey from the shelf. *That's where Dad got it,* Hope thought.

"Why?" Joy said.

Yvette drank straight from the bottle. She slammed it down and looked at Joy. "Why what?"

"Why would you expect more? You thought our mother was trash, and we didn't have a father."

"You certainly had a father. A very good one."

"A drunk one. One who abandoned us."

"How dare you."

"You certainly didn't come looking for us, did you? And now

you're using this stupid house to force us to all be together so that we'll get it when you die. Screw that." Joy threw her napkin on the table and stood. She started to stomp off. She stopped after a few steps and turned to Harrison, who was humming and eating his pancakes.

"Hey," Joy said. "You're supposed to stomp off with me."

"These are really good," Harrison said. "Can't I finish?"

"Since there's not going to be any real love between us," Yvette said, standing up herself, "we might as well go over the other rules." She got up from the table and headed down the hall toward her bedroom.

"Are we supposed to follow you?" Hope called after her.

"No, I'm going to change and then the four of us are going to visit your father's grave." The girls stood, wide-eyed and silent for a full minute after Yvette disappeared down the hallway.

"Did she say?" Faith said. All heads turned to Hope.

"Yeah," Hope said. "She said that."

They ventured out into the thick of the woods where a canopy of trees formed a little circle below. A beautiful spot to spread his ashes. Hope approved. She could think of worse places than being surrounded by this vista. The grave was outlined in baseball-sized rocks and topped off with a wooden cross. The four of them stood looking down. Roger lingered in the background, watching them.

"I thought you said he didn't have a grave," Joy said.

"I didn't think you needed to see this," Yvette said.

"What changed your mind?" Joy persisted.

"All of your arguing," Yvette said. "You girls need closure."

Hope sucked in her breath. *Daddy.* She wanted to lay her body on top of the grave and hug it. She shoved her hands in her pockets and wondered why her grandmother hadn't invested in a real headstone. She would look into ordering one. It could be from the three of them.

"Why doesn't he have a real headstone?" Joy said. Oh, holy night! There went Joy again, reading Hope's thoughts and speaking them out loud. She wanted to rail against Joy for doing it, but she probably didn't actually have a leg to stand on with that one.

Faith kneeled down and brushed leaves off the makeshift cross. "His name isn't even on the cross," she said.

"Your father was a simple man," Yvette said. "And a proud one. I'm doing everything according to his wishes."

"We could have a headstone made," Hope said. "From us. For Christmas."

"Nothing says Merry Christmas like a new tombstone," Faith said.

"Don't make light of this," Hope said. "I want to do that for him. I want him remembered."

"He loved Christmas, right?" Joy said.

"Our names prove it," Faith said.

"That's what we should put on his headstone," Joy said. "Faith, Joy, and Hope."

"I think he'd like that," Hope said.

"We'll come out here on Christmas morning and sing Christmas carols to him," Faith said.

"I always thought we'd see him again." Hope took a deep breath and turned her face to the sky.

"He lives on in each of you," Yvette said.

"I want to be cremated," Joy said.

"Gladly," Faith said under her breath. Hope pinched her.

"You said there were other rules," Faith said, turning to Yvette.

Yvette nodded. "This property is not to be sold as long as Roger is still alive."

"Roger?" Faith said, glancing over her shoulder and lowering her voice. "Why?"

"He could live a long time," Joy said.

"I hope he does," Yvette said. "I hope he lives a very long time."

"You're saying we can't sell the property until he dies?" Joy persisted.

"He's going to live out the rest of his life on this property," Yvette said. "I'd also like one of you to live here. He needs looking after."

The girls exchanged looks.

"What about my coffee shop?" Joy said. "I need start-up money."

"Please," Hope said. "Can we agree not to argue in front of our father's grave?"

Joy had the decency to look slightly ashamed. She stopped talking and nodded.

"We'll go to town and continue our conversation," Yvette said. "I know a good pub."

"It's not even nine o'clock in the morning," Hope said.

"That's what makes it good," Yvette said. She trudged forward and the rest followed. Hope wondered if it was such a good idea, given their current states, to get a few drinks in them.

"I can't just leave the kids here," Faith said.

"I'll watch." It was a gruff male voice and it came from several feet away. They turned to find Roger standing still, staring at them. They all stopped and stared at him.

"Wonderful, Roger," Yvette said. "Wonderful." Yvette clasped her hands by her mouth. She was smiling. Hope couldn't tell if she was applauding the fact that he had spoken or actually agreeing to the suggestion that he was fit enough to watch the kids.

"Why don't we call Austin?" Faith said, her voice cracking. "He could watch them."

"Roger just volunteered," Yvette hissed. "Don't hurt his feelings."

"Harrison can watch them," Joy said. "Unless you have a problem with him?"

"You're hurting his feelings," Yvette said. Her voice shook with anger. Hope looked at Roger, who was indeed staring at the ground and pawing at it.

Hope slowly approached. "Did we hurt your feelings?" Roger continued to stare at the ground. "We didn't mean to. I trust you."

"They're my kids," Faith said.

"You have to understand. We just met you. You don't talk very much. It's not personal." Hope stared at the top of his red cap. She wasn't sure whether he understood or not. "Were you friends with my father?" Roger lifted his eyes, made eye contact, then slowly shook his head no. Hope took a step back.

"He was, he was," Yvette said. "Leave him be now. You're confusing him." Roger continued to look at Hope and shake his head no.

"What about Harrison?" Joy barked again.

"I'll watch," Roger said.

"Let him do it," Yvette said. "He can do it."

Faith smiled at Roger, then turned and lowered her voice. "I'll decide who watches my kids." She threw her arms open. "Roger and Harrison. You'll make a great team." Roger stared at Faith. For a minute Hope thought he was going to speak again. Instead he just nodded.

"I'll go tell Harrison," Joy said. Faith's cell phone rang. She glanced at the screen and a blush spread across her face. She answered and hurried away. Hope stood alone with her grandmother, Roger in the background. They fell into an awkward silence. *And so this is Christmas.*

CHAPTER 22

Austin was at the call center finishing up on paperwork when his cell phone rang. He glanced at the screen. It was a number he didn't recognize. Could it be Josh?

"Hello?" There was a moment of silence. Austin lowered his voice and sank down into his cubicle. He cleared his throat and started again, treating it like the call came in through the switchboard. Hope must have given him the note. Josh might have confused which number to call. Austin took a chance and answered his cell the way he would have answered his work line. "Suicide Prevention. This is Austin. I'm glad you called." There was another moment of silence.

"Why?" the caller said. It was a young male. Austin knew it was Josh. Hope had given him the note.

"Because you're reaching out for help and that takes guts."

"Whatever."

Oh yes. Definitely Josh. "Are you feeling so bad that you're thinking about suicide?"

"Maybe."

"Have you thought about how you would do it?"

"It might just involve Christmas lights."

Austin was glad to hear the sarcasm. That was actually a good sign. But he wasn't going to laugh. He needed Josh to know that he took this very seriously. "You're not alone. Christmas is a really tough time of year for a lot of people. I want to help you."

"You'd want to kill yourself, too, if you had my family."

Did Josh know he was talking to Austin, or did he think he'd called the main line? Austin would pretend it was anonymous unless and until Josh identified him. "What's been going on?"

"How soon do you die if you fall through ice?"

"Are you near a body of water? Are you thinking about drowning yourself?" The pond. It would be frozen solid, so at least that was some relief.

There was a click and the line went dead. "Damn it," Austin said under his breath. He stared at his cell phone hoping it would ring again. He knew Josh was in trouble. Something about the pained look in his eyes reminded him so much of his brother. Austin would have given anything if someone had recognized the warning signs in his brother and told him to pay attention.

What should he do now? He definitely didn't want to say anything to Faith because she seemed like she could really tear into you given half a chance. He'd stop by Yvette's place after work, see what was going on. Maybe he could get to know Josh a little bit more, see if he could get him to open up face-to-face. From what Austin could tell, Josh was in the early stages of pondering suicide. He still had time. If it got to a point where Austin felt like he had to break confidentiality to save Josh's life, he would tell Hope what was going on. She could deal with her sister. At the thought of Hope, Austin's heart beat a little faster. The more time he spent with her, the more he wanted to see her. He had to constantly remind himself that she wasn't here because of him. He didn't want to take the spotlight away from Yvette or Hope spending time with her sisters. But boy would he like to. Was there any chance that she would stay on after Yvette passed away? He hated the thought of Yvette passing away, and he hated the thought of Hope going away. They were both here now and that's what he should focus on. That and helping Josh. Austin was done with his shift for today. He'd go straight to the estate. And he'd definitely check out the pond, make sure no one was in danger of falling through the ice.

The little tavern downtown was practically empty. Just a few old-timers lined the bar. The bartender smiled at Yvette and set them all up at a table. It was dim inside, and the few Christmas decorations that hung about the place made Hope feel sad. This was where Charlie Brown the grown man would have hung out. Soon after they were settled into a booth and their drinks had been delivered, they raised their pints. Faith had asked for a mimosa and was informed they had ale. Light and dark. They all ordered dark, which Hope hoped wasn't a bad omen, and at the last minute she changed her order to sparkling water.

"Party pooper," Joy said.

"To family," Hope said, ignoring Joy and holding up her pint of water.

"To family," they echoed with varying degrees of enthusiasm. They all raised their pints and clinked glasses. At least that was a bit of cheer. Just then something began rattling above them, and just as Hope was thinking, *Earthquake!* a whistle sounded. Hope looked up. A model train was chugging above them, the tracks running along the wall like crown molding. They all took a moment to watch it go by.

"Dad loved Christmas trains," Faith said.

"I love trains too," Joy said.

"Me too," Hope said. The two of them looked at Faith.

"They're charming," Faith said.

"Would you look at that, it's the United Nations," Yvette said.

"You're feisty, Granny," Joy said. "I like that about you."

Yvette actually smiled; then she looked at the girls. "I can see your father in each of you," she said.

"Tell us everything you know about him," Hope said.

"That's a lot to tell," Yvette said.

"What was he like as a boy?"

"He was spirited and adventurous. You couldn't contain him. I had gone completely gray by the time he was three."

"That sounds like our dad," Faith said. A sad smile played at the corner of her lips.

"Where did you live? What was our grandfather like? Why didn't you have other children?" Hope knew she was asking too many questions at once, but she felt an invisible timer ticking away and she wanted to know everything now. "Do you have photo albums?"

"Relax, Hope," Joy said. "Can the rest of us at least get a buzz on first?"

"I have photo albums, of course," Yvette said. "Your grandfather, Jeremiah, could be a very hard man. He left when Thomas was ten."

"Is that why it was so easy for Dad to leave us?" Faith said.

Yvette slammed her fist on the table. "He did not leave you girls! You were kidnapped!" Several patrons looked over and the bartender shot the girls a warning look. Yvette was already so fragile, it pained Hope to see it. She immediately took Yvette's hand.

"We don't want to upset you," Hope said.

Faith shook her head at Hope and plunged ahead with the interrogation. "If he was coming to see us—why was Roger in the car?" she asked.

Yvette shook her head. "He was coming to see you. He never would have let you girls go."

"Why was Roger in the car?" Faith repeated.

"It's a long drive to Florida. Maybe he just wanted the company."

"Was our father drunk when the accident occurred?" Hope had to ask the question. Yvette pulled her hand back.

"You keep asking that!"

"Because you've never answered."

"I don't know. Back then they didn't make a fuss over things like that."

"You're saying they didn't check?" Faith asked.

Yvette rolled a napkin between her fingers. "He died. That was punishment enough."

"He hurt Roger," Joy pointed out.

Yvette's chin jutted up. A look of fierce pride crossed her face. "I've done right by Roger. I've done right by him."

Hope hadn't wanted to escalate the conversation to this stage this fast. She had wanted to hear happier memories of her father. She tried to steer the conversation back to safer subjects. "He must have had good Christmases growing up."

"We didn't spoil him by any means," Yvette said. "But he did always love it. He loved Christmas lights, and Christmas trees, and Christmas songs. He would just light up all throughout the season. And he was a generous boy too. He loved giving gifts more than receiving. One year I think he gave everyone he knew a gift. Even the mailman. He loved *A Christmas Carol* and later *It's a Wonderful Life*."

"We watched those with him," Faith said.

"Over and over," Hope said. "All year round. I loved his love of Christmas. And I loved that he would pick me up and swing me around a lot."

Faith laughed. "Oh, I used to love when he did that. He was so strong."

"And handsome," Yvette said.

"Where did he grow up?" Hope asked.

"It's a very small town, about an hour south of here," Yvette said. "He moved to Seattle when he was only seventeen years old."

"And that's where he met our mother," Faith said.

Yvette kept her lips clamped shut.

"They were so young," Faith said.

"Women and girls were always throwing themselves at your father," Yvette said. "I never expected him to marry so young."

"So you hated her before you even met her," Faith said.

"I have my prejudices. I'll admit it. He was my only son. He was my everything. But it's all in the past. Can't I enjoy my last days on earth with my three beautiful granddaughters?"

Hope reached over and took her hand again. "Of course you can."

"Mom never remarried," Joy said. "Even though she's been with a ton of men. I mean a ton." Faith and Hope gave her a look. "What? Just sayin'."

"I think we should all go sledding," Hope said. "The kids are dying to do that."

"Don't forget we're here to talk about Roger," Yvette said. "I want to draw up a contract where the three of you agree that he's to stay on the property until it's his time to pass away. After that you're free to do whatever you wish with it."

"What if we found him another home instead?" Joy asked.

"He's already home," Yvette said. "You will not move him."

"What if he gets to a point where he needs twenty-four/seven care," Joy persisted. "We're not nurses."

"I'm sure you'll see there's enough money to hire a full-time nurse," Yvette said. "But that man is going to die at home, do you hear me?"

"I definitely hear you," Joy said. "You're loud."

Yvette stared at Joy, then laughed. "It runs in the family," she said. "Now, I'm going to call a taxi and go home."

"No need," Faith said. "We'll take you back."

"No, I want you girls to spend some time together, away from the house. Talk about my terms. If you don't agree, that's fine, but you'll need to let me know so that I can decide who will inherit the property. Roger is nonnegotiable."

"Would there still be enough cash in the estate for me to start my coffee shop?" Joy said.

"Not while Roger is alive," Yvette said. "You might need it."

"My God," Joy said. "You're certainly giving us motive for murder here."

"Joy!" Hope said.

"Oh my God, I'm kidding," Joy said. "Lighten up."

"Let's have another round," Faith said.

"Didn't you take your vitamins this morning?" Hope said to Faith.

"What?" Faith said.

"Your *vitamins*," Hope said. "I don't think you're supposed to mix them with alcohol."

"You're really not supposed to mix anything with alcohol," Yvette said. "That's why I've pretty much given everything up but drinking."

196 • *Mary Carter*

"We'll agree to your terms, Granny," Faith said. Joy shot her a look. "Unless you have a better idea?"

"Fine," Joy said.

"Of course," Hope said.

"I'll have my attorney draw up the contracts," Yvette said. "I want them signed while I'm still alive to witness it." They helped Yvette to a taxi and stood watching as it pulled away. Shops were just starting to open and the sun was peeking through the clouds. Christmas decorations started to glow and the snow sparkled. *Magic,* Hope thought. *It's enough to make you believe in magic.*

"How do we know Roger isn't some kind of scam artist?" Joy said. They were sitting on a retaining wall overlooking the sledding hill. Kids on colorful sleds zoomed by, squealing and shouting. Hope wanted to grab Brittany and Josh and have them all join in.

"I like Roger," Hope said.

"You would," Joy said.

Hope plunged on. "She's known him most of his life. He was friends with our father."

Joy snorted and began kicking her feet on the stone wall. Maybe they should give her ADHD medication for Christmas. Joy in a coffee shop swilling espresso all day would be overkill. "So she says," Joy said. "Do you two ever remember meeting Roger? Did Dad ever mention him?"

"We never met anybody," Faith said. "Any memory I have—besides meeting Granny a few times—was just Mom and Dad."

"We could ask Mom if she remembers him," Hope said.

"That's like being the one to give Pandora the box for Christmas," Faith said. "No thank you."

"Good one," Joy said. "But what does an Internet radio station have to do with Mom?"

"We did kind of live in a bubble," Hope said.

"Some of us still do," Faith said, flicking her glance to Joy.

"What do you think, Faith? Could Roger be a scam artist?" Joy asked.

Faith shrugged, stared off into the distance. "If he is, he's certainly a pro."

"He was in the accident with Dad," Hope said.

"So she says." Joy again.

"Why in the world would Yvette make that up?" Hope couldn't bring herself to call her Granny, or even Grandmother. She was hoping she would feel that connection, that Yvette would morph into something grandmotherly and loving, but it just hadn't happened. They weren't here to bond with her, they were here to make sure Roger had a home. There was no way that woman would go to such extremes for just some man. Would she? People took advantage of the elderly all the time. Did they know for sure that Roger wasn't faking his brain injury? Could he be scamming their grandmother? Hope didn't want to think so, he seemed so sweet.

"We should break into his cabin," Joy said. "See what he's hiding."

"Oh my God," Hope said. "We are so not doing that."

"Well, I'm not agreeing to anything until we check him out," Joy said.

"I agree," Faith said.

"What?" Hope should have known they were going to pull something like this. Sure, she'd been thinking the same thing, but in her head where no one could hear her.

"It's due diligence," Faith said. "We can't just take her word that he's a decent guy. And even if he is. So what? Like Joy said—what if down the road he gets sick and needs round-the-clock care? If this contract says he's to live on the property, who is going to be his nursemaid? It's ridiculous."

"We should just sell it and get on with our lives," Joy said. Joy's money would be gone in a year. Hope knew it, Faith knew it. If she did open a coffee shop it would fold within the year. Joy didn't have experience running a business, let alone starting one from scratch, and she certainly wasn't mature enough to stick with it through the rough patches. It might not be a nice thing to think about her own sister, but it was the truth.

"Can't we just enjoy the time alone with each other right now and figure this out later?" Hope said.

"We could if it weren't for the fact that Granny wants to draw up the contracts," Joy said.

"Why don't we add a clause that if he gets to a point where he needs physical or mental round-the-clock care, that he will be sent to such a place." Hope thought her suggestion was sound.

Faith turned to her. "Do you want to live in the house year-round?"

Did she? The thought had crossed Hope's mind. Austin had crossed her mind too. A lot. "I'd certainly be willing to consider it."

"That's so not an answer," Faith said.

"She totally wants to live here," Joy said. "Although I don't see why."

You don't see why? Hope jumped off the retaining wall and scooped up some snow. She rolled it into a ball.

"What are you doing?" Joy said. Hope hurled a snowball at Joy, aiming for the puffiest spot on her coat so that it wouldn't really hurt. Joy squealed and jumped off the wall. She made a snowball and returned fire.

"You two are so immature," Faith said. In unison, Hope and Joy made more snowballs and shot them at Faith. Faith, too, jumped off the wall.

"Juvenile!" she said. But she was laughing. Nearby kids careened down the hill. After a flurry of snowballs, they stopped to catch their breath.

"You and Harrison could open a coffee hut on the property," Hope said. "Especially if we open the skating up to the public again."

"Small potatoes," Joy said.

"It's a start," Hope said. "Without a lot of overhead."

"Why don't I just buy a coffee truck and drive it around town?" Joy said with disgust.

"That's not a bad idea," Hope said. "Tourists would love that."

"And what about the rest of the year?" Joy said. "We'd go broke."

"At least you'd have a little truck to live in and drive around in," Faith said.

"You two are hideous," Joy said. "I was being sarcastic."

"I think it's a great start," Hope said. "Faith's right, you could drive the truck all over."

"I could drive it straight into the two of you," Joy said.

"What a lovely sentiment for the holidays," Hope said. Joy stuck out her tongue. Hope imagined her getting it stuck to a pole like in *A Christmas Story.*

"I'm getting cold," Faith said. "Let's hit the shops."

"Wait. Let's sled down the hill," Joy said. "Just once."

"Remember the year we went sledding with Mom?" Faith said.

"That was a great day," Hope said.

"I hate you two!" Joy said.

"You were there," Faith said. "Mom held you the entire time."

Hope lunged at Joy and hugged her. Faith slammed in and joined the hug. Any outsider watching would have thought they were the closest sisters in the world. For a second, they felt like they were.

"Let's do it," Joy said, breaking out of the hug and heading for the sledding area. Faith and Hope hurried after her.

"We don't have a sled," Faith yelled.

"They rent them," Hope said. "Yvette's husband used to own it."

"They're used," Faith said. "Anything could go wrong."

"You can just watch then," Joy said. "Hope and I will go." Hope and Joy exchanged a smile and kept moving forward, knowing that any second Faith would blow past them and take the lead.

CHAPTER 23

Austin threw open the door of the barn, where the skates were housed. He wished Hope was here; she seemed really eager to start the skating party; but once he mentioned it Brittany lit up like the star on top of the Rockefeller Center tree, so there was no going back. Luckily, Roger had been shoveling the snow off the pond since the Garland Girls arrived, and its surface was as smooth as a mirror. Josh was lurking at the edges, but at least he was around and safe. He hadn't made eye contact with Austin since he arrived, increasing his suspicion that Josh had been that morning's caller. Until he knew for sure, he was going to make sure the kid was always in somebody's sight.

Inside the barn, skates were stacked floor-to-rafters on the shelves. Although Austin didn't miss the traffic jams that existed in the days when the lodge was open for skating and other festivities, he did miss the music, and the sound of children's laughter, the scratch and swish of the skates as they went round and round. Roger had followed him into the barn and stood looking at the skates as well. He had certainly come to life lately. Austin turned to him.

"How's it going?"

Roger didn't vocalize and answer, but he did give a nod. Now that was interesting. It meant he understood Austin perfectly well. Austin wasn't sure now if that made him more suspicious of the man or less. It would certainly help if he could have a conversation with him.

"Where's Harrison?" Brittany asked.

"Watching television," Josh said. "I think I'll join him."

"Aw, come on," Austin said. "This will be fun." Roger headed farther into the interior of the barn. "Why don't you ask Harrison to join us?"

"I'll do it," Brittany said. She tore off for the house.

"Are you sure the ice is ready?" Josh asked.

"I'm sure," Austin said. *There's no way you can fall through and drown.* It was him. Oh boy. It was definitely him. They stood around for a few awkward moments until Brittany came running back.

"That was quick," Austin said.

"I knocked on the window," Brittany said in between trying to catch her breath. "He's coming." Austin helped Brittany find her size, grabbed a pair for himself, and then asked Josh his size. Josh reluctantly found his size on his own—and the three plopped down on a bench near the pond to put on their skates.

"Where's Roger?" Brittany said. "Is he skating too?"

"He's somewhere in the barn," Austin said.

"He's a nice man," Brittany said.

"He's a weirdo," Josh said. "He's probably just going to lurk on the side and watch us."

Austin wanted to tell him not to judge. That would make him a hypocrite. He'd had his own doubts about Roger. He also didn't want Josh to feel scolded. He was already in a dangerous place. Austin was probably going to have to break some rules and confront Josh about the call. The consequences of doing nothing were too serious. His brother might just be alive today if someone had done that for him.

Brittany glided around the ice like it was the easiest thing in the world. Whenever she fell, she'd mutter a little "Oops!" and bounce back up. Austin stumbled a few times before his body remembered the rhythm. He used to be real good. He found himself imagining going around and around with Hope. Holding her hand. Roger, indeed, stood on the sidelines, grinning and giving Brittany a thumbs-up every single time she passed. Josh sat on the bench kicking the skates near his feet. Harrison emerged and sauntered over to the fence surrounding the skating pond.

"Join us," Austin said when he came around again. "Both of you." Josh just stared.

"I'll be the cheering section," Harrison said, grinning and flashing them a thumbs-up.

"Don't you want to skate?" Brittany said.

"I'll spend the entire time on my behind," Harrison said, taking a seat on the bench.

"But you'd be doing that anyway," Brittany said, coming around and eyeing him on the bench.

Harrison laughed. "Right, but it's not frostbitten," Harrison said, giving a slap to his behind.

"Please, Josh," Brittany said. Roger came near Josh and patted him on the back. Josh jerked away.

Roger finally got the hint and left. A few minutes later, "Jingle Bells" started to play. Roger had found the stereo system they'd used back in the day. The music rang, loud and clear, into the air. Austin looked at him and gave him a thumbs-up. Roger just stared at him for a moment, then nodded. "Our own personal holiday soundtrack!" Austin exclaimed.

"'Jingle bells! Jingle bells!'" Brittany sang out. God, it was great to have someone around who was truly excited about the season. No matter how bad adults felt at this time of year, a wide-eyed child could sure make you remember what it was all about. Harrison began to sing along as well, enthusiastically and loudly. He had a fantastic voice.

"Yea, Christmas carols," Austin said, pumping his fist.

"You're weird," Josh yelled to Austin as he zoomed past.

"Sometimes weird is good," Austin said with another glance at Roger. "Sometimes weird is good."

* * *

The minute they were all seated on the sled, Hope began to have second thoughts. Was this sled really big enough for all three of them? She was in the middle, no surprise there, with Faith in front, and Joy squeezing her from the back. Joy's legs were straight out, making a V—also making Hope feel trapped. She was just about to tell them she'd changed her mind when the kid manning the operation gave them a push and the sled was launched. Joy whooped as it picked up speed. *Oh God, oh God, oh God.* Faith was right. They were going to crash at the bottom and someone was going to break a limb. Faith was laughing, and Joy was screaming, and Hope knew her face was frozen in terror. The ride wasn't smooth, probably due to their combined weight. She could feel every little bump in the terrain. Her bum was already hurting. But, God, the mountains in the distance, so clear, so beautiful. The sky, the snow, the twinkling village below.

"Whoo-hoo," Hope heard herself yell.

"Whoo-hoo!" Joy answered. Joy's arms tightened around Hope's waist and she in turn squeezed Faith. Faith pumped her fist. They were halfway down, pine trees appeared to whiz by on either side. Hope could see the bottom of the hill coming up, the terrain was designed to slow the sled, and employees were waiting to make sure the path was clear in order to avoid collisions. Maybe now Faith would let Josh and Brittany do this, although Hope wasn't going to go again. By the time they reached the bottom and a kid helped Hope off the sled, she was certain she was going to be sick. She took a few wobbly steps, then fell on her face. She could hear Joy and Faith cackling behind her.

"And she didn't even drink!" Joy said. Hope heard the click of someone's camera phone.

"That's going to be my new profile picture on Facebook," Faith said. Hope just lay there. Soon she was being lifted, Joy yanking on one arm, Faith the other. They were both laughing so hard they couldn't talk.

Hope wanted to wipe snow off her face, but her arms were trapped by her sisters. She spit out ice. "Not funny," she said.

"So funny," Faith said.

"Hilarious," Joy said.

"Let's go again," Faith said.

Hope waited at the bottom while they went again. It had been her suggestion in the first place, so why wasn't she happier that they had such a good time? She'd tried to get them to wait, to do it again with Brittany and Josh, but Faith and Joy were off in tipsy-land. Maybe they'd be in the mood for a little Christmas shopping when they came down. Hope imagined being on a sled with Austin. He'd sit behind her and wrap his arms around her waist. She probably would have done it a second time with him. She wondered where he was this very moment and what he was doing.

"I'm too worn out for shopping," Faith said when they finished the second round.

"Drinks?" Joy said.

"We had drinks," Hope said. "We should get back so we can spend time with the kids." Faith shot her a dirty look, as if she was angry for Hope saying that instead of her.

"They like you better," Joy said to Hope. "You're the favorite aunt."

"Don't start," Faith said. "We were actually having fun."

"Let's go home and go skating with the kids," Hope said.

"We could hit the hot tub," Joy said.

"That's a fabulous idea," Faith said, poking Hope. "You could make those candy cane martinis."

"Yum," Joy said.

Had they not heard a word about spending time with the kids? "Let's skate with the kids and then do the hot tub," Hope said. "Or we could all make cookies. Snuggle around the tree."

Joy and Faith looked at each other. "Hot tub and cocktails?" Joy said.

"Hot tub and cocktails," Faith said. Faith barged ahead to the car. Joy tugged on Hope's sleeve. "I'm going to get her drunk and find out who she's sleeping with."

Hope just stared at Joy, mouth slightly agape.

Joy flounced ahead, catching up with Faith, linking arms with her, giggling like they were schoolgirls. She watched their hair bounce, heard their laughter mingle together. Hope, too, wanted details on who Faith was sleeping with and why. But she was giving Faith space, waiting for her to tell them in her own good time. Maybe she wasn't really related to Faith and Joy. Maybe she was adopted. Maybe that's why she was so drawn to orphaned dogs. Maybe they were all adopted.

Josh sat on the bench, freezing his behind off with Harrison as Brittany and Austin continued to skate and laugh, but his mind was elsewhere. He was playing out the fantasy that his mother would once, just once, leave her phone where he could get at it. He'd thought about sneaking into her room while she was sleeping, but the thought of getting caught terrified him. If he could just get the phone and find out who this guy Charlie was, then he'd get the information to his father so he could do something about it. He would do something about it, wouldn't he? His father still loved his mother, he could tell. Not only could he tell, he could see how much his father was hurting. All you had to do was look in his eyes and see the pain. Sometimes he saw the same pained eyes when he looked in the mirror. Sometimes he felt so sad he just wanted it all to stop. He spent a lot of time imagining his death, and even more time imagining everyone's reaction. He'd play it over and over again in his mind. He knew it wasn't right to do that, and the really sick part was—he actually enjoyed it. Not imagining he was dead, but imagining everyone else reacting to it. It felt so satisfying to be the one to finally make them get it. To make them see that they just didn't appreciate anything, especially him. In his fantasies it felt so good to show them.

Brittany was clueless, going on and on about Christmas as if they were children, acting like a child, getting all of Aunt Hope's attention. Josh was just waiting for Brittany to declare that she still believed in Santa Claus. Everyone around here was pretending. Josh was tired of watching them skate, but he got the feeling Austin was keeping his eye on him. Josh had to act normal so the guy would leave him alone. He was tired of everything. Would anything ever seem fun again? He wanted to snap out of his bad moods and he tried, really he did, but they always came back. Like a Ninja pouncing on him, hijacking his brain. It was an impulse, that's all, like when the doctor hit your knee with that little silver hammer and it bounced up. His knee kept bouncing up even though he wanted it to stop. Stupid, stupid, stupid.

You're an idiot, Josh. Now he'd be watched like a hawk. Not that he really intended on killing himself. It just made him feel calmer, having the option. An escape hatch when things got too jumbled inside his head. A way out. A way to show them. But he would never do it. He knew that now. It was time to stop all this pretending.

He just needed to get his mom's phone and find out who Charlie was, and why his mom was calling him all the time with that goofy look on her face. Then he had to make sure his dad came out here.

Drowning. Did he really ask Austin about drowning? The pond was way too frozen. Maybe he could go sledding and aim directly for a tree. But what if he just ended up brain-damaged? Like Roger? Of course he probably wouldn't know it, so maybe it wouldn't matter. Roger seemed happy enough.

No. He didn't want brain damage, and he didn't really want to end his life. He just wanted things to go back to the way they were. It was all his mother's fault. She was planning on destroying the only thing he liked about his family: his dad. It would be one thing if his dad was happy about it. Josh could go live with him. He'd have his own room. They'd go to baseball games and order pizza every night and leave the television on full blast overnight. Cleaning would only be when necessary.

"Your mother and sister are coming over," his father would say. "Let's throw these boxes out and turn down the television." Josh wouldn't mind that. His mother would miss him so much she'd bring video games and cupcakes. Brittany would be squirming with jealousy.

But his father wasn't acting as if he wanted to get a place with

Josh. His father was scuttling around like a tortured man. He didn't want to be cheated on and he didn't want a bachelor pad with or without his son because he didn't want a divorce.

"Come on. Put those skates on and get out here," Austin called, breaking Josh out of his daydream. Just then Roger plopped down next to him on the bench. Josh scooted away. Did he notice? Had he just hurt his feelings? Roger didn't seem to notice. He picked up the skate closest to him and began loosening the laces, as if preparing it. He handed it to Josh. Josh pointed at Roger.

"You skate?" Roger shook his head. He offered the skate again to Josh.

"I suck," Josh said. Roger grinned. His teeth were nicer than Josh expected.

"Fun," Roger said. His voice was throaty, as if it had been packed away in a dusty attic for a dozen years.

"You'll have all the fun," Josh said. "Watching me fall on my ass."

Roger laughed. Austin stopped skating and stared. Josh shook his head and tore off his boot, then put on the skate. Roger was still laughing.

"If you're going, Big Dude, then so am I," Harrison said, striding across the lawn. Brittany and Austin cheered. Harrison headed to the barn for a pair of skates. Josh had just finished lacing his left skate and was putting on the right when his great-grandmother came tearing out of the house. She had some speed on her for an old lady. She was wearing a nightdress and running in the freezing cold. Old people were crazy. They could do whatever they wanted and get away with it. She could shout out mean things, too, and nobody sent her to her room. His great-grandmother could drink whatever she wanted, whenever she wanted, even for breakfast. It might not be so bad getting old.

"Yvette?" Austin said. "Are you okay?" Breathless, she ran to Roger, stood over him, staring. Roger stopped laughing and stared back. Yvette placed her hands on Roger's face.

"You laughed," she said. "I saw you from the window. You

were laughing." Tears dripped down his grandmother's face. Roger just stared.

"You didn't know he could laugh?" Josh said.

"Yvette, you're going to freeze to death," Austin said.

"Don't take your work home with you," Yvette called to Austin. Josh felt his face flame red. He didn't dare look at Austin. If Austin said anything to anyone he was going to kick his ass.

"I laughed," Roger said. Yvette started to cry harder. God, these people were weird. It made him think of his grandma Carla. She was old, too, but she wasn't crazy. Just fun. He wished she were here instead of in Cuba. Maybe he'd call her. Maybe she would know how to get her daughter to stop cheating on her husband. Now that would be a Christmas miracle. Josh wobbled out to the pond and stepped onto the ice. Too bad it wasn't fall. If it was fall, the ice would crack, and maybe he would fall through. He could definitely see himself going under and never coming back up. They'd be so sorry. They would all be so sorry.

When the Garland Girls arrived at the property, Hope was surprised to see Austin and Harrison skating with the kids. She wanted to join them.

"No," Faith said before they'd even gotten out of the car. "This is a perfect time to sneak into the hot tub."

"Maybe another time," Hope said.

"Not a chance," Faith said. "You're the one always insisting that the three of us do things together, so you're getting in that hot tub and drinking one of your own cocktails whether you like it or not."

"Shazam!" Joy said.

"I'm not making cocktails before noon," Hope said.

"Then don't," Faith said. "But you're getting in that hot tub if we have to wrestle you in."

"Fine," Hope said. "But you'd better take the blame if Brittany is upset."

"I'll get the booze," Joy said. "You guys don't have swimsuits with you, do you?"

"No," Faith said. "Bra and panties, underneath winter coat. Once the hot tub is cooking we'll slip our coats off and get in. We'll make sure we have enough towels, and when we're done we'll just race for the house." Faith and Joy giggled. Hope wanted to skate and she definitely didn't want to drink, but she also didn't want to leave Joy and Faith alone to bond and share deep secrets without her. That's why twenty or so minutes later she was actually slipping into the hot tub in her bra and panties. The hot water enveloped her, but every inch of skin exposed to the cold tingled. Hope soon wished she'd made cocktails. Joy held up a bottle of whiskey, drank, and passed it to Faith. Faith drank and passed it to Hope.

"We have to stay in here until that bottle is gone!" Joy exclaimed.

Hope groaned and took the tiniest sip possible. "Again," Faith said. The two of them, little pushers. Hope was saved by Joy grabbing the bottle out of her hands.

"So," Joy said, turning to Faith after the bottle had gone around twice. "Who is he?"

Faith sank deeper into the hot tub. "What?"

"You can't tell us you're having an affair and not give us details," Joy said. "Who is he?"

"Just someone," Faith said.

"Don't you trust us?" Joy said.

"Are you in love?" Hope said.

Faith's face opened up. "I think I am," she said. "Oh, I really am." Then, she started to cry. "How can I do this? How can I destroy my husband? My kids?"

"Is it too late?" Hope said. "Can you make things work?"

Faith slowly shook her head. "No, even if it weren't for Charlie I would leave Stephen. He's so great. Just not great for me."

"And Charlie is?" Hope asked.

"Oh yes. Charlie is a total match for me."

"Who is Charlie?" Joy pressed.

"We met at a book club," Faith said. "Can you imagine?"

"Were you reading *Fifty Shades of Grey*?" Joy asked.

"Of course not," Faith said. "We were reading something so-phisticated and literary."

"You can't even remember what it was, can you?" Hope asked.

Faith laughed. "I can't remember a word of it, or what it's called. Except that I hated it and Charlie loved it."

"How long have you been seeing him?" Joy asked.

"Four months," Faith said. "And we're still in the honey-moon phase."

"Do you have a picture?" Hope asked.

"In my phone," Faith said. "I'll show you when we're not in a hot tub. Although I think I should tell you—"

"MOM!" Brittany was racing across the lawn toward them.

"We've been spotted," Hope said, ducking down. "Act sober."

"Act sober," Joy mimicked.

"Act sober," Faith said. They dissolved into laughter again. The snow was coming down harder now. Brittany was a blur running toward them.

"It's snowing!" Joy cried out, her face turned to the sky.

"Mom?" Brittany said, coming to a stop near the deck and looking up at them.

"Baby!" Faith said.

"Hey, kiddo," Hope said. "You went skating, huh?"

"Are you guys drunk?" Brittany said.

"We're just terrible actors," Joy said. She and Faith dissolved into giggles.

"I'm not," Hope said. *Only slightly tipsy.*

"We are, honey," Faith said. "We are so drunk." She splashed Joy and Joy splashed back.

Hope got out of the tub. God, it was like ice! She reached for a towel and hurriedly dried herself. She turned to grab her coat. Austin was standing next to Brittany staring up at her. "Oh!" Hope said. "I didn't know you were there." She hurriedly put on her coat as Joy and Faith cackled behind her. Austin's mouth was hanging open.

"She's looking good, don't you think?" Faith said.

"She's hot," Joy said. "Don't you think, Austin?"

"Stop it!" Hope's face flamed.

"Are they drunk?" Austin said.

"We are so drunk," Joy said. Hope shoved on her boots, hat, and scarf and jumped off the deck. She headed for the house.

"Are we just going to leave them there?" Brittany asked.

"It's a heck of a lot nicer than what I'd like to do to them," Hope said.

CHAPTER 24

Josh couldn't believe his mother and Aunt Joy were acting so silly. Like children with their squealing and giggling and inside jokes. And yet, it gave him the exact opportunity he was looking for. She'd left her cell phone in the house, on her bed. Josh had passed by the room several times now and he was pretty sure no one was paying any attention. Hope was making dinner; the smell of roast chicken filled the air. Brittany and Austin were building a snowman right by the window. Roger was watching them. Granny was on the sofa wrapped in blankets, drinking tea—although Josh had seen her pour whiskey into it—and Harrison was playing solitaire. And just as he had entered his mother's room and was about to grab her phone, she and Joy came whooping through the front door. He didn't want to risk taking it now. He hurried out of the room, down the stairs, and grabbed his coat from the mudroom. He was going to be wherever his mother was not as often as he could. At least until his dad could straighten this mess out. And that wasn't going to happen until he got Charlie's number off the phone. For now he was going to video call his grandmother in Florida. Maybe they hadn't headed off for Cuba yet. He took his iPad past the dorky snowman and to the side of the house. Roger was only a few feet away putting up more Christmas decorations. He waved at Josh, but then went back to minding his own business. Josh pulled up the info for Grandma Carla and tried to reach her.

"Joshua!" He heard Grandma Carla's voice first and watched as her face appeared on the screen. She looked tanned and smiling. He wanted to live with her.

"Hi, Grandma," he said. "Mom is drunk."

"Good for her," his grandmother said with a wink. She held up a frozen drink. "I'm working on it." *God, my family is weird.* "Is it snowing there?" she asked, leaning forward. She was in a swimsuit, on a sailboat.

"Are you in Cuba?" he asked, squinting.

"No, that didn't work out. God, this society and their rules. Fernando needing ID and a permanent address to travel. The Bohemian spirit is disappearing. This planet belongs to all of us. Mark my words, there's going to be a revolution. We'll go to Cuba next year, Joshie; you'll come too."

"Can I drink rum?"

"Of course. It'll put hair on your chest."

"Can I live with you?"

Grandma Carla didn't answer the question. Instead, she leaned forward as if trying to enter the screen. "Is that snow I see behind you?"

"Yeah," he said. "There's a ton of it."

"God bless," she said.

"I'd rather live with you. In Florida. Can I?"

"Wouldn't your parents miss you?" Carla was still leaning close to the screen.

Josh shrugged.

"Well, show me this ski lodge." Josh began to pan the camera around to the house.

"Yvette in a place like that," Grandma Carla said.

"They have twenty acres here," Josh said.

"How much will the girls sell it for?"

"I dunno," Josh said.

"Has to be worth a fortune. Has the witch said anything bad about me?"

"Granny?"

"Is that what you call her?"

Josh shrugged. "That's what Mom and Joy call her."

"She's not your grandmother. Not in the real sense of the word."

"Okay."

"You can tell me. Has she said anything nasty about me?"

"I don't know," Josh said. "I don't get to hear everything."

"Have you heard how much the place is worth? Maybe we can buy a yacht and we can all sail to Cuba next year."

"Joy wants to buy a coffee shop in Seattle across from another coffee shop."

"Of course she does."

"She has a new boyfriend. He's black. I like him."

"Did Granny freak out? She always was a . . ." She stopped, then shook her head. "Never mind. What's his name?"

"Harrison."

"I'm happy for her. I hope she doesn't hurt him."

"He's bigger than she is," Josh said.

His grandmother laughed. "I meant break his heart, darling. Joy goes through men like . . ." She stopped again. "How old are you again, Joshua?"

"Fifteen."

"Ah. Well, you're old enough then, aren't you?"

"I guess."

"I would love to talk to Granny," his grandmother said. "I bet she'd keel over this instant if you showed her my face on-screen." Grandma Carla sat back and lit a cigarette, as if really waiting for Josh to show Granny his iPad.

Josh frowned. He really didn't want to make Granny keel over. "I think she's taking a nap," he said.

Carla flicked her cigarette and shrugged. "Well, tell her I say hello at least. We can start small."

"Sure."

"Twenty acres, and a ski lodge. Good Lord, I never would have guessed. She married rich. Funny. She hated me for marrying her son for love."

"I think they have to share the place," Josh said.

"Share? Share with who?"

Josh panned the camera over to Roger. "Roger. He works here." He brought the camera back to his face. "Do you want me to go inside and show you how drunk Mom is?"

"Just a minute," his grandmother said. She put her drink down, crushed out her cigarette, removed her sunglasses, and unfolded her legs until her bare feet were on the floor of the sailboat. She moved her face closer to the screen.

Josh instinctively pushed the iPad back. "What's wrong?"

"Dear heart. Will you bring the camera closer to that man?"

"Roger?"

"Roger," his grandmother said. "Yes. Will you bring the camera closer to Roger?"

Josh glanced up. Roger was already looking at him. Why would his grandmother want to see him? "He's kind of creepy," Josh said. "I heard Granny say he was in a car accident."

"When?"

Josh shrugged. "I think a long time ago. I was listening, but I didn't hear everything."

"He said his name was Roger?"

"Granny said. He doesn't talk much."

"He lives in the house?"

"No, in a cabin. I've never gone in it."

"What has he said?"

Why was she so interested? Maybe she didn't want him around her grandchildren if he was creepy. "I think he hurt his brain. He doesn't talk much. I don't want to get closer."

"He's got a beard, and a cap, and sunglasses," his grandmother said.

"So?" Josh said.

"Sorry. I'm just . . ." His grandmother was clasping her hands together, staring at the screen. "Pan over again, like you're showing me the scenery."

Josh sighed, then did as she asked. Roger turned his face away, so he zoomed in on the back of him. Just then, Roger turned his head toward the phone. That ought to give her a good look. After a few seconds Josh turned around and pretended to pan the rest of the place. When he turned to see his grandmother again, he was surprised to see tears spilling out of her eyes.

"Grandma Carla? What's the matter?"

"Are they all drunk?" she said.

"Aunt Hope doesn't seem like she's drunk. She's making dinner."

"I need to talk to her," his grandmother said. "Right away." He didn't even get a chance to tell her that his mom was cheating on his dad. What was the big deal about Roger? He was the one who called his grandmother, and she didn't even want to talk to him.

"Okay," Josh said. "I'll take you inside." Josh stepped inside. Granny scolded him and told him to come in through the front entrance so he could take off his boots. He thought he heard his grandmother call her a witch. "Where's Aunt Hope?" he said, glancing at the empty kitchen.

"She's taking a shower," Granny said. "Now go around front." Josh closed the door and headed around to the front.

"Aunt Hope is in the shower," he said.

"Tell her to call me the minute she's out," his grandmother said. "Tell her it's urgent."

"Okay," he said. "Well, nice talking to you."

"Let me talk to Granny."

Uh-oh. What had he done? Grandma Carla sounded strange. Was she mad?

"Okay, bye," Josh said, then pushed END. Oh boy. He made her cry. Then he made her mad. And then he hung up. He'd pretend it was an accident next time he talked to her. He shut off his iPad in case she tried to call back. Why was he always messing things up? It wasn't really his fault, though. It was Roger. Roger made her cry. Why would Roger make her cry? Did she feel sorry for him for being brain-damaged? Someone else was always getting the attention around here.

By the time Hope showered and dressed and came down for dinner, Faith and Joy were passed out on the sofa, snoring like a couple of old men. Brittany was soon at Hope's side, helping her set the table. Faith had found some holiday-themed plates in the china cabinet and was using ones with snowmen on them.

"I can't believe you went sledding without me," Brittany said. She sounded truly hurt. Hope forgot how painful everything could be when you were a kid.

"Your mom wanted to make sure it was safe first," Hope said. That sounded way better than *Your mom was so loaded we could have talked her into anything.*

"Austin skated with me," Brittany said.

"Was it fun?"

"It was so much fun," Brittany said, jumping up and down.

"Sounds wonderful. I can't wait to skate with you."

"Austin is a really good skater."

Hope smiled, but she didn't want to start thinking about Austin, and she definitely wasn't going to replay the look she saw on his face when he saw her in her wet bra and panties; she'd save that for tonight when she was alone and could daydream. "Did Josh skate?"

"He just slumped on the bench at first, but then Roger got him to skate."

"Roger got him to skate?"

"And he laughed."

"Josh?"

"Roger. And Granny came running out of the house because she heard Roger laughing."

"Oh." Sounded like a nice enough afternoon. "Where is Josh?"

"It wasn't my turn to babysit him," Brittany said.

218 • *Mary Carter*

"Funny," Hope said. They finished setting the table. Brittany counted the plates.

"Who all is coming?"

"You, me, Josh."

"That's three."

"Granny, Faith, Joy."

"Six. Harrison is seven."

"And Austin and Roger."

"Nine," Brittany said, confirming the number. She turned her head to the window. "You think he'll come inside?"

Hope didn't have to ask who she meant. "I'm hoping he will."

"I like him too. He's nice. A little weird. But nice."

"Do you want to go ask him if he'll come in for dinner?"

Brittany's eyes widened. "Me?"

"If you feel comfortable. And can you find your brother while you're at it?"

"It's snowing and cold out there."

Hope laughed. "I'll go with you."

"Okay."

Harrison was watching television in between the snoring women. Hope asked him to keep an eye on the oven; then she and Brittany bundled up. Hopefully Austin would answer his cell phone and all they would have to do was find Roger and Josh.

"It's really coming down," Hope said the minute they stepped outside. She turned to Brittany. "Why don't you go back in, sweetie. I didn't realize it was this bad." Brittany looped her arm in Hope's.

"I want to stay with you."

"I don't want you to get frostbite."

"I don't want *you* to get frostbite."

"I'll be quick." She turned Brittany around and gently shoved her toward the door. "We'll go sledding all day when this clears up. I promise."

"If you're not back in twenty minutes I'm coming back out," Brittany said.

"I'm just going to find Roger and Josh," Hope said.

"Twenty minutes," Brittany said.

"Yes, ma'am. Put on Christmas carols and see if you wake up the sleeping beauties," Hope said. She pulled her hood tighter and sank into the snow. It almost covered her entire boot, at least a foot already. She hadn't been paying attention to the weather, and wondered how much they were in for. It was starting to get dark, and the wind was whistling through the trees something fierce. It was stunning, and sharp, and bitter, and beautiful.

"Josh?" she called. "Joshua?" She headed for the barn. Just beyond it was Roger's cabin. She thought about calling Austin first, but that would mean taking her cell phone out of her pocket and taking her gloves off to dial. Roger had plugged in the tree, and the mechanical creatures, and although the falling snow had rendered all the lights a bit fuzzy, Hope felt a surge of Christmas spirit. Maybe that's what they all needed, to get snowed in for a few days and work out their differences. Or maybe they'd kill one another and their bodies wouldn't be discovered until a spring thaw.

"Josh?" she yelled into the wind. "It's Hope. Come in for dinner." She stopped. Snow swirled all around. "Roger? Roger, are you out here?" His cabin was in view now, but she didn't see any lights on. Did he sit in there in the dark? Surely it was too early for bed.

"Hope?" She turned at the sound of Austin's voice to find him running toward her. "It's a blizzard. What are you doing?"

"Josh is out here. And I wanted to invite Roger to dinner."

"We'd better find Josh," Austin said. He sounded worried. Was the storm worse than Hope thought? She called his name again, and then Austin's voice shouted it out.

"You sound really worried," Hope said. "Is the weather that dangerous?"

"Not yet," Austin said. "But it's a big piece of property. Easy to get lost in the woods."

"Josh really isn't the type to wander away," Hope said.

"Are you sure he's not in the house?"

"I didn't look under beds, but pretty sure."

"We can go to Roger's cabin. He knows these woods better than anyone."

"I was going to call you next, invite you to dinner," Hope said as they trudged toward Roger's cabin.

"There's no light on," Hope said. "Where could he be?"

"The door is ajar," Austin said. Hope squinted and sure enough she could see the door to Roger's cabin was indeed open a few inches.

CHAPTER 25

Hope and Austin stood in front of the cabin door. "I hope Josh isn't sneaking around in there," Hope said.

"Roger?" Austin called. "Are you in there?"

"Josh?" Hope called.

Austin stepped closest to the doorway and snuck his hand around. A few seconds later the cabin was lit up. Once Hope's eyes adjusted she could see into a small kitchen with a card table. Josh was standing by the fridge. He'd whirled around and was staring at them with a stricken look plastered on his face.

"Josh!" Hope said. "What are you doing in here?" The cabin was sparse. A rocking chair was positioned by a small wood-burning stove, a ratty sofa faced the windows, and a coffee table bridged the gap between the two. Dishes were piled in the sink. Hope wondered if Yvette was the one who usually washed them. Other than that there was no personality to the cabin. No photographs on the fridge, no knickknacks that Hope could see, no bookshelf filled with books. It made her a little sad. Who was Roger? What was it like to be him?

"Is Roger here?" Austin said. Josh shook his head no. "This is private property, let's go." Josh skittered toward them and the minute he was out the door, Austin switched off the light. "Was the door open like this?" Austin said.

"Yes," Josh said. "I swear."

"We can't just leave it open," Austin said. He closed it.

"Do you think he's in there?" Hope said.

"He's not," Josh said. "He's in the barn."

"Why would he leave the door open?" Hope said.

"I think he wanted me to go in and look around," Josh said.

"Why would he want you to do that?"

"How should I know?" Josh snapped.

Hope stopped, as she realized she sounded like her sister when she squabbled with him. She was supposed to be the fun aunt. "Dinner's ready. Let's get inside."

Josh shrugged, then shoved his hands into his pockets and headed for the house. "Grandma wants you to call her," he said.

"Carla?" Hope said.

"I don't have to call her that," Josh said.

"When did you talk to her?"

"I dunno. A little bit ago. She only wanted to talk to you. Said it was urgent."

"Is she stuck in Cuba? She'd drive Castro to distraction." Hope laughed.

"They didn't go to Cuba."

"Oh," Hope said. "Did she say why?"

"Some Bohemian disappeared."

"What?"

"And there's going to be a revolution."

"Okay." Her mother was a piece of work. What was she up to now? "I take it she was drinking?" *Or was she smoking something?*

Josh shrugged. "She wants you to call her."

"And we're talking about?" Austin said.

"My mother."

"You call your mother Carla?"

"Says it all, doesn't it?"

"I think she was freaked out by Roger," Josh said. "That's why I was looking in his cabin."

"Why? What did you tell her about Roger?"

"I told her we might have to share the property with him."

"Ah," Hope said. "Mystery solved." She shook her head. Her mother was like Joy when it came to wanting something for nothing.

"She wants to buy a yacht so we can all sail to Cuba for Christmas next year."

"Of course she does." They were passing the barn. Hope stopped.

"You said Roger is in the barn?"

"Are you going to tell him?" There was a tinge of panic in Josh's voice.

"I'm going to invite him to dinner."

"But are you going to tell him?"

"Did you take anything?"

"No."

"Are you ever going to do that again?"

"No."

"Then I won't tell him."

"Thank you."

"He deserves his privacy. And Grandma had no right saying anything about him at all."

"She didn't say anything. Not really."

"Why don't you two go to the house. I'll look for Roger in the barn."

"We're in this together," Austin said. "We'll all have a quick peek."

"Why is he in the barn anyway?" Josh asked.

Hope entered the barn. There was a single bulb hanging from the ceiling emitting a soft glow. Her eyes took in bales of hay lining the dirt floor, the wooden planks making up the walls, the stalls, a shovel propped in a corner, and several parked tractors. There was a hayloft with more hay. So far no sign of Roger.

"Were there ever animals in here?" Hope asked.

"Oh yes," Austin said. "Rupert kept some of the horses here. The ones that pulled the sleighs in town."

"What happened to them?"

"He arranged for them to be adopted by another horse farmer," Austin said. "He knew Yvette wouldn't be able to handle them."

"He sounds like he really loved her," Hope said.

"I think he had a hard life growing up. His first wife died in a car accident. I think he felt Yvette was a kindred soul."

Because her only son died in a car accident. "It must be tough having your job," Hope said. "You must hear a ton of sad stories."

"I do," Austin said. "I hear a lot of stories."

"But you're not allowed to tell us because they're all private, right?" Josh asked.

"Right," Austin said. "They're all private. Anybody can call anytime and not worry."

Suddenly a bell jingled. The three of them halted.

"What was that?" Josh asked.

"Santa Claus?" Hope said.

"Funny," Josh said.

Austin looked up at the ceiling and laughed. Hope looked up to see what was so funny. Mistletoe hung directly above them.

"What's that?" Josh said. Austin and Hope locked eyes. A jolt of electricity ran through her. He gave a little smile.

"Somebody is playing matchmaker," he said. Hope had a sudden and awful thought. She wished Josh wasn't right behind them. Would they have kissed if he wasn't?

"Roger," Hope said, calling out to the dark recesses of the barn. "I want you to come into the house for dinner. Please?" Silence greeted them. "Ring the bell if you'll come," she added. Again, silence.

"It's cold," Austin said. "Let's get inside."

"Do you want me to bring you a plate then? Bring it to your cabin?" Hope asked. A second later came the ring of the bell. Hope smiled. At least he wanted to eat. They exited the barn.

"Race you to the house," Austin said to Josh. Josh sprinted ahead. Austin started forward, then suddenly whirled around and latched his arm around Hope's waist. He pulled her into him and kissed her. It was a passionate kiss, and it didn't take long before she was kissing him back. Warmth shot through her entire body. When he let go, they were both out of breath.

"It's bad luck to ignore mistletoe," he said with a wolfish grin. Then before she could reply he took off across the snow, trying to beat Josh to the house.

CHAPTER 26

Dinner began as a quiet affair. In addition to the roast chicken they had mashed sweet potatoes and a green bean casserole. They didn't fight or burn anything and Harrison, who was thrilled to discover Yvette owned a bread maker, impressed all of them with homemade bread. Turns out he had gone to culinary school and hoped to open his own restaurant someday. The bread practically melted in your mouth. "You should sell loaves of this at the coffee shop," Faith said, practically humming into the bread. "I'd drive to Seattle for this." Everyone was at the table on time except for one. Hope eyed the empty place setting, wishing Roger had changed his mind and joined them. She'd bring him a plate as soon as they were done.

"I can't remember the last time this table was filled with people," Yvette said, looking them each in the eye as if thanking them. The lights of the Christmas tree were on and Bing Crosby was playing in the background.

"How did you and Rupert meet?" Hope asked. She was still thinking about that kiss with Austin. And trying not to look at him across the table. Every time she even thought about him, a smile threatened to break out. She watched as Yvette's face relaxed and a smile came upon her face as well.

"In a pub downtown," she said. "Isn't that cliché?"

"Totally," Joy said.

"Did he have some smooth moves?" Harrison teased.

"He had a horse and carriage outfit, a sledding outfit, and a log house on twenty acres," Yvette said.

"Those are some smooth moves all right," Harrison said with a wink.

"Tell us more about his Christmas antics," Hope said.

"What antics?" Brittany said.

"Skating, a light show, caroling, roasting marshmallows over the fire pit. You name it, he did it," Yvette said. The more she spoke, the younger she appeared. A smile even slipped out before sneaking back in.

"Did you enjoy it?" Faith asked.

"I never thought I'd like strangers crawling all over the property," Yvette said. "But Rupert loved it so much that, yes, I'd have to say eventually it brought me joy too."

"Dad would have loved him," Faith said.

"Oh, he did," Yvette said.

Hope stared at Yvette, waiting to see if she understood what she just said. Was she starting to go senile?

Faith cleared her throat. "Dad never met Rupert," she said softly.

Yvette frowned. "Is that right?" she said.

"He passed away long before you two ever met," Faith said.

"I'm on a lot of medications," Yvette said.

"It's okay," Hope said. "I bet you've imagined them meeting a thousand times. And Dad definitely would have loved anyone who was just as crazy about Christmas as he was."

Yvette nodded, and her fork shook as she brought it up to her mouth. She'd probably be more coherent if she stopped drinking the whiskey, but if Hope were faced with dying by the new year she'd probably be doing the same.

Yvette was coming around to the idea of Christmas, and she even lit up when she mentioned the celebrations from when

Rupert was alive. They should have one more Christmas like that. For Yvette. They should have at least three days that the property was open to the public again. They could come and skate, and sing, and roast chestnuts in the fire pit, and enjoy all the lights and decorations. Hope felt herself smiling as she imagined it. She looked up to find Austin staring at her, and soon he raised an eyebrow. He wanted to know what was making her smile. She gave a little nod and hoped he'd interpret it as *I'll tell you later.*

"Why did you set a place for Roger when he said he wasn't coming?" Joy asked, looking at Yvette.

"I'm the one who set his place at the table," Hope said. "I was hoping he'd change his mind."

"It's not good to force him," Yvette said.

Hope didn't want an argument. "I wasn't," she said. "Just encouraging."

"I'm surprised you didn't set a place for Mr. Jingles," Faith said.

"Poor guy," Hope said. "I'll have to bring him some scraps when I take Roger his plate."

"Have you ever considered putting Roger in an assisted care facility?" Joy asked. Hope couldn't believe what she'd just heard. Joy didn't regularly use phrases like *assisted care facility*. That meant she'd been talking to someone. Of course she had. She still wanted nothing more than to sell the property.

Yvette's face immediately hardened. Joy might be scheming, but she wasn't thinking ahead on this one.

"You won't be inheriting any of this property," Yvette said.

"Because I asked a question?" Joy's mouth hung open.

"I made my wishes very clear," Yvette said. "I'm not even in the ground and you're trying to defy them."

"It was a simple question. We're not nurses. I only want to know if you've considered other places for Roger."

"This is his home," Yvette said. "It's where he will stay."

"Why don't you just leave the entire place to him then?" Joy said.

"What are you doing?" Faith asked Joy.

"Order in the court," Joy said to Harrison.

"Excuse me?" Faith said.

"You're like a judge, always trying to direct us," Joy said.

"No fighting," Josh said.

"Josh is right," Hope said. "Let's just eat. Try to enjoy the meal. You know. Like normal people."

"It was a mistake inviting you girls here," Yvette said.

"What?" Hope said. That hurt. And here she'd almost started warming up to Yvette. Was starting to like her even.

Yvette continued. "If it weren't for Roger you wouldn't still be here."

"Here we go with Roger again," Joy said.

"I have an idea," Hope said.

"I bet it's good," Brittany said. Her eyes lit up. Why couldn't everyone be that sweet?

Hope threw Brittany an appreciative smile before continuing. "We've all been tense. Very Scrooge-like around here. Except for the kids." She smiled at them again. Josh hadn't exactly been cheery, but she didn't want to single him out.

"What are you driving at?" Faith said. Faith didn't like any idea that wasn't hers.

"Christmas is about giving. It's about love and sharing. Let's pay tribute to Dad, and Rupert."

"How?" Yvette said.

"Why?" Joy said under her breath.

"What did we talk about?" Harrison said to Joy. "No picking fights until after we finish dessert."

"What is this brilliant idea?" Faith asked.

"I think we should open the property up to the public for Christmas again."

"Yeah, right," Joy said.

"I mean it," Hope said. "Skating, Christmas lights, hot cocoa, Christmas carols. We could invite the whole town!" She looked around the table. Most mouths were open. "Like it used to be," she added. "It's a shame to have all those decorations on the lawn and use up all that electricity and not share the joy." *Besides, none of you appreciate it anyway.* One by one those at the table glanced at Yvette to see her reaction.

"It wouldn't be the same without Rupert," Yvette said.

"You're right," Hope said. "It would be different. But we'd all be giving back. And since none of us seem capable of just enjoying each other's company—why wouldn't we do it?"

"I think it's a great idea," Austin said. "In fact a lot of my coworkers could use an evening skate. We've been trying to think of a place to celebrate. Downtown gets way too crowded."

"That's perfect!" Hope said. "We'll invite your coworkers and the people who live here year-round and work at the shops. Give them a break from the tourists too."

"We're tourists," Faith said.

"Skating, Christmas carolers, roasting chestnuts," Hope said. "It could be so sweet. We can put up even more decorations and start a toy drive for children in need."

"Can we, Mom?" Brittany said.

Faith pushed back her plate. Hope noticed that she'd left a bit of everything except for the vegetables. Those were all gone. She glanced at her own plate. She hadn't touched the veggies. It was like all the food had fallen off a cliff, leaving the veggies stranded on a porcelain deserted island. She jabbed her fork into the greens. *Coming to save you,* she thought to herself as she started to force them in. She wasn't sure if it was her, or Faith, but one of them was not normal. Totally not normal.

"Are we going to have the town over for Christmas, Mom?" Brittany piped up again.

"I don't have any say in this," Faith said.

Yvette leaned forward. "If we're going to do this, then you all have to agree."

Faith turned to her. "A few days ago you didn't even want to celebrate Christmas. Are you really considering this?"

"I like the idea of my last Christmas being in tribute to Rupert," Yvette said. "I think that would be a nice way to go out."

Faith shrugged. Joy shrugged.

"It's settled then," Hope said.

"I can start spreading the word," Austin said. "I know the right folks in town."

"This is so exciting," Hope said.

Josh got up from the table. "Where are you going?" Faith said.

"I'm calling Dad," Josh said. "If the whole town is coming for Christmas, then he is too."

"Pass the wine," Faith said.

"It's gone," Joy said.

"Pass the whiskey," Faith said.

"Granny has it," Joy said. The girls all looked at their grandmother.

"Blood only goes so far," Yvette said.

Hope and Austin headed for Roger's cabin with a plate piled with food. "That was a great idea," Austin said. "I think Yvette really liked it."

"My sisters didn't seem too keen," Hope said.

"They'll come around. I truly think that when you start doing for others, you can't help but open up, become a happier person."

"Now that would be a Christmas miracle," Hope said.

"Do you think Josh's father will come here for Christmas?"

"I don't think so. They're actually having some issues. Waiting until after the holiday to resolve them."

"I thought as much." Austin stopped. "Listen. I'm in a bit of a pickle here."

"What is it?"

"I just think it might be a good idea if Josh's father comes for Christmas. It might cheer him up."

Hope frowned. "That's your pickle?"

"Yes, it's a pickle because it's none of my business. But he seems troubled."

"And you work with troubled people so you would know," Hope said.

"Exactly," Austin said. "I think he could use some support."

"I'll talk to Faith."

"Thank you." He seemed to hesitate.

"Is there more?"

"Would you mind not mentioning me when you have that conversation with Faith?"

Hope laughed. "Afraid of her, are you?"

Austin laughed and nodded. "Terrified."

"Mum's the word."

"Thank you."

He seemed genuinely relieved. In some ways he reminded Hope of a grown-up male version of Brittany. There didn't seem to be a mean bone in his body. She couldn't help thinking that if she had stayed with Michael and he were here with her that he wouldn't have cared less about inviting the town for Christmas. In fact he probably would have been annoyed. If it wasn't for him, or about him, he wasn't interested. Hope would take Austin any day. "Are you always more concerned about other people than you are yourself?"

Austin smiled. "It gets boring thinking of yourself all the time."

"Don't I know it," Hope said. They were a few feet from the cabin. The lights were on inside. Mr. Jingles was in the cabin curled up at Roger's feet by the sofa. "So that's where he's been all the time," Hope said. Roger bent down and patted Mr. Jingles on the head.

"Maybe that's the reason for his improvement," Austin said. "Canine therapy."

"If I lived here, I'd have a dozen dogs running around," Hope said. "Don't repeat that to Faith."

Austin laughed. Then stopped. "Are you seriously considering living here?" His voice was lower, huskier. He sounded like he loved the idea.

"I am," Hope said. "But I don't think my sisters are going to let that happen."

"Let me know if there's anything I can do," Austin said. He held her gaze. Her stomach gave a flip. They were at the door of the cabin. Mr. Jingles barked and made a beeline for the door.

"He's switched sides already," Hope said. She knocked. Soon

the door opened. Roger took the plate, gave her a nod, and then closed the door. Hope didn't even have a chance to say anything. A few seconds later the curtain on the window closest to the door came down. Then the other window. They had been officially sealed out.

"At least he took the plate," Austin said. They began to walk back to the house.

"How would you like to go into town with me tomorrow?"

"To start planning the Christmas extravaganza?"

"If that's more agreeable than a date, absolutely." He kept a smile on his face as he held eye contact. She felt her cheeks heat up.

"Are they mutually exclusive?" she asked.

"Not at all," he said, linking arms with her as they walked. "I love to mix romance with planning extravaganzas."

The next day passed quickly with a doctor's appointment for Yvette in the morning, skating on the pond with Brittany in the afternoon, and starting a to-do list for Christmas. Before Hope knew it, evening was nearly upon them and it was time for her date with Austin. The best thing about it is she didn't even have to get ready. He said to dress casual, and so all she did was slip on her coat and jump into his truck when he stopped to pick her up. She told him to hurry, hoping no one else would even catch on that she was with Austin. The first thing they did was to go on a horse and carriage ride through the snow. It was magical. The horse clopped through town at a reasonable pace, and from atop the carriage Hope could take in all the Christmas lights and decorations. Everything was aglow. Hope couldn't stop smiling.

"Can I ask you something?" Austin said.

"Of course."

"Do you regret breaking up with that guy?"

"Michael?" Austin nodded. "No, I'm relieved actually."

"Good." His hand slid across the red satin lining of the carriage and soon it was holding hers. "I just had to ask."

"My turn," Hope said.

"Uh-oh," Austin said.

"When was your last relationship?"

"It's been about three years."

"Does she still live around here?"

"No, she moved to New York."

"Is that why you broke up?"

"It is, actually. I don't think I ever want to leave here. I don't mean I won't travel. But this is home."

"And she didn't feel the same way?"

"She did for a while. And then she didn't. She wanted to go back to New York."

"And you never regret not going with her?"

"No, there were other reasons too. Who knows. Maybe I would have gone if she had been the right girl. But I know I made the right decision."

The carriage made a loop around to the starting place at the top of a small hill that overlooked the entire village. Hope gazed out at the shops and the mountains, and the backdrop of the trees. "I can see why you love it here," Hope said.

"It's magical, isn't it?"

"It is."

"This is where we get off," Austin said, doing just that and holding out his hand to help her off. "Would you like to go get some hot chocolate and a piece of pie?"

"That sounds fabulous."

"Good." He held out his arm and she linked hers, and soon they were walking to town.

"Do you think Joy has a point about Roger?" Hope asked.

"How do you mean?"

"What if he does need medical care in the future?"

"There would be options of course. The bigger question is— why in the world would she even ask this of you or anyone else?"

"I'm not really surprised. I think she's come to think of Roger as a son."

"But she shouldn't expect you to treat him like family."

"Are you still suspicious of Roger?" Hope asked. She found herself crossing her fingers, praying he would say no. For some reason she found herself growing extremely attached to Roger. Like her grandmother, she had an urge to make sure he had a place to live the rest of his life. Who in the world would want to throw an old man out of his modest cabin? Joy and Faith, for two, but that was another matter.

"Actually," Austin said, "I'm not. Whatever his story is he seems to genuinely care about Yvette. And you girls."

"I like him too. And it's not really based on facts. Just a feeling."

"You are a really special person, you know that." Austin stopped and put his arms around her waist, then pulled her closer.

"I'm just average," she said. "Just the girl next door."

"Literally," Austin said, and threw his head back with laughter. Hope realized what she said and then joined in. "I've always wanted to fall for the girl next door," Austin said. He leaned in and kissed her. They went to the Winter Biergarten for dessert. Austin excused himself to go to the restroom. Hope was still replaying the evening and smiling to herself, not caring at all that the waitress seemed to be ignoring her, when she felt her phone vibrating madly in her purse. By the time she retrieved it, she'd missed the call. She stared at the phone, dumbfounded. She had forty-two missed calls from her mother.

CHAPTER 27

Josh snuck around the back of the barn. He'd finally been able to snatch his mother's cell phone when she was in the shower, and Brittany and Granny and Joy were downstairs watching Harrison make a pie. Josh didn't see what was so exciting about that, but he was glad to be able to slip out unnoticed. Charlie. He now had his phone number. There was no picture next to his name. Josh scrolled through the most recent texts.

CHARLIE

I miss you

FAITH

Josh curled his fist. Disgusting! How could she do that to his dad? That's it, he wasn't celebrating Christmas. Not with her at least. His dad would fix it now. He had to. Josh didn't want to read any more. He would give his father Charlie's phone number. His hand shook as he called his father. Maybe he would sneak one of his mom's pills, just to calm his nerves.

"Hey, buddy," his dad said on the fourth ring. Relief washed through him.

"Dad," Josh said. "You have to come now."

"Too much estrogen over there?" his father joked.

"What?"

"Too many women?"

"I know about Charlie." Josh could feel the silence on the other end. "Dad?"

"Is she there?"

"Mom? She's in the shower."

"Is Charlie there?"

His father wasn't making sense. Why would Charlie be here? "Of course not."

"So your mother told you she was seeing someone?"

"You knew?" Josh demanded. Why wasn't he doing anything about it? Probably because he didn't have Charlie's phone number. Well, he would have it now.

His dad sighed. "I know," he said. "We were waiting until after the holidays to tell you. Does Brittany know?"

"Yes," Josh said.

"I'm sorry, buddy. I'm sorry you found out like this."

"How could you let Mom date another man?"

"You're talking about Charlie?" his dad asked.

Why did his dad sound so stupid? Was he drunk too? "Who else? Is she dating more than one other man?"

"No," his father said. "Charlie is the only one your mother is dating."

"Dad! Don't you care? You don't even sound like you care."

"I do care. But it's complicated."

"It's not complicated," Josh said. "It's simple. You have to do something. You have to fix it."

"You're missing key elements of the situation," his dad said. He still sounded so freaking calm.

Josh couldn't understand why he was so calm. Maybe his dad was taking Xanax too. Maybe they were the Xanax family. Josh was keyed up enough for all of them. "What key elements?"

"This is not a conversation we're going to have over the phone. Tell your mother to call me."

His dad sounded mad now. But he sounded mad that they knew, not that his mom was dating another man. "Are you dating someone else too?"

"No," his dad said. "I'm not."

"Dad. You have to come get me."

"You'll be home soon."

"I won't stay here. I won't."

"I thought it was a ski lodge with a skating rink."

"I don't care. All they do is fight. I want to come home."

"Just do your best to enjoy it."

"You're coming here for Christmas, right?"

"That wasn't the plan."

"I won't stay unless you say you're coming. I won't celebrate Christmas."

"What will you do?"

"I'll hitchhike back to California."

"That's not funny."

"I'm not joking."

"I'm going to call your mother."

"Why don't you call Charlie instead? I have his phone number."

"What are you doing with Charlie's phone number?"

"I snuck it off Mom's phone."

"Why are you behaving like this?"

"You don't want the number?"

"Josh. Sit tight. I'm going to work this out with your mom."

"You mean you're going to kick Charlie's ass?"

"Don't go anywhere. I'll talk to you soon." His dad clicked off. Josh couldn't believe how that just went down. His dad really didn't care. He didn't even ask for the phone number. Josh stared at the number. He'd wait and see what his dad said when he called him back. He'd wait. But if his dad didn't come around, then Josh was going to have to take care of this. He would call Charlie. He would tell Charlie to stay away from his mother. And he'd hitchhike back to California.

He shouldn't have called Austin. Now Austin thought he

wanted to kill himself and he was hanging around all the time. Maybe if he tried it would finally wake people up. All they did was argue. He hated it. Forget taking just one Xanax. You could probably kill yourself if you took enough of them. That's what he'd do. He'd take the rest of the bottle and float in the hot tub until he was gone.

Josh felt a nudge on his thigh. He turned around. Mr. Jingles was behind him, looking up at him, his big mouth open in a smile.

"Hey," Josh said. Mr. Jingles whined and then licked Josh's hand. Josh patted his big head. Mr. Jingles nuzzled up to him. "You want to go play in the woods?" Josh began to run, and Mr. Jingles followed. Josh would think about killing himself later. And maybe he wouldn't even do it. But he'd definitely start sneaking some of his mom's pills just to have some on hand. Just in case.

Brittany thought Granny was funny. Maybe she wasn't all sweet and cuddly, but neither was Carla. She'd rather have grannies with personality. But she got the feeling that this one really didn't know how to make a pie. And her hands shook every time she picked up a knife. So Brittany started to do all the cutting. Her mom never let her use sharp knives like this. But she was doing a good job, slicing the apples. She thought pumpkin pie or cherry pie was better for Christmas, but her granny had all these apples lying around and Harrison said he knew how to make the best apple pie. From the smells coming out of the oven, he was not lying.

Outside, Josh was sneaking around the barn. He was up to something. Brittany knew it had something to do with their mom. Brittany didn't want to believe her mom was seeing another man. She didn't even want to think about it. She was glad Josh was planning on doing something. She wondered what it was. She wondered if it was too late. Brittany was standing by the window looking outside when Granny came up to her.

"Did your mother ever tell you about your grandfather?" her granny asked.

"Who?"

"Thomas. Your mother's father. Did she ever tell you about him?"

Brittany shrugged. She didn't like the tone of Granny's voice. Like she was already mad. "I know he really liked Christmas," Brittany said.

"That he did," Yvette said.

"I love Christmas. Don't you?"

"I love that you love Christmas," her granny said.

"I want to get everyone a present for Christmas," Brittany said. "But I can't get to town by myself."

"We should draw names," Granny said.

"Draw names?"

"You'd go broke buying a present for everyone. We could put everyone's name in a hat and whoever you pick—that's who you buy a present for."

"Oh," Brittany said. She didn't like that idea at all. Of course she had to get a present for Mom, and Dad, and Josh. But she also wanted to get a present for Aunt Hope and Aunt Joy, and Granny. Maybe even Roger. A new cap for Roger. And Mr. Jingles. She was definitely going to get him a present. And Austin. And Harrison. Her grandmother's idea was never going to work. "I don't mind buying lots of presents," Brittany said. "I've been saving my allowance."

"That's very nice of you."

"Is there a Ninety-Nine Cent store in town?"

"No."

"I could make presents."

"We're making a pie right now." The tune of "Jingle Bells" rang out.

"That's for me!" Brittany reached for her phone on the counter. She saw Carla's face light up her screen. "It's my other granny."

"Don't answer it," Yvette said. But it was too late, Brittany had already accepted the call and said hello.

*   *   *

Hope replayed her date with Austin over and over in her head. Was this really happening or was it a dream? She was bursting to tell someone, but Faith had her own complex problems when it came to love, Joy was too preoccupied with herself, the kids were too young, and she didn't feel a close enough bond with Yvette to confide in her. Although the moment she came back into the house, Yvette gave her a look that fully conveyed she knew of the budding romance.

The scent of sweetly baking apple pie filled the air.

"You missed dinner," Brittany said. She and Yvette were seated at the kitchen island playing Scrabble. Joy and Harrison were curled up on the couch watching television. They were there so often Hope was starting to imagine them as an actual part of the furniture, like decorative throw pillows.

"Aunt Hope?" Brittany said.

"Yes, darling?"

"I'm going to make presents for everyone this year."

Hope went over and kissed Brittany on the top of her head. Her hair was so soft and this time smelled like peaches. She loved this girl to death. "That is so sweet of you. Homemade presents are the best."

"What do you want me to make you? A bookmark? Or a picture?"

"Surprise me," Hope said.

"Where is Faith and Josh?"

"Mom's in her room," Brittany said.

"And Josh?"

Yvette looked around, as if she'd never seen her living room before. "I thought he was here."

"Joy? Harrison?" Slowly, they turned their heads toward her. "Have either of you seen Josh?"

"I think he's out by the barn," Harrison said.

"This late? Again? In this weather?" Hope tried to relay a bit of scolding, but nobody took the bait.

"Grandma Carla is coming for Christmas," Brittany said. Hope's head jerked toward Brittany. Her face was still, not a twitch of a smile on her face. Hope's eyes flicked to Yvette, who locked on her.

"We should really have a discussion," Yvette said. "In fact, I need to discuss something with all three of you."

Hope had tried to call her mother back in the restaurant, but there had been no answer. Why on earth would she be coming here? Had something happened with her boyfriend? Did she get in trouble in Cuba? No. Josh said she didn't go to Cuba. She must have gotten into trouble in Florida. Or was she racing out here to try to claim part of the inheritance?

"It will have to wait," Hope said. "We have to locate Josh." She went to the bottom of the stairs and called out to her sister. Soon Faith appeared at the top of the stairs, face flushed.

"What do you want?"

"Is Josh in his room?"

"I don't think so. Why?"

"Would you please check?" Faith stared at Hope for a minute, then nodded. A few seconds later she was back.

"He's not in his room," Faith said. "What's wrong?"

"It appears he's been outside for a while," Hope said.

"This late?" Faith said. "Why didn't anyone tell me?"

Why didn't you notice? "No worries," Hope said. "I'm going to go look for him. Thought you might want to join in."

"I'll be two seconds." Faith flew into her room and came back out dressed and ready to go.

"When was the last time anyone saw him?" The panic in Faith's voice was clear. She tripped down the steps.

"Did he join you guys for dinner?" Hope went on one little date and everyone fell apart.

"No, he was moping. He went outside. But that was hours ago."

"Joy. Harrison. Boots and coats."

"I think he's with the dog," Joy said. "That thing follows him everywhere."

"Mr. Jingles is his name," Hope said. "And I'm relieved to hear that."

"Why?" Faith said. She was still in a near-panic.

"Because Mr. Jingles has an excellent sense of direction, and at his size he would definitely protect Josh against the elements—or whatever." Hope didn't want to make it sound too dire. Should she call Austin? No, they'd just parted ways, he said he was looking forward to his chair and book. She loved that about him. There was no need to involve him. They would probably find Josh out by the barn. Or even in the cabin with Roger. She hoped so, because it was freezing out there. One could definitely get frostbite if one weren't careful.

CHAPTER 28

They huddled together with flashlights and checked the barn first. Along the way they called out for Josh and Mr. Jingles. The barn door was closed tight and there were no lights from within.

"He wouldn't be hiding in a dark barn," Faith said.

"Let's check Roger's cabin," Hope said. *Where we found him and Mr. Jingles last time.* They headed for the cabin with Faith in the lead even though she had never been to Roger's cabin before. The moment the cabin became visible, they could see lights were on and smoke was coming out of the chimney.

"Someone's home," Faith said, breaking into a jog. "Josh?"

"Mr. Jingles?" Hope called out, just in case the dog was inside and could hear her. By the time Hope reached the cabin, Faith was already pounding on the door. The curtains were closed tight so it was impossible to see whether or not Josh was inside.

"Roger?" Faith called. "Please open the door."

Hope, Joy, and Harrison stood in a line behind Faith. Brittany latched on to Hope's hand. They shouldn't have included her in the search, Hope knew that now. What if something had happened to Josh? Brittany shouldn't be around to witness anything like that, not to mention it was freezing cold and pitch-black out here.

"If he's not here, we're dropping you off at the house," Hope said to Brittany.

"I want to stay with you," Brittany said. Just then the door opened. Roger stood in the doorway with Mr. Jingles at his side.

"Mr. Jingles," Brittany said. Roger patted Mr. Jingles on the head and smiled at Brittany.

"Is Josh here?" Faith asked.

"I'm fine," Josh called from inside.

"Oh, thank God," Faith said. She looked at Roger. "We didn't know where he was."

"He's fine," Roger said.

"Josh, let's go," Faith said. "I'm sorry he bothered you."

"Mother!" Josh said. Roger still hadn't opened the door more than a crack and Josh still hadn't appeared.

"He not bother me," Roger said. The sentence seemed labored as if it had taken a lot out of Roger to formulate it. She wondered if he would benefit from speech therapy. She'd never seen him go into town for groceries or a pint at a local tavern, let alone doctors' appointments. Had Yvette been enabling him all this time instead of really helping him?

"Roger said I can stay here," Josh said.

"Get your coat and let's go," Faith said. "We're all freezing out here." Roger looked stricken, as if he knew the polite thing to do was to invite them all in, but Hope could see the terror in his eyes at the possibility. Even letting Josh and a dog into his cabin was probably a huge step for him.

"We're playing blackjack," Josh said.

Blackjack. Their father loved that game. "Our father played blackjack," Hope said. "Did you used to play with him?" Roger shook his head no. Hope frowned. Any time she mentioned anything about her father Roger would shake his head no. Did he remember her father? Hate him? Did he blame him for the accident? Her father paid with his life, you would think Roger would have some forgiveness for that. Then again she didn't know the struggles he had been through. She just wished he was more forthcoming about their father so she could delight in new stories about him, turn them into new memories.

"You can come back another time," Faith said.

Josh finally appeared at the door. His hair was disheveled and he had dark circles under his eyes. Hope almost laughed. One evening in Roger's company and Josh was turning into a little hermit himself. Then again, those bags under his eyes were proof that it was him Hope often heard sneaking around at night. He'd definitely not been sleeping. Should she mention it to Faith? You had to be careful what you said around Faith. Any whiff that you were suggesting a better way of parenting would be met with swift and severe punishment. Telling another parent how to raise their children was tantamount to swiping a picnic basket out of the paws of a grizzly bear.

"I want to stay here instead," Josh said. "Roger doesn't mind. Do you mind, Roger?"

Roger looked at Faith. Then at Hope. When his eyes connected with hers, she felt something. Something electric, and loving, and so, so familiar. Roger usually had sunglasses on. She was surprised that his eyes were blue. And not just any blue. They were her father's eyes. Not only were they his eyes, but they were giving her a look only one other person had ever given her. *Daddy*. It was like she was looking into her father's eyes. It couldn't be, though. He couldn't be. His name was Roger.

Then why did he shake his head no every time she said something about her father?

Why did Yvette treat him like a son?

Why hadn't they ever heard about Roger?

Why did she have forty-two missed calls that evening from her mother? *She seems freaked out by Roger.* Hadn't Josh said something like that? Of course they were in the accident together because they were the same man. He was her father. Their father. Roger wasn't his name. This was Thomas Garland. He was her father. Their father. She gasped.

"What?" Faith said, sounding annoyed. Roger disappeared from the doorway.

"Good night," Hope heard him say from within. Seconds later Josh's coat was tossed his way. Hope would have asked about Mr. Jingles, but her entire body was nearly paralyzed. She didn't even remember the walk back to the log house. As the others were in the mudroom tugging off boots and coats, Hope grabbed Faith's hand and dragged her outside.

"What are you doing?" Faith said.

"It's Dad," Hope said. A huge lump formed in her throat and tears stung her eyes.

"What about Dad?" Faith said.

"Roger," Hope said, her voice coming out husky, almost like his. "He's our dad."

Faith started to open her mouth, then closed it. Her hand fluttered to her mouth. "No, I would have known. I knew him better."

"I was the one looking into his eyes. Blue. Just like Dad's."

"Tons of people have blue eyes."

"Think about it. Why does Yvette act like she loves him better than us? Why is she so insistent he keeps living here? Why would some man we'd never even heard of have been in the car with Dad if he was coming to see us? Why has he suddenly come to life since we've been here? Why isn't there a name on the tombstone? Why did he shake his head no every time I asked if he knew our father? And did you catch what he was playing with Josh?"

"Blackjack," Faith said.

"And just now—the way he looked at me—I *recognized* him, Faith. It's him. He's our dad. I'm sure of it."

"I can't believe this."

"Think about it, Faith. Just close your eyes and think about it." To Hope's surprise, Faith followed her instructions. Soon she gasped and her eyes flew open.

"Do you think I'm right?" Hope heard the desperation in her own voice. She so wanted to be right.

"I think you're right," Faith said. "Oh my God."

"I know, right?"

"How could that woman lie to us?"

"Who? Yvette?"

"I can't even call her by name. How could she do this to us?"

"First things, first. He's alive, Faith. Our dad is alive." Hope started for the cabin. Faith pulled her back.

"Wait."

Hope jerked free from Faith's grasp. "I have to see him right now." She was close to tears. She wanted to tear across the lawn and throw herself into his arms.

"Just wait. We have to think about this."

"What is there to think about?"

Faith started to pace in the snow. Not an easy task when it was so deep. "Maybe Dad had a brother. Maybe he's our uncle."

"And they both like blackjack and Christmas, and love us, and they were both in the car accident?"

"Why not?"

"And we never met him? Never even heard that Dad had a brother?"

"We can call Mom."

"She's never once mentioned a brother or our uncle. You know she would have. And look." Hope showed her the missed calls on her phone.

"Oh my God," Faith said. "She's on her way here."

"I'd say so," Hope said.

"Why did she call you? Why not me?"

"Seriously? You have to do this now?"

"You're right. He's alive. Daddy is alive."

"I think we're too old to call him Daddy. But I'm doing the same thing in my head."

"Yvette. She's evil. Do you think she planned on telling us at all?"

"I don't know. But I don't care about her right now. Our father is just over there." Hope pointed to the cabin and once again headed for it, and again Faith pulled her back.

"What if he doesn't know?" Faith cried.

Hope stopped dead. She'd never considered this. "What?"

"He has brain damage. His own mother is calling him Roger instead of Thomas. What if he doesn't know who he really is?"

"Oh my God," Hope said. "Oh my God."

"He was standing right there when she showed us that phony grave. Do you think he would have allowed us to see that if he knew who he was?"

"Never," Hope said. "Never."

"I'm right," Faith said. "I'm right."

"You're right. You're so right. Our dad would never hide from us. And he never would have left us. That's the reason he's never come for us."

"So he wasn't a spy," Faith said softly.

Hope gave a bittersweet laugh. "But he didn't mean to leave us. You're right, Faithy. He has no idea who he is."

Faith and Hope stopped talking, too stunned in the revelation. They stared at the cabin, then at all the Christmas decorations on the lawn. They were glittering, and moving, and in this moment seemed to be crying out just like them.

"He still likes Christmas," Faith said softly, taking it all in. Hope could hear a sob forming in her voice. She felt a lump of her own.

"He still likes us," Hope said.

"Do you think so?" Faith said, the hurt little girl clearly taking over her voice. "Do you really think so?"

Hope grabbed Faith's hand. "I know so."

"Make me believe," Faith said.

"Look at this lawn," Hope said. "It's all around us. These decorations haven't come out since Rupert passed away. Even Yvette said he hasn't behaved like this. Talking, laughing, decorating for Christmas. He's reacting to us. On some level he knows."

"And blackjack," Faith said.

Hope laughed. "And blackjack."

"That's why Yvette is going through so much trouble to make sure he's all right after she dies." Excitement grew in

Faith's voice. Hope refrained from mentioning that she'd already pointed this out.

Hope felt like jumping for joy. Well, not for her sister, but out of true joy. "It was right in front of our face this whole time. He's alive, Faithy. He's right here."

"Don't cry."

"I'm not."

"You are." Faith tried to wipe the tears from Hope's face with her big mittens. "Stop it."

"Don't yell at me." Hope swatted her hands away. The tears came harder.

Faith groaned. "If you start, then I'm going to start and I might not ever stop."

"Can I at least have a Xanax?"

"Yes."

"Yes?" Hope said. She'd been half-kidding.

"If ever a situation calls for a little Xanax, this is it," Faith said.

"Hear hear."

"We're just going to go back inside and talk about this. We're not going to do anything tonight."

"I agree," Hope said. "I totally agree."

"Although we might have to have a word with Granny Dearest first," Faith said. "Okay, okay. Tea. Xanax. Talk."

"This is the best Christmas present I could have ever imagined," Hope said.

Faith clasped Hope's hands. "Even if he doesn't know who we are?"

Hope squeezed back. "Even if."

"What about Joy?"

"Oh God," Hope said. "She's going to kill me for telling you without her."

"It's okay. It's okay because we're not completely sure."

"You're not sure?"

"Oh, I'm sure. I'm sure. But Joy doesn't have to know that. I mean, a little white lie in order to avoid a nuclear reaction from our little sis is quite acceptable, don't you agree?"

"Totally agree. Okay. Right. When we're sure. We'll tell her when we're sure." Hope looked back in the direction of the cabin. "God, I just want to run up there right now and hug him."

"He may be our father, but he doesn't look like he showers very much."

"Just like Joy!" Hope said. "She'll be thrilled to know she inherited that from him." She and Faith shared a little laugh.

"We may not want to mention she got that particular trait from him."

"Do you really think he doesn't know who he is?" Hope said.

Faith stared at the cabin. "The only thing I know for sure is that I don't know anything."

"I'd like to shake our grandmother awake right now. Because she certainly knows." The more Hope thought about it the more furious she became. If that was their father and Yvette deliberately lied about it, well, there was no forgiveness, was there? Maybe their mother had been right all along. She was a cruel woman.

"Pajamas. Tea. Xanax," Faith said. "We'll figure out a plan of attack."

Josh lay on his bed in his clothes. They had come looking for him, but they hadn't even cared that he didn't want to come back with them. He much preferred hanging out with Roger. They had fun. Roger had Coke and potato chips and a jar of coins he brought out to play blackjack. It was the most fun Josh had had since he'd been there. He would have slept much better on Roger's sofa. He didn't think Roger would have minded. Heck, maybe he could convince his mother to leave him here with Roger permanently. Especially if his dad didn't want him and Charlie was going to move in. It figured. The minute Josh was having fun his mother just had to step in and ruin it. His door creaked open. It was Brittany.

"What's wrong?" he asked.

"I can't sleep," she said. "I'm too excited about Christmas. Aren't you?"

He smiled. He wished he could be more like her. It wasn't her fault she was so happy. "Come in."

"Really?" Her voice perked up and she skipped into the room.

"You can sleep here tonight."

"Will you tell me a story?"

"Sure," Josh said. She snuggled under the covers. Josh looked outside at all the twinkling lights. He took a deep breath. " 'Twas the night before Christmas and all through the house . . .' "

Joy lay in bed wishing Harrison would join her. Except for two times, he'd been the one who insisted they follow Granny's rules. She could hear him snoring from his room across the hall. She smiled. He was enjoying himself. His mother was furious with him, though; she'd heard him talking to her on the phone the other day. She didn't want to spend Christmas without her boy. Joy couldn't blame her. Maybe they should go back to Seattle for Christmas. This was turning out to be a nightmare anyway.

She could hear Hope and Faith in Faith's room. What were they doing in there and why hadn't they invited her? She supposed they figured she was with Harrison. Still, it would have been nice to be asked. She always felt like the unwanted one. She didn't get to know their father. Faith left when she was young, and Hope had been absolutely brokenhearted. Joy always thought Hope loved Faith better, and that Faith must have loved Hope better—for why else take off before really getting to know Joy?

Now that she was older, she knew logically that it was just life. Faith had been pregnant and scared. Their father died. Hope, of course, was going to miss her older sister. But in her heart, Joy had carried a world of hurt. She wanted to be close to her sisters, repair the broken bits, she just didn't know how. She liked being around them, though. They were actually having fun some of the time. She wondered if Hope had been serious about the coffee truck idea. Grudgingly, Joy had to admit it was a pretty good one. They could take it everywhere. Especially downtown in the winter. This place was growing on her. They certainly had a lot of tourists at this time of year, and tourists loved coffee. They could have hot chocolate for the kids. Maybe Harrison could even bake his bread and pies. Some of those trucks were even big enough to sleep in. Oh, who was she kidding. A truck might be cheaper than a store, but that didn't mean they could afford it. The only way they would be able to afford anything was if they were allowed to sell this house.

Granny and her rules. Can't sell it until some old man dies? That was crazy. And crazy couldn't be legal, could it? And what had Josh been doing in that creepy cabin? What kind of man lets a teenage boy into his cabin at night? In this day and age?

Thank the Lord they found Josh quickly. She was surprised Faith wasn't harder on that old man. It wasn't right to have someone else's child over at your house for hours without telling anyone. Joy didn't know why everyone else was tiptoeing around the guy. Joy just thought he was weird. Were Hope and Faith really considering keeping him on after Granny passed? She'd noticed the office for a lawyer in town when she was there last. She was going to make an appointment. There was no way what Granny was asking them to do was legal. And then she was going to confront Roger. Tell him that everyone else might be fooled, but she knew he was putting on an act with all that brain-damaged stuff. Scamming a rich old lady about to die.

Joy crept into the hall. She could sneak into Harrison's bedroom, or she could join Faith and Hope. She stopped by Harrison's room and opened the door a crack. Loud snores snaked out into the hall. She smiled and shut the door. She headed for Hope's room. This time she didn't bother to knock or even open the door a crack. She pushed the door open and took a flying leap for the middle of the bed. Hope and Faith, who were sitting on the bed, squealed as Joy landed between them, laughing.

"So nice of you to drop by," Hope said.

"We thought for sure you were busy," Faith said, using air quotes.

"He's in his own bed, snoring," Joy said. "And I'm wide

awake." She looked at her sisters. They looked all red-eyed and funny. "Are you two drunk?"

"No," Hope said.

Faith just blinked rapidly.

"You both have red eyes," Joy said. "Did you smoke a joint?"

"No," Faith said.

"We were standing too close to the fire pit outside," Hope said. "That smoke is killer."

"I can't sleep," Joy said. "Harrison is snoring loud enough to wake the whole house."

"Do you want me to make you some warm milk?" Hope joked.

"Actually, yes, I do," Joy said.

"Mom used to make that for you all the time," Faith said.

"I know. Didn't she make it for you guys too?"

"Nope," Hope said. "She didn't start doing that until you."

"Because I was a terror about sleeping," Joy said.

"She would spike it," Faith said.

"Why do you think I always pretended I couldn't sleep?" Joy said with a wicked smile.

"I think I could use some warm milk too," Faith said.

"Are you sure that's a good idea?" Hope said. Joy resisted rolling her eyes. Who made Hope the permanent hall monitor? Joy would have to sneak some extra alcohol into Hope's warm milk just to loosen her up a bit.

"Come on, bitches," she said, throwing her arms around her sisters. "Got milk?"

It was nice being in the kitchen late at night with her sisters. They were talking in whispers just in case Yvette could actually hear them from down the hall. The milk was warming in the pan and Joy was making a big deal out of examining each coffee cup in the cupboard and putting herself in charge of who drank out of which one. She gave Faith a cup with a bulldozer on it, Hope one with an enormous turkey, and she drank out of the one that said, WORLD'S BEST MOTHER. Probably just to stick it to Faith. Faith and Hope exchanged a look. Had Roger given Yvette the mug?

When the milk was hot, and Faith's and Joy's spiked with just a bit of rum, they sat at the kitchen island. Hope kept glancing at Faith, wondering if they should tell Joy about Roger. They'd decided to wait until they were a hundred percent sure. That was probably wise when it came to Joy. She was like a spring, always ready to bounce.

Roger. It was going to be impossible to call him that. First thing in the morning they were going to call Carla. Hope wasn't even sure their mother was really on her way here. She could have been reacting to Roger getting a piece of the inheritance, not Roger being Dad. But it was him. Hope knew it. She just didn't know if he knew it.

"What's up with you guys?" Joy said.

"It's about Roger," Faith said. What was she doing? They'd just agreed not to tell Joy until their theory was irrefutable.

"Ugh," Joy said. "I couldn't believe you didn't let him have it."

"What?" Hope said.

"Who lets some strange kid in their cabin without checking in with the mom?" Joy said. "I don't care if he is brain-damaged. He has to know he can't do that." Faith glanced at Hope. Joy's eyes narrowed as she caught the look. "What?"

"That's not what Faith was trying to say," Hope said. A loud rap on the door startled her. Hot milk slopped out onto her arm.

"Oh my God," Faith said. "Is someone at the front door?" The knock came again.

"What time is it?" Joy hissed.

"It's one a.m.," Faith said.

"I suddenly wish that beast of a dog was in here with us," Faith said.

"Maybe it's Mom," Hope said.

"Mom?" Joy said. "Why would it be Mom?"

"There's no way she got here this fast," Faith said.

"Mom's coming here?" Joy said. "What happened to Cuba?"

"She changed her mind," Hope said.

Joy slid off the stool so she could literally stomp her foot.

"Why am I always the last to know?" Hope resisted looking at Faith. Joy was going to kill them for keeping the secret about their dad. Another loud bang on the door interrupted Hope's thought.

The Garland Girls advanced to the door together. Hope flipped on the light to the mudroom. A woman could be seen standing on the porch. She was petite, with blond hair. Not Carla, although she could have introduced her head to a bottle of bleach.

"Oh no," Faith said. "Not now."

Joy and Hope exchanged a look as Faith hurried to the door, raced through the mudroom and had the front door thrown open in seconds flat. Hope and Joy followed and watched as Faith hugged the woman, then scolded her. She smiled broadly at Hope and Joy and they smiled back.

"What are you doing here?" Faith said. Her voice sounded intimate.

"I missed you," she said.

"You should have called."

"I did. Several times. And texted. Why are you ignoring me?"

Faith glanced behind her at Hope and Joy. "Can you give us some privacy?"

"I don't think so," Hope surprised herself by saying.

"Not a chance," Joy said.

"Great," Faith muttered.

"These must be your sisters," the woman said. She held out a dainty hand. "I'm Charlie."

"Charlie," Joy said, slowly, as if she were wine tasting, savoring the sights and smells.

"Charlie," Hope said.

"I was going to tell you," Faith said.

"Stayed in the closet, did you?" Charlie said. Her laugh was much bigger than she was. "Oops!" She winked at Hope and Joy. Hope had to hand it to Faith, she was cute.

"Guess who's coming to dinner?" Joy said.

CHAPTER 29

Yvette was up with the birds. Bright red cardinals and little brown sparrows, and if she was lucky Yvette could spot the occasional hawk gliding by the window. The house was quiet for a change. Hope was usually up messing about the kitchen, and Yvette was surprised to realize that she missed her. The girls hadn't quite taken to her, not that she expected them to, but they sure did bring Roger back to life. She fixed his breakfast, a hardboiled egg, warm oatmeal with apples, and a thermos of coffee, and then put on her boots and coat and headed for his cabin. She glanced at all the Christmas decorations. Roger had been putting up a little more every night, and now almost half the lawn surrounding the log house was filled with one moving creature or the other, all lit up and heartily embracing Christmas. She was even allowing herself to get into the Christmas spirit. When she was a child they didn't make a big fuss over Christmas, but oh, she loved it anyway. Their gifts were modest—Clementine oranges, a pair of shoes, or a hairbrush—something practical but new. And oh, how Yvette cherished her gifts. Nowadays kids were so spoiled. Brittany and Josh were an exception. What wonderful children. She felt closer to them than she did the girls, but Yvette had always had an easier time relating to children than adults. Brittany was so fresh-faced and agreeable. And she didn't mind Josh being a bit moody—he reminded her so of Thomas.

She approached Roger's door and knocked. He opened within seconds. "Good morning."

He nodded and moved back. Yvette stepped inside and set his breakfast up at his card table. She saw a jar of coins and a deck of cards. She looked at him.

"Josh," he said.

Yvette smiled. She felt tears coming to her eyes. Maybe she had been wrong about the extent of Roger's damages all these years. Maybe he understood and remembered a lot more than she once thought. She sat down with him. He noted his surprise by the raise of an eyebrow.

"Thomas," she said, trying it out. Roger didn't move. His body stiffened. "Your girls are lovely."

"Lovely," he said.

"Your daughters," Yvette pressed.

"My girls," he said.

Oh God. He did know. Yvette trembled. She started to cry. After the accident he didn't speak at all. The doctor said his brain was permanently damaged. There was no way of knowing what he remembered. He wouldn't answer to Thomas. The only word he muttered was "Roger." If she'd ask him to do something, he'd say, "Roger, Roger." She eventually started calling him that. It was easier. This man was not her son. She still loved him, but he was not her son.

"I think you should tell them," Yvette said. "Tell them your name is Thomas."

Roger's head snapped up and he looked stricken. "Roger," he said.

"They're still your girls," she said. "They will love you."

"No!" he said. He began to pace, smacking himself over and over on top of his head. "No, no, no, no."

"Okay, okay." Yvette hurried to her feet and waved her arms. "We won't tell, we won't tell." She had to shout it and repeat it several times before he stopped. "Okay, okay," she said. She took his arm and guided him back to the table. He sat, but his hands shook violently. She fetched his medicine from the cabinet and doled it out.

"Roger," he said. "Roger."

"I know," Yvette said. "Roger." Oh, the doctors they'd been to over the years. Even with all the advancements in medicine the brain was a strange and befuddling thing. Because he wasn't completely himself, but there was a flicker of Thomas inside him. The girls had turned that flicker into a flame. But he didn't want his girls to know. He knew enough to know that he wasn't himself. He didn't want them to know him like this. Or Carla. Yvette knew Roger still kept photos of Carla and the girls around the cabin. Bringing the girls here had been a risk that had paid off. She didn't know how Roger was going to react, and it was better than she could have ever suspected. She'd hoped he would come around enough to tell them.

She wasn't surprised they couldn't recognize him. He even walked different since the accident, and twenty years had aged him considerably. And they'd been so little. They still saw young, handsome, standing-up-straight, clean-shaven, laughing, wild Thomas. But Carla had certainly recognized him. Even on video camera. She didn't like the woman, but she had to grudgingly admit, she and her son had had quite the connection. Apparently they still did.

Despite that, Yvette didn't want that woman anywhere near him. Roger wasn't Thomas, couldn't be a husband again in any sense of the word, and Yvette hated to think of what heartbreak he might incur by seeing her again. But she hadn't been able to figure out a way to stop Carla from ever visiting. And yet Brittany said the foul woman was on her way here. She hoped it wasn't true. If it was, she had to stop her from seeing Roger. In order to do that, she'd have to tell the girls the truth. And if she did that, she'd be betraying Roger. His entire life had been ruined with one accident. He'd lost absolutely everything, how could she deny him the only thing he'd ever asked of her? If he wanted her to keep her mouth shut, she was going to keep her mouth shut.

"Go now," he said. Yvette nodded and stood to leave. She never got insulted when he spoke his mind. That was one thing about his brain injury, it had removed all social filters. Roger told you exactly what he wanted when he wanted it. She normally kissed him on the head before leaving, but he was still upset. She simply nodded and left.

Hope was in the kitchen drinking coffee when she looked out and saw Yvette returning from the cabin. She brought Roger most of his meals. Correction, she brought *her son* most of his meals. She wondered where the name Roger had come from. She was dying to say something to her grandmother, but Faith had made her swear on her grave that she wouldn't confront anyone about this without her. Joy would be the first person they would tell. But now Faith was off with Charlie, and who knew when she'd be back. Hope was dying to say something to someone, anyone. Her mother still wasn't answering her phone. Hope had left several messages, and in the last one even hinted she knew why her mother was coming, but begged her not to do or say anything until she had talked to them first. Hope still didn't know what Roger did and did not understand, and Carla could be a hurricane. She certainly didn't want her barreling through and upsetting everyone.

Faith and Charlie had gone to a hotel downtown last night. Faith said she'd be back before the kids were awake, but so far no sign of her. Then again the kids were known to sleep in. Hope missed that about being a teenager.

She and Joy had actually bonded last night, staying up another hour in Hope's bed going over the bombshell.

"Did you ever think she was a lesbian?" Joy said.

"If anyone was going to go that way, I thought it would be you," Hope admitted. "Just to be different."

"I haven't ruled out bisexuality," Joy said. "But I never once thought Faith was that cool."

"She was always good at sports," Hope said. Then giggled. It was so surreal, and besides women could be straight and good at sports. "Do you think Stephen knows Charlie is a woman?"

"Uh, yes," Joy said. "Faith said he caught them on the living room sofa, remember?"

"Oh, right."

"Imagine that moment."

"I'd rather not." Stephen might not have been her favorite brother-in-law, but he was her only one, and she certainly didn't wish him any pain. He might not have been the man Hope envisioned for Faith, but he was a good father. And regardless of whether Charlie was a woman or a man, Hope knew this really had to hurt. She could see why Faith had been trying to hide it. And they hadn't had any time at all to grill Faith or even get to know Charlie. Faith was dressed, packed, and out of there before Hope or Joy could get in a word.

Thank God for coffee. Life would be impossible to process without it. She laughed, remembering Joy's ambition. Maybe Hope had been too quick to judge the coffee shop idea. Her sisters were living their lives. Going for what they wanted. Hope actually felt a bit of excitement for Faith. It must be a relief to realize who you are, or be honest about who you are, no matter what stage of life you were in. But how could she and Joy not know? Then again they hadn't known Roger was their father either. Secrets. Families were filled with secrets. Hope was more than a little hurt Faith had hid something this huge from them. From now on, she wanted them to be the kind of sisters who told one another everything.

Like the fact that Roger is their father. For a second Hope could relate with how betrayed Joy was going to feel. Maybe they should just pretend they were finding out about it along with Joy. Or should Hope tell Joy right away? No. Faith would kill her. God, three was such a horrible number sometimes. And there was too much going on at once. The revelation of Roger. Yvette dying. And Charlie showing up at the door last night.

It was still going to be difficult on the kids and Stephen. But

Hope had liked Charlie straightaway. She wanted Faith to be happy. She needed to lighten up, that was for sure.

She heard heavy footsteps above and soon Josh was thunking down the stairs.

"Where's Mom?" he said before he'd even reached the first floor.

"She went into town," Hope said.

"This early?"

"You know how people are around Christmas time," Hope said. "They're full of surprises." She hated herself the minute the lie was out of her mouth, but what choice did she have?

Josh squinted. "Are the shops even open this early?"

"It's nine-thirty, sleepyhead. I'm sure some of them are open." Josh settled himself onto a counter stool. He looked outside. "Did you have fun with Roger last night?" Hope tried to keep her voice casual, but it wasn't easy. She wanted to know every single thing her father said and did.

Josh shrugged. "He knows how to play blackjack." Hope laughed. Then bit her lip as tears came to her eyes. Josh narrowed his eyes and studied her. "Do you like Roger?"

"I do," Hope said, hoping her voice wouldn't betray her secret grief. "I like him a lot. I look forward to getting to know him a whole lot better."

They heard the front door opening and minutes later Yvette came in from removing her coat and boots.

"Ah, we have two awake I see," Yvette said. "It's as if you're all sleep-deprived."

"Mom is in town," Josh said.

"In town?" Yvette said. "At this hour?"

"That's what I said," Josh said.

"Christmas secrets," Hope said. "My lips are sealed." She only wished Charlie had come at another time. She didn't like waiting to confront her grandmother about their father. Faith told her they'd waited twenty-four years, she could wait another day, but it wasn't going to be easy. She had hoped to actually go with Yvette to deliver Roger's breakfast, but Yvette had beat her to it.

Joy and Harrison tripped down the steps next. Hope wondered if their grandmother was suspicious about the fact that they often came down at the exact same time, but she'd never voiced a complaint.

"I'll make us all breakfast," Hope said. "Are you hungry, Yvette?"

"I'll just have some toast," Yvette said. "You can make whatever you want for the rest of them."

"Do you think Roger would want to join us?" Hope said. She heard her voice crack. She'd better watch it or she was going to tell everyone what she suspected. Faith would kill her. Then again, why did Faith have to call the shots? Hope was the one who recognized him first.

"No, he's already had his breakfast," Yvette said.

"Do you have any idea how we could get him to come inside the house?" Hope asked.

"We could tell him we're playing blackjack," Josh said.

"Why are you suddenly so obsessed with him?" Joy asked.

"I'm not," Hope said. Joy was more astute than Hope gave her credit for.

"Gawd," Joy said, dropping onto a counter stool and waiting for Harrison to do the same. "I'm so freaking tired."

"That's because you and your sisters were up all night giggling like schoolgirls," Harrison said.

"You were?" Josh said. "Mom too?"

"You're lucky you didn't hear them, little man. They were totally obnoxious. Your mom too."

Joy gave Hope a look. "Where is our dear sister?" she said. Hope frowned. Joy knew perfectly well where Faith was. She just enjoyed stirring the pot.

"French toast, anyone?" Hope said. Joy loved French toast. Maybe if she had her mouth full she would keep it shut.

"Yum," Joy said. "Should I go wake up Faith?"

"She's in town," Josh said. "It's a secret."

"You told him?" Joy said.

"Told me what?" Josh was on high alert.

"I told him Faith was up to some secret Christmas errands in town," Hope said in a very measured voice. She was going to throttle Joy. This was exactly why they hadn't shared their suspicions about Roger with her.

"Right," Joy said. "Top-secret Christmas activities."

"This early?" Harrison said.

Finally, Brittany emerged and made her way downstairs.

"Hello, Princess," Yvette called.

"I'm making French toast," Hope said.

"I love French toast," Brittany said.

"Do you have potatoes, Granny?" Harrison said.

"I do," Yvette said.

"I'll make some of my famous hash browns," Harrison said.

"Yummy," Joy said.

"It's snowing again!" Brittany said, running to the window. "Can we build a snowman today?"

"A snowman?" Hope said, looking outside. "With this much snow, we can build a fort."

The door opened and Austin strode in. He stopped halfway as if surprised to see them all here. "Hello, everyone," he said.

Hope felt her insides warm and she had to stop herself from jumping into his arms. She'd been meaning to call him but had held back, hoping he would contact her first instead.

"Glad you could make it," Yvette said.

"You said you needed my help?"

Hope turned to her grandmother. She wouldn't meet her eyes. "Whatever it is," Hope said, "we're all going to eat French toast and Harrison's famous potatoes first."

"Amen," Harrison said.

"Brittany, Josh, would you help set the big table?"

"Should I set a place for Mom too?" he asked.

"Or two," Joy said.

"Why two?" Josh said.

"Just a joke," Joy said. Hope glared at her.

"I don't get it," Josh said.

"She eats a lot," Joy said.

"No, she doesn't," Josh said.

"We can always add a place if she shows up," Hope said. "Let's assume for now she's eating breakfast in town."

"Indeed," Joy said.

"I sure hope I don't run out of French toast before you get yours," Hope said to Joy. Joy stared at Hope, then mimed locking her lips and throwing away the key. *If only.*

CHAPTER 30

Austin helped Hope clear the breakfast plates. He had come to take Yvette to her doctor's appointment, but Joy and Harrison had offered instead. Austin had asked Yvette if she was sure she didn't want him to take her, and even now he was glancing at the door often, as if expecting her to come crashing through. Brittany and Josh were skating on the pond. Austin looked toward the door again.

"What is it?" Hope asked.

"The doctor is helping her with the exit plan today," Austin said.

"The exit plan?"

"Medication for when it gets too bad," Austin said. "That's the only reason she agreed to go."

"Oh." Hope put the last of the dishes in the rack. There was a machine, but today she'd wanted the distraction so she'd washed them by hand. "Sometimes I forget she's sick."

"Your visit has really perked her up," Austin said.

"No," Hope said. "Our visit has perked Roger up, and that's

what perked Yvette up." She could hear the bitterness in her own voice, only now it went much deeper. Yvette should have told them, should have told Carla, a long time ago what happened. Instead she let them wait and wonder all these years. Maybe there was something that could have been done. He was functioning, and talking, and on some level he recognized them. They could have had him back in their lives. She'd robbed them of the most important gift of all. The truth.

Hope wiped her hands on the towel and threw it down. "Are you okay?" Austin said.

"What happened to your brother?" Hope didn't even know she was going to ask him that until the words were out of her mouth.

Austin looked at her, then leaned against the counter. "He was my half brother, although that's neither here nor there. I didn't grow up with him, but I did love him like a brother. He took his own life."

"Oh my God." Hope's hands fluttered up to her mouth. "I'm so sorry."

"He was sixteen. It was a few days before Christmas. And he had been staying with me."

"Oh my God."

"I didn't recognize the signs. He'd been acting out with my father and stepmother so they sent him to live with me for a while. I underestimated what he was going through."

No wonder Austin hated Christmas. "Wait. Is that why you've been so worried about Josh?"

"Did you read the note I asked you to give him?"

"No," Hope said. "I figured if you wanted me to, you would have directed me to read it."

Austin gave her an appreciative look. "I like that about you," he said softly. He sighed. "It was my phone number along with a number for the suicide hotline."

"You think it's that serious?" Panic fluttered in Hope's stomach.

"I will never underestimate someone's pain again." Austin glanced toward the pond. "There's more."

"What?"

"I shouldn't be telling you this."

"Please."

"He called me."

"The hotline?"

"No, my cell. But he might have thought it was the hotline."

"Why? What did he say?"

"The good news is that he didn't have a plan to kill himself. But he is having thoughts of doing so."

"Oh my God. When? When did he call?"

"A few days ago."

"And you didn't tell me? You didn't tell Faith?"

"Hope. It's confidential."

"The hotline is confidential. But you said he called your cell."

"I think it was a mistake. I think he meant to call the hot-line."

"But he didn't."

"Hope. I swear. He's only in the early stages of contempla-tion. I've been keeping an eye on him."

"When we went on our date? You knew then?" Austin looked at the ground. "I can't believe this." She was furious with him, but Josh was more important. "What do we do? We have to tell Faith."

"I don't think that's the best idea."

"Why not?"

"Because you don't want him to feel cornered. He won't even talk to me in person. He's waiting to see if I'll betray his confidence. Which I just did."

"Shouldn't we get him into a hospital?"

"Maybe."

"I can't believe this is all happening at once. I have to tell Faith. If anything happened and I didn't tell her . . ."

"Okay. But let me talk to Josh first," Austin said. "Let me ex-plain to him why I have to betray his trust."

"I just can't keep that kind of secret from my sister."

"I understand. I'm very sorry I didn't say anything before. I was going to. I just wanted to make sure I was doing the right thing. Because of my brother. I didn't want to jump to conclusions."

"Is there any doubt that it was Josh who called you?"

"It was shortly after you gave him the note. It was a San Francisco number. And it sure sounded like him."

"What exactly did he say?"

"He just expressed frustration about the family. He asked if you could easily kill yourself by drowning."

"Oh my God."

"But the pond is frozen. And he tried to make a joke out of it. Look. I know it's not a joke. I truly think he's only in the very early stages of considering it."

"I can't believe this. This hurts so much." Hope looked out the window again. Josh and Brittany were headed their way. "I want to follow him around every second now."

"Are you angry with me?" Austin asked softly.

"You shouldn't have kept this to yourself."

"I was trying to figure out how and when to say something. I was torn. I still am."

Hope was torn too. Should she confront Josh or talk to Faith first? Faith should know before she brought her girlfriend to the log house to meet the kids. That was the last thing Josh needed right now. Suddenly Hope remembered something Josh said in the restaurant. Something about Faith keeping the butter knives away from him. "I think he might have attempted suicide before," Hope said. She told him about the incident at the restaurant. She expected to see a bit of relief in Austin's eyes. If Faith already knew, then Austin couldn't be entirely blamed. "What's wrong?" she asked.

"We have to find out. If he has threatened it before, it raises the level of concern," Austin said. "The longer he's actively been contemplating it, the more danger he's in."

Hope nodded. "We'll talk to Faith before we confront Josh. Get all the facts."

"Let's do it quick," Austin said.

Hope grabbed her phone and called Faith. It went directly to voice mail. Hope left a message asking Faith to call right away.

"There's so much going on," Hope said. "All at once." And to think. Just a few weeks ago, Christmas was the biggest thing on Hope's mind. Now it seemed so unimportant. Their grandmother was actively dying. Her father was alive. Brain-damaged but alive. Their mother was on her way. Faith was breaking up her family. And Josh was contemplating suicide. There just wasn't any reason to celebrate Christmas this year. She could hear Josh and Brittany in the mudroom now. She took a deep breath. All these secrets were getting to be too much to bear.

Hope and Austin played blackjack with Josh and Brittany. Hope was doing her level best not to stare at Josh. She'd practically accosted him when he said he was going to his room, and thus the game of blackjack.

"Why don't we go into town?" Josh asked. Austin looked at Hope. She was thrilled Josh wanted to get out and about, that was probably a good sign, but what if they ran into Faith and Charlie?

"I'm free," Austin said.

"We could go sledding and Christmas shopping," Brittany said.

"I thought you were making presents," Josh mimicked.

"I need supplies," Brittany said, biting her lip.

"Great," Hope said. "Let me call your mother and see if she wants us to meet her somewhere."

"I don't want to hang around her," Josh said. How painful to hear him talk so of her sister. But he was hurting, and what Faith was doing was reckless.

"I'll just let her know that I'm kidnapping her two favorite people in the world so she doesn't worry," Hope said with a wink. She purposefully averted her gaze from Josh so that she didn't have to take in his sarcastic reaction.

Hope hurried to the window as she listened to Faith's cell

phone ring. Roger, correction, their dad, was outside, rear-ranging the Christmas decorations. Faith's voice mail kicked in.

"Where are you?" Hope said. "Josh and Brittany want to go into town and I'm bringing them." She clicked off. She sounded angrier than she'd meant to. But seriously. She didn't want to start lying and covering up for Faith, but she certainly didn't want to encourage a collision either. Roger was just outside and it appeared as if he was just plugging and unplugging Christmas decorations. Hope was determined to get him to come to town with them. She whirled around and headed for the mudroom.

"What did Mom say?" Brittany asked.

"I just left a message," Hope said. "I'm going to invite Roger."

"Good luck," Austin said. Hope threw on her coat and shoved her feet in the boots. There was at least a foot of snow on the ground so she wasn't exactly racing across the lawn but tromping, her feet sinking deeply into the snow as she went. Roger stopped and watched her. She was breathing heavy by the time she was a few feet from him. He watched her, then broke out in a smile when she was near. She took a moment to really look at his face. It was still hard to know for sure. People definitely aged differently, and this was not the handsome young father she remembered. Was it him? Were these the same eyes? Tears pooled in her eyes before she could stop them. Roger appeared startled for a moment and then reached a gloved hand toward her. A dam broke in her then and she threw herself into his arms, weeping. At first he was stiff; then his arms went around her and he hugged her.

"My girls," he said. "My girls." Hope heard him say it and she cried harder, but when she pulled back and wiped her tears, she did not question him any further.

"Thank you," she said.

"Don't be sad," he said.

"You made me feel better," she said. "Please come into town with me. And Josh, and Brittany." *Your grandchildren.* "And Austin. Please. I want you to come with us."

"Town," he said, frowning.

"Just for a little while. As soon as you want to come home, you let me know and we'll come right home."

"No," he said. "No town." Then he turned around and headed for his cabin.

My girls. He said *my girls.* Hope was lost in thought as Austin's truck bounced along the road. "Are we going sledding?" Brittany said.

"Why not?" Hope said. Screw Faith. She still wasn't answering her phone or calling her back. Why not go sledding? "Does that sound good?" Hope asked Josh.

"Sure," Josh said. It was way better than his typical "Whatever." Austin and Hope exchanged a little smile. After they parked they headed directly to the sledding hill. Butterflies danced in Hope's stomach at the thought of Austin's arms around her waist. It had been several days since that kiss and she'd been thinking about it nonstop. From the looks he was giving her, so was he. It was early in the day and there wasn't a long line to sled. Before she knew it, they were up next. Josh wanted his own sled, which left Brittany, Austin, and Hope to share one. The threesome took off first with Brittany in the front, Hope in the middle (as always), and Austin in the back. He did indeed sneak his arms around Hope's waist shortly after the sled started its descent. Brittany's delighted screams filled the air. They were halfway down when they heard another raucous scream from behind. Josh was a wild man on the sled, and he seemed to be purposefully zigzagging down the path, leaning his body side to side to produce the slaloming effect.

"Careful," Austin shouted just before Josh's sled slammed into the back of theirs. The sled veered off path and headed straight for a tree. Hope screamed, as the image of Brittany's head colliding with the trunk terrorized her. She threw her hands over Brittany's head as Austin desperately tried to right the course of the sled. Josh flew past them, zooming sideways down the hill. Why hadn't Hope listened to Faith? Austin managed to steer them away from the tree, but the violent change in course tipped the sled and soon they were careening down the final leg of the hill, precariously balanced on the side, in danger of falling out. And as soon as the fearful thought struck Hope, it happened. Brittany tumbled out of the sled, and then to Hope's horror the sled tipped upside down. Hope's face was crushed into the snow as she felt the sled run over the top of her body. Where was Brittany? Was she okay? This time it was Hope's screams that filled the air and they were anything but joyful.

CHAPTER 31

Hope, Austin, and Josh were in the waiting room of Cascade Medical Center. Hope's eyes were swollen from crying. She couldn't stop replaying the event in her mind. Although he hadn't meant for them to get seriously hurt, she couldn't help but think that Josh had purposefully clipped their sled. By the time Hope's body had stopped rolling down the hill and she'd crawled over to Brittany, she'd been relieved to see that Brittany was conscious and crying, then horrified to see the position of Brittany's leg, twisted behind her at an unnatural angle, and realize it was broken. Faith still wasn't calling her back, so Joy and Harrison were out looking for her. The doctor had just popped in to say that they were almost finished setting Brittany's leg and they could visit in a moment. Faith was going to kill Hope. Austin kept reaching over to squeeze Hope's hand, but she was finding it a challenge to accept the comfort. Josh was wide-eyed and worried sick about Brittany. Hope had to admit to herself that that alone brought her some relief. He had snuck off to the bathroom and when he came back his eyes were red and his lashes wet with tears.

"Come here," Hope said. Josh took the seat next to her and she put her arm around him. "It was an accident."

"I was trying to pass you, not hit your sled," Josh said.

"I know," Hope said. She suspected he might have hit their sled on purpose, but she knew in his teenage brain that he thought it would be funny and didn't intend on driving them straight for a tree, flipping them over, or breaking his sister's leg.

"The guy who worked there said I was being reckless," Josh said. "Are they going to arrest me?"

"No," Austin said. "You just can't sled there anymore."

"Good," Josh said. "I don't want to. Mom was right. It's too dangerous. You should have listened to her, Aunt Hope."

And now the blame was squarely on her. Austin squeezed her hand again. "Brittany is going to be okay," he said.

"She has a broken leg," Hope said. "She's going to spend the rest of the holidays in a cast."

"I want to be the first to sign it," Josh said. Hope swallowed. "Aunt Hope?" Josh said.

She looked at him and waited. "What are you going to tell Mom? I mean, are you going to say it was my fault?"

Austin and Hope exchanged a look. She didn't know much about boys, or boy energy, or what all their teenage hormones made them do. "Here's the thing," Austin said. "We know you were trying to have fun, but you were also a bit reckless."

"It was an accident, I lost control," Josh said.

"I know you didn't mean for us to get hurt," Hope said.

"That's right, I didn't," Josh said.

"But I think you knew you were going to bump into our sled," Hope said.

Josh jumped up. "Don't tell Mom that. You're going to, aren't you? You're going to tell her it was all my fault."

"Josh, please sit down," Hope said.

"Everybody always thinks everything is my fault. Now it's going to be poor little Brittany. I wish I had broken my leg instead. Nobody would care then, would they?"

"Of course we would care. How can you even think we wouldn't?"

"Nobody wanted to come here for Christmas. Just you. You made everyone come." Josh had never spoken to her like that or glared at her like that.

A nurse came into the waiting room. "She's in her room. You can go in."

Josh barged ahead, almost running. Hope followed, her eyes once again filling with tears. Austin grabbed her hand. "This is not your fault," he said.

"I think he hit us on purpose," Hope said. "But I don't think he meant for this to happen."

"I know," Austin said.

"So what do I say?"

"You tell the truth. He's going to have to deal with the truth."

"What about his state of mind?"

"You mean the suicidal inclinations?"

Hope nodded. "This adds stress," Austin said. "We're definitely going to have to tell Faith everything. I'm sorry. I should have done this from the start."

"It's not your fault," Hope said. "It's mine."

"Don't say that," Austin said.

But Hope pulled back from his touch. "Josh is right. I pushed for this. A happy holiday. A happy family. I pushed for this."

"There's nothing wrong with wanting a happy Christmas. Or a happy family."

"Makes me a bit naïve, don't you think?"

Austin slipped his arm around Hope's shoulder and this time she didn't shrug it off. "You're being too hard on yourself. Let's go see Brittany." Hope nodded and hugged the teddy bear she'd bought in the gift shop. Austin held the flowers and cards. Hope's cell phone rang and she headed for the room. It was Faith. Hope answered, but the minute she said hello the connection was cut. Cell phones weren't allowed in all areas of the hospital and the reception was shoddy. Hope texted Faith.

Cascade Medical Center
Sledding accident
Brittany okay but has broken leg

A few seconds later her phone dinged.

Ha-ha. On my way back to the house

Turn around
Not joking

Enough. You're joking.

Hope entered Brittany's room. The poor girl was grinning despite her leg in a giant cast and propped up on pillows. Her grin grew when she saw the teddy bear and flowers. Josh stuck to the side of her bed, nervously playing with the sheets. Hope engulfed her in a huge hug. "Your mom thinks I'm joking. Mind if I take a picture?"

Brittany smiled for the camera. Josh jumped out of the picture at the last minute. Hope sent it to Faith. When her phone dinged back, the sound went straight through Hope's heart.

OMG!!!!!! I'm seriously going to kill you

Hope showed Austin the text. He smiled and squeezed her arm. "I'll do my best to stop her," he said.

Brittany was propped up in the living room of the loft near the Christmas tree and the roaring fire. Austin and Hope were still waiting to talk to Faith privately, but she wasn't giving them the time of day. Josh, on the other hand, was watching every move they made, still seemingly terrified that they were going to tell Faith he had rammed them on purpose. Which, of course, they were. Hope was getting so weary of secrets. Especially Yvette's. She was resting, having just come back from the doctor, and Joy was the bubbliest Hope had ever seen her. Hope hated the thought that Joy was secretly thrilled that Faith was livid with Hope. Roger was standing particularly close to the window, every so often holding up something for Brittany's delight: a pinecone, an ornament, an ice skate.

"Roger is so funny!" she said. Hope couldn't help but notice the look Joy and Harrison exchanged. Joy didn't have any idea that Roger was their father, and why would she? Hope was dying to tell her, but of course she had already promised Faith they would do it together and Faith was once again in the driver's seat, now playing the martyr, the loving mom who had tried to protect her children from breaking a leg sledding, but defeated by dumb Aunt Hope who had never raised anything but dogs. Austin was the only bright spot in all of this.

"Do you want to go to my place later?" he whispered.

"I want to go now," she said. He laughed. "Yes," she said. "Later." Later couldn't come soon enough. Christmas was a week away, the only saving grace—would they all just part ways after Christmas? Wait for Yvette to die? The doorbell rang. Faith hurried over to it and soon Charlie came into view, smiling. Hope smiled back but felt sick. How could she bring her here? What was this going to do to Josh? They hadn't had time to tell Faith about Josh's call to Austin. This was a nightmare. Faith was introducing Charlie around the room as her friend Charlotte who just happened to be in the area. Hope gathered from the look on Charlie's face that Charlotte wasn't her real name at all. Regardless, she smiled and started to hand out presents.

She was like Mrs. Claus, distributing sudden cheer. She had presents for Brittany and Josh, and even little tins of cookies for Hope, and Joy, and Granny. Faith allowed the kids to open them, which was a relief to Hope given that she had already opened hers and was on her second cookie—a delicious chocolate and almond concoction. These were much fancier than the sugar cookies Hope made. Would you look at that? Faith was in love with a woman who baked cookies. She wondered if she made kale chips. It somewhat endeared her to Charlie. Still, the timing couldn't be worse. Wasn't Stephen on his way?

As soon as he'd found out about Brittany breaking her leg, he announced he was coming to spend Christmas with them. Josh seemed thrilled, so at least there was that.

None of them had heard from Carla, her Facebook page had gone quiet, and she wasn't answering her phone. This was so typical of their mother. To dramatically announce she was coming here and then disappear.

"We need to do something positive with this group," Hope said to Austin. "Something to get us in a Christmas mood."

"Skating is out," he said. Hope gave him a look. He laughed.

"I need to make my Christmas presents," Brittany said.

"Now there's something we could do," Hope said. "We could all make each other's presents this year."

"Great," Josh said. "Just another way to ruin Christmas." Tears came to Hope's eyes, but she quickly hid them.

"What is it you would rather have for Christmas?" Austin asked Josh.

"A faithful mother," he replied.

"You told him?" Charlie said. Up until now she had been helping Brittany sort through the gift she brought her, a jewelry-making kit. It was actually quite an appropriate present for Brittany. It was still so weird to think of Faith being with another woman, but in another way it all seemed to fit. They heard the sound of a car horn. Faith leaned in and whispered in Charlie's ear. A strange buzzing sound soon rang out.

"Someone is at the gate," Austin said.

"Dad!" Josh said.

"It could be Grandma Carla," Joy said. At the mention of her mother, Hope's head snapped to the outside window. Roger wasn't anywhere in sight. They had to tell Joy about Roger, then confront Yvette before Blizzard Carla barreled through.

"Stephen's coming?" Charlie said. The panic was obvious in her voice.

"We have to get you out of here," Faith said.

Josh suddenly lasered in on Charlie while Austin went to see who was at the gate. "What did you say your name was?"

"Ms. Gates," Faith interrupted. "You can call her Ms. Gates."

Charlie tried to smile, but she looked slightly deranged. Josh's eyes narrowed, but then he tossed it off and made a beeline out the door.

"Coat, coat, coat," Faith yelled after him.

"Faith," Hope said. "We have to talk."

"Kind of busy right now," Faith said. "Thanks to you."

"It's not my fault."

"I told you I didn't want them to go sledding."

"We need to talk in private."

Faith shook her head. "You're always trying to control things," she said.

"Me?" Hope said. "Me?"

"Who else?"

"Uh, hello pot, it's me, kettle."

"Whatever."

Austin stepped up. He kept his voice firm but low. "We're concerned about Josh," he said.

"Excuse me?" Faith's eyes flashed. She was furious. "Just what the hell gives you the right to say that to me?"

"What's going on out here?" Yvette emerged from the bedroom. Poor woman. Their arrival had brought nothing but stress.

"Austin works at a suicide prevention center," Hope said.

"So?" Faith said.

"That's what I meant by we're concerned about Josh," Austin said.

Faith's mouth clamped shut at first. "He told you?" She closed her eyes. "I'm surprised. He said he didn't mean it. The cuts weren't deep enough to do any real damage."

"He tried to kill himself," Hope said. So that's what the "hide the knives" comment had been about after all.

"Isn't that what you're referring to?"

"He called Austin's hotline," Hope said. "Just a few days ago."

"What?" Anger was back in Faith's voice. "And you're just telling me now?"

"He actually called my cell or I wouldn't have been able to tell you at all. Even now I'm betraying a confidence. But I thought you should know."

"Of course I should know. I'm his mother."

"I don't think he's in the planning stage, or at least I didn't—but I had no idea he'd attempted it before."

"There's something else," Hope said.

"You'd better tell me everything."

"He purposefully rammed into our sled."

"What?" Faith headed for the door. "He's not getting away with this."

"Wait," Hope said. "I don't think he meant to hurt anyone. But he was being a bit reckless."

"I'll handle it," Faith said.

"Let's think everything through," Austin said.

"Here you are again, telling me how to parent my own son."

"I had a brother," Austin said. "He committed suicide when he was just a year older than Josh."

Faith stared at him. "I'm sorry," she said.

"I'm not trying to tell you how to parent. But I do think this is a critical time. I think you and your husband need to figure out a plan, and have a united front."

Faith nodded. "I'm going to see if that's him at the gate," she said. Faith left. Charlie was soon at Hope's side.

"If that's Stephen I should leave," she said.

Hope turned to Charlie. "I'm not trying to be rude. You seem very nice. And thank you for the cookies. So good. But I think you should leave either way. It's just not a good time."

"I think I'll let Faith tell me when she wants me to leave," Charlie said.

"Aunt Hope?" Brittany called. Hope hurried over to Brittany.

"I'm sorry you had to hear that," Hope said. "I was trying to get your mom somewhere private."

"I'm glad you told her. I've been worried about him too. I don't want to lose my brother." Brittany began to sob.

Hope tried to comfort Brittany. She put her arms around her and made soothing noises. Austin plugged in the tree and put on Bing Crosby. Hope glanced over to see what Yvette was doing. She'd almost forgotten she'd come into the room. She was nowhere to be seen. Had she gone back to bed? Hope wouldn't blame her. She'd like to go back to bed. Charlie was planted at the kitchen island; so much for getting out of here. The gate swung open and a red car pulled in.

"That's Dad!" Brittany said.

"Would you like to become acquainted with the back door?" Hope said to Charlie.

"I can give you a ride back to your hotel," Austin said. Charlie nodded, slipped off the stool, and headed for the back door.

"He'll find out she was here anyway," Hope said. "Let her stay. I think today we should get all secrets out in the open."

"What secrets?" Yvette barked from behind.

Charlie is Faith's lover, Josh is suicidal, and Roger is our father, Hope wanted to shout.

"Yes, what secrets?" Joy said. She and Harrison had just come in the back door. Hope hadn't even heard them leave.

"Where have you been?" Hope said.

"Nowhere," Joy said. She said it fast.

A little *too* fast.

CHAPTER 32

Hope studied Joy. She definitely looked guilty. Like she'd been caught doing something. A dozen instances of Joy sporting that look flashed through Hope's mind. Sneaking into the fridge late at night. Getting into the presents before Christmas. The first time the cops caught her shoplifting and brought her home in the cruiser. What was she up to now? "Did you see Roger while you were out there?" Hope asked.

"Why are you suddenly fixated on Roger?" Joy asked.

"What about Roger?" Yvette said.

"You know what we all need?" Harrison said. "A snowball fight. What do you say, Mrs. G?"

"You'd be surprised," Yvette said. "I still have two good arms." The door opened and Stephen walked in, Josh literally hanging on his coattails.

"Hello, everyone," Stephen said. Hope was struck by what a handsome man he was. Young-looking for his age, with all his hair. He'd find someone else, she thought. This was going to be the hardest on the kids.

"Dad!" Brittany yelled.

"Pumpkin," Stephen said. He dumped his suitcase and headed over to Brittany, Josh still on his tail. "Oh, sweetheart, I'm so sorry."

"She's okay," Josh said.

"I'm okay," Brittany echoed.

"I think she likes it," Josh said.

"Not really," Brittany said.

"Well, we're going to spoil you," Stephen said. "Who wants cookies?"

"Me!" Brittany said.

"They haven't even had dinner," Faith said.

"Cookies for dinner," Stephen said. He kissed Brittany, ruffled her hair, then approached Yvette and introduced himself.

"I'm sorry my granddaughter is leaving you," Yvette said after they shook hands. "You seem like a nice man."

Hope could tell Stephen was taken aback by the comment, but he managed to smile. "We'll get through it." He glanced at Charlie sitting at the kitchen island. "I'm sorry. You are?" Charlie stood still, wide-eyed, as if no one would be able to see her if she didn't move a muscle. Then, her eyes slid to Faith.

"That's Hope's friend, Jackie," Faith said haltingly, just like someone improvising on the spot would do. "From the shelter."

"Hello, Hope's friend Jackie," Stephen said.

"I thought you said her name was Charlotte," Josh said. "And you're the one who brought her here—she's your friend." Maybe Josh was actually the healthiest of all of them; at least he was the one speaking the truth.

"Charlotte?" Stephen said. "You're Charlotte?" He overpronounced her name, then turned to Faith with a withering look, then glanced at Charlie again. "I didn't recognize you." His look clearly finished the sentence. *With your clothes on.*

"I'm sorry," Faith said. "She just showed up. I swear."

"It's true," Charlie said. "I did. But I'm here now and everyone knows."

"Great," Stephen said. "That's just great."

"Everyone knows what?" Josh said.

"That she's my friend," Faith said. "Everyone knows she's my friend."

"Why was it a secret in the first place?" Josh asked. "Why did you tell Dad she was Hope's friend?"

"I just didn't want him to think I was spending time with my friend and ignoring you guys," Faith said.

"You're spending time on your phone and ignoring us," Josh said.

"Well, we're all here now, so why don't we do something fun?" Hope said.

"We're inviting the whole town here for a big Christmas celebration," Brittany said. "I wish I could show you the whole place."

"I can get the carriage out," Austin said. "Pull you around in it."

"I won't be too heavy?" Brittany said.

"We could pull you around in a sled," Josh said.

"You won't be too heavy at all," Austin said.

"Would you like that, Dad?" Brittany said.

"She has to leave," Stephen said, pointing at Charlie.

"Fine," Charlie said. "I'll go back to the hotel."

"No," Stephen said. "You'll crawl back to wherever it is you came from."

"Stephen!" Faith cried.

"What's going on?" Josh said.

"You can't tell me where to go," Charlie said.

"Let's get the carriage and get Brittany and Josh out of here," Hope said.

"Brittany, Josh?" Austin said. "Would you like to see my cabin?"

"Yes," Brittany said.

Josh shrugged, which in his book was a resounding yes.

"You two will have to help me pull the carriage," Austin said. "You up for that?"

"I'm going to the cabin to give Roger his dinner," Yvette said.

Joy and Harrison snuck a look at each other, then dashed up the stairs the minute Yvette was out the door. A few seconds later they all heard Joy's bedroom door slam.

"We'll let you three have some privacy," Hope said, glancing at Faith, Charlie, and Stephen.

"You guys are weird," Josh said. He really wasn't putting it together and for that Hope was grateful. "Totally weird," Josh added.

"I'd hardly call that a newsflash," Hope said.

The carriage was a two-seater with giant wheels. Austin held Brittany in his arms while Josh and Hope dragged it out into the snow. Then Austin laid Brittany in the seat while Hope and Josh held the metal posts that would have attached to a cart led by a horse. "Just a sec," Austin said. He went back into the barn, then came out carrying a box.

"What's that?" Brittany asked.

"My place doesn't have any Christmas decorations," Austin said. "I thought you guys could help remedy that." Brittany clapped her hands, Josh rolled his eyes.

"Why don't you get in next to Brittany," Austin said to Josh. "Hope and I will pull first."

"Are you strong enough?" Josh asked Hope, raising an eyebrow.

"We're going to find out," Hope said. Austin winked and Josh took a seat next to Brittany. Austin and Hope each picked up a handle and then began to pull the carriage toward Austin's house.

"Mush!" Josh said.

"Hush," Hope answered. Brittany's laughter rang out through the darkening sky. Even with a broken leg she was the cheeriest of them all. Pulling the carriage took a lot of concentration, and halfway there Hope was sweating through her down coat. Now this was a workout. Soon they were crossing onto Austin's property. Once they passed through a small section of trees, Hope could see the cabin just ahead. It was about the size of Roger's cabin.

"Looks small," Josh said.

"It will be easy to decorate," Austin said.

"Why doesn't my father like Charlotte?" Josh said.

"I like her," Brittany said. "She's nice. And pretty."

Hope ignored the question. What could she say? *Because she's named after a spider and your father is an arachnophobe . . . ?* She wasn't going to be the one to out her sister to her children.

Austin kept quiet too. "We made it," he said as they came alongside the cabin. Hope set her side of the carriage down, her arms were killing her. Austin dropped his side just as the kids were starting to slide across the seat.

"Sorry," Hope said.

Austin laughed. "Let me unlock and open the door and then I'll come get you," he said to Brittany. Josh hopped off the sled and picked up the box of Christmas decorations. Austin unlocked his cabin and flipped on a light. Despite its small size, it was very tidy and well decorated. He had a leather sofa and chair facing a rustic slate coffee table, a red wood burning stove, stainless-steel appliances, a pine table in the kitchen painted green with matching chairs, and a tan shag throw rug in the living room. Lastly there was a nook with a computer and chair. The door to the bedroom was closed. He hurried out after Brittany as Josh and Hope took in the space. When he returned he laid her out on the sofa.

"You can tell us where to put everything," he said with a wink. He closed the door and immediately set to building a fire in the stove.

"This smells better than Roger's cabin," Josh said. Austin laughed and set the box of decorations on the coffee table in front of Brittany. She pulled out a string of lights first.

"Where shall we put these?" Austin asked. Brittany pointed to the set of windows across from the sofa, facing the property. "Perfect," Austin said.

"We need a little tree," Brittany said.

"A Charlie Brown tree," Josh said.

"I love Charlie Brown trees," Austin said. He handed one side of the lights to Josh and headed for the windows. "Can you bring me a chair?" he asked Hope. She removed one of the kitchen chairs and brought it to him. Austin positioned it near the window, stood, and looped his side of the lights over a nail.

"Why do you have a nail there?" Josh said.

"There's one on your side too," Austin said. "Failed curtain project." He slid the chair over to Josh. Josh stood and even though he had to stand on tiptoe and reach, he managed to loop his side above the window as well. It hung halfway down. Austin removed a brown extension cord from a drawer in the kitchen, then plugged in the lights. They lit up immediately, twinkling against the top portions of the windowpane.

"Beautiful," Brittany said.

"She's easily amused," Josh said.

"Then I am too," Hope said. "It is beautiful." She wondered if Austin had ever decorated his cabin for Christmas before now. Given what she knew about his brother, the answer was probably a resounding no. He was doing this for the kids. He was a good man. She hoped it wouldn't be too painful for him.

Austin grinned. "What's next?" he said to Brittany. She reached in the box and began pulling out items. A big red bow, a pinecone wreath, and a pair of ceramic chipmunks wearing Santa outfits. Hope spotted a radio on the kitchen counter.

"Do you mind?" she asked Austin, as she pointed at it.

"You read my mind," he said. "I could also make popcorn, and I think I have a few sodas."

"Popcorn!" Brittany said.

He winked, turned the radio on, and fiddled with it until he found Christmas tunes, then took a large pot out from the cabinets. "Can you guys handle the rest of the decorating?"

"Thanks to all these nails you have in the walls, we're set," Hope said. She tied the bow to the pinecone wreath and found a nail hanging on the door. It was so simple, but it really did bring the place to life. Josh was holding a chipmunk in each hand.

"Where do you want these?" he said to Brittany. She squinted and began concentrating on every inch of the cabin. Hope was prepared for Josh to lose his patience, but to her relief, he gave Brittany time and space to decide.

"One near the woodstove," she said. Josh nodded and placed a chipmunk near the woodstove.

"The other on the kitchen counter next to the toaster," she said. Josh followed suit. Brittany found a silver rope of tinsel in the box.

"Uh-oh," Austin said. "Now we're getting crazy."

"'Tis the season for crazy," Hope said.

Josh put the tinsel around Brittany's neck. "You're the Queen of Christmas," he said. She giggled.

"I like it there," Austin said. "As long as you take it with you." He winked at Brittany, then poured oil into the pot and turned the burner up. Next he pulled a tin toward him and opened it, revealing popcorn kernels filled to the brim.

"Nice," Hope said. He grinned. God, she loved his smile. Just like the landscape of Leavenworth, Washington, Austin Rhodes had such a pure and natural essence about him. Simple, yet powerful. A girl could get used to both—the place and most definitely the person. How many bachelors keep popcorn in a tin? She loved it.

"Do you have a television?" Josh said.

"No," Austin said. "But sometimes I watch movies on my laptop." A bark sounded at the door.

"Mr. Jingles," Brittany said.

"Can he come in?" Josh said.

Austin nodded. "The more the merrier."

Josh opened the door and Mr. Jingles bounded in. "I think he has a nose for popcorn," Hope said, nuzzling the big dog as he jumped on her.

"Lucky dog," Austin said right after Hope planted a big kiss on his furry face. They shared a long look, and Austin smiled. She looked away before the kids picked up on the fact that she was crazy about him.

"I think I even have some candles that have that pine tree smell," Austin said. "They're in one of these kitchen drawers."

"I'll look," Hope said. "If you don't mind."

"Not at all." He gave her another smile and Hope began to look through the drawers. Josh was right behind her. Mr. Jingles ambled over to Brittany, who hugged on him until he tired of it; then he wedged as much of his body as he could underneath Austin's coffee table and soon began to snore.

In the third drawer Hope opened there was a photo of a teenage boy sitting on top. She knew it must be his brother. The dark hair, the deep eyes—she could definitely see the resemblance. Hope was about to shut the drawer when Josh reached beside her and snapped up the photograph.

CHAPTER 33

"Who's this?" Josh asked, waving the photograph around like a lawyer discovering new evidence in court. The first kernels of popcorn had just begun to pop. The sizzle and scent filled the air.

Hope reached for the photograph. "Why don't we put that away," she whispered.

"It's okay," Austin said. He turned to Josh. "That's my brother. His name was Tommy."

"Was?" Josh said, picking up on the tense right away.

"He died," Austin said.

"Can I see?" Brittany said.

Hope wanted to tell them both to forget about it, but it wasn't her place. Josh took the photograph over to Brittany. Hope was watching Austin closely, but he didn't look at her. Instead he turned his concentration to the popcorn, shaking it as if someone's life depended on it.

"He's a kid too," Brittany said.

"He was," Austin said. "He was just a kid."

"Where does he live?" Brittany asked. She obviously hadn't

heard the earlier exchange. Hope wished she had remote controls that mute anyone in a flash. Now that would be a fantastic Christmas gift.

"He passed away three years ago," Austin said.

"What happened?" Brittany cried. Josh took the picture back and studied it even closer.

"My brother took his own life," Austin said. He said it calmly and matter-of-fact, although Hope could hear the heartbreak in his voice. She made a point not to stare at Josh.

"What?" Brittany said, near-panic in her voice. "Why?"

"I think the popcorn is done," Hope said. The lid was being pushed up by the white fluffy kernels.

"I'll melt some butter," Austin said. He brought butter and cans of Coke out of the fridge.

"Coke!" Brittany said. "Can we, Aunt Hope?"

"Mom would say no," Josh said.

"It's a special night," Hope said.

"I really only have it on very special occasions," Austin said.

"Like close to Christmas," Brittany said.

"Exactly," Austin said.

"How did he do it?" Josh asked.

"Josh!" Hope said. She knew Austin was used to the subject and probably wanted Josh to have a reason to talk about it, but the admonishment was out of her mouth before she could stop it. Then hot flashes of guilt began to pulsate. "I'm sorry," she said, not knowing whether she was talking to Austin or Josh.

"It's okay," Austin said. He removed the popcorn from the burner and removed a large wooden bowl from the cabinet. He heaped the popcorn in the bowl and poured melted butter over it. Then he sat the bowl on the coffee table along with a roll of paper towels. "I'd be happy to talk to you about it in private," Austin said to Josh. "I don't think the girls want all the details."

"Is that why you work at a suicide prevention center?" Josh asked.

"It is," Austin said. His eyes were kind and steady on Josh.

Josh looked at Hope. "Does she know?"

Austin nodded. "Normally it would be protected information, but you called my cell phone and I was worried."

"It's okay," Josh said. "I would never do it."

"You tried it once!" Brittany cried out. Real fear was in her voice.

"I didn't mean it," Josh said quickly.

"I was so scared," Brittany said. She reached her buttery fingers out and after a minute Josh took her hand.

Hope reached over and took Josh's other hand. "I'm glad you called Austin," she said. "It's healthy to talk about your feelings, and it's very healthy to reach out for help when you're overwhelmed." She tried to keep her voice steady and light, although she wanted to burst into tears. Josh didn't pull his hand away, which was also a very good sign.

"I wouldn't do it, I wouldn't," Josh said.

"You can't predict how you'll feel in the future," Austin said. "But there is help. And if you ever need it, all you have to do is ask for it."

"I just want my family to be happy and normal again."

"Your mom and dad, and Brittany, and me, and Aunt Joy, we love you more than anything. If you're not okay, we're not okay. No matter what else is going on."

"But we can't even enjoy Christmas," Josh said.

"I'm enjoying it right now," Hope said. "How about you, Brittany?"

"Yes!"

"Austin?"

"I'm like you, Josh," Austin said. "I haven't enjoyed Christmas in a long time. But ever since you guys arrived—well, I'm finding myself enjoying it against my will." He laughed and soon Josh joined in. Hope reached over and hugged Josh, then kissed his cheek.

"And if you ever need to call again and want it to be anonymous, just use the 1-800 number," Austin said.

"Okay," Josh said. "Or maybe I'll just talk to you guys."

"Pain passes," Austin said. "If I could say one thing to my brother it would be that pain passes."

Josh nodded. "I know that," he said. "I do."

"I would just die if you died," Brittany said.

"So would I," Hope said.

"I know that now," Josh said. "I do."

"Let's eat, drink, and be merry," Hope said. Austin gave each one of them a can of Coke and they turned their attention to the popcorn, and the soda, and the music. *He planted that picture there on purpose,* Hope thought. He was still keeping his eye on Josh, still keeping the conversation going. Hope wanted to throw her arms around Josh and pour her heart out. Tell him over and over again how they would all be scarred for life, and heartbroken forever if he ever did something like that. They'd never get over it. Just like Austin had never gotten over it. Life was challenging, and holidays could be stressful, but it was still worth fighting for. Family was worth fighting for. They were everything. She thought of Roger. Of all he'd missed out on. His girls. The love of his life. His life, period. She so wanted to tell Austin and the kids who he really was. They were going to be all right. No matter what, they were going to get through this.

"This is fun," Brittany said.

Hope took her hand and held it. Then she reached over and took Josh's hand. She looked at Austin and smiled. "If I had a third hand I'd hold yours too," she said.

"If you had a third hand I'd toss you out on your two feet," Austin said. Josh threw his head back and laughed. Not just any laugh, but a deep belly laugh. It was the sound of a small miracle. Hope smiled and then felt tears rolling down her cheeks. Outside, snow began to fall.

When Hope, Josh, and Brittany were delivered back to the house, Stephen, Faith, and Yvette were playing Scrabble. Charlie was nowhere to be seen, ditto for Joy and Harrison. Hope asked of their whereabouts.

"Joy and her boy are with Roger," Yvette said. *You mean your son.* Hope sighed, wanting to call her grandmother out, but also quite convinced it wouldn't lead anywhere positive. What in the world was Joy doing hanging around Roger so much all of a sudden? She couldn't possibly know who he was, so there had to be a motive. Hope was too tired tonight for any more drama, which was why she wasn't going to ask about Charlie.

"Where's Charlotte?" Brittany sang out.

"She was eager to get back downtown," Faith said. "I told her how lovely everything is decorated for Christmas."

"I want to go downtown," Brittany said. "We have to start inviting everyone here for our Christmas celebration."

"I already let a few know, darling. Believe me, the news has spread already. We'd better start planning the activities or we'll have three nights of the peasants revolting," Yvette said. She sounded cheerier than usual.

"What?" Brittany said.

"We get to start planning so people don't complain," Faith said.

"Skating, Christmas carols, all the lights," Hope said. She walked up to the window. "I think Roger adds something new every day." She fixated on a penguin holding a candle. When he was turned on, he glowed from within and slowly moved the candle up and down, like marching in a Christmas parade. The little flame at the top even flickered. She definitely hadn't seen that little guy before. He was adorable. Roger. She realized with a start that that's how she saw him, thought of him still, as Roger, not her father.

"Triple letter and triple word score," Yvette sang out, setting down a word.

"Zelda?" Stephen said.

"She was quite the gal," Yvette said. Stephen glanced at Faith.

"Her house, her rules," the group called out. Yvette nodded.

"Zelda it is," Stephen said.

"Can I steal Faith for a second?" Hope said. Yvette didn't even look at them or acknowledge their comments about having a private word with her.

"Want to play for your mom, Josh?" Stephen asked.

"Sure." Josh took a seat in front of the Scrabble board. Faith put on the television for Brittany; she squealed when she found out *Rudolph* was playing. Hope planted a big kiss on her head; then she and Faith hurried to the mudroom to get their coats.

On their way to the cabin, Hope filled Faith in on their time with Austin, and how Josh told them he'd never try to take his own life again.

"I should be furious," Faith said. "Austin should have told me the minute it happened."

"He kept his eye on him until he was positive it was Josh. And the fact that he's talking about it is good news, Faith. It really is."

"It's all my fault. Even if he didn't know the details, he knew something was wrong between me and Stephen. Kids know everything. Even when you think they don't."

"Did he actually attempt to take his life?" Hope asked.

"He had a stash of sharp objects—razor, knife, and a piece of glass in a shoebox under his bed."

"Oh no," Hope said.

"At first he just said he liked collecting things that were sharp. I actually bought that one for a while."

"And then?"

"And then I walked in one day and he was holding the piece of glass above his wrist, as if thinking about cutting himself. He'd already taken a few swipes—what he called *practice swipes*. None of them deep. But seeing that—it was the most horrifying moment of my entire life."

Hope's heart broke open. The thought of Josh being in that much pain—and then the thought of him actually following through with it. Hope would give her life for her niece and nephew. She didn't want anything bad to ever happen to them. No wonder Faith was popping so much Xanax. If anything ever happened to either one of those precious children, it would be a life sentence for all of them. "Why didn't you tell me?"

"He was so mortified. I promised not to tell anyone. As long as he agreed to go to a counselor. I've been taking him to one ever since, but he's refused to talk. Austin has done more in this past week than anyone else."

"He's a special guy," Hope said.

"And you're falling for him," Faith said.

"I won't deny that."

Faith laughed and put her arm around Hope. "I approve. And I'm so relieved Josh is finally talking to someone, even if it's not me. Did he say why he was so upset? Is it all my fault?"

"He didn't put it together that Charlotte was Charlie if that's what you mean."

"He's going to hate me."

"No," Hope said. "He's going to be surprised. Like I was. And Joy."

"I was having such trouble admitting it to myself that I didn't tell anyone else," Faith said. "I'm sorry."

"I just want you to be happy," Hope said.

"Why is Josh so sad? What did I do wrong?" Hope could hear Faith's heart breaking. God, life was difficult. No wonder everyone needed their family. Nobody should have to get through all these crazy things alone. Hope took her hand and squeezed it.

"I'm sure it's a combination of things. Including hormones and normal teenage angst. But I think it makes it doubly important that we all remind ourselves what really matters. Family."

"Family," Faith said. "Our father."

"What happened with you, and Stephen, and Charlie?"

"It wasn't World War Three, but Stephen made it clear that until we're officially divorced and the children know about me and Charlie that he doesn't want us to see each other."

"How did she take it?"

"Her feathers were ruffled, but that's just Charlie. I was the one who was relieved. I'm actually with Stephen on this one. I'd rather start with a clean slate. But the holidays were starting to make her nostalgic and romantic and she's hurt that I don't want to spend them with her—or can't spend them with her."

"Did you always like women?" They were almost at Roger's cabin.

"That's a conversation for another time," Faith said. "We've got to tell Joy who Roger really is before anyone else does."

They approached the front door. The curtains were closed, but through the gaps Hope could see that Roger's lights were on and she could hear voices from within. She knocked. A few seconds later Joy opened the door. She didn't even crack it open wide enough for Hope to see Roger.

"Harrison," Joy yelled. "Let's go."

"What are you doing?" Hope said.

"Let us in," Faith said.

"No, we're done here," Joy said. She glared at her sisters. "Don't ruin this," she hissed.

"Ruin what?" Hope said. "What are you doing?"

"Investigating," Joy said.

Did she suspect? "Investigating what?"

"I think he's a con artist," Joy said. She slammed the door shut in their faces. Hope shook her head, Faith threw up her hands.

"We should have told her," Hope said. Faith stepped up and banged on the door. When it opened again, Joy and Harrison barreled out in their winter coats. Hope caught the briefest glimpse of Roger as he shut the door. The lock clicked behind them and the lights went off.

"What did you say to him?" Hope called after Joy, who had already plowed ahead.

"It's cool," Harrison said. "We were cool." He took off after Joy.

Faith stood staring at Roger's door. She put her hand on it. "Why is he shutting us out?"

"Don't forget. We don't know what he knows. I want to hug our father, I want to hit him, I want to yell at him, I want to cry at his feet and tell him how much I love him. But we don't know the damage he's suffered. I can't inflict any pain or confusion on him if it's going to make him worse. I can't. We have to talk to Yvette."

"Joy is out of control!"

"That's our fault. We should have told her straightaway."

Faith looked in the direction Joy and Harrison had gone; they were already distant figures. "She's not exactly accessible these days."

"Let's kidnap her," Hope said.

"Kidnap her?" Faith asked.

Hope threw open her arms. "I'm up for a better idea."

Faith's eyes narrowed. "Do you have any duct tape?"

CHAPTER 34

Joy and Harrison were already in their room with the door shut. Faith paced in front of it as if considering barging in. Hope touched her shoulder.

"We'll talk to her first thing in the morning."

"We're talking to Yvette first thing in the morning."

"We have to tell Joy first or she'll never forgive us." Faith reluctantly turned away from the door. The house was dark; everyone was in bed. They crept downstairs.

"Have you heard from Mom?" Hope asked.

"Shit," Faith said. "I was just about to ask you that." Hope sat at the counter and Faith rummaged in the cabinets until she found a bottle of whiskey. "Are you joining me?"

"Yes," Hope said. Faith poured them each some whiskey and they clinked glasses.

"Cheers," Faith said with a laugh.

"When should we start to panic?" Hope said. "She hasn't even posted on Facebook lately."

"She must have booked a flight, right? I mean, would she actually drive here from Florida?"

"No, she would fly."

"But she didn't tell anybody when she was flying in or where she was staying, right? Does she even know exactly where the house is?"

"I never gave her the address."

"Me neither." Faith sighed and they were silent as they sipped their whiskey. "Do we have her boyfriend's phone number?"

"I don't. Tomorrow I'll try to get on his Facebook page and see what's what."

"Who do we call if she's missing? The Florida police? Leavenworth?" Faith sounded panicked.

"Mark Zuckerberg?" Hope joked.

Faith laughed. "She is addicted to Facebook, isn't she?"

"She certainly likes to be in the spotlight."

"If she drove—she could be anywhere."

"I think you just file a Missing Person's report wherever you are."

Faith frowned. "You mean file it from here?"

"It's a start. If we need to do it in Florida they'll probably help us with that. Let's not go to the dark place quite so fast, all right?"

"Okay."

"So what do you want for Christmas? A kale farm?" Faith laughed and punched Hope on the arm. "Peace," she said. "That's all I want. What about you?"

"A new family," Hope said. Faith frowned at first and then laughed. It was a stressful laugh, one that gained momentum and grew in strength until Hope joined in with her. By the time they were done, tears were streaming down both their cheeks.

"Is Christmas over yet?" Faith said.

"That's what I want for Christmas," Hope said. "I want it to be over."

The next morning Faith was on their mother's Facebook page trying to reach her boyfriend, while Hope watched Joy like a hawk, waiting for any opportunity to get her alone. So far it wasn't easy. She and Harrison were almost like a pair of slippers, always cozy and side by side. The plan for the morning was to get more decorations set up in the yard and start planning the menu for the Christmas celebration. Roger was already outside stringing lights. Hope watched him and tried to see some resemblance of the father she once knew. Had she ever seen him concentrate so intently on a string of lights? Roger didn't drink either. Not a drop, Yvette had mentioned once. That was enough to make him a new man.

"Faith and I need to talk to you," Hope said to Joy when the breakfast plates were cleared and Harrison had gone upstairs. Faith had to help Brittany with a sponge bath and to get dressed, but after that they were going to have her outside on the carriage, or sled, or in a wheelbarrow, Josh hadn't quite decided, and Brittany seemed equally excited about all those choices. Stephen had gone downtown to check into an inn. He said he would stay through Christmas, but he wanted a bit of his own space. He promised he'd be back up to the house every day to be with the kids.

"I'm going outside to help," Joy said.

"Later," Hope said. "It's urgent."

Joy put her hands on her hips. "Is it about Mom?"

Hope squinted. "Why? Have you heard from her?"

"No, but I'm sure she's fine. She probably went to Cuba after all."

"Faith's looking into it. Mom was definitely on her way here."

"What aren't you telling me?"

"We have to wait for Faith." How long did a sponge bath take?

"You just said we have to talk."

"Right. I'm letting you know so that when Faith is finished the three of us can go somewhere and talk."

"Good God, Nancy Grace, just tell me now."

"You know I hate that woman," Hope said.

"Well, you are being rather dramatic." Joy stuck out her tongue.

"It's about Mom, and us, and Roger," Hope said. She couldn't help but sneak another glance out the window. He was now setting up another mechanical Santa. She wanted to run out and leap into his arms. He was doing all this for them, working hard in the snow and cold to give them a merry Christmas. He was the best present they could ever ask for. She hoped Joy saw it that way as well.

"Roger?" Joy said. Her attention snapped to him as well, although she was hardly giving him a daughterly look. "What have you found out?"

"Please. Stay inside and we'll tell you everything."

"I was right, wasn't I?"

"What now?"

"Don't play games. Is he a con artist?" Joy sounded uber excited.

She'd probably prefer he was a con artist, Hope thought bitterly. "No, you've got it all wrong," Hope said.

Joy sighed. "I'm going outside. When you're ready you can come get me."

"You can't ever make anything easy, can you?"

"If by that you mean letting you control my every move, no, I can't."

Hope threw the dish towel down. "Don't say we didn't try," she said. She stomped up the stairs as Joy fled to the mudroom.

By the time Faith and Hope were outside looking for Joy, the grounds were deserted with the exception of Yvette, who was wandering through all the Christmas decorations. "They went into town," Yvette said when Faith and Hope approached.

"Even Joy?" Hope asked.

"It was her idea," Yvette said.

Hope was going to kill Joy. She took off on purpose. Just to stick it to Hope for not telling her when she demanded it. My God, she was stubborn.

"How did they get there?" Faith asked.

"They borrowed your car," Yvette said.

"It's not borrowing if the owner is unaware of it," Faith said.

"So? File a police report," Yvette barked.

She was testier than she had been in a while. Hope thought

about Yvette's most recent doctor's appointment. *Help with her exit plan.* She gently touched Yvette's arm. "We really need to talk to you."

"We're not going to wait for Joy?" Faith said.

Hope threw up her arms. "We can't keep putting this off."

"Whatever it is, let's go in the barn where it's warmer," Yvette said. Hope and Faith followed Yvette to the barn. Once inside they could see the electric panel where a majority of the lights were plugged in.

"I can only imagine the utility bill," Faith said.

"Me too," Yvette said. "Only I won't be here to pay it." She threw her head back and cackled. Finally Hope and Faith joined in.

Inside the barn Yvette went to a corner where bales of hay were arranged in a circle. "What's this for?" Hope said.

"I used to be in a book club," Yvette said. "I didn't want a bunch of old ladies tramping through my house with their dog-eared copies of *Fifty Shades of Grey*."

Yvette sat on a bale and waited as Hope and Faith did the same. The hay was scratchy to the touch but surprisingly comfortable. Hope didn't know whether or not Yvette was kidding, but it would be fun to have a book group out here. It would also be fun to snuggle with Austin on a bale of hay. She could really see this as her forever home. It was startling. And worrisome. Her sisters might never allow it.

"What is it?" Yvette asked in a harsh voice, cutting through Hope's daydream.

"Roger," Faith said, emphasizing the name.

"We've been over this," Yvette said.

Hope put up her hand. "Stop. We know the truth."

Yvette laughed. "Hardly anyone knows the truth," she said.

Hope had had enough. "He's our father. Isn't he?" She watched Yvette's composure crumple.

"Please." Yvette glanced around as if he might be hiding behind them. "Don't tell him. Don't tell *anyone*."

Hope's hands flew up to her mouth as she let out a little cry. "You've certainly lived by that rule, haven't you?" Hope had planned on being calm, but the confirmation that he was their dad made her livid. She'd kept this from them for all these years! They thought he'd abandoned them. Or that he was dead. She showed them his grave. It was unforgivable. Wasn't it?

"Don't tell him?" Faith repeated.

"He doesn't know," Hope said. "He doesn't know who he is."

Faith stood and squared off with Yvette. "How dare you?"

"We had every right to know," Hope said. "You did a horrible, horrible thing."

Yvette sat straighter and took a deep breath. Then she looked Faith in the eye. "He may technically be my son and your father. In the sense that he occupies the same body, has the same DNA. But that man is not Thomas. Nor does he wish to be."

"How do you know that?" Faith said. Hope was too heartbroken to speak. Now that it was confirmed, all doubt gone, she wanted to go to him and throw her arms around him, and she wanted him to remember. She wanted her dad back. But Yvette was right. That man wasn't the father in her memories. He wasn't capable of apologizing or explaining. At least Faith was capable of asking questions while Hope sat and just tried to keep breathing.

"Was he the only one in the car?"

"Yes, after which he was in a coma for two months."

"Oh my God," Hope said.

"You rotten woman. How dare you not tell us."

Yvette stood up. "You're right, is that what you want to hear?"

"It's too late," Faith said.

"It's never too late," Yvette said. "I know that now."

"You were never going to tell us," Hope said.

"That's not true," Yvette said. "I was getting around to it."

"It's not a grocery list, for God's sakes," Faith said. "It's not something you get around to. It's something you do. Right away. Like right after it happens!"

"I can't change the past," Yvette said.

"Our mother was right about you," Faith said. "All you do is put her down. But she was right about you. You don't care about anybody but yourself."

"Calm down," Hope said to Faith. She suddenly felt sorry for Yvette. No matter what, she had taken care of Roger all these years. And she was dying. They didn't need to pile on no matter how furious they were. What good would it do? Were all families like this? Pain heaped upon pain?

Yvette took a step toward the girls. "Death has a way of making you realize how foolish you are. But hear me out. He has suffered major brain damage. His intellect is probably that of a ten-year-old. When he was first back from the hospital he wouldn't let me call him Thomas. Every time I asked him anything—he would say, 'Roger that.' So I started calling him Roger. I could tell he liked it."

"You should have told us," Faith said. "His daughters. His wife."

"You really don't think he remembers?" Hope said.

"I wasn't sure. Until you girls came. You've seen how he acts around you."

"So he does remember us?" Hope could hear the desperation in her voice.

"I don't know what goes on inside his head or what he knows of the past. But he certainly still loves you. He's been showing you that since the minute you arrived."

Hope thought about the pinecone he'd left by her shoes just minutes after she had arrived and she wanted to cry. "Why didn't you just tell us who he was from the beginning?"

"Because I didn't know he was going to remember you. I wanted to see how he reacted. I was going to tell you."

"We've been here almost two weeks," Faith said.

"What are you going to do?" Yvette said.

"We're going to go up to him, hug him, and say, 'We're your daughters,' " Faith said. "How's that for a start?"

"Wait until after I'm gone," Yvette said. "I don't want to see any more pain in anyone's eyes."

"We're thrilled he's alive," Hope said. "I wish he were a hundred percent, but if you think for a second this isn't better than—"

"You showed us his grave," Faith cut in.

"Roger made up that grave."

"Roger did?" Hope said.

"He saw how agitated you were getting. He doesn't want to be Thomas."

"Then he must know. He can't hide it if he doesn't know, right?" Faith said.

"I'm not an expert," Yvette said. "His memories may come and go. The only thing I know for sure is that if he does know who he used to be—he's also fully aware that he's no longer that man. And he's deeply ashamed of that. It's too painful to watch."

"That's why we have to tell him we know," Faith said. "Tell him how much we love him."

"But what if it backfires?" Yvette said. "He's come so far. It would kill me to see him backslide again."

"I'd like the name of his doctor," Hope said. "We need more information."

"I'll make sure you get all the information. As long as you promise to do whatever is best for him, not whatever is best for you."

"He's our dad. How can it hurt to acknowledge that?" Faith argued.

"I told you. He knows enough to know he isn't the man he once was. That he couldn't be a father, or a husband. He knows what he's missed out on. He chose not to reach out to you girls or your mother after the accident. He wanted you to remember him the way he was."

"Or maybe Roger didn't think about us at all," Faith said. She headed for the barn door. Yvette and Hope followed.

Yvette took ahold of Faith's arm and spun her around. She pointed at the grounds. Twinkling lights hanging from trees, mechanical reindeer and Santa, and other characters, red bows, and wreaths, and glass balls dangling from tree branches. Skates all organized, and the sound system ready to play. Firewood piled up by the fire pit. "I dare you to look at all he's done since you've arrived, for you girls and you girls alone, and say that again."

Tears came to Faith's eyes. "I'm just so overwhelmed," she said. "I just want to tell him we know. I just want to tell him how much we love him. How much we've always loved him." Hope wrapped her arms around her sister.

"It's going to be okay," Hope said. "It's all going to be okay."

"Is it?" Faith said. "Is it really?"

"He's here and he loves us," Hope said. "And we're here, and we love him." The sound of sobbing filled the air. It startled Hope, for she hadn't realized Faith was crying that hard. And then Faith pulled back and Hope could see it wasn't her. They turned to find Yvette, bent over, shaking from her tears. Hope's heart broke open. In unison they reached for her, wrapped their arms around their grandmother, held her up, and together they cried. They cried for the barren years they'd wasted. They cried for the father they'd lost in the accident. They cried for the wife whose husband never came back. They cried for the grandmother they never knew. And they cried for the man who, no matter how changed, was showing them with every fiber of his being that they still mattered. That he was still their dad, and they were still his girls.

CHAPTER 35

It wasn't until the next day that Hope and Faith were able to kidnap Joy. A Christmas hike through the mountains did not thrill Joy, which was why Faith and Hope kept it a secret until they had already pulled into the parking lot where the trail began. Mr. Jingles was the first to dash out of the car, and since there weren't any other cars parked in the lot, Hope simply kept his leash tucked in his bag and allowed him a bit of freedom. The snow on the ground was several feet deep, but the skies were blue and clear.

"Why are we doing this?" Joy said. "We could eat, shop, or drink instead."

"Exercise and fresh air does wonders for the soul," Faith said. She failed to mention that they wanted to isolate Joy in a remote mountain location before telling her that Roger was their father.

For the moment Hope was enjoying what was in front of her. She loved the smell in the air, crisp and earthy. She was looking forward to the hike—not to breaking the news to Joy—but to exerting her muscles and taking deep breaths, and communing with nature. She suddenly felt filled with the Christmas spirit, and was even thinking fondly of Yvette and looking forward to an evening Scrabble game in front of the fire. Her number-one goal was still to get their father to come inside the house. She couldn't imagine future gatherings—holding her child up by the window so he could "meet" the new baby.

But it was more proof that they didn't know what they were dealing with when it came to his cognitive issues. Yvette was right. They shouldn't make any major moves until they'd spoken with his doctor. But there was still a strong connection between them, and that was something, and for now that would have to be enough. She just prayed that Joy would see it the same way.

Mr. Jingles took off ahead of them, leading the pack. They had only just started on the path, Faith surging ahead, Hope in the middle (always!), and Joy was bringing up the rear, when she made the announcement. "I think we should see a lawyer."

Faith stopped abruptly and Hope plowed into her. The padding from their winter coats helped soften the blow.

"What for?" Hope asked.

"Roger," Joy said. "I think we need to find him a new home as soon as Yvette departs."

"I thought we agreed not to discuss any of this until after the holidays," Hope said. "And for all we know, Yvette might live for years."

"I hope she does," Joy said. "I like her. But I can see her getting weaker every day."

"Me too," Faith said softly. "She's growing on me too."

"So do you agree? We need to seek out a lawyer?"

"Let's get to the top of this trail," Faith said. "It's healthy to be silent."

"Is that a fancy way of telling me to shut up?" Joy said.

"Yes," Hope said. Joy shook her head, but the pair resumed their climb without the chatter. A hawk was perched on a tree just ahead of them and the three stopped to admire it.

Mr. Jingles's excitement grew the higher they climbed. He would run ahead and then race back as if to check on them. The snow wasn't as deep the farther in they went, probably due to the cover of the dense tree branches above them. Patches were a bit icy, which was why they had on their best snow boots and Faith was even carrying a walking stick despite the fact that she was probably in the best shape to handle a slip. At one point Hope slipped and her body slid down a few feet. Joy grasped on to her before she could be slammed to the ground and the two slipped together, furiously trying to get traction while Mr. Jingles ran in circles around them. Finally, they reached the top. From here there was a bit of a clearing to the left and they had a bird's-eye view to the mountains and downtown. Far below, one of the horse and carriages could be seen making its way through the center of town, and shoppers appeared in miniature, carrying their tiny, colorful bags. The three stood in silence, enjoying the scenery, the moment, the peace.

"Harrison and I have decided to take your advice, Hope," Joy said. Hope rifled through every bit of advice she'd doled out to Joy lately and came up blank. "We're going to save up for a coffee truck."

"Seriously?" Hope said. She wasn't sure whether or not to congratulate her. If she accepted the credit, then she would also have to accept the blame if things went south.

"You're moving here?" Faith said.

"Well, it will be a truck, so really we can drive it wherever we want, but yes. We're moving here. We'll stay with Granny while she's still with us."

"You can't do that," Faith said.

"It's already done," Joy said.

"Haven't you already put down money on a place in Seattle?" Hope asked. Not only did she not want to be blamed if the coffee truck failed, she also couldn't push away the thought that Joy was just conniving to get what she wanted, and using Yvette in the process. She was already one meeting with a lawyer away from kicking their father off the property, and even if they only thought of him as Roger, the man had been living there for the past twenty years.

"We've already lost that deposit," Joy said. "We weren't able to pay the next installment."

"We have bigger things to discuss," Faith said.

"Such as?"

"Mom is missing for one."

"I told you she went to Cuba after all," Joy said.

"No," Faith said. "She was coming here."

"Do you hear yourself? Why on earth would she come here?"

Faith looked at Hope. She was handing over the Olympic Torch. Hope faced Joy. "First of all, we tried telling you earlier, but you were always busy."

"Telling me what?" Anger was on the surface, but Hope could also hear the fear in Joy's voice.

"Roger is our father."

Joy broke out in a fake smile, as if to say, ha-ha; then it slowly faded as her eyes bounced between Hope and Faith. "Excuse me?"

Faith took the reins. "Roger is Thomas Garland. He's our father. He's your father."

"Get out," Joy said. She kicked snow with her boot, trying to aim it at Hope, then kicked a pile toward Faith. Joy shook her head, smiling, eyes ping-ponging once again from Faith to Hope, waiting for one of them to admit it was a joke. Once again Hope and Faith remained serious. Joy flapped her arms. "What are you talking about?"

"There was a moment when he looked at me and I just knew," Hope said.

"I didn't know," Faith interjected. "Until I knew. And now every time I look at him I wonder why I couldn't see it."

Joy shook her head. "He died in a car accident. Granny said so. We saw his grave."

"We saw a cross in the dirt that Roger—I mean, our father—stuck there," Hope said.

"I'm sick of this. You two aren't making any sense."

"He was in a coma after the car accident," Faith explained. "He was never the same again. Yvette isn't even sure if he's fully aware of who he is."

"Oh my God," Joy said. "Oh my God." She stumbled forward. Hope caught one arm and Faith the other, as the most unexpected thing happened. Joy began to sob. Faith and Hope held her close. "It's not fair," she said. "It's not fair."

Faith gently pushed Joy back so she could look her in the eyes. "It's a miracle," she said. "It's more than fair. We're getting him back."

"But he's brain-damaged!"

"Yes," Hope said. "And that's the reason he never wanted us to know he was still alive."

"I thought he was a con artist. Are you sure he's not a con artist?"

"We're sure," Faith said.

"This is crazy. How can that man be our father? He's nothing like you said he was."

"He was in a serious accident," Hope said. "But he's still our dad."

"He's not my dad," Joy said. "He never will be."

"Don't say that," Faith said.

"He's a total stranger," Joy said. "I don't feel anything."

"He still loves us," Hope said. "He loves you."

"How can you say that?"

"He's decorating the entire grounds for Christmas. For us. Don't you see?" Hope pleaded.

"I don't see," Joy said. "You two are nuts."

Faith stepped up. "It's not about us. It's about him. We're all going to mourn the father we lost. This doesn't change that. But he's still here. And he's ours. He's yours."

Joy started sobbing again. "I was going to try to have him institutionalized."

"Not the best Christmas present," Faith said. Joy swiped at her.

"Wait," Joy said. "That's why Mom is coming?"

"Yes," Faith said. "But she doesn't know that he's not exactly himself—well—I don't know what she knows because she's missing."

"Does Roger—Dad—know that you guys know?"

"No," Hope said. "We can't tell him yet. We have to talk to his doctors, make sure we're not going to set him back in any way by confronting him with it."

"My God," Joy said. "How long have you two been leaving me in the dark, like a chump?"

"I told you, we've been trying to tell you. It's only been a few days."

"A few days!"

"Please," Faith said. "We love you, Joy. We're not trying to leave you out. Can we please not pile onto the stress here? I think a dying grandmother, an injured daughter, a suicidal teenager, a disgruntled soon to be ex-husband, a secret lesbian lover, a disabled lost father, and a missing mother is quite enough to deal with for one holiday season. I don't even know if I can fit all of that into our annual Christmas letter. So can I please, please just have my relationship with my sisters intact?" Hope and Joy stared openmouthed at Faith.

Joy started to laugh first. Then she began to softly pummel Faith with mittened fists. "I hate your annual Christmas letter."

"Stop it," Faith said, but her laughter betrayed she was enjoying it. Hope grabbed her around the neck and messed up her beautiful hair. "Stop."

"You didn't mention Mr. Jingles," Hope said. "You like him."

"I do not!" Mr. Jingles jumped on Faith and licked her lips. "Gross!" Faith shouted.

"You have the worst life!" Joy said, breaking into laughter again.

"I have the worst sisters," Faith said. Mr. Jingles barked and circled them, then once again jumped up and licked Faith's face with his giant tongue from chin to forehead.

* * *

They stopped in town. Joy wanted to buy Roger a present. She'd agreed not to say a word to him about who they were, but insisted on the gift. For someone who said she wanted nothing to do with the man, she was coming around awfully quick. Hope was so grateful. It just so happened that Joy found her gift in the same store where Hope had her eye on that sweater for Austin. So while Joy was buying their father a scarf, she bought Austin a sweater.

"Who's that for?" Faith asked with a smile, nudging Joy.

"None of your beeswax," Hope said.

"Would Dad like a sweater?" Joy asked.

"Let's get him one that's big and soft," Faith said. The three of them picked out a sweater that matched the scarf, and finally a new cap. They would have bought the entire store for him if they could have.

"Do we have to wait for Christmas to give these to him?"

"That's usually how it goes," Faith said.

"I want to give it to him as soon as we get back," Joy said. "That's how it goes with me."

Hope laughed. "You always had all your gifts opened before Christmas. Except when Mom started locking them in the cedar chest."

"Oh no. I figured that lock out in no time." Joy smiled.

"You did not."

"I did too. I'd open it, unwrap them, then wrap them back up."

"Unwrap them?" Faith said. "You opened ours too?"

"Of course," Joy said. "I switched them sometimes too."

"Oh my God," Hope said. "I knew that purple radio was supposed to be mine. I asked for it." Joy shrugged. "I've been mad at Mom for years over that."

"It's not my fault," Joy said. "I always expected her to confront me, but she never did."

"She hated Christmas so much she couldn't even remember what she bought us," Faith said.

"Or she had somebody else buy them," Hope said. "Speaking

of which—shouldn't we check with a few of the hotels in town to see if she's here?"

"I have to check my phone and see if her boyfriend answered my message," Faith said. "But I agree, let's check the inns in town."

"What do we do if there's no room at the inn?" Joy dead-panned. Hope and Faith raced to see which one would be the first to smack her.

CHAPTER 36

"Well, that was a waste of time," Joy said. They had checked all the lodging in town and no sign of their mother. They stood at the corner of Main Street watching shoppers come and go. Hope was really starting to worry about Carla. She gravitated toward drama, not away from it. It wasn't like her to disappear.

"At least we managed to spread the word of our Christmas Extravaganza," Faith said. The managers of the inns seemed excited about the invitation. Several of them mentioned how generous of a man Rupert had been; nobody commented on Yvette.

"How much are we going to charge per person?" Joy asked.

"We're not charging," Hope said.

"Of course we are," Joy said.

"No," Hope said. "We're giving back. For Christmas."

"We can give and take at the same time," Joy said. They piled in the car and were headed back to the estate.

"Faith," Hope said. "Would you like to jump in here?"

"We're not charging," Faith said.

"Thank you," Hope said.

"Harrison is going to make donuts and I'm going to make coffee, and we're selling those," Joy said. "You can't stop us."

"You're entirely missing the point of the season," Hope said.

"We might need the reward money to find Mom," Joy said.

"See?" Faith said. "There's the selfless Joy we know and love."

"Who's buying me a coffee truck for Christmas?" Joy said.

Hope glanced ahead as they were approaching the estate. The gates were open and everyone was standing outside. She was thrilled to see Austin among them. He turned as their car pulled up and Hope smiled. He smiled back, then stepped to the side, revealing none other than their mother. Carla Garland was wearing a hot-pink trench coat, her highlighted hair piled on top of her head in a messy bun. She was holding court with Josh and Brittany, flapping her arms in high animation. Yvette was to her side, scowling. "She's alive," Hope said. "Thank God."

"I didn't know they sold winter coats in Miami," Faith remarked.

"She looks like a flamingo," Hope said. The two of them laughed.

"Mom!" Joy said. "Looks like I get to keep the reward money." She had the car door open before it had even come to a stop.

"Wonder if she's seen Dad yet?" Faith said. Hope had been wondering the same thing. They quickly scanned the grounds, but their father wasn't in sight. The girls barreled out of the car and ran to their mother.

"There you are," Carla said. "Some welcome." They gave their mother a group hug.

"We were looking all over town for you," Faith scolded.

"I see you didn't tell me that my only granddaughter was crippled," Carla said the minute the hug was over.

"I'm not really crippled," Brittany said.

"Like Tiny Tim!" Josh said.

"Where's Roger?" Faith said.

"Don't call him that," Carla said. She turned to Yvette. "How dare you."

"Thank God," Joy said. "We got here just in time for the good stuff."

Faith stepped forward. "Not in front of the kids," she said.

"Why is Grandma so mad?" Brittany asked Faith.

"Why is the sky gray?" Faith answered.

"You know what?" Austin said. "I was thinking of taking the kids downtown."

"Yay!" Brittany said. "I can practice my crutches."

"There's still a lot of ice," Austin said. "We'll take the sled just in case."

"That's what got her into this in the first place," Faith muttered.

"Not downhill this time," Austin said with a wink. "Just down the sidewalk."

"Can I have some money, Mom?" Josh asked.

"Sure," Faith said.

"How come that never works for me?" Joy said.

"Because you're not my child," Faith said.

"Where's Harrison?" Joy asked.

"He's out in the woods chopping firewood," Yvette said.

"What has this place done to him?" Joy said.

"I need to see *Roger*," Carla said. She drew the name out and glared at Yvette, then headed for his cabin.

"Not so fast," Yvette said, lunging forward and grabbing a hot-pink sleeve. "We have to talk."

"You've had years to talk," Carla said. "Too little and much too late."

"Mom, please," Hope said. "She's right. We do have to talk. All of us." Carla's eyes flicked to Faith. Hope cringed. She would never be seen as a decision maker.

"I second," Faith said. Hope and Faith looked at Joy. For a second Joy seemed startled that they included her. Then she straightened up and looked Carla in the eye.

"Third," Joy said. "I third."

It took a lot of whiskey and repetition, but Carla finally heard what they all had to say. They were huddled on the sofas in front of the fireplace, tucked under blankets, as if trying to squeeze out any bit of comfort they could. Tears were pooling in Carla's eyes and running down her cheeks. Streaks of black mascara ran down her cheeks. Hope handed her a tissue. She clutched it, then looked at Yvette.

"You still should have told us," Carla said. "He was my husband. Their father. We loved him."

"I know that now," Yvette said. "And I'm sorry."

"So what? We just pretend he's not Thomas?" Carla looked to the girls for an answer.

"At the least we need to speak with his doctor," Faith said. "It's obvious he's not the dad we knew. But he functions and seems relatively happy. I couldn't forgive myself if we made things worse."

"Me neither," Hope said.

Harrison entered the house. Joy ran to him and jumped into his arms. Carla looked him over.

"Hi, Mrs. G," Harrison called.

"Hi, Harrison."

"You two know each other?" Faith said.

"We're Facebook friends," Carla said.

"Top friends," Harrison said, putting Joy down.

"Lovely to meet you in person." Carla unfolded herself from the sofa and wiped the mascara off her cheeks. Then she sauntered over and hugged Harrison. Their mother. The eternal flirt.

"Was Roger with you in the woods?" Carla asked, eagerly scanning the windows. Hope found herself doing the same thing. They were going to have to watch Carla or she was going to go rogue.

"For a bit. He went back to his cabin," Harrison said.

"Do you think he saw me?"

Harrison was sporting a grin, but it faded slightly as he frowned. "I don't think so. Why?"

"He's my father," Joy said. "Her ex-husband."

Harrison looked behind him as if expecting someone to jump out. "Who?" he said. "What?"

"Not ex-husband," Carla said. "Husband. I never had him declared dead, and we never divorced."

"I'm lost," Harrison said.

"Roger, the caretaker, is our father," Joy said.

"Funny," Harrison said.

"Not joking," Joy said. She pulled Harrison aside and began to quietly fill him in. A few seconds later he was hugging Joy, wrapping her into his arms. *I really like him,* Hope thought. She never imagined anyone who could calm Joy down like that.

"You're still married," Yvette said slowly, turning to Carla. "I never even thought of that."

"It means whatever decisions get made for him are mine," Carla said.

"I'll change my will. The girls won't get the house. Is that what you want?"

"Let's all calm down," Hope said. "It's Christmas." She walked up to Yvette, took her hands. "You can leave the house to whomever you want. You won't get your way by hanging that over our heads anymore. We actually like you now. We're not just here for the inheritance."

"I second," Faith said. They turned to Joy. Joy stared for a long time.

"Third," Joy said finally, albeit in a dejected tone.

"How is that possible?" Yvette said. Her tone still had an edge to it, but she looked hopeful, as if she wanted to believe them.

"We like you," Joy said. "It's a Christmas miracle."

"I don't like you," Carla said.

"Mom," Hope said. "You will not start pushing your weight around."

"Wouldn't do any good," Carla said. "I've been on the South Beach Diet. I've barely anything to push. Not that anyone noticed."

Hope faced her mother. "You have to agree not to say anything to Roger until after the holidays and after we've talked to his doctors."

322 • *Mary Carter*

"Why don't we talk to his doctors right now?"

"We can make an appointment," Hope said. "We were waiting for you."

"Fine," Carla said. "Call them right now."

"I'm on it," Faith said. The door opened and Austin and the kids piled in. Stephen followed them in.

"I heard you were here," he said to Carla. "I wanted to say hello." Carla practically flew over to his side and enveloped him in a hug.

"Don't you look handsome?" she said. Hope could only imagine how she was going to react to the news about Faith and Charlie.

"That was a quick trip downtown," Faith said.

"It's been two hours," Austin said.

"Wow," Faith said.

"Would you look at that. Time flies when you're also *not* having fun," Joy said.

"You should see the lights downtown," Brittany said. "They're so pretty!"

"As pretty as ours?" Hope teased.

Brittany pondered the question seriously. "Well, they have more downtown, but ours are really special."

"They sure are," Faith said. She looked at the kids. "Sit down," she said. "We have something to tell you."

Josh groaned. "Great. More surprises." He glanced at his dad.

Stephen held his hands up. "Nothing to do with me this time," he said.

"What?" Carla said.

"Later," Faith said. "Guys, we need to talk to you about Roger."

"What's he done now?" Josh said.

"Oh, honey, he hasn't done anything." She knelt in front of the kids and gave them the news.

"Our grandfather?" Brittany said. Her eyes lit up. "I knew I liked him!"

"That's weird," Josh said. He seemed at a loss for words. Silently, everyone turned and looked out the window toward the cabin. Hope wished more than anything that Roger was inside with them right now. Hope turned to Harrison. "Was Mr. Jingles out there with you?"

"Sure was. He went back to the cabin with Roger. I mean your dad. What are we supposed to call him now?"

"Roger," Yvette said. "He wants to be called Roger."

Harrison nodded. "Mr. Jingles and Roger are thick as thieves."

"I'm so happy," Hope said. She thought about how burdened she felt when that woman dumped Mr. Jingles on her. And here it was meant to be.

Carla lurched forward. "I want to see him. I want to see my husband."

"She's not getting this," Yvette said. "She's going to ruin everything."

"I just want to see him. Say hello."

"No," Yvette said.

"It's going to happen sooner or later," Faith said.

"She ruined his life!" Yvette said.

"Me?" Carla said. "You're the one. You ruined all of our lives."

Hope sidled over to Austin. "If this doesn't change your mind about how joyful Christmas can be, I don't know what will." Austin took her hand and squeezed it.

"I have an idea," he said.

They stood outside, with every single Christmas light on the lawn aglow. A practice run, Austin called it. He turned on the stereo system from the barn and soon carols played into the night air. A roaring fire leapt and crackled in the fire pit where Josh and Brittany were roasting chestnuts with their dad. Harrison and Joy were putting the finishing touches on a snowman and snowwoman.

"He's a white dude," Harrison said. "Otherwise, he's fine."

Joy threw a snowball at him and a fight commenced. Yvette refused to come out. She was watching from the windows. Roger had yet to emerge, but Austin insisted on letting him do it on his own. Carla was pacing in the snow, never taking her eyes off the cabin.

"The community is going to love this," Hope said, gesturing all around her. "Even if we can't."

"It's not so bad," Austin said, holding up a sprig of mistletoe above their heads. Hope laughed and kissed him.

Soon they heard the excited barks of Mr. Jingles from the direction of the cabin.

"I'm not sure this is a good idea," Faith said. "Mom looks like a rocket about to launch."

No sooner had Faith said it and it happened. Carla bolted toward the cabin, racing across the snow like a madwoman, sending snow flying behind her. From inside the house, Yvette pounded on the windows as if that would be enough to stop Carla. A few seconds later the cabin door opened and Mr. Jingles came racing out, in a direct beeline toward Carla.

"Uh-oh," Hope said. Mr. Jingles leapt on Carla and tackled her to the ground. Screams filled the air. Everyone but Brittany raced toward her.

"Not fair," Brittany said, hopping on one foot. "Not fair."

Hope kept her eyes peeled on the cabin door as she ran. It was closed again. Had their father seen Carla and refused to come out? Did that mean he understood a lot about what was going on, or did it mean he didn't know who Carla was? The sooner they talked to his doctors the better. Maybe Yvette was right, maybe this should have waited. By the time Hope reached her mother, Austin and Faith had already pulled her up. Mr. Jingles was literally running circles around them and barking, as if to herd them in.

"That's Mr. Jingles," Hope said to her mother. "Sorry."

"He's a horse," Carla said. Once again she was looking at the cabin door. "He doesn't want to see me," she said softly. "My heart is breaking."

Faith looped arms with her mother, and so did Joy. Hope completed the semicircle by standing in front of her.

"It's not about you," Hope said. "I think he's embarrassed for you to see him like this. I actually think it means he understands a lot more than we gave him credit for."

"Or he is just shy around strangers," Faith said.

Hope gave her a look, but Faith shrugged it off.

"I've waited twenty-four years for this," Carla said. "And he's just going to shut me out."

"Let's find some pinecones to leave by his door," Hope said. "A little gift of love from all of us."

Carla arched a severely tweezed eyebrow. "Pinecones?"

"Trust me," Hope said. "He'll love it."

Faith stepped up and clasped her mittens under her chin. "Then let's go inside, pop some corn, and drink hot chocolate."

"Yay!" Brittany said.

"Pinecones?" Carla repeated.

"Dad left one for me on the porch as soon as I arrived," Hope said. "Before I knew it was Dad."

"I want to leave one from me too," Josh said.

"Me too," Brittany said. They all whirled around.

"Sweetheart," Faith said. Brittany had hopped all the way on one foot.

"It's okay," Brittany said. "I'm getting good at balancing."

Austin stepped forward. "Harrison and I will go in and start the popcorn. Why don't you guys take care of the pinecones as a family?"

"I'll join you two," Stephen said.

"You're family too," Faith said.

"Thank you," Stephen said. "But I think you guys can handle this one. I'm going to humble myself for a game of Scrabble with Yvette."

"I'll get the sled," Josh said to Brittany. "Stay here."

"Thank you."

"Oh my God," Faith whispered to Hope. "Are my children actually being nice to each other or am I hallucinating?"

"'Tis the season," Hope said.

"A miracle indeed."

They left a total of six pinecones in front of Roger's door, all bunched up like a miniature family waiting for him to come outside. It was dark in the cabin and the curtains were shut, but Hope felt that somehow he was watching, somehow he knew they were there.

"Shouldn't we put glitter on them, or a bow or something?" Carla said.

"Glitter!" Brittany said. "And a bow!"

"I think they look good au naturel," Faith said. Her eyes flicked over Carla. "Unlike some spectacles."

Brittany indeed found a red bow and set it gently on top of their family of pinecones.

"Now what?" Carla said.

"Now we leave him in peace for a while," Hope said. Once again they took Carla by each arm and gently led her back to the house.

"Do you think he'll know they're from us?"

"Have a little *me*," Faith said.

Hope and Joy laughed. She used to say that joke all the time.

"*Me* to the world," Joy said. She elbowed Hope.

"I *me* it snows on Christmas Eve."

Carla groaned. "Not that old joke again." The girls dissolved into giggles.

"It never gets old," Faith cackled.

Carla shook her head. "And they think I'm the crazy one."

"I don't get it," Josh said.

"Have a little faith, Joy to the world, and I hope it snows on Christmas Eve," Brittany chimed in.

"Oh," Josh said. Then he started laughing. And Brittany started laughing. It was like music to Hope's ears, so she could only imagine how good Faith felt in the moment. Her children, finally sounding happy. Hope wondered how much it had to do with the fact that their father was here. No matter what, kids always wanted the family together. Just like they still longed for their father. She understood how her mother felt. She, too, wanted to bust open the door. She glanced back at the pinecones, huddled by the entrance, waiting for him to greet them. For now, it would have to be enough.

CHAPTER 37

After taking Yvette's advice and each drawing a name, the motley crew was in town doing their Christmas shopping. Although Hope understood the spirit of it, she still wanted to buy Christmas gifts for everyone. Especially since she had drawn Stephen's name. She couldn't imagine not getting a gift for her niece and nephew, not to mention her sisters, or her grandmother, for goodness' sake, and then of course there was her mother, and father, and she'd already bought the sweater for Austin. Rules be darned, she was going to buy a little something for everyone. It was one of her favorite parts of Christmas. Buying gifts she thought others would like, wrapping them, addressing them, placing them under the tree. She wouldn't go overboard, or anything, but she had to follow her heart. She hadn't waited all these years to be together to not celebrate to the max. Horse and carriages were out in great numbers, and the shops were filled. Christmas was in the air. Their celebration was going to start a day after the Christmas lighting ceremony in town. They didn't want folks to have to choose. It was to take place this evening and excitement was in the air. Every time she stepped into a shop and heard a bell jingle and felt the rush of warmth and sound of laughter within, Hope felt a surge of the Christmas spirit. This was what it was all about. Roger still hadn't emerged, but when they woke up in the morning the pinecones were gone. Hope thought it was a fabulous sign, although Carla was still obsessed. They had an appointment with his doctor the next afternoon. It felt funny to be meeting without Roger, but Yvette had Power of Attorney, and would soon have to pass that on to one of them.

Yvette had surprised Hope by coming out with them on the shopping trip. After they'd all finished they were going to have lunch together.

Hope bought coffee mugs for Joy and Harrison with the town of Leavenworth on them, she bought new ice skates for Brittany for when she could skate again, she bought a new yoga mat for Faith, but then drew a complete blank on Stephen, Yvette, her mother, and her father. She met up with Faith in the cooking store and Faith told her that Stephen was going to take up painting, so Hope bought him some paints and brushes and a few small canvases.

"We'd better get all those bags into my trunk," Faith said. "Before the others see you're cheating."

Hope laughed and they hurried out to Faith's car. When she popped the trunk Hope saw a pile of shopping bags. "I see I'm not the only one," Hope laughed.

"Draw names," Faith said. "Ridiculous!"

"I'm going to say mine are from Santa so I don't get in trouble," Hope said.

"Always the peacemaker," Faith said. She shut the trunk, then looked left and right before speaking again. "I have an idea for Joy and Harrison," she said. "But I need you to go in on it with me."

"I already got them coffee mugs," Hope said.

Faith laughed. "Busting the bank, I see." Hope didn't have a lot of money. Not the kind of money Faith had. What did she expect. Faith gently punched her. "I'm just kidding. And I'm not asking you to spend anything you currently have."

"What does that mean?"

"It means we're going to need Yvette's permission for this one—some future inheritance."

"You've piqued my interest," Hope said.

"Get in," Faith said.

"What about lunch?"

"They can start without us," Faith said. "Christmas is about surprises."

On the ride to the surprise, Faith gathered her thoughts. It was time to tell Hope the truth. Why she really left her. The truth of that summer. Faith had had crushes on girls, only girls, ever since she could remember, but she never acted on her feelings. Never dared to think about what would happen if she did. That just wasn't who she was, who she imagined herself to be. Then, a few days after Faith turned seventeen, it happened. She met a girl on the beach. A beautiful, funny girl. A summer girl with chestnut hair and green eyes, and an infectious laugh. Whenever summer girl looked at her, Faith got butterflies in her stomach.

"Why don't you want Joy and me to go to the beach with you anymore?" Hope asked her one day.

Faith remembered how a wave of shame enveloped her, how she couldn't imagine telling her sisters how she really felt. That wasn't how they saw her. It wasn't how she saw herself. "No one's stopping you from going to the beach," Faith said. "And Joy complains too much about her sunburns."

"Fine. Just me then. You never want me to go with you. Why?"

"Because I go there to meet boys, silly." Lie, lie, lie. She was going there to meet summer girl.

One day when they were in the ocean, underneath the bluest of blue skies, summer girl kissed her. And Faith had kissed her back. Boy did she kiss her back. Maybe that would have been the end of it. Or maybe it would have happened a few more times. Faith probably would have kept it as a memory, a delicious secret. If not for Melanie Hayes.

Melanie Hayes was the most popular girl in school. And she'd always been jealous of Faith. And she saw her. She sat on her towel on the beach, watching Faith and the summer girl kiss. And it didn't take long before she confronted her. *Lesbian. Dyke.* And worse. Lots worse. *Wait until everyone hears this,* Melanie threatened. The thought of everyone at school talking about her behind her back paralyzed Faith. But even more, she couldn't imagine her sisters seeing her in a different way. They had her on a pedestal. She was ashamed. Ashamed of who she was and ashamed that she was ashamed of it. Faith did the only thing she could think to do. She slept with the first boy she could find, a geeky trumpet player on vacation with his rich parents. They did it on the beach, her first time, her first boy, her sacrifice, her salvation. Only this time, she saved *herself.*

From the girl she didn't know how to be, from the names she didn't want to be called. When she found out she was pregnant, it was like angels had come down from the heavens to give her a do-over. Melanie Hayes was the first person she told.

But she didn't tell her sisters. Because that would mean telling them everything. Things she wasn't even ready to admit to herself. At the time she didn't want them to think of her that way, to have pictures in their head. Pictures like her kissing the girl on the beach. Her green eyes, her silky chestnut hair, her soft, insistent lips.

Lie, after lie, after lie. That year, Faith told a lot of lies. Mostly to herself. Not that she'd do anything differently if she had it to do over. Because she had Josh. And Brittany. Hopefully that would one day be enough for Stephen too. Hopefully he would forgive her. How terrifying the thought of being a lesbian was to her then. How freeing it was to admit it now. Thank God the world was starting to become a place where you didn't have to be ashamed of who you loved. It was time to tell Hope she never meant to abandon her. She never stopped loving her and Joy. And she was never going to spend another Christmas away from them again.

They took a few roads out of town and twenty minutes later pulled into a long drive. A gleaming silver food truck sat on the lawn with a FOR SALE sign on it.

"A coffee truck," Hope said.

"Right?" Faith said. "Isn't it perfect?"

"How did you find this?"

"I've been looking in the papers."

Hope kept looking at the gleaming silver truck. "How much is it?"

"They're asking forty-five hundred dollars, but I think we can get them down."

"Wow."

"I know. But I think we owe this to Joy." She reached in the backseat and brought up a book. *Coffee and Cream* was written across it. "Harrison showed this to me. It's Joy's."

Hope took it and began to leaf through it. Page by page Joy had been writing down her plans and dreams for the coffee shop. Prices. Varieties of coffees with cool names. Pictures of décor she liked. Even a script for how she wanted her employees to interact with the customers. Hope felt tears come to her eyes.

"She's put a lot of thought into this."

"More than we gave her credit for." Faith and Hope locked eyes. "I'm so sorry I left you two," Faith whispered.

"Don't," Hope said. "You had to. For your baby."

"It was more than that," Faith said. "I was ashamed."

"Ashamed? You?" Faith never had anything to be ashamed of. She was an "it" girl.

"Melanie Hayes saw me kissing a girl on the beach and she threatened to tell everyone I was a dyke. And worse. I slept with Stephen a few nights later. All because I didn't want you and Joy to find out and look at me differently."

"Oh, Faith." Hope could feel her heart breaking. "You were our world. That would have never changed. Never."

"I know that now. I'm sorry I didn't know that then."

Hope lunged forward and squeezed Faith until it hurt. "Let's buy that coffee truck for Joy," she said when she finally let go.

Faith looked worried. "What if she takes it the wrong way?"

"How could she take an extravagant Christmas present the wrong way?"

"She could think we're saying that we don't believe she could make a go of a real shop."

"Last she spoke about it she was into the truck idea. She wanted to stick around here."

"It is true that a truck fits her personality better. If she gets tired of Leavenworth, all she has to do is drive away."

Faith and Hope laughed. "I'm kind of jealous."

"How so?"

"She's young. Starting a new business with her handsome boyfriend. Hitting the open road. Drinking coffee. Sounds like the smartest of all of us, doesn't it?"

"We'd need to buy her a sign."

Faith gestured to the book. "We know what they want to call it."

"True. And she could always change it, but wouldn't it just be complete with a sign?"

"And a wreath. And a giant red bow."

"Oh God. We have to get it."

"Let's take a few pictures, talk to the owner, and then approach Granny. See if she's willing to finance it."

"I'm so excited," Hope said. Giving was better than receiving. Their father had taught them that.

"Me too," Faith said. She reached over and squeezed Hope's hand. "Thank you."

"For what?"

"For forcing us to be together. We needed this."

"We should do this every year."

"Don't push it."

"How are you doing? Have you heard from Charlie?"

Tears came into Faith's eyes as she shook her head. "I told her we needed to take a break from each other until after the holidays. Now my heart is aching. I can't imagine not talking to her on Christmas."

"Have you tried calling her?"

Faith shook her head. "I'm the one who drew the line in the sand. It's too cruel to go back and forth."

"I'm sure a call on Christmas won't hurt. And a little text wouldn't hurt now."

"Are you sure?"

"If I learned anything, it's that we have to hold on to the people we love."

"No matter how flawed," Faith said, grabbing Hope with a grin.

"Just for that I'm ordering a cheeseburger for lunch," Hope said.

"You know what?" Faith said. "We should all order a cheeseburger."

Hope grinned. Faith was finally feeling the Christmas spirit. *Here comes Santa Claus.*

"Where were you two?" Joy asked the minute they stepped into the restaurant.

"An elf's job is never done," Faith said. "Have we ordered yet?"

"We were waiting for you," Josh said.

"I'm getting a cheeseburger and fries," Faith said, squeezing in between Brittany and Josh. "What about you two?"

"Yay!" Brittany said. "Yes!"

Josh nodded. A smile escaped his lips before he could catch it.

"What's happening here?" Joy said.

"Baby," Harrison said, looping his arm over her shoulders. "Can I get a cheeseburger and fries too?"

"I'm going to have to sit at another table," Joy said.

"We can live with that," Faith said with a wink. "And after lunch, I'm going for a five-mile hike in the woods if anyone wants to join me."

"Why don't you just walk back to the house from here?" Joy said.

"Ha-ha," Faith said. "We should all go."

"What about me?" Brittany said.

"I'll pull the sled myself," Faith said.

"But I won't be able to burn off the calories," Brittany said.

"You'll catch up when you're all better," Faith said. "I'm sorry I've been so consumed with that."

Josh grinned and stuck his index finger up. "Cheeseburger

and fries all around!" he shouted. It was the happiest Hope had ever heard him.

"What's with the waitress in this joint?" Stephen said. They all laughed. "What?" he said. They laughed harder.

"She's horrible," Yvette said with a shake of the head. "She's just horrible."

"Brain injuries are a mysterious thing," Dr. Kaplan said. "No two are like. We can't even be sure that your father is aware he even has a brain injury." They learned that there were two types of TBI, mild and severe, and that their father had suffered the latter. Symptoms could include limited function of arms and legs, abnormal speech or language, loss of thinking ability, and emotional problems.

"His arms and legs are good," Joy said.

"Could he improve?" Faith said.

"Recovery is variable," Dr. Kaplan said. "He could. Or he might backslide. I'm afraid we simply don't know." He set his clipboard down and adjusted his glasses. "I'm going to be honest. You should be celebrating his condition. I saw him when he first came in. We never thought he'd make it out of the coma. The fact that he's as high-functioning as he is is a gift."

"What about more treatment?" Hope asked.

"Your grandmother had him in treatment for years. He reached a certain point and stopped coming. But that in itself was a good sign. The ability to make decisions for oneself."

"I'm his wife," Carla said. "But he hasn't seen me in twenty-four years. Will I be inflicting more damage on him if he interacts with me?"

"Does he seem to recognize you?" the doctor said.

"He's been avoiding her," Hope said.

"We think that means he does recognize her but he's embarrassed," Faith said.

"Or," the doctor said, "he's just not comfortable around a new person."

"He recognizes us," Hope said. "On some level anyway."

"He may feel a bond with you without knowing why," the doctor said.

"But you don't think we run the risk of traumatizing him further?" Faith asked.

"Not if you let him take things at his own pace. I wouldn't force anything on him. If he's avoiding you, that's his choice, isn't it?"

Tears came to Carla's eyes, but she nodded. "It is. I won't stand in his way. I'll leave tomorrow."

"Mother," Faith said. "You will not."

"It's beyond painful. I want to look him in the eyes again. I want to hug him. I don't care about his injuries. He's my Thomas. I just want to hold my Thomas." She started to sob. The doctor glanced at Hope and motioned her to the corner of the room.

"She may need to see someone," he said. "Get something to keep her calm. The more calming and loving influences around Thomas, the better."

Hope thought of all the fighting they'd been doing around him. "Got it," she said. Give their mother a tranquilizer. Nothing new there.

"Come on, Mom," Hope said, linking arms with Carla. "We know a great dive bar just around the corner."

CHAPTER 38

The entire gang gathered downtown for Leavenworth's Christmas lighting ceremony. The streets pulsed with people. Brittany grabbed Hope's hand as the crowd was instructed to sing "O Christmas Tree." As soon as they reached the end, the tree in the center of town lit up like a giant firecracker. The crowd cheered. "Let's all count down from ten for the lighting of the shops," the announcer called over an intercom. "Ten, nine, eight . . ." Voices chanted in unison. "Three, two, one!" Up and down the street, the chalet shops flipped on their lights, setting the strip ablaze. This time the cheer was raucous. Last, but not least, the trees on the perimeter came to life, white lights twinkling like stars. The crowd began to follow along with the next song, "Hark the Herald Angels Sing." Voices swelled up and out into the night air.

Hope marveled at the spectacle. Kids were sledding, costumed Santas led lantern parades, and everywhere people were embracing the old-world Christmas traditions. "Light and love to you all," the announcer called. "To your homes wherever they may be, from ours." The Gingerbread Factory had all their gingerbread houses on display, from mini-cabins to ginger-bread mansions, and every shop had their doors thrown open for guests to wander in.

"Has Dad ever come down here?" Joy asked, turning to Yvette.

"Not since his accident," Yvette said. They'd invited him, which meant talking to him through the closed door of his cabin, but he hadn't come out. Hope hated to admit it, but their mother's arrival had set him back.

"Do you think crowds at our place will bother him?" Hope asked.

"He stays in the background for sure," Yvette said. "But it never seemed to cause him great distress. Then again, he hadn't shown much interest in anything until you girls showed up."

"Interest in them, but not in me," Carla said.

"You said it," Yvette said.

"I should leave then," Carla said.

"Mom," Faith said. "You're not going anywhere."

"It's almost Christmas, Grandma Carla," Brittany said. "You have to stay."

"He'll come around," Faith said.

"He's still stubborn," Carla said. "I should sit in front of his door until he opens it."

"Let's just enjoy the evening," Hope said. "Who wants some hot cocoa?" Everyone, it turned out, and soon they were strolling by the shops taking in the lights and the carols, and the characters, hot cocoa in hand. "It's magical," Hope whispered to Austin.

He gazed at her and grinned. "It is this year," he said. He leaned over and kissed her cheek.

"Get a room," Joy said.

"Good one," Harrison said. "Why don't we do the same?"

There were only six days until Christmas and the Garland Girls had finally settled into their sweet spot, making breakfast together in the mornings, putting finishing touches on the grounds in the afternoon, and playing Scrabble with Yvette in the evenings along with hot cocoa, and popcorn, and Christmas specials on the television. At night they would light up the grounds and play Christmas carols through the loudspeakers, and delight in the sights and sounds. Roger still wasn't coming out of his cabin, and Yvette was now the only one who could bring him his meals.

Every day Mr. Jingles would come out and join the rest of them, but in the evening he was always back at the cabin door waiting to be let in. It was bittersweet for Hope; she was so grateful their dad was bonding with Mr. Jingles, but sad he was shutting the rest of them out. Yvette seemed to be getting weaker, although she was still as feisty as ever, which Hope took to be a promising sign. Austin said she was now refusing to go to her doctor's appointments, which in a way made complete sense to Hope. If she was terminal she wouldn't want to waste time at the doctor's either. They needed to get Roger engaged with them again, that would lift Yvette's spirits. Family was so connected, Hope realized. When one was hurting, they all hurt. Likewise sometimes all it took was one genuine smile from Brittany to lift the entire group. Tomorrow would be day one of the public festivities on their grounds and as they erupted in a flurry of activity, the excitement became palpable.

The lights and decorations were ready, the skates were dusted off and organized by size, there was plenty of firewood for the fire pit, and the menu of hot chocolate, chestnuts, popcorn, and S'mores were also stockpiled and waiting. And although admission would be free, they would be taking gift donations for children in need, as well as donations for the local animal shelter and suicide prevention.

"Suicide prevention?" Stephen asked.

"Austin works for a suicide prevention center," Hope said.

"I see." Stephen glanced at Faith, who made a point of not making eye contact. She hadn't told him about Josh's call to Austin. Maybe there had been too much going on to mention it, or maybe Josh's earlier cries for help was a point of contention between them. Hope made a mental note to ask Faith about it later.

* * *

The grounds were set to open in thirty minutes and there was already a line of people waiting to get in. The lights were on, the music was playing, and the skates were ready. Hope kept expecting Roger to come out of his cabin at any minute. Was he really going to miss this? Were they doing the right thing, letting him withdraw like this? Would it be better if they confronted him, or should they ask Carla to leave? Now that their mother was here, Hope wanted her to stay. She wanted all of her family, no matter how flawed, to be together for Christmas. Especially their father. He was the one who was supposed to love the holiday more than any of them.

Austin came up, his eyes bright. "Do you think we should let them in early?" he said, glancing at the line of people just beyond the gate.

"Let's do it," Hope said. "We're ready."

"Great. I'll tell the others." Hope hurried to the fire pit; her first assignment was to make the S'mores and roast the chestnuts. They'd all assigned themselves roles, and they would switch out every hour. She grabbed a few sticks and marshmallows and smiled as she held them over the roaring fire. Even Yvette seemed to be getting into the spirit of things; she was manning the donation booth. Brittany and Josh were passing out the ice skates, Harrison was overseeing all the lights and making sure they stayed on, and Stephen had somehow been talked into wearing a Santa suit. Even Mr. Jingles was sporting his antlers and trotting around sniffing all the guests. Big dogs were a lot less scary when they were adorned in Christmas gear.

Faith and Joy were supposed to be helping Hope, but so far Joy seemed to be eating more chocolate than she was melting, and Faith was sneaking sips out of a thermos that Hope suspected was spiked. She'd seemed on edge ever since Stephen had asked her why they were giving donations to a suicide prevention organization. Even though Josh had certainly seemed to pull himself out of his dark pit, Hope could tell that Faith and Stephen were still traumatized from the earlier incidents. Faith was probably debating whether or not to tell Stephen what had gone down here. Oh, life was so complicated. Beautiful, but complicated. Soon Hope was too busy handing sticky S'mores to outstretched hands to worry about anything else. The sound of children's laughter and conversation filled the air along with the swoosh of skates and music over the loudspeaker.

"Rupert would have loved this," Yvette said an hour later when Hope went to man the donation table.

"I was hoping Roger would come out," Hope said.

"He's been watching from the barn," Yvette whispered. "Don't look." It was so hard not to turn her head, but Hope was obedient. Watching from the barn was progress.

"Where's Carla?" Hope said.

"I thought she was with you," Yvette said.

"No, Faith and Joy were with me."

"Oh no," Yvette said. In unison, they began scanning the grounds for a pink trench coat. It wasn't long before they spotted her, trotting toward the barn.

"I knew it," Yvette said. She headed for the barn herself, Hope trotting after her. "Look after the booth," Yvette called over her shoulder.

"Maybe we should just let her approach him," Hope said.

"It's obvious he doesn't want to see her," Yvette said.

"We can't control people," Hope said. "I think I'm finally learning that." Carla was at the barn door. Roger was on the other side of it. They stared at each other. Slowly, the barn doors started to close. Carla tried to take a step forward, but Roger was able to shut the doors before she made it inside. Even from ten feet away they could hear the sound of it being latched shut. Carla started to pound on the doors.

"I think we're going to need more whiskey," Hope said.

That evening the Garland Girls sat in the living room trying to console Carla. It was just after midnight when the last of the guests had left the grounds. The kids were in bed, exhausted, Stephen had gone back to his room downtown, Austin was back in his cabin, and Yvette and Harrison had gone to their rooms to give them some privacy. Carla had been crying nonstop since Roger had shut the barn door in her face.

"He's not my Thomas," she was saying over and over. "I thought I was going to have my Thomas back."

"We tried to tell you, Mom," Faith said gently.

"I thought it would change when he saw me. I thought our love would make it change."

"Traumatic brain injury made it change," Hope said. "We can't undo that."

"I have to leave," Carla said. "This is too painful."

"He still needs us," Hope said. "Maybe more than ever."

"He needs you," Carla said. "It's obvious he wants me gone."

"We just need to give him space," Joy said.

"Why is Stephen staying at a hotel?" Carla said, eyeing Faith.

"Because we're getting a divorce," Faith said simply.

"Didn't I tell you?" Carla said to Hope.

"You have no idea," Joy said gleefully. Faith shot her a look.

"Tell me," Carla said.

"I'm in love with someone else," Faith said. "I'm in love with another woman."

Carla laughed. The girls all stared at her until she stopped. Then she gasped and her hand flew to her mouth. "That's not funny," she said.

"That's why we're waiting for you to stop laughing," Faith said.

"You're not a lesbian," Carla said. "You're just athletic."

Joy laughed. "I'm going to put that on a T-shirt."

"Stop this right now," Carla said. "You are not a lesbian."

"I don't care what you call me," Faith said. "I'm probably bi-sexual."

Joy turned to Hope and flashed a grin. "Told you!"

Hope reached over and grabbed Joy's ankle. "You're psychic," she said. "What a waste buying you that crystal ball for Christmas." Joy kicked her.

"Well, where is this woman?" Carla said.

"She was here, but then Stephen showed up," Faith said. "We

agreed it was best to wait until after the holidays to see each other."

"What did Granny Dearest have to say about that little development?" Carla asked.

"I don't think Yvette is worried about anything but Roger," Faith said. "Dying has brought out a softer side of her."

"I see she has you all fooled," Carla said. "How can you forgive her for keeping him from us for all these years?"

"I think we're all just worn down," Faith said. "We'd rather just get along, enjoy the time we have."

"Well, enjoy away," Carla said. "I'll be leaving first thing in the morning."

"It's five days until Christmas," Faith said. "You're staying."

"I could be smoking a Cuban cigar right now," Carla said.

"Why didn't you go?" Joy asked.

"Fernando had a few complications with his identification," Carla said.

"Just like you," Joy said to Faith.

"Ha-ha," Faith said.

"Fernando hasn't posted on Facebook for a while," Joy said. Faith and Hope looked at her. "Harrison got me hooked," she added.

"He's in jail," Carla said. They stared at her. "If you haven't bought my Christmas gift yet I'd appreciate if you'd donate to his bail fund."

"You should start a Kickstarter," Joy said.

"This family is so dysfunctional," Hope said.

Faith shook her head. "My annual Christmas letter just keeps getting longer."

"He's innocent," Carla said. "They've got him mixed up with his cousin who's in a smuggling ring."

"And better," Faith said. "It just keeps getting better."

"I mean it," Carla said. "They could be twins."

"I wish they gave prizes for the most dysfunctional family Christmas," Joy said.

"Sadly we probably wouldn't even be in the top ten," Hope said.

"I've never loved anyone like I loved your father," Carla said. "But I still have to spring Fernando from the pokey."

Nothing says Merry Christmas like getting your mother's boyfriend out of the pokey, Hope thought. Her phone buzzed. It was a text from Austin.

Would you like to come over for a nightcap?

Does Santa say ho, ho, ho?

Later, Faith and Joy would recall that Hope was off the sofa, into the mudroom, and out the door before they could even say, "*And to all a good night.*"

CHAPTER 39

Hope and Austin lay under the covers, holding each other and listening to the wind whistle outside. Just like everything else about his nature, being with him had been so easy and had felt so right. Fireworks, actually, and she was still a bit stunned. They just fit. In more ways than one. She protested when he got out of bed. "You stay," he said. "I'm going to make us coffee and French toast." She bit her tongue before she could ask him to marry her. A half an hour later they were eating breakfast in bed.

"I like your mother," Austin said. Hope felt him for a fever. He laughed and gently knocked her hand away.

"I wish Roger felt the same," Hope said.

"Do you think of him as your father or as Roger?" Austin asked.

"I guess I think of him as Roger," Hope said. "But I also love him because part of my father still exists in him."

"I get that," Austin said. "You have to mourn the loss of the father you once knew."

"I've spent my life doing that," Hope said. "We all have."

"Have you guys talked any more about what you'll do when Yvette is gone?"

Hope shook her head. "We haven't known her very long, but it's already impossible to imagine being here without Yvette."

"I know," Austin said. "I feel the same."

"I want to move into the house," Hope said. "But we have to see if Joy and Harrison will go for the coffee truck. Faith isn't sure what she wants either."

"But you all want Roger to stay on the property," Austin said.

"Yes, we all agree. And Yvette could surprise us all. Live another couple of years."

"Are you going to move in either way?"

Hope smiled and rested her head on Austin's shoulder. "Eager to be neighbors?" she teased.

"Yes," he said, and kissed the top of her head. As imperfect as they all were, this was turning out to be the best Christmas she could ever imagine. She even had hope that Roger was going to come around. They were together. She smiled every time she imagined all of them gathered around the Christmas tree on Christmas Eve. Only three days away. The silver coffee truck was parked in Austin's driveway. Yvette was more than willing to let them borrow against their future inheritance, and Faith had talked the seller down a thousand bucks. That was her bossy sister. Hope smiled. She couldn't wait to surprise Joy and Harrison. She had almost fallen back to sleep when there came a furious pounding on the door.

Austin was out of bed first, and Hope scrambled to put her clothes on. By the time she got to the door, Josh was already inside.

"It's Granny," he said. "Come quick."

She was in bed, and thrashing from a fever. Faith and Carla were tending to her with cold compresses. Her eyes were open, but it was as if she had no idea anyone was in the room with her. She wouldn't make eye contact with any of them. "Thomas, Thomas, Thomas," she repeated over and over. "My Thomas."

"We need to give her the morphine," Faith said.

"Thomas, Thomas, Thomas," she said.

"Just start with the smallest dose," Austin said. "I'll call the doctor."

Hope hurried out of the room. Roger needed to know what was happening. She had to believe that telling him was the right thing to do. She hurried out to the cabin. Mr. Jingles ran out of the barn, barking and running around her in circles. In the distance she spotted Roger, lumbering into the woods. She hurried after him with Mr. Jingles on her heels. She wondered if he knew she was following him for he seemed to pick up his pace. She just hoped he wasn't going to go too far into the woods. The wind was picking up, and the cold was biting. "Roger," she shouted. "Please. Wait up."

Stephen was seething. How dare Faith not tell him about Josh's call to a suicide prevention line? He had to hear it from Brittany. He pulled up to the estate and honked. Brittany and Josh thought they were just going to breakfast. Instead, he was taking them home. They'd be angry at first, but it was for their own good. Their mother was too distracted by other family matters to take care of them. They all seemed convinced that Josh was perfectly fine, but he wasn't going to take that chance. Josh would be angry, sure, but it was for his own good. Stephen had already spoken with his doctor back in San Francisco and arrangements were being made to admit Josh into a psychiatric unit. One threat was all that he was willing to let go by. This was the second cry for help and everyone, including a so-called professional, was just ignoring it.

He smiled as Josh helped Brittany into the car. It's too bad they couldn't pack their things or say good-bye to their grandmother, but the longer Stephen waited the less he'd be able to hide his emotions. The sooner he got Josh checked in the better. Holidays were a high risk factor among those considering suicide. He'd been going along to get along, but not anymore. Losing his wife was one thing. He was not going to lose his son.

*   *   *

Snow was starting to fall. Hope could barely see the back of Roger anymore, and he was completely ignoring her pleas for him to stop. Mr. Jingles was running back and forth between them, and seemed to be getting more and more frantic.

"All right, boy," Hope said the next time he came around. "I'm going back." Roger knew the woods much better than she did, she would have to trust that he would be okay. She hated the thought that he wouldn't get to say good-bye to Yvette. She turned in his direction.

"Yvette is very sick," she yelled. "I thought you might want to see her." *She's not going to make it.* Just ahead Roger stopped moving. Well, that was progress. "If you want, we'll all leave the room so you can be alone with her." There was no response from him, only the whistling of the wind. "She's dying," Hope finally said. "Your mother is dying. You should say good-bye." She turned and headed back for home, tears pooling in her eyes, and prayers already forming on her lips. She had followed her gut. She only prayed she was right to do so.

"Where have you been?" Faith asked the minute she was back inside.

"I thought Roger should know," Hope said. "I followed him into the woods."

"Your face is beet red."

"It's windy and cold," Hope said.

"I'll start a fire," Harrison said. He headed to the fireplace.

"Where is everyone?" Hope asked.

"Joy and Carla are with Yvette, Austin went to get the doctor, and Josh and Brittany are having breakfast with Stephen."

"What can I do?" Hope hated standing around; she felt as if she were waiting for something awful to happen.

"Why don't you plug in the tree and put on some Christmas music," Faith said. "I don't want the kids to be sad when they get back."

"Got it." Hope didn't think they would be fooled that easily, but a little cheer couldn't hurt. They all knew this was coming, and they had to pull together. Hopefully Yvette could turn a corner, get well enough to enjoy one last Christmas. And if not, she wanted her to go peacefully with all her family at her side. She looked outside again, into the gray sky. "Should I turn on all the outside lights too?" Maybe that would get Roger's attention. Oh, who was she kidding. He had heard every word she said. It was his choice whether or not to come and hold his mother's hand. And if he didn't, it wasn't his fault. The doctors were right. Nobody knew what was going on inside Roger's head. The best any human being could ever do was to love everybody they could as long as they could. Everything else was completely out of your control.

"No," Faith said. "No, no, no." She was standing at the kitchen island, dumping items out of her purse.

"What's wrong?"

"It's gone," Faith said. "My entire bottle of Xanax is gone." Just then Faith's phone vibrated on the island. She looked at the screen. "It's Charlie." She snatched it up. "What? There must be some mistake. They're just having breakfast." Hope didn't like the panicked sound in Faith's voice. "I'll call you back," Faith said. She looked at Hope. "Charlie just said she just saw Stephen peeling out of town with the kids in his car."

"Call them," Hope said.

"They're just having breakfast," Faith said. Hope grabbed the phone and called Stephen. It went to voice mail. She called Josh. His went to voice mail too.

"Try Brittany," Faith said. "She always answers." Hope brought up Brittany's name and called. Voice mail picked up after one ring.

Joy ran out from Yvette's room. "She's getting worse," she called down. "How long until the doctor gets here?"

Faith looked at Hope. Her face was stamped with worry. "I don't know what to do. For the first time in my life, I have no idea what to do."

"Keep calling Stephen," Hope said.

"Do you think Josh has it?" Faith said. "Did he take the Xanax?"

"What are you guys talking about?" Joy called down.

"Stephen seems to be taking Josh and Brittany out of town and Faith's bottle of Xanax is missing."

"A full bottle," Faith said. She looked at Joy. "Tell me you took it. I won't be mad at all. Please tell me you took it." Joy shook her head, her face too overwhelmed with a look of fear. Hope never wanted to see that look on her sisters' faces again.

"Should I call the police?" Faith said.

"We're not even sure what's happening yet," Hope said.

"He's not answering!" Faith hung up her phone and swore. "What do we do?"

"Is the doctor here yet?" Carla emerged from Yvette's room. "We have to give her a higher dose of morphine," she said. "I think we have to give her the final dose."

"Did you take my Xanax, Mom?" Faith said. "Tell me you took my Xanax."

"You have Xanax?" Carla said. "Sure I'll take one if you're of-fering—" She stopped talking and her head jerked up. For a second Hope thought Carla was trying to work out why her daughters looked frightened to death. But then Hope noticed she was looking beyond them. Harrison turned from tending the fire and let out a low whistle. The back door was open. Roger was standing inside the house.

CHAPTER 40

For a second nobody moved. Hope stepped up. "Come in," she said to Roger. She took his hand and helped him over to the rug where he could take off his boots. He gripped her hand as he kicked them off. "Coat?" she said, reaching for it. He shook his head. "Okay. Come with me. You too, Mom." She led him down the hall and into Yvette's room. He didn't look at anyone, including Carla, but rather kept his eyes glued to the floor as he followed Hope. Hope stopped when she got to Yvette's door. "Carla is going to go in with you."

"What?" Carla said from down the hall.

"She's very sick," Hope said. "Do you understand?" Roger looked Hope in the eyes and nodded. "I have to help Faith now. Carla is going to stay with you in case you need her. But she won't bother you. Okay?"

"Okay," Roger said. He still wouldn't look at Carla, but he waited until she entered Yvette's room and then followed her.

"Please, Mom," Hope said.

"I won't upset him," Carla said. "This is about Yvette."

"Thank you." Hope hurried back down the hall. She took Faith's hands in hers. "Go after them."

"I'm too upset to drive," Faith said.

"I'll drive," Harrison said.

"I'll come too," Joy said.

"Keep calling Stephen," Hope told Joy. Joy nodded.

"What are you going to do?" Faith said.

"Stay here and wait for the doctor," Hope said. "If you don't find Stephen in the next half hour, call the police and then call me."

"Okay," Faith said. "Okay." Joy took Faith's arm.

"I've got you," she said. "We're going to find them."

Roger came to the edge of the bedroom. Yvette could barely lift her head off the pillow, but her eyes lit up when she saw him.

"Mom," he said. She lifted a shaking hand. After a brief hesitation he stepped forward and took it.

"My boy," she said. "My boy." Hope left the room as tears spilled out of her eyes. She found her own mother, also crying, standing in the kitchen.

"He knows who he is," Carla said.

Hope nodded. "He does in this moment," she said. "But he's not the man you used to know."

"I know," Carla said. "I know."

Faith sat in the back next to Charlie, giving directions to Harrison as she tried to keep her panic under control. She wanted nothing more to find Stephen and ram the back of his car, although she couldn't do that with her children in the car. She'd never known him to be so vindictive. Then again she'd hurt him a lot this past year. And she should have told him about Josh reaching out to Austin. Her poor boy. They were going to have to get him to a psychiatrist, especially if he had taken her bottle of Xanax. She prayed he hadn't done anything with them yet. Joy was still trying to reach Stephen on the phone. As per Faith's instructions, Joy told him they feared that Josh had Faith's bottle of Xanax.

"This is useless," Faith said. "He had a head start." A few minutes later the phone rang. "Please," Faith prayed aloud.

"It's Stephen," Joy said.

"Thank God." She was going to kill him, but for now she was going to be thankful.

"Where are you?" Joy said into the phone. "Did you get my message?" Faith pulled over to the side of the road as she listened to Joy's end of the conversation, which wasn't much at first.

"Oh my God," she said.

"What?" Faith said. "Don't do that."

"Josh took off," Joy said.

"What do you mean?"

"Stephen pulled over to a gas station. Josh said he had to use the bathroom. He's gone."

Faith swore to herself while Joy wrote down where they were. "He called the police," Joy said when she hung up. Tears spilled out of Faith's eyes.

"Let me drive," Charlie said. Faith didn't even argue.

"I'll tell Hope to call Austin," Harrison said. "Josh called him once, maybe he'll call him again."

"He has to be trying to come back to us, right?" Faith said as Joy got in the back with Harrison and Faith took the passenger seat.

"We'll find him," Joy said, scrolling through Faith's phone. "Is it under 'Josh'? I don't see it."

"It's under Baby Boy." Faith could feel the tears pooling in her eyes.

"Found it," Joy said.

"Put it on speaker." Faith held her breath as Josh's phone rang. A man's voice answered after the second ring.

"Who is this?" Faith said. "If you hurt my son I'll kill you."

"It's Austin. Josh called me. I've got him."

"Is he?" Was all Faith managed to squeak out.

"He's fine," Austin said.

"Tell her I'm not going with Dad. I'm going to see Granny."

"He said—"

"I hear you, Josh," Faith said. "Austin can take you back to Granny's."

"Brittany is with Dad at a gas station—"

"I know. We're going to get her right now."

"Are you mad at me?"

"No, no, I'm not mad. But, Josh—please. Do you have my bottle of Xanax?"

"What?"

"Please, give it to Austin."

"I don't have it," Josh said.

"Did you already take them? Should he drive you to the emergency room?"

"How many fingers am I holding up?" Joy said.

"We're not on camera," Josh said.

Faith glared at Joy. "I'm just trying to keep him talking," she said.

"I didn't take your Xanax," Josh said. "I swear."

"He seems fine," Austin said.

"Oh, thank God," Faith said.

"Is Dad going to get arrested?" Josh said.

"No," Faith said. *Possibly run over.*

"He did try to kidnap us," Josh said.

Your mother is your kidnapper. Did crazy run in the family?

"We'll work it out," Faith said. "I can't tell you how glad I am that you're all right." She followed Joy's directions to the gas station. Two police cars were pulled up next to Stephen, who was outside pacing while an officer took notes. Brittany was leaning against the car, crying.

"Let me handle this," Faith said. "You guys stay in the car." She slammed the door and glared at Stephen. She'd wanted to drag out the news that she knew where Josh was as long as possible, torture him a little, but she couldn't do that with the police involved.

"Josh is with Austin," she said.

Stephen bent over and let out a sob. One of the officers squared his shoulders. "Who is this Austin?" he said. "Do you have a description?"

"No, it's okay. He's a friend of the family. He's taking Josh back to the house now."

The officer turned to Stephen. "Is this true, sir? You can trust this Austin?"

Stephen lifted himself and gasped a few breaths. Then nodded.

"Austin is Aunt Hope's boyfriend," Brittany sang. Faith ran to her little girl and threw her arms around her.

"I guess we're done here," the officer said. "Unless there's anything else?" He stared directly at Faith. She held the eye gaze, hoping the silence would offer some small amount of torture, then shook her head.

"Thank you," she said.

The officers headed back to the car. "Happy endings at Christmas," the one called out. "It doesn't get better than that."

"Merry Christmas!" Brittany called back to them.

"Brittany, will you wait in the car," Faith said.

Joy and Harrison got out of the SUV. "We'll help you," Joy said.

"I'm getting pretty good at hopping," Brittany said. Joy and Harrison helped Brittany to the SUV. Brittany looked back at her father. "Are you coming back with us, Dad?"

"I don't think so, pumpkin. I'm so sorry."

"But it's Christmas," Brittany said. "You have to come."

"Let me talk to your mom," he said. As soon as they were back in the SUV, Stephen looked at Faith.

"I'm so sorry," he said. "I was so angry. And impulsive."

"I wanted to run you over with the car," Faith said.

"Thank you for not telling the cops I took them without your permission," Stephen said.

"I called you a million times. I thought Josh had taken my bottle of Xanax."

"Oh my God."

"This could have been our worst nightmare."

"Does he have it?"

"He said he didn't take it."

"Do you believe him?"

"Yes, I do."

"Good. That's good."

Faith took a deep breath. "I should have told you about Josh's call to the center. Not that it's any excuse, but I found out late in the game myself. But I think he's okay. I really think he's okay."

"We still have to watch him."

"Oh, we will. We certainly will."

"I'd better get going."

"Stephen. It's Christmas. We've all had such a tough year. Come back to the house with us."

Another sob broke from him. "Do you mean that?"

"Yes, but Charlie is with us. She's the one who saw you with the children. She called me."

"I understand. Brittany recognized her. She waved at her." Stephen gave a wry laugh.

"Our Granny is dying. I don't think she'll see Christmas Day."

"Are you sure you want me to come back with you?"

"I'm sure."

He wiped his eyes. "Thank you."

"Hurry and get in your car before I run you over," Faith said.

Hope put down the phone. "They found them."

"Oh, thank God." Carla poured herself some more whiskey.

"I thought you were drinking because you were worried," Hope said.

"Now I'm drinking because I'm celebrating," Carla said. "Did they arrest Stephen?"

"I don't know. That was Austin on the phone. He's on his way here with Josh."

They both glanced down the hall. Roger was still in with Yvette.

"How do you feel about Dad?" Hope asked.

"I won't lie," Carla said. "My heart has been pattering nonstop. But not for Roger. For Thomas. And he's gone. I see that now."

"I feel like he's half here," Hope said.

"The dad half," Carla said. "The half we need to take care of."

"We?"

"This place has like a dozen bedrooms. I'll be in and out." Carla began pulling baking pans out of cabinets.

"What are you doing?"

"I'm making Christmas cookies."

"You don't bake."

"How hard can it be?"

They all gathered in Yvette's room. Hope thought Roger would leave the minute others started to come in, but he was in a chair by Yvette's bedside, and there he remained. Mr. Jingles was sitting beside him, wearing, to Hope's surprise, reindeer antlers. He didn't seem to mind them. Yvette was breathing slowly, but awake, and her eyes actually lit up when she took them all in.

"Look at all my gifts," she said, holding her hands out. Josh took a hand, and so did Brittany. Yvette smiled and looked everyone in the eye.

Joy leaned over to Hope. "Did she just call us gifts?"

"She's heavily medicated," Hope said. "Go with it."

Yvette looked at Carla. "I'm sorry I called you a trashy whore."

Roger laughed, startling all of them. He and Carla made eye contact and he immediately stopped laughing, looking instead like a child caught doing something naughty. Then, Carla started to laugh and soon everyone joined in.

Suddenly they heard the sound of cars honking. Simultaneously came the smell of something burning.

"Someone is always trying to burn me out," Yvette said.

"My cookies!" Carla said. She flew out of the room.

"We forgot about the second night of festivities," Faith said. "We have to cancel."

"No," Yvette said. "I want to celebrate." They all stared at her. "I won't make it until Christmas."

"Are you sure?" Hope said.

"I'm sure," Yvette said. "I want to see lights, and laughter. And all of you. Celebrating."

"Okay," Austin said. "I'll turn on the lights and let them in."

"Me help," Roger said.

"That's my boy," Yvette said. Roger shuffled out of the room after Austin with Mr. Jingles at his heels.

"Look, Mom," Josh said, picking up an orange bottle from the table near Yvette's bedside. "The Xanax!"

"What's it doing there?" Faith said.

"You were taking too much," Yvette said. "I thought it would be safer hiding amongst all my pills." She saw the looks exchanged around the room. "What?" she barked.

"Nothing," Faith said. "You're right. I don't need it."

"I want to go out there," Yvette said. "I can't walk."

"We can put you in the wheelbarrow," Brittany said. "I'm getting good at hopping now."

"What a smart girl," Yvette said. "But I won't need to take yours. There's a second wheelbarrow in the barn."

"I'm on it," Harrison said. "It's okay if I wheel it in here?"

"I'm dying," Yvette said. "You can ride a horse in here if you want."

Josh jumped up and down. "Can we?"

"No," Faith said.

Josh shook his head, and Yvette laughed. "It's my house and I'll have a horse in it if I want to."

Yvette and Brittany were the queens of the evening. They rolled them up to the bonfire in their heavily blanketed wheelbarrows and gave them long sticks to roast S'mores. Yvette couldn't actually eat, but she seemed delighted by all the sights, and sounds, and lights. Roger was meticulously making the rounds, checking all the moving parts and lights and every once in a while returning to squeeze Yvette's hands. Her eyes were constantly wet with tears.

"Can Granny open her presents tonight?" Brittany said.

"That's a great idea," Hope said.

"I have all my presents," Yvette said. "Every single one of them."

"You mean you peeked?" Brittany said.

Yvette laughed. "You're priceless," she said. "I can't wait until you open the ones from me."

"You didn't have to get us anything else," Brittany said. "You've already given us so much."

"I'm just sorry I didn't cop on a year ago," Yvette said.

"What does that mean?" Brittany said.

Yvette laughed. "It means I should have mended fences a long time ago."

Brittany ambushed Yvette in a hug. "I forgive you."

Yvette hugged Brittany back as carolers began to sing "We Wish You a Merry Christmas." Hope looked around at this crazy group of people she called family. Definitely not perfect. At times downright annoying. Perhaps a little unconventional. And she couldn't imagine it any other way.

"Mr. Jingles just stole a bag of marshmallows!" Brittany said.

"I'll get him," Josh said. He tore after the dog.

Harrison came to push Brittany around the grounds. Hope, Faith, and Joy wheeled Yvette to a private spot in the yard where they could gaze upon all the glittering lights and happy people.

In the distance Roger and Carla were walking together, weaving their way through the people and the lights.

"Thank you," Yvette said. "You girls have performed true miracles."

"We love you, Granny," Joy said. She leaned down and hugged her. Soon Faith joined in and then Hope.

"Killing me with love," Yvette said. "I guess it's better than burning down my house."

CHAPTER 41

They sat in the living room. It was well after midnight, but they were all still wide awake. Yvette seemed to have a new burst of energy, as if summoning everything she had to make every second count. She sat in front of a sea of presents.

"We were supposed to draw names," she said. "What's all this?"

"Turns out we're not much of a name-drawing family," Hope said.

"I'd rather you give these to someone else," Yvette said. "You're my gifts. Love is the only thing I get to take with me."

"Start with this one," Hope said. She handed her a package. Yvette's hands were shaking too much, so Brittany and Josh helped her tear into it.

"Clementine oranges," she exclaimed, running her fingers over them. "Like when I was a little girl."

Once she got into it, Yvette seemed to have a blast opening all her presents. Ornaments with their pictures on them. A bottle of top-shelf whiskey. A mug for tea. A box of chocolates. A soft blanket. She exclaimed over each and every one of them.

Roger stepped up and handed her a gift. They all watched as she unwrapped it. It was a picture frame that said: MOM.

"I never knew that people cried so much when they were happy," Brittany said.

"Life is full of surprises," Faith said. "Now go to sleep."

"Will Granny make it until Christmas?"

"I don't think so. But I think we've given her the best Christmas she could have ever asked for."

"She'll get to be an angel," Brittany said.

Faith kissed her and pulled her blankets up. "Just like you," she said.

Hope knew the minute she saw Roger's face the next morning. She found him standing in the hall between Yvette's room and the living room. Tears were running down his face and he was shaking.

"I'm so sorry," Hope said. She reached out for him. He sidestepped her and headed out. She stood still and soon heard the slam of a door. She bit back her own grief and resisted the urge to go after him. She hurried to Yvette's room and was at least grateful to find that her eyes were closed and she looked entirely at peace. She went and held her hand and kissed her cheek.

"I love you," she said.

As per Yvette's wishes, she was cremated. They had planned to spread her ashes in the woods, but they were waiting for Roger. He'd locked himself up in the cabin and not even Mr. Jingles had been allowed in. The dog paced through the house, whining. It was Christmas Eve Day and the festive mood they'd been in yesterday seemed so far away. Josh and Brittany had been crying all day. Harrison and Charlie had busied themselves in the kitchen, creating one comfort food after the other. Piles of bacon and coffee, and donuts for breakfast, macaroni and cheese for lunch, and now it smelled as if a roast was on for dinner. Stephen was being a good sport, bringing offerings to

Roger's cabin, and although Roger had opened the door each time and accepted the offerings, he still hadn't let any of them in or come out himself. It was hard to lose a mother at any age, but they had no way of knowing for sure what mental age Roger was operating at, and impossible to know it on an emotional level. Hope wanted nothing more than to comfort him. The slam of his door and his tightly drawn curtains kept her from breaking in and forcing comfort upon him.

"I don't feel right about celebrating Christmas anymore," Brittany said.

"Me neither," Josh said. "Can we just skip it?"

"We don't have to force anything," Faith said. "But Granny had a wonderful day with all of us yesterday. She would want us to be happy too. She would want us to celebrate with the best gifts we could ever ask for."

"Xbox games?" Josh said.

"Each other," Faith said. Josh didn't look convinced.

"And Xbox games," Joy said. "What?" she said off Faith's look. "We all need a little something to boost our ratings."

"I just want Roger back," Brittany said. "I don't want to celebrate Christmas without him."

"Me neither," Josh said. "And it looks like Mr. Jingles feels the same."

"We'll try," Hope said. "But first things first. I think we should all call him Thomas, or Grandpa, or Dad."

"Roger that," Joy said. Hope threw a biscuit at her. Joy caught it in her mouth.

"Do we get to each open one present on Christmas Eve?" Joy said.

"Ah, the old tradition," Faith said.

"Can we, Mom?" Brittany's eyes lit up.

"You didn't carry on the tradition?" Hope said.

"We only did it because Joy couldn't stand to wait," Faith laughed.

"And even then it was just a farce," Carla said, biting into a piece of coffee cake. "Joy had already opened and rewrapped them all anyway."

"You did?" Brittany sounded horrified and fascinated in equal measure.

Joy turned to her mother, mouth agape. "You knew?"

"We all knew," Faith said. "The best part was watching you pretend to be surprised the next morning."

"Well, I didn't do it this year," Joy said.

"It's not Christmas yet," Hope said.

"I'll lock her in her room," Harrison said. "She won't be peeking this year."

"Good luck with that," Joy said. "You'll be asleep before I can say 'Twas the night before Christmas.' "

"How about a Scrabble tournament," Austin said. "In Yvette's honor."

"We can make up words," Hope said. "Tonight they all count."

"I hope I get 'glitty,' " Austin said. Hope looked out across the grounds. The lights were off out of respect for Yvette and Thomas. She glanced at a set of candles on the mantel.

"Are any shops still open?" she asked suddenly.

"It's dark, but it's actually only five p.m.," Austin said. "There will be plenty open for those last-minute shoppers."

"I knew you didn't get my gift yet," Joy said.

"Har, har," Hope said.

"You've got that look in your eye," Faith said.

"What look?" Hope said.

"She's right, you do," Joy said.

"What look?" Hope said.

"Don't tell me you're about to adopt every stray dog in the neighborhood on this Christmas Eve," Faith said.

"Can we?" Brittany said. "Can we?" Mr. Jingles, either from hearing the word *dog* or from Brittany's excitement, barked rapidly.

"We need candles," Hope said. "Tons of them."

Austin stared at her. "You do have a look," he said. "What are you thinking?"

"Forget Scrabble," Hope said, putting away the board. "What do you say we make real words instead?"

* * *

They bought all the candles they could get their hands on, plus used every one from their house and Austin's house. It wasn't an easy job, and it took hours, but they worked together and when they finished and lit them all, and stood back to gaze upon their efforts; it was all worth it. In large letters facing his cabin, with a heart before and after the words, the candles spelled out:

MERRY XMAS DAD

They didn't have enough candles or time to spell out *grand-father,* but Hope assured the kids he would understand. The candles were flickering in the wind, but each person held a lighter and would be quick to ignite any that burned out.

"Now what?" Joy said.

"Now, we sing," Hope said.

"Should we start with his favorite?" Faith asked.

The girls exchanged a look, then they started in on "Here Comes Santa Claus." Finally, in the middle the curtain twitched. Then opened. Seconds later, Roger opened the door to the cabin and stood staring at the message. He looked up to find Faith, Hope, and Joy standing in front of him.

"My girls," he said.

"Our dad," Hope said. They competed to be the first to throw their arms around him, then held as if they were never going to let go.

"Merry Christmas, Thomas," Carla said from behind them.

"Carla," he said with a nod.

"Merry Christmas, Grandpa," Josh and Brittany chimed. Thomas stepped outside, tears rolling down his cheeks.

"My family," he said. "My family."

CHAPTER 42

Christmas Day found the gang surrounded by a sea of colorful wrapping paper, with snow falling lightly outside, and all the lights on the lawn gleaming. The aroma of pancakes and bacon and coffee wafted through the room as Bing Crosby sang. Thomas sat in the center of them all, with Mr. Jingles at his side.

"We all made out like bandits," Hope said. Austin looked so handsome in the sweater she'd given him. He had bought her one from the very same store and she was wearing it as well as a bathrobe from Faith and slippers from Joy. Thomas had no less than three new caps and the sweater from his girls. He was wearing the sweater and every single cap, one on top of the other, which thrilled Josh and Brittany to no end. Faith and Hope had yet to take Joy over to the coffee truck, allowing Joy to think the coffee mugs were her only gift from them. Faith couldn't stop smiling.

"These are great," Joy said for about the fourth time, holding up her coffee mug. "Not disappointed at all."

"I got you rum," Carla said.

"Oh, it's in here all right," Joy said, lifting up her mug.

"Why don't you put your coat on and take a walk with your sisters," Faith said. She tossed Joy's winter coat and it landed on top of her head.

"Maybe later," Joy said. "I'm busy thoroughly enjoying my gift of a coffee mug."

"We won't be gone long," Hope said. "Up and Adam," she said to Joy.

"You always get that wrong," Faith said. "It's up and *at 'em*."

"That sounds aggressive," Hope said. "At who?"

"I don't know," Faith said. "Who is Adam?"

Hope shrugged. "Adam and Eve?"

"Dumb and Dumber," Joy said. "Either way. I'm not going."

"You're going if we have to drag you," Faith said.

"Be a sport," Harrison said. Faith and Hope had shown him the truck last night. He helped keep his eye on Joy all night.

Joy huffed. "A walk," she said. "How lovely." She threw on her coat, and the three of them tromped to the mudroom to put on their boots.

"What are you two up to?" Joy said.

"We just want to take a walk with our sister," Faith said. "What's wrong with that?"

"Are you guys okay if I leave my coffee mug here. I mean, I wouldn't want you to think I don't appreciate it or anything."

"Get out," Faith said. She kicked her lightly on the rump. They trudged toward Austin's cabin, Joy trailing behind. When they were halfway through the woods and almost to Austin's property, Faith and Hope stopped and pulled out a red scarf.

"We're going to blindfold you," Faith said.

"I knew it," Joy said. "You're going to get me lost and leave me to find my way home."

"Poor thing," Hope said, looping the scarf around her eyes. When they were convinced she couldn't see anything they each took one of her arms and began to lead Joy toward the coffee truck.

"What's going on?" Joy said.

"We're taking you to your other Christmas present," Faith said.

"Not that you weren't appreciative of the coffee cup," Hope said.

"I was," Joy said. "Although you could have at least thrown in some coffee beans."

"We thought you'd have plenty of those when you start your business," Faith said.

"I'm having second thoughts about that," Joy said. Faith and Hope stopped and gave each other a look. Joy plowed into them.

"OW!"

Hope laughed. "I told you," she said to Faith.

"I guess it could be anything they want it to be," Faith said.

"What?" Joy said. "What could?" They were out of the woods now. The silver coffee truck, rimmed in little white lights, positively gleamed. A neon sign had been attached to the outside: J&H: Coffee and Cream. A giant red bow was wrapped around the hood. They stood back.

"Merry Christmas, Joy," Faith and Hope said at the same time. Joy hesitated, then removed her blindfold. She stared at the gleaming truck, blinking several times. For once in her life, Joy was at a loss for words.

"It's the nicest gift anyone's ever given me," Joy said. She wiped tears from her face with the sleeves of her coat. Faith and Hope put their arms around her. Joy let out a sob.

"You can always turn it into a taco truck," Hope said. From behind them came singing. "It's Beginning to Look a Lot Like Christmas" rang out as the rest of the family joined them. Harrison was holding a platter of pancakes.

"Let's get in this baby and start making coffee," he said. He winked at Joy as he got in the truck. "Come on, Mr. T," he called to Thomas. Thomas laughed and followed Harrison into the truck. Soon their two faces grinned out from the serving window.

"Who wants a cup of java?" Harrison said. "Or hot chocolate?" he added with a wink to Brittany and Josh.

"Can I have a cup of coffee?" Josh asked.

"Sure," Faith said. "It's Christmas."

The Garland Girls stood smiling, holding hands. Thomas beamed down at them. "Merry Christmas," he said.

"Merry Christmas, Dad," they returned.

"I'll take my coffee black," Joy said.

"Don't I know it," Harrison said. Joy squealed and then joined them in the truck.

"Can I come in?" Josh said.

"The more the merrier," Harrison said. "In fact, let's all get in. It's cold outside." One by one they started to pile in the truck. Austin caught Hope's hand just as she was about to step into it. She looked up to find him holding mistletoe.

"Merry Christmas," he said. "Here's to the first of many." Before he could lean in, she beat him to the punch, pulled his head down to her, and kissed him. Afterward, a shiver ran through her.

"Are you cold?" he asked, smiling.

"Not at all," she said.

His eyes twinkled as he understood what she meant. Hope threw her head back to the sky. "Look," she pointed. A bright star twinkled, even though they should have all disappeared from the sky.

"It's Granny," Brittany said, popping her head out of the truck. "Our angel." Hope and Austin stepped inside.

"Look at all my gifts," Hope echoed, squeezing Austin's hand and gazing at the smiling faces of Carla and Thomas, and Stephen, and Charlie, and Brittany, and Josh, and Harrison, and Mr. Jingles. And, of course, her sisters. Faith and Joy. Always Faith and Joy. Laughing, not forced, not phony, but true laughter, a bit of happiness on this Christmas Day.

Suddenly her father was in front of her, holding a wrapped gift. It was about the size of a magazine and soft. Faith and Joy had the same ones. "I helped out a bit," Carla said.

"She helped," Roger said.

"We have to open at the same speed," Joy said. "Because I think they must be the same." Carla shook her head and laughed. Hope opened hers and caught sight of a red T-shirt. Sure enough, they each had one. They each held them up:

OLDER SISTER

I make the rules

MIDDLE SISTER

I'm the reason we have rules

YOUNGER SISTER

The rules don't apply to me.

"Let's wear these every Christmas," Joy said.

"I'll be the judge of that," Faith said.

"You guys," Hope said. "Already planning next Christmas. I'll have to check my calendar and see if I can pencil either of you losers in."

Joy squealed and picked up a can of whipped cream, then held it up as if aiming it for Hope's face. Faith grabbed another and did the same thing.

"Don't you dare," Hope said, already backing up.

"On the count of five," Faith said.

"You'd better run," Joy said. Mr. Jingles barked. It was every man for himself as Hope squealed, grabbed a bottle of maple syrup, and prepared herself to battle the whipped-cream-toting nightmares that were her sisters. She readied the maple syrup for optimum flying distance (like Santa and his reindeer), and knew for certain that this was going to go down in Garland Girl history as one of the worst and best Christmases of their entire lives. Perhaps it wasn't ever possible to have one without the other. Not that she was going to get any credit for it. The middle child never did. Her thoughts were interrupted by a string of whipped cream landing in her eye.

"This is war!" Hope cried, and squeezed the bottle of maple syrup in the direction of her sisters' evil, smiling faces.

"I just love Christmas!" Brittany cried out. "Don't you guys?" The Garland Girls stopped, then after exchanging knowing glances with one another, turned their sticky terror onto Josh and Brittany.

"I'm not cleaning this truck all by myself," Harrison said as the children's squeals filled the air.

"I'll help," Austin said.

"Me too," Carla said.

"Roger that," Thomas said. Everyone stopped in their tracks and looked at him. "Thomas," he said with a smile. "I'm Thomas."

> *Merry Christmas to all*
> *And to all a good night.*

HOME WITH MY SISTERS

Mary Carter

ABOUT THIS GUIDE

The suggested questions are included to enhance
your group's reading of Mary Carter's
Home with My Sisters.

DISCUSSION QUESTIONS

1. When the novel opens, Faith and Joy brush off Hope's invitation to get together for Christmas. What does this say about the relationship between the three of them?

2. Hope breaks up with Michael shortly after meeting Austin. Coincidence?

3. Hope wants to visit their grandmother primarily to find out what happened to their father. What is Faith's and Joy's motivation for going?

4. Joy is the sister who missed out on knowing their father. How does this shape her behavior?

5. How does their birth order affect each sister's personality, or does it?

6. Faith is the only sister with children of her own. Do you think because of this that she's not as stuck in the past as Hope?

7. Yvette is dying and is worried about Roger. Do you think this is the only reason she allows Austin to contact her granddaughters?

8. How does Yvette react to Josh and Brittany? Is she more or less open to them than to her granddaughters?

9. When Roger first meets Hope he leaves her a pinecone. Do you think he's fully aware in this moment of who Hope is?

10. Yvette has a few words to say when she first meets Joy's boyfriend Harrison. She says in her day they only drank one kind of milk. Is she really talking about milk, or like Joy believes, is she making a racist comment?

11. Josh, we learn, has recently made a suicide attempt. Do you think his state of mind has anything to do with the secrets that Faith is keeping?

12. Does Christmas approaching help everyone to heal, or does it make it worse for all of them? Or both? Please discuss.

13. How do the sisters change and grow at the end of the novel, if at all?

14. Will Hope stay with Austin? Will Joy and Harrison make a success out of their coffee truck? Will Faith make her new blended family work?

15. What do you think their relationship will be like with Roger from here on out?